Cruise Ship

MICHAEL LLOYD

Monument
A Division of Witherby Publishing Group Ltd
4 Dunlop Square, Livingston, Edinburgh, EH54 8SB, Scotland, UK
Tel No: +44(0)1506 463 227 - Fax No: +44(0)1506 468 999
Email: info@emailws.com - Web: www.witherbyseamanship.com

First edition published 2013

ISBN: 978-1-85609-582-2
eBook ISBN: 978-1-85609-592-1

British Library Cataloguing in Publication Data
A catalogue record for this book is available from the British Library.

Printed and bound in Great Britain by Charlesworth Press, Wakefield

Published by

Witherby Publishing Group Ltd
4 Dunlop Square, Livingston,
Edinburgh, EH54 8SB,
Scotland, UK

Tel No: +44(0)1506 463 227
Fax No: +44(0)1506 468 999

Email: info@emailws.com
Web: www.witherbys.com

ALSO BY MICHAEL LLOYD

Non-Fiction
In Command - 200 Things I wish I'd known before I was Captain
The Complete Chief Officer
Captains' Legal
Masters Pocket Book Series - Standby Vessels
Masters Pocket Book Series - Checklists
Masters Pocket Book Series - The Pocket Book of Anchoring

Co-Authored
The Work of the Harbour Master (published by the Nautical Institute)
Command (published by the Nautical Institute)
The Ice Navigation Manual

Fiction
Devil's Cauldron
Cruise Ship

Coming Soon
Broken Ship
Convoy Ship

Preface

This book was conceived in 2009 as larger cruise ships were being built. It is not based on any one cruise or hotel ship company.

Just because we build larger ships with all the benefits of modern technology, it does not mean that the sea is any safer than it was a century ago. Shipping companies do what they can to ensure that their ships are as safe as possible, but many ships still sink every year. Ships continue to disappear without trace and many who venture into this hostile environment are killed. Seafarers know this, and this is why they exercise and drill in the various emergencies that can beset a ship. Of all these, abandonment is the most essential.

A Captain of a ship has one duty above all the others. This is not to save the ship, as many would believe, but to safeguard the lives of those under his command. It may be that the best option is to stay on the ship, and in that case every effort must be put into keeping the ship afloat. Alternatively, abandonment might be the only course of action.

This is the Captain's decision, and his alone. There are no committees on a ship, just the Captain's seamanship, knowledge and judgement.

A number of professional seafarers have read this book, and their remarks and comments have assisted with the accuracy of the general aspects of the story. I sincerely thank them all, in particular Gary Dickinson, a colleague and friend, with whom I have sailed on many ships and oceans.

This is a story of people and the ships they sail in. Irrespective of the ships, situations, rank or ratings they hold, they have my profound admiration.

For the seafarers who read this book, I ask for tolerance as the book is also written for those who are not familiar with the sea, the language or customs. For this reason, there must be a balance between professionalism and readability.

Finally, it is a novel and, of course, we must not let fact stand in the way of a good story.

Personnel

This book involves three ships as well as shore staff who are pertinent to the story. Owing to the large number of crew and passengers on board these ships, only those who appear with some regularity or who are relevant to the events are mentioned.

Southampton Shore Staff

Sue Selsby	Manager, Human Resources
Eric Bellfield	Fleet Safety Manager
Jamie West	Fleet Safety Manager/ Group Safety Manager

Fort Lauderdale Shore Staff

Bob Hinchley	Senior Vice President
Adam Falconi	Fleet Safety Manager
John Zachary	Fleet Operations Manager

M.V. *Sea Breeze*

Captain	Dave Benson
Staff Captain	Gabriel Sattori/Charlie Clayton
Safety Officer	Anthony Marvin/Jim Clariby
Hotel Manager	Henri Larou
Cruise Director	Peter Bramby
Security Guard	Bert Fallows

M.V. *Vacuum Pioneer*

Captain	Karl Johnsen
Chief Officer	Eric Aasland
Chief Engineer	Trond Johnsen
Second Officer	Arturo Emita
Third Officer	Ivo Milanovic
Quartermaster	Corazon Montejo
Captain's wife	Gerdy Johnsen
Captain's daughter	Briget Johnsen

M.V. *Majestic Sea*

Captain	Augusto Cota
Staff Captain	Adama Ricci/Jim Clariby
Joint Secretary	Celine
Safety Officer	Jan Weekers
Assistant	Janice Beerman
First Officer	Peter Allway
Senior Second Officer	Gaspar Bandissi
Junior Second Officer	Mike Prentiss
Third Officer	Alan Drury
Senior Cadet	Zhou
Cadet	Matheson
Cadet	Kemp
Cadet	Bindra
Senior Security Officer	Bert Fallows
Security Officer	Mark Davies
Security Officer	Samuel Gully
Senior Fireman	Carlos Benito
Bosun	Jose Domingo
Staff Captain's Steward	Rodrigo
Chief Engineer	Iain Macgregor
Staff Chief Engineer	Patrick Connor
Senior Surgeon	Dick Brentwood
Ship General Manager	William Shelby
Cruise Director	Scott Pierre
Entertainment Director	Vivien Pierre
Hotel Manager	Henry Milau
Purser	Bella Winchester/Jean Sinter
Pianist	Helen Shreiber
Passengers	Harvey and Shirley Inch
	Andrew and Nicola Inch
	David and Isobel Chancery
Ice Pilot	Graham Chesney

Content

Part One

M.V. *Sea Breeze*

"Ships are designed for the sea, but the sea isn't designed for ships or for those who venture onto it."

Chapter 1

Jim Clariby waited anxiously for the post. He had been waiting for more than two months now and his wait was becoming increasingly desperate. Redundancy and the failure to find a new position had eaten away at his confidence and left him questioning his abilities, particularly as there should have been employers falling over themselves for an experienced Captain with a proven record.

It was a warm spring day. He should have been out in the garden with his wife, Jenny, relaxing on leave between ships. Instead, he sat waiting for a bell like a tired boxer in the last few rounds of his fight. There was a rustle of paper at the front door. Instantly, Jim sprang up and went to pick the letters up from the hall floor. He flicked through the usual junk mail and bills, but there was nothing. He knew the sickening feeling that came over him. Another day with no apparent future.

He went back through the house, out the kitchen door and into the garden where Jenny was kneeling by the rose bed. They had been very lucky in their life together. They had met on the Australian run of a passenger ship when Jenny was coming home to England after a visit. He was a young Fourth Officer then, hurrying along the boat deck in his crisp white uniform with its tight collar and immaculate uniform cap when he saw this dark haired girl playing deck tennis. That was that and for the rest of the voyage he devoted his time to enthralling himself to her. She thought he was good looking, arrogant and naïve but still amusing. He had potential. She may have thought that, but when he was on leave in England and turned up in his red MG sports car, her parents realising that it might be serious had a very different opinion. They had not brought up their daughter to marry a merchant seaman, particularly as she was on the verge of marrying a nice young lawyer in the city. Jenny, however, was not going to be dictated to by her parents. At twenty two, she had her own mind. The result was a wedding with reluctant parents and a quick voyage to sea together before Jenny settled down ashore, to make a home and prepare for the family which would inevitably appear.

Time went by too quickly. They found their cottage in the country; Jenny's parents mellowed as Jim progressed up the ranks of various companies until he obtained his Master's Certificate. Next, Jim moved to a small company specialising in ice class ships. He was promoted to Chief Officer, then finally command. He was on different ships until the company purchased an ex-Finnish ice class passenger vessel, which specialised in cruising in ice waters. For the last three years at sea, he had command of this ship. These were happy years until five months ago the company sold their ships without warning. Within two weeks, Jim and his officers were replaced by cheaper foreigners and they were on the beach with a month's redundancy pay.

At first he wasn't worried, but as the months went by and bills continued to flood in, he realised that British captains and officers were no longer a sought-after commodity and that the age of the accountant had arrived. One agency told him that they were 'too independent' and that foreign officers from the third world were more subservient. If it were true, it was hardly their fault as they had been trained to be leaders and to think for themselves. Who wanted subservient officers anyway? The answer came immediately; the ship operators, apparently.

So here he was in his late forties, on the beach, school fees and a mortgage to pay and wondering what would come next.

Jenny heard him approaching and looked up shading her eyes. She was still a lovely looking woman. She had a country look, little make up, freckles showing faintly on her brow, her dark hair with the occasional fleck of grey; there were fine lines around her eyes but she was still slim. She complemented Jim, who was just as slim, although after being on cruise ships he was carrying a few extra pounds. His fine head of hair was beginning to thin, and grey was creeping in around the edges. His eyes were more deeply crinkled from peering out for endless hours on the bridge, particularly into the incredible brightness of the ice.

Jenny got up from her flower bed. She didn't need to ask; his face told the story. She went to him and put her arms around him.

'Don't worry darling. A Captain like you won't be left on the beach for long.'

'I wish I had your confidence, Jenny. It's getting serious. We can't live on savings for ever.'

'What about a shore job?' She saw his face and added hastily, 'Just temporary until something comes through.'

'Hell, Jenny. What can I do in Somerset? Maybe in London but they don't want a captain in his late forties. Anyway, I don't want a shore job. I'm a seafarer. It's all I know.'

'Well, we could take the children out of school. That would save us a fortune.'

'We may have to, but not yet. Let's see what comes along. We can manage for a bit longer.'

She kissed him. 'Come on, Birdseye. Go and make me a cup of tea.'

They were in the kitchen when the phone rang. Jenny answered it, then looked at Jim. She put her hand over the speaker. 'It's for you. It's an agency.'

Jim took the phone; he had sent his CV to a number of marine employment agencies.

'Captain Clariby? George Southwall, Seacraft Marine Ltd.'

'Good morning, Mr Southwall. How can I help you?' asked Jim.

'We sent your CV to a company a few days ago and they would like to meet you if you're available.'

Jim's heart leapt. Don't be too eager, he thought, although it was hard to keep the excitement down.

'Which company is it?'

'Seaborne Cruises.'

Jim was surprised. They were a big cruise group with dozens of ships.

'If you're interested, they want to meet you at their headquarters in Southampton.'

'When?'

'Monday at 1030, if that is convenient?'

'I can make that.'

'Good. I'll tell them to expect you. When you arrive, ask for Human Resources, Marine. You are meeting Mrs Selsby. Good luck, Captain.'

Jim put the phone down. Jenny was eagerly waiting.

'Well?' she asked.

'Seaborne Cruises want to see me next Monday.'

Jenny shrieked with joy. 'You see! What did I say?'

'Hey, calm down,' Jim said. 'It's just a meeting. We don't know what they want yet.'

'They want you! They're not stupid.' It was hard not to become caught up in her excitement.

'We'll see,' he said. 'Meantime, we could go to the pub for lunch. You can buy me a pint.'

She hugged him. 'Don't drink too much if you want an afternoon siesta.' Her eyes sparkled.

'You're on,' he laughed.

Just after ten on Monday morning, Jim stood outside the impressive entrance to Seaborne Cruises. The flags of the various cruise companies in their group were outside snapping on their flagpoles in the stiff breeze.

He looked at his watch for the third time.

Sod it, he thought, I'm going in.

He approached the huge reception desk with several receptionists behind the counter. One looked up and smiled at him.

'Can I help?' she asked.

'My name is Captain Jim Clariby. I have an appointment with Mrs Selsby in Marine Human Resources.'

She tapped the keys of her computer.

'That's right,' she said. The printer whirled and a slip of paper was ejected, which she passed to Jim. 'Here you are. Go over to the security desk where they will issue your pass. Then go to the third floor and see the reception desk there.' She smiled again.

Jim went to the security desk where he was given a clip with his pass inserted. He then passed through an electronic security check which, after detecting his mobile phone, allowed him access. The lift took him swiftly to the third floor and opened directly in front of the reception desk. Another smiling receptionist was waiting. Once he identified himself and she checked his badge, he was directed to a waiting area. There was a drinks dispenser; he pressed the button for a coffee and then sat flicking through the latest Seaborne cruise brochure. Time went by. He looked at his watch - it was after 1030. The phone rang occasionally behind the reception desk and was quietly answered. Various office staff passed through, but no one spoke to him. Impatiently, he got up and approached reception again. He got the same smile. It was now 1045.

'Can you tell me what's happening?' he asked.

'I have told Mrs Selsby that you are here, but unfortunately she is in a meeting at present. She will be with you shortly.'

Jim sat down again. This wasn't starting very well.

More time passed. 'Mr Clariby.' Jim started and looked up. Standing over him was a tall young woman, immaculately groomed and wearing a smart dark business suit. He guessed she was in her early thirties. She smiled. Everyone smiled here.

'Captain,' he said.

'Sorry?'

'Captain Clariby.' He held his hand out.

'Oh I see. I'm Sue Selsby. Sorry I'm late. I told them I had an appointment, but they said it was urgent and that it would only take a minute. Unfortunately, it took longer than I thought. Please come with me.'

She set off down the corridor at a brisk pace with Jim following. They turned into an open office door. She indicated to the seat in front of the desk.

'Do you know much about us, Captain?'

'I know you are one of the largest cruise outfits in the world, that you've acquired a number of other cruise companies and you now have a fairly modern fleet with new builds coming on line periodically.'

'In a couple of years, we will be the largest. Now, I have your CV here; it's very impressive. I see that all your certificates are in date, which is essential. You went to sea when you were 16, passed your Master's Certificate at 26, were given command in your early thirties and then were on a number of different ships culminating in ice class cruise ships. You must excuse me, but I don't know the company that ran them.'

'They were a relatively small outfit, based in France, but they had an office in Cape Town that ran cruise ships to the Antarctic.'

'How big were they?'

'Around 18,000 deadweight. They carried up to 400 passengers and were usually pretty full,' replied Jim.

'We prefer to call them guests. It's more welcoming that way. Your ships were very small compared to our ships.'

'You will see on my CV that I commanded ships that were up to 80,000 tonnes in the Arctic. The largest ship I commanded was over 200,000 tonnes.'

She smiled faintly. 'But that wasn't a cruise ship was it?'

'No, but it required more skill because it only had one propeller and no thrusters. It also had a much deeper draught and was bigger than any cruise ship.'

She did not reply but instead carried on looking through his CV.

'So you were made redundant from that company and since then you've been unemployed. Any reason for that?'

'I really don't know. You've seen my CV. Perhaps you can tell me as you are in human resources.'

Jim felt it wasn't going well. He mustn't bite, he told himself. She felt his impatience.

'Look, Captain, this is just as difficult for me. We don't normally look to recruit someone as old or senior as you. We prefer to bring in younger staff and train them up in our ways from the start. That is easiest for us. However, a situation has arisen.'

Jim kept silent and waited.

'We are going to start cruises to the Arctic and Antarctic, and as a result we need ice experienced officers.'

'When do they start?' asked Jim.

'At present it's in the planning stages, but it will be some time later this year. We will be sending one of our latest ships, the *'Majestic Sea'*.'

'I didn't know she was ice class.'

'She isn't.'

'Is that wise?'

'We have been assured that it is fine. The classification society and flag state are quite happy, on the basis that we are not going in winter or into heavy ice.'

'What is the flag state?'

'Panama.'

'With respect, Mrs Selsby, they don't have a lot of experience with ice in Panama.'

'Captain, you're really talking to the wrong person. But I assure you we would not endanger one of our new ships if there was any risk. The intention is to show the guests the ice so that they can say they went to the Arctic and saw it. In and out as you would say.'

Jim shrugged. The last thing he wanted was to talk himself out of a job.

'That is why we are interested in you. Let me tell you what we are looking for first, then we can decide.'

She took a deep breath. 'We can't consider you for Captain, at least not yet. The company and shipboard management will probably be very different from what you are used to and it is essential that you learn about our methods. You will find that the hotel side of the ship is very much in the forefront compared to normal ships or possibly your own. If we decide to offer you employment, we would want you to start as Safety Officer.'

She saw Jim about to speak and held her hand up.

'Wait, let me explain. Today the Safety Officer is the new title for the Chief Officer's position. The Staff Captain is the head of the deck department and the Safety Officer is his deputy. Next is the First Officer who is the navigation officer, then we have two Second Officers and three Third Officers as well as cadets. We would place you on one of our older ships for several cruises in that position until you are familiar with our management system, then you would move to the 'Majestic Sea' as Staff Captain in time for the ice cruising season. How does that sound to you?'

Jim thought for a moment, then replied, 'You know I don't have a job at present.' She nodded. 'You've seen my CV and you wouldn't have invited me here if you didn't think I could do the job. I think the question is could I accept going back to being a Chief Officer or Safety Officer as you call him, especially when he is not head of the deck department.'

'It would only be for a short time until you are ready for the 'Majestic'.'

Again Jim paused. 'If that was the case, then yes. However it depends on the salary. We haven't discussed that yet.'

'We could not initially match what you were earning in your last company, but when you are promoted to Staff Captain it would be closer. Once you became Captain, it would be the same or better. Now there is one other requirement and please don't blame me for this. The company has a policy of psychological assessments.'

'Presumably they feel that my years in command are not enough.'

'I am afraid there are no exceptions. I did mention that I felt this would not be required, but it is the policy.'

'When would this be done?'

'If you like, we could do it today before you leave. It only takes about half an hour to complete.'

'Will I be meeting anyone else?'

'Not today. Once the assessment is completed, I will meet with the senior management involved and then we'll make a decision. We will let you know within a week either way.'

'Let's get it over with then,' said Jim.

She picked up the phone and spoke for a moment.

'It's all ready for you. This way please.'

They went down the corridor to another room where they were greeted by a young man behind a desk; he was David Benson, the company psychologist. Set out on a separate desk was a form and beside it a pencil.

'Please sit down, Mr Clariby.' Demoted already, thought Jim sadly.

'There is no pass or fail mark and there are no trick questions. Some questions may seem strange, but please answer all the questions on the form. Take your time. If you have any questions during the assessment, please ask me. I will be here throughout.'

'I'll see you later,' Mrs Selsby said as she left the room.

Jim sat down and looked through the form. What three things would you take to a desert island? Easy, a sat phone, power boat and fuel. What did the cloud shapes remind him of? Bloody clouds of course.

He began working his way through the questions; some he could see the purpose of, but others made no sense to him. Eventually he finished and he put down his pencil.

Benson looked at his watch. 'That's a good time. Thank you, Mr Clariby.'

He called for Mrs Selsby. 'I'll see you down, Captain,' she said.

She escorted Jim down to the foyer, where he left his security badge.

'Don't ask me what he does with those questions,' she said. 'They go further up the line. If or when they are acted on, they don't tell me. As far as I am concerned, you are what we're looking for, but let's see what they say.' They shook hands. 'We'll contact you in a few days.'

Chapter 2

They were in the kitchen having breakfast when the letter arrived. It was three pages long and confirmed the offer for the position as Safety Officer on the *'Sea Breeze'*, joining in two weeks' time. It listed the joining salary and allowances. It also asked him to phone Mrs Selsby to arrange a time to meet with the Fleet Safety Manager and to visit the company outfitter for his uniforms.

Jim showed the letter to Jenny.

'It's not as much as we've been used to, but at least it's a job and we can manage until I am promoted.'

'They don't mention the promotion in here.'

'Well, I can keep my name out there with the agencies in case anything better turns up.'

'I can see if the surgery wants me full time, but the last time I asked they only wanted me part time.'

'No, we'll manage. At least the duty tours are less than I have been doing. Three months on and two months off.'

Jenny leant across and kissed him. 'Are you happy?'

'Yes, a bloody sight happier than without a job.'

She laughed. Jim phoned Mrs Selsby.

Three days later, Jim entered the company building again and went to the third floor. This time Mrs Selsby came immediately with the same friendly smile.

'We're going up to the fifth floor where you'll meet with the Fleet Safety Manager. His name is Eric Bellfield. Then you'll meet the Group Safety Manager for your ship. Each group of ships has its own Group Safety Manager.'

'What about Marine Superintendents and Operations Managers?'

'The same applies to the Operations Manager, but we don't have Marine Superintendents. We do have Technical Managers, although they are engineers. The nautical side of things tends to be on the fifth floor, and the rest of the building is mainly devoted to the hotel side and finance.'

They arrived at the Safety Manager's office. Jim noticed the title Captain in front of Bellfield's name on the door. Many left the sea with their Master's Certificates and called themselves captain when the nearest they had ever come to being in command was on a pleasure boat. They went in. Jim saw a large beefy man in his fifties sitting behind his desk. His sleeves were rolled up and he was tapping into a computer.

He looked up and came round his desk.

'Good to meet you, Jim. I've heard a lot about you from Sue here and of course I've read your CV. Welcome to the fleet. Come and sit down.'

'I'll disappear now,' Mrs Selsby said. 'You're in these guys' hands now. Eric, he has to be at the outfitters by twelve so when you're ready call me and I'll arrange for him to get there. Did you come by car or train?'

'Train.'

'Okay we'll organise a taxi to take you there and then on to the station. I won't see you again before you join your ship, Captain Clariby. I wish you a good voyage.' They shook hands and she left.

'Come and sit down, Jim.'

Eric let Jim settle down before passing him a bound booklet.

'This covers all your duties on board and the usual company crap about their safety policy. Don't try to read it now. I put it together for all new senior officers who join us as things are often quite different to what they have been used to. I got a bit of a shock when I joined some years ago and things have changed since then as well.'

He looked at Jim. 'Just in case you're wondering, I was Master on passenger cargo ships before I joined here, banana boats actually, and then I had command of the ship you're joining. She didn't belong to them then. When they took her over, they took me as well. She's a bit old, the usual tarting up with plastic and chrome. Not large by new ship standards, but she still carries 1,200 punters and has a crew of over 500. She's a good ship and you've got a good Captain there, although a little rough by modern cruise ship standards. He has a varied background, same as me. Redundant and this was all there was. But he's a good seaman and we need them regardless of what the hotel side think. That's why I wanted you. The 'Sea Breeze' is part of the Mediterranean fleet. We separate the fleets depending on where they are based. Australia based ships are managed from Sydney; UK and Med based ships from here. In the US, which is our largest market, we have two fleets, one on the east coast operating out of Fort Lauderdale, the other on the west coast operating out of San Francisco.'

'Do the ships interchange?'

'Not if we can help it. It's a big administrative headache, but they can and do when there is a problem, for example if a major breakdown requires some repositioning. The personnel change though, sometimes at their own request, sometimes promotion or because they are needed elsewhere. Do you have any questions about the operational side?'

'At this stage not really, presuming most of it is in here,' Jim said holding the booklet.

'Some things aren't. I don't intend telling you about safety procedures, documentation and all that. As you are fresh from commanding a cruise ship, you could probably tell me. Anyway, after me, you're meeting the Safety Manager for your ship. Don't mind him. He's a supercilious little prick who undoubtedly will be on the board one day. If he becomes a bigger prick, he'll be the Chief Executive. He's a jumped up second mate who thinks he knows it all. If you have any problems with him while you're on board, just call me. What I do want to do is to put you wise to the company and its ways.

'Don't think of the company as a shipping company. Most of the senior people here wouldn't know a ship if it was parked outside. This is a hotel company and the hotel side rule the roost. You see, in marine we spend the money, the hotel people make it. It's as simple as that,' explained Eric.

'They thought the same in my last company, but luckily there was a good office team who put seamanship before anything else. That helped us to keep the hotel people in line.'

'Well, not here. And they're political. This is a very political company. It could give parliament a run for their money. Now, a word of advice, especially as you're new and settling in. Don't make waves. You'll see things you're not happy about. I shouldn't say this, but you're a seaman the same as me. If you really are concerned about something then call me. Or you can go to the Captain. He's a good man. Enough said?'

'Yes, Sir. Thank you for that. Can I ask about security? Do they come under us?' asked Jim.

'Theoretically, yes. I don't know who is running them on your ship, but they are usually ex-Petty Officers from the Royal or Merchant Navy, but they could also be from private industry ashore. I say theoretically. They like to be a law unto themselves and it depends what the Staff Captain allows them to get away with. One more thing, do you drink?'

'Not much, no. An occasional glass of wine or a pint, that's all.'

'That's good. There's nothing the hotel bastards like more than reporting a deck officer for drinking. They think that's all we're good for, drinking and screwing. If you want to drink, do it in your cabin.'

'That won't be a problem.'

Bellfield picked up his phone. 'Jamie, he's all yours. Come and collect him.' He turned to Jim. 'Take it easy. The job is a doddle compared to real seagoing. The pay's not bad, good food and you are steaming around in good weather. Women whenever you want them but be discreet; no port problems; lots of junior officers to do the paperwork - enjoy it!'

The door opened and a younger man came in. He was slim, fair haired and well groomed, the opposite of Bellfield. Jim put his age at mid to late thirties.

'Jim, meet Jamie West, your Group Safety Manager.' They shook hands.

'If you're finished, Sir, we'll go to my office.'

Bellfield waved them away. 'Have a good trip, Jim.'

Jamie's office was two doors down.

'So, how did you find our Fleet Safety Manager?'

Jim was careful. 'He's interesting.'

'He's a dinosaur,' snorted West. 'A nice one, but still in the past. Now Clariby, let's understand each other. You work for me and I expect you to fully understand the company safety management systems. You will comply with them completely. If there are any problems, you will advise me immediately. Is that understood?'

Jim nodded, not trusting himself to speak.

'This company is very successful and that is due to their operational procedures. Our guest numbers are increasing every year, because they enjoy being on our ships. Remember those words. Enjoy being on board.

Now, your job is to ensure that the safety requirements are complied with, without causing undue disturbance. Understand?'

Again Jim nodded.

'Remember, I am always available to you if required.'

'Surely my first duty is to report any problem I have to the Staff Captain and the Captain?'

'Well of course I expect that, but regardless I want you to inform me as well. Do we understand each other?'

We certainly do thought Jim. 'I will do my best, Mr West.'

'That's what I want. Now you have to go to the outfitters, so if you go down to the foyer I will ensure the taxi's on its way.' He stood up and held his hand out. 'I hope you have a good voyage, and don't forget I am here any time you want me.'

Jim's visit to the outfitters was relatively short and he was soon on the train heading back to Somerset. The company livery was gaudy compared to the standard merchant navy uniform he was used to, but that was a minor issue. He had a job and that was all that mattered.

Chapter 3

Jenny watched as Jim packed. She had learnt over the years to let him pack, but to also remind him of what he had forgotten.

'You've got more gold braid as a Safety Officer than you had as Captain,' she remarked.

'I've a feeling there'll be a lot more braid on board. I just hope it's not trying to make up for a lack of ability.'

He stepped back from the cases, 'I think that's about it.'

'No it's not,' she said. 'You forgot your bow tie.'

'Thanks.'

'And your cummerbund. You'll need that soon if you continue eating all that good food.'

'A strict diet, I promise,' he said giving her a hug.

'I don't mind the food, just watch out for the women.'

Jenny always said that whenever he went away, but she never questioned him when he returned.

Jenny drove him to the station in their old estate car. She glanced across at him as she drove. His mind was elsewhere. It was always the same; the last few days were not leave. He had already gone aboard the ship long before he got there. She sighed. The house would be empty without him, and although it had been worrying, it had been lovely having him at home for so long.

'What are you smiling about? Glad to get rid of me?'

'No. I was just thinking you've become quite a handyman these last few months.'

'Well, now you've got an excuse to see the plumber again,' he laughed.

'Hah! Have you seen him? He's as old as the hills and has a beer belly that rolls as he walks. I can do better than that!'

They arrived at the station.

'Make sure he pays rent.'

She kissed him. 'I love you. Take care.'

She never came onto the station platform or lingered. She drove off into the distance and he headed off to his train.

He picked up his gear and headed for the train which, after a few changes, would take him to the airport and then on to Barcelona where he would join his ship.

He had seen pictures of the ship so there was no surprise when the taxi pulled up at the passenger terminal where the ship was berthed. She didn't look old, but Jim knew that, under the new aluminium, paint and plastics, there was a thirty year old hull. Although it was only morning, passengers were already swarming on and there was the usual bustle that existed around any ship that was due to sail.

He pulled out his crew pass as he approached the security at the gates. He passed through without any problem and continued to the reception area. From the desk, he was directed to a side door leading to the crew gangway. It was on the jetty and led to the ship's working alleyway.

He identified himself to the security guard on duty at the gangway.

'Continue on, turn left and walk straight down until you come to the lift. You want deck level 2. You'll see a door marked crew only. That's where the deck officers live.'

'Thank you. Would you get a steward for my bags, please.'

'They're not stewards any more, they're waiters. I don't know if there are any available.'

Jim could feel himself becoming pissed off already.

'Let's start again. Try the magic word 'Sir' and call for a waiter. Do it now.'

The guard hesitated. Jim could see he was wondering whether to chance it or not, but he picked up his walkie-talkie and spoke into it.

He turned to Jim. 'It'll be a few minutes.'

'Sir.'

He hesitated again. 'Sir.'

'There,' said Jim. 'That's better. Easy isn't it?'

A few minutes' silence followed.

'Are you new here, Sir?' The Sir was reluctant but it was there.

'Yes and new to the company. I joined a few weeks ago.'

'She's all right. The hotel crowd are a bit snotty as usual, but I've been on worse.'

Jim looked at him with interest. He was in his late forties, probably about the same age as Jim, stocky in build and there was an air about him.

'Which company did you sail with?' asked Jim.

'Quartermaster and Master at Arms with Union Castle, Sir.'

'So what are you doing as a security guard?'

'They don't want British seafarers do they? All the seamen here are Filipinos. They're good lads, but much cheaper than us.'

'So are all the security guards British?'

'No. There are six of us and only two are Brits. The others come from all over. There's one from Russia, one from Romania and two from Poland.'

'Are they all ex-merchant navy?'

'The other Brit is from the Royal Navy and the Poles are from the Polish navy.'

'Who's the senior man?'

'I am.'

'So you're the Chief Petty Officer?'

'I suppose so. They don't call me that though; they call me Senior Security Officer. There are more officers on board than you can shake a stick at. Any time they want more money, they give them another stripe instead. The difficulty is knowing who really is an officer or a jumped up waiter.' He looked around. 'Talking of which, here's the lad for your bags. Sorry about that at the beginning, Sir. Just having a bad day.'

'It happens to us all. I'll see you around. What's your name?'

'Bert Fallows, Sir.' Jim held his hand out and they shook.

Jim followed the waiter up to the Officers' deck. They stopped outside a cabin where the sign above the door said Safety Officer. Jim knocked and entered. No-one was in, but two suitcases were sitting in the small dayroom/office. The waiter put Jim's bags down and disappeared. There was a small bedroom off the dayroom and also a bathroom. It was compact but adequate accommodation. Jim moved his bags into the bedroom, then left the cabin and went out into the alleyway. It was quiet so Jim went forward and found stairs leading to the next deck, which was labelled bridge deck. After a short walk, he arrived at the bridge door, but it was closed and he needed an unlock code. He banged on the door and waited, but there was no reply.

'Can I help you?'

He looked behind him. It was a young Filipino officer with two stripes on his shoulders. Jim assumed he was one of the Second Officers.

'I'm the new Safety Officer, Jim Clariby,' he said.

'Good morning, Sir. We are expecting you. I think the Safety Officer and Captain are on the bridge.' He reached forward, typed in the code and opened the door.

The bridge was wide and spacious. A large chart table separated the main bridge area, which spanned the width of the ship enclosing the bridge wings. A meeting was going on, and the participants turned to look at Jim. Three of them were in white uniform and had four stripes. Jim approached the group and introduced himself to the person who looked the oldest and most likely to be the Captain.

'Jim Clariby, Sir. Your new Safety Officer.'

'Dave Benson, your Captain.' He was much older than the others gathered around him. Possibly early sixties. He was bald, stout and had glasses perched on the end of his nose. 'You've caught us all together. Let me introduce you. Henri Larou the Hotel Manager, Peter Bramby the Cruise Director, Gabriel Sattori the Staff Captain and the man you're relieving, Anthony Marvin.' They looked a mixed bunch. The Cruise Director was wearing a light tropical suit and looked exactly as he should, expansive with a florid face and in his fifties. The Hotel Manager was dark, small and looked worried. The Staff Captain was the youngest; he had a thin moustache and an air about him. Jim guessed he was in his late thirties. Marvin was black, tall, slim and a little older than the Staff Captain.

'As the new Safety Officer, this concerns you. We're discussing when to hold the passenger boat drill. We are due to sail at 1900 this evening. The first sitting for dinner starts at 1830 and the last of the passengers arrive from the airport at 1730. So when do we have the drill? Tony wants it at 1800 before we sail, but everyone else wants it tomorrow morning. What do you think?'

'1800 before we sail,' replied Jim promptly.

There was an immediate storm of protest from the others while the Captain watched calmly. Larou and Bramby were the most vocal. The passengers wouldn't have time to get ready, and the hotel staff would be preparing the first dinner sitting. Even the Staff Captain was supporting them.

'Captain, we must consider the guests. It's unreasonable to send them immediately to their drill.'

The Captain thought for a moment and then said, 'OK gentlemen, I've had enough. 1800 it is. You will have to sort out your staff. If the first sitting is delayed a little then so be it. Just make an announcement. Tony, take Jim off and do your handover, and give him his orientation at the same time. I'll see you after we sail, Jim.'

Jim followed Tony to his cabin. As soon as they closed the door, Tony erupted.

'Those shits, every time we try to do things properly, they scream about their precious 'guests'. Thank Christ we have a proper Captain here, otherwise who knows what would happen. Even then the drill is watered down. We mustn't panic the punters, you understand. Anyway it's your problem now. There's nothing to it from your point of view as the bridge broadcasts what to do. It tells the passengers to put their lifejackets on and then assemble in the lounges in the specific areas for their boats. The hotel side are supposed to make sure that the passengers listen to the broadcast and put their lifejackets on correctly. I say supposed to, because most wouldn't say boo to any of the passengers. It's really more like an airline drill. Those who are interested watch and those who aren't don't. Let's go for a tour around and your orientation.'

They left the cabin and went down to the next deck and entered the passenger accommodation. Passengers were milling around and one or two asked for directions, which Tony politely provided.

They continued down to another deck and went further forward, entering a door in the bulkhead. Behind this was a working alleyway leading to another door marked Emergency HQ. Inside there was an array of fire suits and breathing apparatus hanging on hooks on the bulkhead. On the opposite bulkhead was a comprehensive array of equipment.

'Your emergency party is a total of 34 crew, which is half sailors and half hotel staff. Half assemble here under you and the other half go to the after station under the senior Second Mate. They are also under your orders. The problem is that the boat parties are mostly hotel staff. We don't have enough seamen to go round. They have all got their boat certificates, but we know what they're worth. If we want properly trained people for the boats we have to strip the fire parties of the seamen. So either we have a fire or an abandon ship, but not both together!'

'The engine room have their own fire equipment and the Chief is pretty hot on their training. He's Polish, bloody good but his English is not so great; you have to speak slowly. Sometimes the Old Man forgets and the conversations from the bridge between him and the Chief can be quite interesting. He has a Staff Chief Engineer who's a Brit. He looks after the admin, as well as all the accommodation machinery, lifts, galley plumbing, that type of thing. He also looks after the cranes and boat davits except the wires, which come under the deck department.'

'Who are the coxswains for the boats?'

'We have six boats on each side and a Fast Rescue Craft for each side. The FRC crews are fully trained up; they do their courses in the UK. The crews are all seafarers so no problems there. All the junior officers have done the coxswains course along with the Bosun and three of the ABs.'

'How often are they exercised?' asked Jim.

'When we can. It's usually about once a month when we get time in port, and if the port allows us to put the boats down.'

'Not at sea?'

'No, company orders,' said Tony shaking his head. 'There was an accident a few years ago when boats were put down at sea. So now it's only in port.'

'That doesn't make sense.'

Tony clapped him on the back. 'You'll learn. Ours is not to reason why. Come to the safety office. I'll show you the station cards there. You have an admin officer by the way. She's Filipino, a very clever lady.'

The office was a short walk from the emergency station HQ. When they entered, a small smiling woman in a white uniform stood up.

'Jim, this is Mary, the most efficient Safety Officer on the seven seas. Mary, Mr Clariby, the new Safety Officer. I'd marry her but my wife would kill me.'

'So would my husband,' Mary said smiling. She was small and chubby with a round shining face and a lovely smile.

'Mary belongs to the hotel side, but we have diverted her.' The printer was whirring away. Tony went over and took a sheet out.

It was part of an updated emergency station bill with the crew changes already on it. 'Safety matters like this I have distributed by one of the cadets. That way I know they get there.'

Tony took Jim over to the state board.

'This is the main state board. It shows where all the different fire equipment is positioned around the ship and also where the hydrants are. You have a phone bank here with direct lines to the engine room and bridge. Over here are the various electrical areas divided up for ease to isolate as required. The engine room will do that on your orders. If there is an emergency, one of the Third Officers will come down here and man the communications for you.'

'What about stability and flooding control?' asked Jim.

'That's under the Staffie, whose station is on the bridge with the Old Man. They get on with that as required.'

He pointed to a long line of files in a bookcase. 'Those are all the safety certificates. Everything is up to date. I never look at them as it's easier leaving it to Mary. The bridge has duplicates of the ones required for port entry - occasionally they want the originals and we send them up as required. One other thing, there are three firemen on board. They are responsible for keeping all the equipment in good order and up to date. They are on watches, same as the bridge. In day time they do the equipment and at night they do fire patrol.'

'Where are they normally?' asked Jim.

'Outside the engine room, there is a small office where all the fire detectors and smoke alarms are. They are duplicated on the bridge. That's where they hang out when they're not working, either that or in the crew bar.'

Jim looked at him. Tony shrugged.

'They're ex-firemen from the Ukraine and were trained by the Soviet Navy. You have to watch them. They're good at their job, but they enjoy their drink. They will also join your fire parties and do the fire training on board.'

'In the locker over there is all your safety equipment. It's kept by the Bosun and he is responsible for its issue and collection. You'll meet him later. He's a good seaman, but don't expect too much leadership from him. He'd prefer to follow decisions rather than make them. The hotel people look after their own equipment.'

'Does that come under me?'

'Theoretically, yes. All aspects of safety come under you, but their own safety guy tends to look after that. He is one of the deputy head waiters. I meet with him periodically, usually when they are filing an accident report. Mary deals with those as well. Next, the lifeboats.'

They went up to the boat deck and outside. It was deserted. The boats were stowed in their davits in a row broken by the large tenders, two on each side.

'Each tender carries 150 passengers. The crew have good boat experience in the boat ports, but because terminals are being built everywhere, they are being used less and less. Still the good thing is that the company is always looking for cheap ports so they are still in use. The FRCs are at the end of each row of boats.'

Jim looked down the boat deck. 'At least there is space to muster the passengers and crew by the boats.'

Tony feigned shock. 'Good God, we don't do that. The poor darlings might get cold and wet. No, they assemble in the lounges. It's not too bad as they're on the same deck as the boats so it's easy to get them out and on board.'

'How often do you lower the boats?'

'When we can. I usually try to get them down to the embarkation deck about once a month, and when I can I put one into the water for a drive around. Come on, let's continue round the ship.'

The tour covered all the decks and the safety equipment. They also made a quick visit to the galley, which was a bedlam of noise and shouted orders.

'It's like this until late at night when they go and the cockroaches come out.'

'Do you have many?'

Tony smiled. 'She's an old ship, what do you expect? That's one of the reasons why they're very strict about not allowing any of the punters in.'

Chapter 4

Eventually they arrived back at the cabin. Tony looked at his watch.

'I still have plenty of time. I'm not flying out tonight. I'm going to a hotel then getting a flight in the morning.'

'Where are you heading?'

'South of France, near Antibes. What about you? Have you got out yet?'

'I'd like to but my wife is firmly rooted.'

'Before I forget,' Tony said, 'here's your pass key. Guard it like gold dust. If you lose it, there will be a major inquiry.' He passed it to Jim. 'You also have a passenger table in both sittings. Table number 12 in the main restaurant.'

'Is there an officers' mess?' asked Jim.

'Yes, but Staffie likes the senior officers to attend the restaurant.'

'What about the Old Man?'

'He couldn't give a toss. He doesn't like going down and is always looking for an excuse to duck out.' He went to a refrigerator in the corner of the dayroom and took out two beers, passing one to Jim. 'Here's to a good trip.' Jim nodded his agreement.

'What about the company Safety Management System?' asked Jim.

'Mary keeps the amendments up to date. She sends a copy of any new amendments to the department head concerned unless it's a major one, in which case it goes to all heads. Each department is responsible for their hours of work. I used to think we flogged the books a bit but you should see the hotel side. Anyway, one of the Third Mates does the deck ones. At the end of each month, they come in to Mary and she files them. It's the same with risk assessments. Each department keeps their own. I usually go through them each month to check they are being updated and that work card comes in here at the end of each month. I meet with all the department safety officers each month in the command conference room, which is on this deck near the bridge. It can last all morning so you have to pick your time carefully. Of course they can come to you at any time.'

'What about the Staff Captain?' asked Jim.

'This one isn't really interested unless it affects him. He's just waiting to get ashore so he doesn't want any problems. In some ways it's good. He'll leave you to do your own thing, but don't expect any support. Theoretically, the deck department comes under him with you looking after safety. He likes his social life so he relies on you to deal with most of it. I meet him each morning, tell him what I'm doing and get on with it unless the hotel people have been whining in his ear, then you'll find him suddenly interested. For example, today the cadets have been spirited away to mess around with one of the swimming pools.'

'How many cadets do we have?'

'The deck department has four and the engine department has two.'

'I suppose I should meet them, and the Bosun for that matter,' said Jim.

'The Bosun will normally come to see you before eight every morning and around five in the afternoon, that's when he's free. The problem is we are constantly in and out of port with a night at sea. Is it very different to what you've been used to? I hear you were in command of a cruise ship.'

'Word travels fast. Yes I was, but a much smaller one than this. We carried 400 passengers. We had a mix of South African and British crew. They were a good crowd of experienced seamen and officers. We had to be, working in the Antarctic. The company was very seamanship and deck department orientated. There aren't many ports in the Antarctic so we had long spells at sea.'

'I dream of that, but I'm afraid we are in the hotel ship age. One day we'll look out of the window and ask what is the sea? Let's finish our drinks and head to the bridge. I know you're not a watchkeeper, but they might let you drive one day. I've been here for over two years and not had the chance yet.'

'It'll feel strange to sail without having any responsibility on the bridge.'

'Enjoy it while you can, Jim.'

They walked along the alleyway and came to the bridge door.

'The pass number is 1441,' said Tony.

As they entered, an officer Jim had not met glanced up from the automated chart display system which had been built into the chart table.

'Peter, this is Jim, the new Safety Officer. Peter's from Poland but living in Sunderland. Why, God knows. He navigates this mighty vessel.'

Peter smiled. 'Welcome on board.' They shook hands.

'What's the schedule?'

'Look here.' He played with the chart display and the whole western half of the Mediterranean showed up. 'We sail this evening at 1900 to Genoa, then on to Livorno, Palermo, Naples, Corsica and then back to Barcelona. It's a standard cruise run so I don't need a chart for that. I can do it in my sleep.'

Tony continued to show Jim round all the bridge instruments, lingering at the radars to show their setup.

'Once you get away, I'm sure the others will show you in more detail.' Jim was looking at the watertight door indicator board.

'How often do you close them?' he asked.

'We test them weekly, but only close them in fog. All the indicators and safety equipment on the bridge are tested by the officers. They'll advise you when they've been tested and Mary will then log the tests. Same with the engine room. They have their own safety officer who is one of the Third Engineers. He's not really interested so Mary has to chase him for his test reports.'

'What about fire exercises?'

'We do drills rather than exercises, although I do keep trying to arrange them. Again, it's dictated by time restrictions and pressures of schedule. Drills are carried out in port when the punters are off the ship and before the next batch join. Come on, let's go and find the Bosun. We'll go outside and get some fresh air.'

They went out the back of the bridge and down the ladders to the promenade deck.

'The deck planking looks well cared for,' commented Jim.

'They were renewed a short time ago, but it's nice to see it. The crew are kept busy having to hose it down in the mornings. We still haven't managed to stop the engineers from dropping soot on it though.' They found the Bosun and a party of seamen cleaning out one of the pools in the large swimming pool complex at the after end of the deck. When he saw them approaching, he put his deck broom down.

'Good afternoon, Bosun. What happened here?' asked Tony.

'Passengers last night, Sir. They had a party here and put all the chairs and tables into the pool.'

'It's not that unusual, so we just pull them out,' commented Tony.

'No, Sir. They also threw in bottles and glasses so we have to get broken glass out. As it is empty, I can get it clean.'

On the other side of the pool, the cadets were looking at the damaged deck furniture. Jim was used to cadets in their teens, but three of them looked older. He remarked on this.

'One is twenty three and the youngest, the female cadet, is nineteen,' replied Tony.

'What are they like?'

'Spoilt. They think this is normal seagoing. Staffie has them mostly on the bridge, making checks or something. Every time you see them, they're on the gangways or running around with checklists.'

Jim went over to them. 'Good afternoon. I'm the new Safety Officer, Mr Clariby, and you are?'

There was a pause while they looked at him. The female cadet spoke first. 'I'm Julie.' After another pause, the oldest one said 'I'm Dave, this is Arun and Stephen.'

Jim thought for a moment. 'Let's get a few things straight. I am a senior officer and you are cadets. I don't want to know your first names. I am unlikely to ever refer to you by them, at least until you become officers. Next, you will address me as Sir. So, let's start again.'

He pointed to the oldest one. 'With you.'

The cadet looked sullenly at him. 'Jameson.' He paused deliberately. 'Sir.' They all followed accordingly.

'The Staffie calls us by our first names,' Jameson said.

Jim rounded on him. 'I don't care if he calls you arsehole, which is how you're behaving. I'll call you what I bloody well like. Is that understood?'

They stood in shock.

'Well?'

There were mumblings of 'Yes, Sir.'

'Good, now carry on with your work.'

Jim returned to Tony who had been listening.

'That was good; they need more of that. It's obvious you've been in command for a while,' said Tony.

'That's got nothing to do with it, Tony. Their attitude is our fault. They've been allowed to get away with it. We're supposed to be making officers of them, but they won't be any good like that.'

They walked slowly back along the decks to the accommodation. Tony looked at his watch.

'It's late but shall we go to the officers' messroom and grab a sandwich for lunch?'

'Good idea.'

They got into the service lift on the officers' deck and went down several levels.

When they got out, the alleyway was busy with various crew members passing by. The doors ahead of them led to a large cafeteria style messroom. It was almost deserted except for a couple of officers in white boiler suits at a corner table. They took trays and, after selecting their food, Tony led Jim to a table in an alcove.

'There are no set tables, but this is regarded as the senior officers' table.'

'Is there an officers' bar or wardroom?' asked Jim.

'There is a lounge on deck four, but that tends to be full of hotel people and entertainers, so I use my cabin.'

'What about a bar?'

'There's a crew bar, but because the officers are allowed to use certain passenger amenities when they are off duty, there isn't a specific bar for officers.'

'That's a pity. I find it helps if the officers can relax away from the passengers.'

'I guess what we've never had, we don't miss,' Tony said.

They finished their meal and returned to Tony's cabin.

'There's probably a lot I haven't told you,' he said, 'but I've written handover notes, which are here on the desk, so hopefully you've got most of the necessary information.'

'I'll probably think of questions once you've left,' said Jim. 'That's normal.'

Tony went into the bedroom but continued the conversation. 'You have a steward who does your room. The problem is that he has another 15 officers' cabins to do, so there isn't much time for niceties.'

'Where do the cadets live?'

'They have cabins at the end of the alleyway here. The steward does their cabins as well.'

'What!'

'Company instructions.'

'That's ridiculous! They're cadets. Cleaning their quarters is part of their training.'

'I said exactly the same thing when I joined the company, but no one listened.'

'Never mind. When you become Staff Captain, you can change things on your ship.'

Tony came back into the dayroom dressed in casual clothing. 'Fat chance of that.'

'There's a first time for everything,' said Jim.

Tony laughed. 'I'm not interested, Jim. I have a nice place in France, a happy family and no hassle. I get on the ship, keep my head down, do my job and leave. I'll leave it to you to fight over the spoils.'

Tony held his hand out. 'Best of luck, especially when you get to the *'Majestic'*.' He picked up his bags and paused by the door.

'Watch out for Staffie. He's so slippery that nothing sticks to him. If the shit doesn't stick to him, you can guess where it does stick.'

With that, he was gone. Jim checked his watch. It was almost 1700. He had time to unpack, shower and change into his uniform before the passenger boat drill.

At 1730, he walked along the alleyway to the Staff Captain's quarters. He was in his office, which led through to a dayroom. It was compact but still pleasant.

'Come in, Clariby. Sit down. I trust the handover went smoothly?'

'Yes, Sir. Mr Marvin has left the ship now.'

'Good, good. He's a good man Marvin. He could be more committed but he's not a career man like you and I. I believe in a 'hands off' approach. With your experience, I'm sure you know the job and what is required, so carry on. Always remember I am here if required. The main thing is I want to be kept informed about what is going on and what you are doing. There is a heads of department staff meeting every day, so each morning I would like a small written report about any problems, what is planned, that kind of thing. It is important that you understand the delicate balance between sailing the ship and running a hotel. The hotel doesn't concern us, but we should support the running of it as much as possible. If you feel there are any problems with the hotel side of things then before acting come to me and I will deal with it. Is that understood?'

'Yes, Sir.'

'For example, this nonsense of having this boat drill this evening. It is upsetting for the hotel staff and could have been done tomorrow morning.'

'Sir, I was new to the ship and was asked my opinion out of the blue.'

Sattori raised his hand. 'It's all right. I completely understand. Marvin was really at fault wanting it this afternoon. Anyway, what is done is done. But in future leave these decisions to the department heads, understand?'

Jim nodded.

'Good. I'm sure we will get on very well.' He looked at his watch. 'It's almost time for the drill. Are you going down?'

'Yes, I want to go round the boat assembly points and see how it goes.'

'That's good. Jump right in. I will see you later then. You have your table number for dinner?'

'Yes, but I was hoping to settle in this evening, read the handover notes and the safety management manual.'

'You can do that after dinner. It is important that the guests see you and are made to feel welcome. I hope you realise that this is the balance I was talking about.'

'Very good, Sir. I will attend dinner.'

Chapter 5

Jim went directly to the main forward lounge where the forward lifeboat passengers were to muster. He waited patiently until the first announcement was made warning the passengers that there would be a drill in ten minutes. Five minutes later, another announcement was made warning that the boat signal would be sounded and that this would require them to get their lifejackets from their cabins. He noticed some passengers were sitting in the lounge with tea and cakes who had not moved.

'Excuse me,' Jim said, 'but I think you should go and get your lifejackets, then go to your muster station ready for the drill. You only have a few minutes.' He said this with a smile. One of the men in the group turned round and spoke to Jim.

'It's quite all right, officer. We are regular cruisers with the company and have been on this ship many times before.

'I understand that, Sir,' said Jim. 'However, it is company policy that all passengers should follow the instructions and have their lifejackets. It is entirely for your safety.'

'Look,' said the man. 'We've only just arrived on board and are having a cup of tea. We will listen to what is being said. Why this couldn't be done in the morning as usual I don't know. I will speak to the Captain about this.'

'It was his decision, Sir.'

'Then it was wrong. Now please stop bothering us.'

Then I hope you fucking well drown, thought Jim, just as the alarms sounded.

Jim realised he wasn't getting anywhere and left them to go and watch the other passengers assembling. Most did take it seriously and put their lifejackets on according to the instructions. The lifejackets were bulky and had hard plastic floats in the front. Unless they crossed their arms over the float they would spring up and break their necks if they did have to jump from any height. He noticed the announcement didn't mention that. He took out his pen and began to make notes. Each boat had a hotel officer with a stripe or two in charge who was checking off the passengers. Others went round checking the lifejackets were being worn correctly, but it was obvious they were hurrying. In the centre of the room stood a woman with grey hair who was in charge. He walked up to her and introduced himself.

She was the Embarkation Manager, whatever that was.

'What do you do about any passengers who don't turn up?' he asked.

She looked flustered. 'We send the checklists to the ship's office.'

'Which one?'

'The main reception desk.'

'So they will see the names of those who haven't bothered?'

'I suppose so.'

'And is it the same for those who aren't wearing lifejackets?' he asked pointing to the table with the group having tea. She became even more flustered.

'Well, we don't list those.'

'I don't see anyone making any effort to tell them to get their lifejackets.'

'It's not that easy,' she protested. 'We only have a limited amount of time and we can't force them to get them.'

'Why not?' asked Jim.

'I don't know. You're the Safety Officer, you should know. I would like to make them get them, but we have no authority to do that.'

Jim tried another tack. 'How long does it take to get the passengers from here onto the boat deck by the boats ready for boarding?'

She sighed. 'I really don't know. Look, I'm from the accounts department. I have done the abandon ship courses but everybody passes, so that shows you the standard. I think they chose me because I can count.'

He could see she was becoming agitated.

'Please excuse me. I'm new here and I wanted to find out how things are done. I know you're doing your best.'

She relaxed a little. 'Let's hope that nothing serious ever happens,' she said.

Another announcement was made thanking the guests for their attention and asking them to return their lifejackets to their cabins.

'My thoughts exactly,' muttered Jim.

Jim went up to the bridge for departure. The Captain was on the starboard side looking down at the berth with the Pilot.

'Do you mind if I come up for departure, Sir?' Jim asked.

'Be my guest, Jim. Pilot, this is Jim Clariby, the new Safety Officer. He was a Captain on a cruise ship in the Antarctic. He's doing a few trips here as Safety Officer before going as Staffie on the 'Majestic Sea'.' They shook hands.

'You'll find she's a bit different to this,' said the Pilot. 'I brought her in once, before they moved her to the States. She has state of the art manoeuvring. All done by computers. Just tell the computer where you want her to go and it does the rest.'

'I prefer this,' said the Captain. 'Wheel, engines and thrusters. At least you know when they don't work, and you can get a couple of tugs to assist if you want them. What was yours like, Jim?'

'Same as this.'

'You can let go when you like, Captain,' the Pilot said.

The orders were given and the ship smoothly eased away from the berth. Then with the tugs assisting she turned and headed out down the harbour for the breakwater.

The pilot boat arrived alongside.

'You can get off inside the breakwater if you like, Pilot,' said the Captain. 'I can then turn out to sea as soon as I am clear.'

The Pilot disappeared. Once the boat was clear, the Captain ordered full ahead. The ship surged through the breakwater and turned almost 90 degrees to port and headed out to sea. The weather was calm, but the Captain still ordered the stabilisers out.

He turned to Jim. 'Well that's that. Another day, another cruise. Are you going to the restaurant for dinner?'

'The Staff Captain thinks I should put in an appearance.'

The Captain grunted. 'At least on the first night you don't have to put your penguin suit on. I'm not going, navigational duties,' he smiled.

'When you finish dinner, come up to the cabin for a chat.'

Dinner wasn't as bad as he expected. He had two retired couples and a single lady who was a school teacher on his table. They were all from a different planet, but were still interested in the sea and ship. Jim declined wine and made his excuses early, telling them of his tiredness on joining that day. As he was leaving, there was a loud gust of laughter from a nearby table. Glancing over, Jim saw it was the Staff Captain's table. On it were the couples who had refused to get their lifejackets.

Birds of a feather, thought Jim.

Jim tapped on the Captain's door and entered the spacious outer office. There was a conference table at the side and a large desk looking out over the bow. There was a compass repeater on the bulkhead which ticked occasionally. There was no sign of the Captain so he tapped on the inner door. It opened revealing a homely cabin with a three piece chintz suite and light wood panelling. 'Come in,' a voice called. 'I'll be with you in a minute.'

Jim entered and stood looking out the windows over the bow.

He heard the Captain come in. Turning round he saw he had on an old dressing gown and was drying his hair. 'In the good old days we had baths didn't we? I wonder how many professions can say that things are worse now than thirty years ago. You know, when I came to sea, Captains were paid more than twice what doctors got ashore; now it's the other way round.' He finished drying his hair. 'I'm sorry, I'm rambling. I'm going to make myself a cup of cocoa. Would you like one or something stronger?'

'Cocoa's fine with me.'

'Good. Sit down.' He busied himself at his sideboard where a kettle was boiling. Soon two cups of steaming cocoa were on the low table in front of the settee.

'Tomorrow morning, I'm going to call you into the office out there and give you a mild bollocking.'

Jim looked up surprised.

'Did you have cadets on your last ship?' asked the Captain.

'Yes, same as here. We had four.'

'And I bet you drove them hard.'

'Well, not me, but my Chief Officer did. We had to because the training time at sea has been cut so much we don't have much time to make officers of them.'

'Good, I'm pleased to hear that. That's how it should be.' He paused and then added, 'But not here. The company has a 'friendly' training policy set out by human resources based ashore. It's called a modern approach, whatever that is. It means you don't swear at cadets.' The Captain could see Jim wanted to speak and held his hand up. 'Wait a minute. The little darlings complained to Staffie who scuttled along to see me. He could have dealt with it himself, but I think he is a little intimidated by you. Anyway, now I have it. They could have complained to their parents, and that would have then involved the office. Hell, they could have probably complained to their MP, and then there would have been questions in Parliament. That's what it's like now. They're not being trained as seamen; they are being trained as socialising technicians. You must also take care with the hotel people. They're not seamen either. If truth be known, the two of us and a few others are probably the only real seamen left on board.'

'I'm sorry, Captain. I didn't mean to cause any problems especially on my first day on board.'

'Given your background, Jim, it was inevitable. Now I suggest you spend this first cruise observing. You will see a lot of things wrong and a lot of things you will want to change. By all means put any suggestions on paper for my desk and we can discuss them. A few of us have tried, and the more of us who try the more chance we might have in reminding them that these things are ships. Understand?'

'I will be grateful for your experience, and I mean that,' replied Jim.

'Try to work with the Staff Captain. I know he's a pain, but he's our pain. Anyway he won't be with us much longer. He's destined for higher things, which is good because it gets him off ships.'

The Captain stood up and Jim did as well. 'Good to have you on board. Don't forget, tomorrow morning, act surprised.'

In the morning, once Jim had reported to the Staff Captain, he was taken to the Captain's office, where Sattori made his complaint. The Captain looked serious and reminded Jim of how to treat personnel, including the cadets.

'I think the Safety Officer should apologise,' said Sattori.

'What?' spluttered Jim.

'Apologise to who?' asked the Captain.

'The cadets of course.'

The Captain watched Jim's face.

'Captain Sattori, I don't know how it's done in Italy, but in the UK senior officers do not apologise to cadets for their professional conduct unless they happen to fart, when it may be acceptable if it is noticeable. The matter is closed.'

On the second night at sea, it was the Captain's cocktail party. It was a strange affair. Jim was used to stand up receptions where the ships officers circulated among the passengers. But not here. Instead all the passengers sat down and the senior officers lined up at the front. Worse was to follow. The Captain was introduced by a fanfare from the band and the spotlight was shone on him. He then had to make a welcome speech, which thankfully he kept as brief as possible. Then he introduced his senior officers. Each one had to step out into the spotlight accompanied by a fanfare and the passengers' applause.

'I wonder if they would clap if they knew what we really thought?' the ship's doctor, a dour Australian, whispered.

Chapter 6

Jim spotted plenty to do on the safety side, but found that the security team, especially as they were trained seamen, could be very useful. Tony, while a good officer, had been lax over some of the checks. Jim tightened up the procedures for these. All the time, he made notes. He even managed to change the broadcast made to the passengers to include a warning about holding down the front of the lifejackets, although it was a battle with the hotel side who felt it might disturb the passengers and appear critical of the lifejackets.

'So we should be,' said the Captain. 'Bloody cheap crap.'

During the second cruise, when they were about to leave Livorno, the Captain called Jim to the bridge.

'Nice morning,' he said. 'I thought you might like to keep your hand in. Want to take her out?'

It felt good to be driving again. The bridge officers responded well to Jim's commands and the ship left the port smoothly. Gradually the Captain allowed Jim more ship handling and, by the end of the third cruise, the bridge recognised them as a team. Sattori left the ship after this cruise and, as expected, entered the operations department. The new Staff Captain, Charlie Clayton, was very different and was grateful to Jim for his work and assistance with settling in.

Jim found himself enjoying the ship and his job, something he didn't expect to happen. A lot was due to the Captain. He also managed to stop going to the cocktail parties.

'I'm sorry, Captain. I'm embarrassed by this nonsense of the presentation. We're seamen, not showbiz. It's disgraceful having the band play and the passengers clapping us. For what?'

The Captain thought for a while. 'I agree, but it's company orders. I have to do it, but I don't think there is regulation saying you have to. Tell you what, don't make a song and dance about it. Just don't turn up. I'll deal with Staffie if it's an issue, but I don't think it will be. He doesn't like it either.'

Halfway through the fourth cruise, Jim went to the Captain with his carefully considered recommendations. The Captain perched his glasses on his nose and scanned through them.

'Leave this with me for a few days, Jim, and then we'll discuss it.'

Two days later, there was a meeting in the Captain's office. The new Staff Captain and the Hotel Manager had also been invited.

'Jim, I have invited Henri here as much of this concerns him. You all had a copy of this sent to you a few days ago and I would like to go through it with you now.'

'There's a lot here that I have seen written before,' commented Charlie.

'That doesn't mean we shouldn't discuss it,' said the Captain.

'No, not at all. I'm not disagreeing, just commenting,' replied Charlie.

'Let's start with the first item. Jim has noted there is a lack of discipline with the passenger boat drill. Some of these points we know. We are not forcing the passengers to wear their lifejackets or to even listen to the drill. Jim suggests that, when the list of missing passengers is sent to the office, those passengers are called to a separate briefing and not allowed to get away with this. The same would apply to those who don't bring lifejackets.'

'That's not possible,' said Henri.

'Why not?' asked Jim.

'Because we are here for their pleasure. What are we going to do if they refuse? Chuck them off the ship?'

'Why not?' said Jim. 'That's what we used to do. It will make the others realise we're serious about safety.'

'Captain, this is lunacy.'

'I see his point, Henri, but I agree with you. We can't put them down the gangway, much as I'd like to. They would probably sue us. Tell you what we could do though, we could put a polite note in their cabin saying their presence was missed or that it was noticed that they didn't have their lifejacket and to get in touch with the office for private advice regarding boat drill.'

'That doesn't solve the problem though,' said Jim.

'No, but it shows we are watching, and that's about as far as we can go in this company.'

'Can we turn the volume up on the speakers for the drill briefing? Then even if they are talking, it will override them,' asked Jim.

'Staffie, what do you think?'

'Why not, provided it doesn't distort the audio.'

'Henri?'

'No objections, Captain.'

'OK that's agreed. I see you want to run a full scale fire and boat drill for the entire crew. Where and why? Also that you want to form a 'panic suppression' team. What's that? Are you going to go around clubbing the punters?' asked the Captain.

'The fire parties are made up of all the seamen and added to by the hotel staff,' said Jim. 'If boat stations are sounded, the sailors have to go to man the boats. I want to see the effect that has on the fire teams and also how long it takes for the seamen to get to the boats. I would like to hold it in port when the passengers are changing over.'

The Captain looked at Henri. 'What do you think?'

'It could be done, but that is a busy time for us,' Henri replied.

'All right, Jim, I understand. Liaise with Henri and find a time when it is acceptable. Now the press gang. What about them?'

Jim took a deep breath.

'I believe we would have a problem with panic if we ever had to abandon ship. The problem is control. All the passenger direction is controlled by the hotel staff, who only have very basic training. Many may not understand the concept of passengers first.'

'That's a disgraceful thing to say,' said Henri.

'We must be ready for all eventualities. In addition, the entire hotel department are wandering around the ship covered in gold braid. When there is an emergency, all the passengers see is gold braid. They depend on these people for decisions and I don't believe they will get them. The idea for the panic party is for a group of crew to be established from the deck or engine departments who can be relied on to control the boat deck. They must wear their uniform and cap to separate them from the hotel people.'

'This is nonsense,' said Henri. 'You have no reason to say these things, and the company won't allow such a change.'

'I like the idea,' said Charlie, 'but you won't get away with it. It implies a distrust in the hotel side, who make up ninety percent of the ship's personnel. The company would never admit to that.'

'He's right,' said the Captain. 'Now moving on to the wheelchairs.'

'Sir, the number on board is a major problem, particularly for abandon ship. If these passengers are on decks other than the boat deck, how do they get up the stairs without lifts?'

'We could arrange for the lifts to be available for them,' said Henri.

'But all the power to the lifts is switched off as soon as abandon ship is declared. Anyway the chances are the ship would be listing. Have you tried to push a wheelchair along with a list? You can't do it. So how do we get these people to the boats?'

There was silence for a moment.

'You must have had these on your ship. How did you deal with it?' asked the Captain.

'Certain cabins were allocated to them which were adjacent to the boats. A crew member was delegated to each passenger, and it was their responsibility to assist that passenger in the event of an emergency. Mind you, I have seen passengers on here who are so old or infirm that we wouldn't have accepted them on board in the first place,' replied Jim.

The Captain looked at Henri. 'Over to you.'

Henri looked at Jim. 'Please don't think we're not concerned about this. I know in the past others have drawn the company's attention to this problem, but apart from confidential reminders about care and attention little has been done.'

'The problem is, as always, the cost,' said Charlie. 'It's impossible to redesign existing ships, or even new ships being built for that matter.'

'Then what about reducing their numbers on board? Each ship could be assessed for the number it can safely accommodate and accept.'

'This has been discussed before, Jim,' said the Captain. Charlie nodded in agreement.

'It is a delicate issue. You're correct in what you're suggesting, but retired people are the most infirm and they are the lifeblood of this industry. Move against them and you'll have every pensioners support group coming at us. Also there is the issue of discrimination.'

'Even if it's in the interest of safety?'

'They won't be interested in that. It would be another issue for these groups to hang their publicity hats on. I can already see the civil rights lawyers enjoying themselves on breakfast television. Sorry, Jim. I'm afraid it's something we have to live with.'

'Until there's an incident,' remarked Jim.

'As you say, until then. Even then it would have to be big.'

Jim looked at Henri. 'Could you assign hotel staff to these people and have that as their emergency station?'

'It depends on the number on board. We have no control over that. But I will look into it for you.'

As they continued down the list, Henri became increasingly angry.

'It seems you have no trust in us,' he said to Jim.

'No, you're wrong,' Jim said. 'It's because of the basic training your staff have had. A few days learning about crowd control and boatwork is not sufficient for an emergency.'

'I disagree,' said Henri.

The meeting broke up with just a few changes agreed to.

After the others had gone, the Captain signalled Jim to sit down.

'You'll have noticed that I didn't discuss the administration changes, lifejackets or some of the equipment suggestions. That's because it is for head office. However, I'm not forwarding them to the office.'

'Don't you agree with them?' asked Jim.

'On the contrary, I do agree. Have you heard the Chinese saying of breaking someone's rice bowl? Someone in that office made the decision to give us that equipment or decided on those procedures. By making this report, you are saying they are wrong. Who is going to win, someone new to the company like you or them with friends ashore? Imagine the cost of changing all the lifejackets. You want all the hotel staff to have completely separate uniforms to distinguish them from the deck and engine department. Christ, apart from the cost, they would go ape over that. They love their gold braid. Do you know the cooks have four stripes? Even the barman's got two. You suggest that passengers should have smoke hoods in all the cabins for escape if there is a fire. No cruise ship in the world has that.'

'Yet all the hotels in Japan do.'

'Then they can go on holiday in Japan. It's a good idea, and yes if there was a severe fire in the cabin areas we wouldn't be able to get them out. We know that. We exist to prevent such accidents. We pray it never happens, because we know the consequences. That's what we are here for, prevention and to take the blame if things do go wrong. Jim, a few of your ideas were agreed to. Be happy with that.'

'Now, on to other things. I have been advised you are to go on leave at the end of this cruise. I know it's early but they want you on the *Majestic Sea* in good time to get you settled in before she starts this new Arctic flyby business. I have been asked to give an evaluation of you. Here it is.'

He passed across a confidential report form, which Jim read.

'Thank you very much, Captain.'

'Not at all, you deserve it. You will note that I have recommended that you are immediately promoted to full Captain. They won't do it, but it guarantees your promotion to Staff Captain. You should make full Captain within a couple of years if not sooner, especially if they continue building new ships.'

'What about you, Captain? Are you going on leave?'

'At the end of the next cruise. I'm also retiring at the end of this year. I'll be pleased to get out.'

'What are you going to do?'

'The Princess and I are heading for New Zealand. Then a nice boat with lots of fishing, good food, booze and a small town where they think political correctness is the local politician not stealing.'

The final day came.

He went and knocked on the Captain's office door.

'So, on your way then?' The Captain stood.

'It's been a pleasure, Sir. Thank you for everything.'

'Likewise. I would have liked to have sailed as a passenger on your ship. I'm sure it would have been a bit different to this.'

Jim smiled. 'Just a little.'

'One last piece of advice from an old Captain. You're bright, but don't show it too much. The office don't like clever seamen. They prefer to think of us as only being slightly annoying, a bit like Popeye. Do you know I got a degree from the Open University two years ago in Greek History? Honours too, but I didn't tell the office. Best of luck on the *'Majestic Sea'*.'

Jim walked back to his cabin and saw the security guard, Bert Fallows, standing there.

'I got word you were on your way so I thought you might need a hand with your bags, Sir.' They both smiled.

Bert put Jim's bags in the taxi. 'I won't say goodbye, Sir, as I'll see you again soon. I'm also going to the *'Majestic Sea'*.'

'I'll see you there then. It'll be good to have a friendly face around. Have a good leave.'

'You too, Sir.'

M.V. *Vacuum Pioneer*

At the same time as Jim went on leave, the M.V. 'Vacuum Pioneer' was heading towards Halifax on the eastern Canadian seaboard. She was still a few hours out on a brisk late spring morning. Seagulls already circled the stern of the ship waiting for the galley waste.

The ship was a 60,000 ton petroleum tanker designed specifically for ice. Her bow and forward part of the hull were strengthened against the hard cutting ice. She also had a high, well-sheltered forecastle. She had sailed up from Galveston in the Gulf of Mexico with a part cargo of aviation fuel. After Halifax, she was due to carry on to Quebec with petrol.

She was not a new ship but not that old either, having been built within the last 10 years. She was well built and equipped, her owners were Norwegian and she was currently chartered to an oil consortium. The Captain and senior officers were Norwegian, and the junior officers and crew were Filipino. She was a happy ship with good management, good food, good manning and best of all, being a product tanker, she was relatively small. She could berth close to towns and often had a few days in port, allowing regular shore leave.

The Captain, Karl Johnsen, was on the bridge talking with the Chief Officer, Eric Aasland, while the Third Officer, Ramon Robredo, the Officer of the Watch, was dealing with the navigation. Ramon had mixed feelings about his forthcoming leave in Galveston. He was anxious to get home to his fiancée, but he was sad to be leaving a good ship.

The Captain picked up his binoculars and peered ahead. He was in his early fifties, of average build with a tanned, weather-beaten face and greying beard. On his left arm was a faded tattoo, a souvenir of his cadet days in the Far East.

'We should see the entrance channel buoys soon, Ramon.'

'Yes, Sir. We are 8 miles away now.'

'Let me know when we're 2 miles off and I'll tell the engine room where we are. We'll reduce speed when we're 3 miles from the pilot station. As soon as you pass the first buoy, let the pilots know our ETA.'

He turned to the Mate. 'At least we'll have the night in. It'll give us a chance to get ashore.' Eric was like a younger version of the Captain except he didn't have a beard or tattoo. He was 30 years old and deeply tanned. Both men had vivid blue eyes.

'Suits me fine, Captain. Halifax beats the hell out of Galveston and the beer's better.'

They were both satisfied men. Satisfied with their ship and their life. They had been at sea since they were boys and had an air of familiarity with their environment. Many seamen intend to leave and find work ashore. They talk of it or dream of it, and some even plan it from their first venture onto the sea. But there are also those who are content with the sea. These men and women, as their experience on the sea increases over the years, take on an assurance of competence that reflects in their attitude to work and life. Above all, they have a familiarity with the ocean, which ensures a deep understanding of what the sea is and ensures their respect for what the sea can do.

Part Two

M.V. *Majestic Sea*

'The ship was golden, gleaming in the sun and enchanting the people, but its beauty attracted the sea that desired it and took it for its own.'

Chapter 7

The short leave passed quickly. As expected, Jim's promotion was confirmed and he was requested to visit the office to see the Fleet Safety Manager.

This time he was asked to go to the 5th floor where there was the obligatory reception desk. After a while, a young man appeared. 'I'm James Peters, the Fleet Safety Manager's assistant. Please come with me, Captain.' Jim was looking forward to seeing Eric Bellfield again. He got a shock. When he entered the office, Jamie West was sitting there.

'Good morning, Captain. A little surprised?'

'Yes. I expected to see Captain Bellfield.'

'He was put out to grass last week. He took early retirement and the company decided to make me Fleet Safety Manager. There are going to be changes, I can tell you. You've met my PA already. He is a seafarer as well, so here we are, three seafarers together.'

In your dreams, Jim thought to himself.

'You'll be joining *'Majestic Sea'* in Fort Lauderdale. They want you to fly out early so they can meet you in our office there. It's quite an operation and a very important office because of the number of American guests we carry. The Fleet Safety Manager there is Adam Falconi and the Fleet Operations Manager is John Zachary. Actually, out there they're called Vice Presidents or VPs. You'll meet both of them. I wanted to emphasise that, regardless of the fact that you are with that fleet, you must continue to keep me advised of anything important. I saw your confidential report from your last ship which was excellent. That was very gratifying. I am sure that if this continues you'll be

Captain before long. Remember, it is the blend of safety and guest comfort that keeps us at the top of the game.'

The rest of the morning was spent discussing recent accidents in the fleet, including the few that had occurred on the *'Majestic Sea'*, together with the new company regulations, which were numerous.

'One thing you'll find different is that the ship carries a Ship General Manager. This is because of the ship's size and, of course, our investment. This causes a delicate problem. Under law, the Captain is in command of the ship, which means that everyone is under him. However, in actual fact, the Captain is responsible for all the navigation, operation and safety aspects of the ship, including engineering, but the General Manager is responsible for all other aspects. In a way, he acts as a bridge between the hotel side of the ship and the rest. This is a relatively new position and I am assured it is working splendidly. The Lauderdale office will give you a better picture.'

'Is this General Manager from a seagoing background?' Jim asked.

'No. We didn't consider that important. In fact, it may be good because he is unbiased and able to make considered judgements.'

Jim thought about this as he travelled back home. He was very suspicious when any shore office told him something was working 'splendidly'. In his experience, not much at sea worked splendidly. It usually meant that the person saying it didn't have a clue about what was going on. He talked to Jenny about his concerns, but she was more practical.

'Jim, you got your promotion. It also looks like you'll be back up to full Captain very soon. And the money's better. Give it a chance before you start questioning it. I know you want everything to stay the same, but it can't. You have to move with the times.'

'I know,' replied Jim, 'but I'll keep my name with the agencies, just in case.'

The children were home from school so they were able to be together as a family, which was quite rare.

'Mummy said you can have us on board with you,' Annabel piped up. She was like her mother, vivacious and direct.

Jim looked at Jenny. 'Even I didn't know that,' he said.

'It came in the post from Human Resources. Apparently, families are allowed on board if there is room.'

Jim waited until the children had gone outside. 'You know what I feel about you or the children being on board.'

'But that was on smaller ships. On something like this you wouldn't even know we were there,' she protested.

'That's not the point. I know you wouldn't interfere with my work, but if something happened, my mind would be on you, not where it should be, dealing with the problem.'

'Really, Jim. You do worry. What could possibly happen? The ship is huge.'

'Jenny, that's the problem. Including the crew, there are more than 4,000 people on board. That's a lot of people to get off.'

'If it wasn't safe, they wouldn't build them. You sailors, you see problems everywhere. No wonder the hotel people get frustrated with you all.'

'Tell you what, give me time to settle in and we'll take the children to Disneyland in Florida for Christmas. How's that?'

'They'll love that. Promise?'

'Promise.'

Vacuum Pioneer

A few thousand miles away in Croatia, a young man was discussing his future on the phone with an agency. Ivo Milanovic had just obtained his watch-keeping certificate and was now looking for a job. He wasn't interested in what the job was as long as the money was good.

'It's a modern product tanker,' the agent was telling him. 'It's good money, six month contract, then two months' paid leave. If they like you, you will be offered long-term employment. It's a Norwegian company, so there will be no problem getting your money. She's ice class, but you had ice experience when you were a cadet so that's fine. The senior officers are Norwegian so the accommodation is good and so is the food. She's Liberian flag on a long-term charter to American charterers.'

'Where is the ship?'

'Presently on the American and Canadian east coast. It's a good job; if I were you I'd take it. I've got three others on the books so you must decide now.'

Ivo thought for a moment, then answered.

'I'll take it.'

'That's wise. I'll send your details to them now, and I expect I'll hear back by tomorrow.'

'When would they want me?'

'As soon as possible, so you should start packing. Their present Third Mate is waiting to go home to get married.'

He was excited. This was his first ship as an officer, something he'd dreamt of since he was a schoolboy. Hard years at sea and university had followed, but here he was, qualified and about to join his first ship as an officer. The money was good too. The sports car he had been looking at could be his when he came home on leave. Within two days, he flew out to Houston to join his ship in Galveston.

A week later, Jim flew out to Fort Lauderdale Hollywood Airport. It was warm and sultry, but the heat of the day had gone by the time he landed in the late afternoon. He was met by a driver from the office and taken to his hotel.

'They want you in the office at nine tomorrow morning, Captain. It's only a short distance away so I'll collect you at eight thirty.'

The hotel was typical of a large international chain. If you didn't go outside, you wouldn't know which city you were in. The last thing Jim wanted to do was sightseeing so, after a couple of beers in the bar, he had an early dinner and went to bed.

In the morning, the driver was on time and they sped along the seafront boulevard. The well-groomed frontage with palm trees and modern white buildings provided a gleaming backdrop to the calm blue sea and the white sand on the other side. Soon they pulled up under a white portico in front of a darkened glass wall with a large revolving door in the centre. The driver sprang out of the car and opened the door for Jim.

'Just go to reception, Captain,' said the driver.

The foyer inside was, in contrast to the white building outside, gleaming black marble. There was a white marble reception desk in the centre. Jim noticed the armed security guards discreetly tucked away at the sides of the foyer.

A stunning black woman in a white suit welcomed him.

'May I see your identification please, Captain?'

After Jim produced this, he was issued with a badge which showed he was a guest of Seaborne Cruises Inc.

'You want the fourth floor, Captain. Have a nice day.' A guard responded to a signal from the receptionist and escorted him to the lift.

On arrival on the fourth floor, he found a reception desk identical to the one in the foyer and a duplicate receptionist.

She smiled. 'The front desk told me you were on the way up. Mr Falconi is waiting for you in the conference room. Please come this way.' She took him down the carpeted corridor past heavy solid walnut office doors and into a large reception room. She opened the doors and waved Jim in. There were two men sitting inside.

'Captain Clariby, hi. I'm Adam Falconi and this is John Zachary.'

They were both in their early forties, but the resemblance ended there. Falconi was dark haired and tending to portliness whereas Zachary was blond and slim.

'Sit down, Captain. May we call you Jim?' Without waiting for a reply, he carried on. 'Did you have a good trip? Hotel OK? Any problems just call me.'

'Everything's fine, thank you,' replied Jim.

'That's great. Well it's good to see you here. I'm sure we'll all get along fine. She's a really great ship and I want to tell you how excited we all are by the new cruising schedules up into Canada. It adds a new dimension for us to be able to offer these to the public and they are really going for it, aren't they Johnny?'

'They really are, Jim. We're already booked out for the first cruise up there and mostly full for the second and third.'

They were like two excited schoolboys, but Jim knew from previous experience that he would be stupid to underestimate them. Too many people had already done that to their cost with American businessmen.

'I'm pleased to hear that.'

'If we could fit more cruises in, we could fill the ship again,' said Zachary.

'Well I'm sure your Safety Officer here has told you the problem,' Jim said carefully. 'The season for being able to go into Arctic waters is very short, only July and August. It all depends on what you want. If you stay further south, out of the ice areas and the Arctic Circle, then you can extend that period.'

'Can't do that, that's not what the passengers want. They want to see the icebergs and say they've been in the Arctic. We are calling the cruises 'Voyages of Exploration' and giving them certificates.'

'Well, then you will only manage three trips unless you get ice-class ships,' explained Jim.

'The Captain thinks we could squeeze in four trips. We're putting an ice pilot on board, in addition to yourself.'

'That's good. All help is welcome, but I hope we will stay well away from anything big and white.'

They looked at each other puzzled.

'Icebergs,' Jim explained.

'We hear that you've already been Captain of a cruise ship in the Arctic.'

'The Antarctic, actually.'

Zachary waved. 'Same thing, lots of ice.'

Jim decided now was not the time for elementary education.

'If these cruises are a success, we intend sending her down to the Antarctic during their summer. We would like to send you the plans for the itinerary and have you look them over.'

'I can do that,' replied Jim.

'That's great, Jim,' said Falconi. 'I don't know if you have much experience with American passengers, but they are very cruise orientated. They tend to judge us on our ability to make sure they enjoy themselves and are very quick to point out where they think we are wrong.'

'They also sue at the drop of a hat,' added Zachary.

'This isn't a criticism, but the Brits tend to be very straight when it comes to running ships and there's nothing wrong with that.'

'Absolutely nothing,' added Zachary

Like parrots, thought Jim.

'You must remember, we aren't just in the hotel business but also in the entertainment industry as well as running ships. So the art is to make the ship side as unobtrusive as possible.'

'They want the romance of the sea without any of the problems,' said Zachary.

'We're very lucky with the Captain of the ship, Augusto, Captain Cota. He has been with us for a long time and the passengers adore him.'

'Especially the women,' said Zachary.

'I'm certain that if you follow his lead you will quickly see how our guests on this side of the pond respond.'

'Well I'll certainly bear in mind what you've said,' murmured Jim, not certain what else to say.

'The reason we are concentrating on this is that Captain Cota is very social and will leave you to deal with a lot of the ship's operations. He'll deal with the Ship Manager and the hotel side while you look after the ship's affairs. It's a good arrangement and how we like to operate things over this side. We would like to show you around the office to meet the people here. Then we all have a lunch appointment with the Senior Vice President, Bob Hinchley. After that, you are free to have a look round our little town before the ship comes in tomorrow morning.'

Lunch was in a typical American country club, set in the middle of a pristine golf course and among beautiful people.

'A lot of our customers come from this club, Captain,' said Hinchley. 'America really has taken cruising to its heart. They expect the best and they get that with us. What's it like in the UK?'

'Some like it, others don't,' replied Jim.

'It's all down to marketing, Captain. You guys need to learn to sell. You need to make them feel they are missing the experience of a lifetime if they don't go cruising. Even while you're on the ship, you're selling. Our most valuable customers are repeat cruisers. They only come back if they're happy, and that, Captain,' he said, pointing his fork at Jim, 'means happy with you guys as well. You Brits are uptight about running ships. You know, when we changed the uniform to give it a little more razzmatazz, the only guys yelling were the Brits.'

'Hopefully, we manage to run the ships safely,' Jim said carefully.

'Hell, Captain, I'm not arguing with that. The customers like the Brits. Have you ever had a beard by the way? They love that.'

'No, I haven't. I prefer to get by on my ability rather than my appearance.'

'Hey, Captain. You see, Brits! Don't get so uptight. It was just a suggestion. Do you play golf?'

'No, I don't. Not many courses at sea.'

'You should. It relaxes you. There's a pitch and putt area on the *'Majestic Sea'*. There's even a golf pro.'

As they left the club, Hinchley put his arm around Jim's shoulders.

'I may see you on board some day. I hope to come up to Canada and join one of the new Arctic cruises. Bring the little lady along; she's always wanted to see the icebergs and penguins.'

Jim thought about telling him that he had the wrong end of the world, but there wasn't any point.

'Think about the beard,' was Hinchley's parting remark as he drove away.

That evening, Jim phoned Jenny. 'It's warm, the food's good, and I'm heading off shortly. The ship's coming in early tomorrow and we sail in the evening.'

'Where are you going?'

'A run around the usual islands. We've got a couple of those before heading up to Canada for the Arctic cruises. Just two of those, then I'll be home. By the way, they want me to grow a beard.'

'Over my dead body! You'll sleep on your own then.'

'That's the end of that then. How about a moustache? The American captains have them.'

'Let them, but you're not American. You stay as you are.'

Jim laughed. 'Funny isn't it? They think of the ships as showbusiness.'

'Never mind. It pays the mortgage,' Jenny said.

It was always good talking to her. It reminded him of the normality the English countryside gave.

Chapter 8

As Jim went up the crew gangway the next morning, he was delighted to see a familiar face. It was Bert Fallows, resplendent in an officer's uniform with two stripes.

'Christ, Bert. That's a faster promotion than mine. Congratulations. What do we call you?'

'Good morning, Sir. Chief Security Officer if you please. I have ten security officers on board.'

'Well, you'll need lots of gold braid to control them all then.'

Bert laughed. 'The ship's awash with that, Sir. I think even the ship's cat's an officer.'

'Have we got one then?'

'Wouldn't surprise me. One of the punters bought a bloody great snake at one stop last cruise. We had a hell of a job with it. Silly bugger took it into the Starlight Lounge on the last night to show his friends. If you want to get the punters off the ship in a hurry, that's the way to do it. It cleared the bar in ten seconds flat.'

Jim laughed. 'Good to have you here, Bert.'

At that moment, a waiter appeared. 'This is Rodrigo, Captain. He will be looking after your cabin.' Jim shook hands with them both. Rodrigo picked his bags up and led the way to the lift. Jim looked at the deck numbers, which were at least double the *'Sea Breeze'*. She's certainly big, he thought. They eventually arrived at the bridge deck and Rodrigo led the way to Jim's cabin.

The outer office was spacious. It went through to the dayroom, where the outgoing Staff Captain was talking on his phone. He waved Jim to sit down. Jim looked around; not too large but comfortable enough. There was a three piece suite in green brocade matching the light green carpet. On one bulkhead was a bookcase with a large screen TV, and on the other was a bureau and a door leading to the bedroom. Rodrigo went past and put Jim's bags in the bedroom and then left.

The Staff Captain finally finished his call.

'I am sorry, Captain Clariby,' he said. 'I was talking to my family, telling them when to expect me. I leave tonight and arrive in Rome tomorrow morning. I'm Adama Ricci.'

'Jim.'

They shook hands. 'Come into the office and we can talk there.'

Jim settled into a seat at the conference table and waited for Adama to take his seat.

'How was your last ship, Jim?'

'It was fine. You might know the *'Sea Breeze'*. She's a little old, but we had a good Captain.'

'I hear he can be very tough. Some officers had a difficult time with him.'

'They probably deserved it then.'

'Well, you will find this Captain very different. He is the best Captain in the fleet. That's why this is his ship. I'll miss not being with him. He has taught me a lot.'

'I must say, I am a little surprised to be here this early. I was scheduled to stay on the *'Sea Breeze'* for a further month or so.'

'Me too. I was expecting to stay for another month. Of course, we knew you were coming for the ice trips, but that's just how things happen. Everything is up to date on board. The Safety Officer's report is on the desk for you to read later. He is a good man and will give you a full brief later. He is very reliable, a little serious, but everything is in order. The department is running well. My handover report for you is also on your desk. It is quite extensive, but I think all the major points are covered.'

'Are there any outstanding defects?' asked Jim.

'As you know, there are always defects, but nothing we can't live with or that will cause any undue concern. There is so much equipment on the bridge something is always broken. We have four electro-technical officers on board and between the bridge and the engine control room they are kept busy. They won't admit it, but some of the equipment is so new it even baffles them,' Adama said smiling.

'What department do they come under?'

'For administration, they are under the engine department. All maintenance or repair requirements go to the Staff Chief Engineer. However, for communication functions, they operate under you. For example, for emergency stations, one is stationed on the bridge. They have all done the communication courses and are familiar with all the communications, including the satellite setups. Come and have a look round the bridge.'

They walked along to the end of the alleyway, which was barred by a closed door with a coded entry lock.

'2738,' said Adama opening the door.

'Impressive,' Jim murmured looking at the vast bridge in front of him.

There were various islands of instruments and screens. Technicians in white boiler suits were working at two of the islands and an officer in uniform was at another. He stepped forward to meet them.

'Jim, this is Peter Allway, the First Officer and ship's navigator. Peter, your new Staff Captain, Captain Clariby.' They shook hands.

'All the way from Australia, Peter?'

'Hell no, Captain. All the way from New Zealand,' Peter said laughing.

Jim waved at the bridge. 'You've got quite a job on your hands.'

Peter shrugged. 'As you can see, it doesn't always all work.'

'Anything important?'

'Not really. The reason that there is so much equipment is that everything is duplicated.'

They showed Jim round the bridge. Peter was right. Basically what was there was normal, just newer, more lights and replicated, apart from the manoeuvring system.

'I haven't seen this before,' said Jim.

'Let me show you,' said Peter proudly. He started up the large square screen, which soon displayed a computerised bird's-eye view of the harbour.

'The display is relayed from the automated chart system,' Peter explained. 'You can see the ship positioned alongside the berth.'

He enlarged the display and the ship's image appeared clearly. 'Now I will switch to trial mode.' Once he'd done this, using the control stick he manoeuvred the ship back to the channel leading into the harbour. 'Now you can see the course leading to this position off the berth.'

Jim nodded.

'Right, what speed do you want for the harbour approach?' asked Peter.

'Eight knots,' Jim said. Peter entered the speed and pressed a button. Immediately an image of the ship started approaching down the channel. When it entered the harbour, it altered course to port and carried on to a position off the berth, where it stopped.

'It selects the Azipods as well as the bow and stern thrusters to keep the ship on track. Now watch.' He enlarged the screen.

'Where do you want to berth the ship?' Jim pointed to an empty space along the jetty. Peter moved the image of the ship into the berth, then pressed the button.

Immediately, two images of the ship were visible on the screen. The image of the ship off the berth slowly moved to blend into the image alongside. They came together and stopped.

'There you are, ship alongside.'

'I'll be damned,' said Jim. 'What if I want the ship facing outward?'

'Then you just put the image round that way and the ship will then turn before coming alongside.'

'What if other ships are in the way or small boats?'

'It knows about them from the radars and Doppler sensors along the hull. It will also tell you why it's stopped, but it will hold its position until they are clear or you override the system.'

'It's like a computer game,' Jim said.

'The head waiter could do this,' said Peter.

'Don't say that too loudly,' said Jim. 'You'll fulfil their dreams.'

Peter laughed. 'It's funny really. The punters think the Old Man is a brilliant ship-handler when he's drinking coffee and chatting to the women.'

'Women?'

'Peter's joking,' said Adama hastily. 'Occasionally the Captain will allow important guests on the bridge to observe operations.'

'He doesn't need to do that,' said Peter. 'Look behind you.' Jim turned and saw a large rectangular window set in the after bulkhead of the bridge.

'What's that?' asked Jim.

'That is the latest idea. It allows the punters to see into the bridge.'

'When?'

'During daylight. The screens are closed at night.'

'The guests appreciate it,' said Adama.

'I bet the bridge officers don't though,' said Jim

'You've hit the nail on the head, Captain,' Peter responded.

Jim shook his head. 'At least we still have a ship's wheel,' he said stepping up to the steering console, touching the wheel spokes.

Peter smiled. 'Believe it or not, that's fake. It's for the punters to see the ship's wheel as they imagine it. The steering tiller is here,' he said, indicating a small lever on the front control panel.

'Come on, Jim. We'll have a walk around,' said Adama leading Jim away.

'He's a good navigator,' said Adama as they walked back down the alleyway, 'but not really suited to cruise ships.'

Along with a few others I can think of, thought Jim.

They walked through the passenger areas, where crowds of passengers were still disembarking. He stood in amazement as they entered the main shopping mall, which went up four decks in the centre of the ship. Glass lifts went up and down at the sides, while at the top there was a magnificent chandelier.

'Bloody hell,' said Jim. 'I've never seen anything like this even in a shoreside hotel.' Jim lost count of the number of bars and lounges they went through.

'There are four swimming pools,' said Adama, 'and several Jacuzzis.'

'Can we see the lifeboats please?' asked Jim.

Adama led the way to a lift and they went to the boat deck. At regular intervals along the alleyway were wide doors leading out on deck. Above each door was an illuminated sign indicating the lifeboat number. Carlos opened one of the doors with a key and they went outside onto a narrow deck space. Immediately above them was a huge lifeboat stowed in davits.

'Just lift the brakes and down she goes, once the gripes are removed of course,' said Adama.

'How do you stop a drunk punter from lowering one?'

'They can't get out to that area. I used my pass key, which is yours now by the way.' He passed the key to Jim. 'The doors are activated from the bridge when abandon ship is ordered.'

Jim looked around. 'Where do the passengers assemble?'

'Up in the lounges.'

'Then what?' asked Jim.

'They are led down to their boats.'

'OK, I can see that, but where do they assemble down here?'

Adama looked uneasy. 'They are meant to get immediately into the boats on arrival.'

'And if they can't?'

Adama shrugged. 'They have to stay inside.'

'In the narrow alleyway?'

Again Adama shrugged.

'Where are the emergency control stations?' asked Jim.

'There are four; one amidships, one outside the engine room primarily for the engine department, one forward and one aft. Each team has 22 personnel, of which about half are seamen and half are hotel staff. There is also a separate fire control station where the ship's firemen monitor the detection systems around the clock.'

'How many firemen are on board?'

'Eight. They report directly to the bridge when they are on watch or patrol, except in an emergency when they report directly to the Safety Officer.'

'I'd better meet the Safety Officer.'

'You will at 1230. The Captain's giving me a farewell party. We'll meet up with him in the Captain's cabin. You will also be able to meet the other senior officers there.'

Jim looked at his watch. 'What time is embarkation due to start?'

'1400 and sailing at 1900.'

'Then I had better unpack and get into uniform,' said Jim.

As they walked back through the passenger accommodation, Jim could see that, now the passengers from the last cruise had disembarked, the hotel staff were rushing around cleaning and preparing the ship for the next batch of passengers. Most looked as if they were Asian.

'Are all the hotel staff from Asia?' asked Jim.

'Most,' said Adama, 'but some are from South America and the Caribbean.'

Jim got back to the cabin and unpacked his cases. He then put his uniform on, white trousers and a white tropical shirt with epaulets.

Adama was waiting in the dayroom. He frowned at Jim.

'Your trousers are creased,' he said.

'They get that way when they have been packed for a long time.'

'The Captain is very keen on smartness.'

'So am I,' said Jim, 'but I don't intend meeting any passengers today and I'll iron my uniforms this evening.'

'There's no need for that. Put them out for Rodrigo this evening and he'll have them back by morning. The laundry service is excellent.'

'So, what are the rest of the officers like?'

'No problems. They all know the ship well and I have given them all good reports.'

'What about cadets?'

'There are four of them, a mix of British, Indian and one female cadet from Singapore.'

'Which one is the Senior Cadet?'

'The female cadet, her name is Zhou, but we use the oldest cadet.'

'Who is?'

'Matheson. He's twenty three and in his first year.'

Jim nodded. 'Who is their training officer?'

'The Junior Second Officer. You haven't met Celine yet. She is from the Purser's department but is attached to the deck department. She acts as your secretary and assists with the bridge documentation. She has relatives here so I gave her leave today to go and see them.'

Adama looked at the bulkhead clock. 'Shall we go?'

As they approached the Captain's cabin, they could hear the buzz of noise, which grew louder as they got closer. A bar was set up in the outer office, where two waiters were serving drinks. Jim asked for a beer, and then they moved through into a spacious dayroom. It was crowded with officers and several civilians.

Unmistakeably, in the centre of the cabin was the Captain, surrounded by people, including two ladies.

He was, Jim had to admit, a striking man and the ladies obviously thought so as well, from the way they were hanging on his words. He had blond hair, a tanned face and blue eyes, all star material.

The Captain turned and saw them.

'Here is our guest of honour,' he declared loudly coming towards them. He took Adama by the shoulders and embraced him.

'Adama, what will I do without you? Everyone, Adama is here to say goodbye to us.' The crowd enveloped Adama and the Captain, leaving Jim on the outside.

He felt a tap on his shoulder. Turning, he saw a tall lanky officer with thinning blond hair and a serious face.

'I thought I would introduce myself, Sir. I am Jan Weekers, the Safety Officer.'

'Pleased to meet you, Jan. Do we have these often?' he asked waving his glass in the direction of the party.

'You'll get used to it,' said Jan. 'This is regular; the Captain enjoys parties.' The way he said it made Jim look at Jan.

'I sense you're not a party man.'

'I have too much work to do,' said Jan. 'Sorry, Sir, I didn't mean to criticise but I prefer the quiet life.'

'Nothing wrong with that, Jan. Where do you come from?'

'Do you know Holland?'

'A little,' Jim replied.

'A small village in the country just outside Groningen in the north.'

'I come from a small village in the country as well,' said Jim, 'so we have something in common. Jan, there are a lot of people I want to see in the morning, but I'd like to meet with you first. Come and see me this evening once we've sailed.'

Before Jan could reply, Jim could see Adama beckoning him urgently from the circle.

'I have to go,' he said. 'See you this evening.'

Jim went over to join the circle. Adama took his shoulder. 'Captain, everybody, this is Jim Clariby, the new Staff Captain.'

Captain Cota was watching Jim with a faint smile on his face. His piercing eyes were looking directly at him. He held his hand out. 'Welcome on board, Jim,' he said. 'You've come to a fine ship and have a hard act to follow, but I've heard about you and I know we have a good replacement. Let me introduce you. This is William Shelby, the Ship General Manager.' Standing beside him was a large overweight man and a hard looking woman with too much make up. She looked nervous, her eyes darting around. 'This is Scott Pierre, the Cruise Director, and his wife Vivien, who looks after entertainment. They are locals from Miami.' Next was the Hotel Manager, Henry Milau. He was a small dapper-looking man wearing an immaculate uniform with four gleaming gold stripes. He touched Jim's hand briefly then drew it back quickly. An attractive blonde woman in her early forties was next, Bella Winchester, the ship's Purser, another four stripes. Then the Senior Shop Manager and finally a ship's dancer with more bare flesh than clothing who seemed to have a proprietary interest in the Captain, Gloria Jenkins from London. Her smile was nice and genuine. The group seemed close. After his introduction, they seemed to lose interest in him, allowing Jim to move slowly from the circle. At the side of the cabin was a buffet table where two other officers were standing.

'Can I presume you are the Chief Engineer and the Staff Chief?' asked Jim.

'You presumed right,' said the older one. 'Iain Macgregor and this is Patrick Connor.' Iain had a craggy face that showed wear and tear, but his eyes were bright and intelligent. Patrick on the other hand had an easy carefree look and startling ginger hair. Both were in their fifties.

Jim shook hands. 'Jim Clariby.'

'Aye, we know who you are,' said Iain. 'We thought you were joining the fan club,' he said, indicating the circle around the Captain.

'I'm not a club man,' replied Jim.

'If you want to get on with Errol Flynn, you'd better be,' said Patrick.

'I assume you mean the Captain,' remarked Jim.

'There's only one star on this boat, isn't there Iain?' said Patrick.

'Well it's not you or me,' replied Iain draining his glass. 'Come on, let's go and get a proper drink in my cabin.' He looked at Jim. 'You're welcome to join us.'

'I'll take a rain check today, if I may. It may not be too diplomatic to leave at this moment.'

Iain shrugged. 'Not for us. He's usually pleased to see us go. Come and see us some time. We want to talk to you about the ice trips anyway.'

Jim watched them go. The party showed no sign of ending and just as he turned towards the door, Falconi, Zachary and Hinchley from the office came in.

'Hi Jim!' shouted Hinchley. 'Getting into the spirit already I see. Great. You and the skipper will get on like a house on fire.' Without stopping, they carried on to the circle to cries of welcome.

A good time to leave, thought Jim.

No-one noticed.

Chapter 9

An hour later, Adama came into the office. Jim was sitting at the desk working through the handover documents and making occasional notes.

Adama looked happy. 'I will just go and change, if I may.'

'Of course,' said Jim. A faint whiff of alcohol followed Adama in. Well why not, thought Jim. It's a good way to leave a ship.

Rodrigo, the steward, arrived.

'May I go and get the bags, Sir?' he asked. Jim nodded. Rodrigo soon emerged carrying bags and put them onto a cart outside. Adama then emerged beaming, obviously pleased to be going home.

'Before you go, Adama, where is your safety equipment, helmet, boiler suits and stuff kept?'

Adama looked puzzled. 'I've never had to use that. I suppose if you want it the Safety Officer could get it for you.'

Jim stood and they shook hands. 'Have a good leave, Adama. Any idea where you're going next?'

'No news yet. I'll find out soon enough. Have a good trip, Jim.'

Jim sat for a moment once Adama had left. So, no working clothes. That told him something; either everything was perfect or he had better get kitted up. He picked up the phone and scanned the directory; it gave most of the offices and officers' cabins. He found the Safety Officer's cabin and dialled the number. There was no reply. He then tried the Safety Office. A woman answered.

'Staff Captain, I'm trying to contact the Safety Officer.'

'He'll be on his pager, Captain. I'll call him for you, but you have a list of the pager numbers. When you dial, the pager goes off and they will contact you.'

Jim looked on his desk and there beside the phone under a Perspex cover on the desk was a pager list.

'Thanks for that, I've just found it. Who are you by the way?'

'I'm the assistant to the Safety Officer, Captain.'

'I realise that, but what's your name?'

'Sorry, Sir. I'm Janice Beerman.'

'I look forward to meeting you, Janice.'

Jim continued to work his way through the handover notes. The meetings section was interesting. He saw that he went to the Captain's cabin each morning at 0900 for a short meeting, and then at 1100 when at sea he went to the Ship General Manager's office for a heads of department meeting. Interesting, not the Captain's office.

There was a tap on his door; it was one of the hotel officers.

'Good afternoon, Sir. I'm the restaurant manager's assistant. I have your table seating plans for this cruise.' He placed the list on Jim's desk and turned to leave.

'Hold on!' called Jim. 'Wait till I've read it.' It was small print, reminding Jim that he really needed to get glasses.

'There are three lists.'

'Yes, Sir, one for each sitting in the main restaurant and one for the grill room. The last Staff Captain alternated the sittings in the main restaurant and used the grill room on party nights. Your table numbers are at the top of each sitting.'

'I see that the grill room sitting is for 2100.'

'Yes, Sir.'

'Well you can cancel that one. I'm not waiting until the middle of the night to eat.'

The young man looked shocked. 'But it's already been arranged, Sir.'

'Then bloody well un-arrange it.'

Next Jim looked at the list of passengers on his table. 'I see you have put a single woman on each side of me.'

'Yes, Sir.'

'For heaven's sake, they won't want to sit by me. Surely there must be single male passengers for them to sit with.'

'They are both married ladies travelling without their husbands, Captain. They are regular guests with us and arranged their sitting before they knew Captain Ricci was leaving. They are also friends of the Captain.'

'Look at me. Do I look like a stud? Now please find a married couple, preferably intelligent, and put them in their place. Also while you're here, I will not be dining this evening. I'll go to the officers' messroom instead.'

He handed the plans back to the officer, who disappeared promptly.

The phone rang; it was the Safety Officer, Jan.

'Jan, I want some working clothes, the usual protective equipment please.'

'All of it?'

'Of course. I thought it was a regulation that we all had this issued.'

'Yes, Sir, but it's not usual for the Captain or yourself to have this.'

'What about the other officers?'

'Only the engineers and technical officers have this equipment, Captain. The others can get it when they need it.'

'How often is that?'

'Not often.'

'Meaning?'

'Well I've never issued them with any.'

'You mean to say that none of the deck officers has worn a boiler suit or working gear since you came on board? How long ago is that?'

'Only since the last cruise, Captain, but my predecessor never issued it either. We keep records of the issue.'

'And the cadets?'

'They have the equipment, but don't use it often.'

'Please tell the Bosun I want all the deck officers to be issued with work clothing and safety equipment tomorrow. Make sure that the safety helmets are all marked with their ranks.'

'Yes, Sir, with pleasure.'

'I see you report to me every morning at 0930.'

'Yes, Sir, after you've seen the Captain.'

'That changes tomorrow. I want to see you and the Bosun at 0800.'

'That's better for me, Sir,' replied Jan.

Jim put the phone down. It was proving to be an interesting afternoon.

His phone went again; it was the First Officer.

'Yes, Peter. How can I help?'

'The passage plan is ready for you, Sir.'

'Me? You've got the wrong Captain.'

'No, Sir. The Captain prefers the Staff Captain to review the plans.'

'I'll be on the bridge shortly.'

That was a turn up for the books, he thought. Normally the Captain looked after the bridge and the navigation aspect. Still, different ships, different splices.

Just as he was leaving, the phone went again.

'Good afternoon, Jim. This is Henry. We met in the Captain's cabin.'

'Oh yes. You're the Hotel Manager.'

'That's right. Jim, we have a bit of an issue. The restaurant manager has just been to see me. Apparently there's a problem with your table.'

'Why? Is it broken?'

'What? Oh I see, yes, very amusing. It's regarding the seating arrangements. These were done very carefully. The two ladies in question are very good customers and always sit at either the Captain's or Staff Captain's table. One of their husbands is a congressman and the other a president of an oil company here in the States. We really cannot change these at the last moment.'

Jim thought it really wasn't the time to make an issue over such a small matter.

'Henry, of course I didn't realise this would cause a problem. Leave it as it is and I will do my best to keep them happy.'

'That's very understanding of you, Jim.' Henry sounded relieved. 'In future, I'll make sure your table is discussed with you.'

Never have a fight you can't win, thought Jim as he walked along the alleyway to the bridge. He was sure it would have gone further if he hadn't relented.

Peter was waiting by the electronic chart display. He led Jim through the passages of the cruise. After the general display, he called up the passage to the first port, Kingston in Jamaica.

'That looks good. I see you're taking us through the Bahama Islands.'

'That's our normal route, Captain,' explained Peter.

'That's fine. I'm not disagreeing with the route, but I noticed you're going along to Rum Cay then down very close to the southern tip of Long Island.'

'It's perfectly safe, Captain. We always go that way so the passengers can look at the coast.'

'Peter,' Jim said softly. 'Think. At present the ship is less than a mile off at some points. Some are nearer half a mile. Look where my finger's pointing.' Peter looked.

'What does it say?'

'Wreck, Captain.'

'Yes. It's on Long Island and very recent. I don't think we want to be another one.' Peter didn't answer. 'Let me put it another way. If the steering went, how long would it take to stop the ship? Let's say an emergency stop.'

'The manoeuvring diagram says 7 cables.'

'Forget that. That's like the car companies' claims for petrol consumption. It's carried out under controlled conditions. I reckon if it says 7 cables then it will actually be about a mile. The ship will definitely go on the rocks before a mile is up, so let's be safe shall we? At least two miles off all places where we can't float, then we can sleep in peace.'

Peter was looking dubious.

'Don't worry. One beach is like another. Think of this. If anything did go wrong, who would be for the high jump?'

Jim went back to his office humming. He knew he would hear about that conversation from the Captain. Jim thought to himself, well if I am to look after the navigation, it's going to be done properly and if the Captain doesn't like it, he can do it himself.

Jim went through to his dayroom. He switched on the TV and found the BBC news channel. He had just sat down to watch when Rodrigo silently came into the cabin. He was carrying a tray of tea and biscuits. Also on the tray was the ship's daily programme.

'Thanks, Rodrigo. Now, where is the iron kept?'

'You give it to me, Sir, and I will do it.'

'OK, thanks, but I still want an iron for the cabin. I would also like a kettle and some cocoa. Can you do that?'

'Please, write it down and I will solve it.'

Rodrigo went to the office and reappeared with paper and pen. Jim started writing. While he did this, he looked up at Rodrigo, who stood patiently. He was a small older man, with greying hair, fine features and a patient but tired look.

'Where are you from, Rodrigo?'

'Manila, Sir.'

'Do you have a large family to look after?'

There was a hint of a smile. 'Very large, Sir.'

'How often do you get home?'

'After six months, Sir, but I have been here for nine months now.'

'Do they let you do that?' asked Jim.

'I asked, Sir. Some of the children are at university and it is expensive.'

'How many cabins do you look after?'

'I do all the deck officers and cadets.'

'Do you now?' said Jim thoughtfully. 'You're a busy man then.'

Rodrigo smiled again briefly.

'Well, from tomorrow morning, you won't be cleaning the cadets' cabins.'

'What?' asked Rodrigo, obviously surprised.

'I said no more cleaning the cadets' cabins. They are cadets and learning to be officers. Part of that training is learning how to keep things clean. Don't worry. I'll make sure they are informed.' Rodrigo still looked worried.

'Here's my list, Rodrigo. I've also added the bond I want. I see there are spirits, but I also need beer and soft drinks.' Rodrigo looked, so obviously he could read English.

'Can I bring it tomorrow?'

'Certainly, Rodrigo.' Jim went into his bedroom and came out with a pile of white uniforms, which he gave to Rodrigo.

'Don't forget what I said about the cadets. No cleaning.'

Jim sat and watched the news while he drank his tea. Then he scanned the ship's programmes. There were two, one for passengers and another for the crew. On the crew's programme, he saw there were a number of training sessions scheduled for tomorrow, a couple of staff meetings, including one for the heads of department at 1100. Two birthdays were due to be celebrated in the crew lounge bar in the evening and one member of the crew had had a baby daughter yesterday. There was a notice about the smoking areas, another about throwing garbage over the side and finally one saying farewell to Captain Ricci. He was obviously well liked.

The passenger programme listed all the available activities that evening, reminded guests that it was not necessary to dress up on the first night, and set out the general onboard dress policy. Guests were requested to remove their hats in the saloon, to wear a shirt or some form of top when eating, and not to wear swimwear in the restaurants. He wasn't surprised, having seen it all before. One thing did disturb him - no lifeboat drill was scheduled before sailing. It was too late to do anything about that now. He went back into the office and made a note of this. His list was growing.

Outside the cabin, he could hear the occasional background noise coming from the loudspeakers. He went to the speaker in his cabin and found it was turned down. Once he had turned it up, he could hear the various messages. It was obviously on the crew circuit as the messages all related to ship operational activities. He left it on and carried on reading the handover.

He was absorbed in the notes when the speaker announced hands to station for leaving harbour. He stood up, stretched and took his uniform cap off the coat hook. It felt good to get the oak leaves back, even if he was second in command. Looking out of the window, he could see it was now dark outside, but there was no rain or wind. A good evening to sail.

Chapter 10

He arrived on the bridge and immediately entered a well-ordered world where reports were given of various actions being passed and orders given. From the quayside came the noise of a band playing. Peter stood at the central control panel. Two of the Third Officers were at radar stations, while two cadets were dealing with communications through the walkie-talkies in their hands and the VHF sets. A quartermaster stood by the central control steering panel and in the corner there was a steward in a white jacket making coffee.

Captain Cota was sitting in the starboard command chair with the Pilot seated beside him in the port chair. The secondary lighting on the bridge was still on and, as Jim approached the Captain, he noticed that the window overlooking the bridge from the passenger library still didn't have the curtains drawn and that it was crowded with passengers looking in. As he approached, Cota looked up.

'Hello, Jim. Come to help us out? Pilot, this is Jim Clariby, the new Staff Captain.' They shook hands briefly.

From the bridge, the ship didn't look so big. This was because the bridge was in the forward part of the ship with the mass of the hull behind. Apart from his time on passenger and cruise ships, Jim was used to huge tankers and bulk carriers where the mass of the ship was in front of the bridge. Jim remembered trying to manoeuvre these huge ships with a single engine, wheel and no thrusters. This was infinitely better.

The final reports came in saying the gangways were clear and that the ship was ready for letting go. Cota looked at the bulkhead clock; it was two minutes to go.

'Bridge and forward lights off please.'

The lights went out immediately and the bridge was dark until their eyes gradually became used to the gloom. The whole bridge sparkled with twinkling lights coming from the various controls and patches of light from the many screens. They waited.

'One minute,' called Peter.

Cota waited a few seconds. 'Let go forward and aft,' he ordered.

At almost exactly 1900, the stations reported the lines all gone.

'May I, Captain?' asked the Pilot.

'Please,' Cota replied.

There was a remote control panel between the command chairs. The Pilot barely seemed to move his hand yet the ship slowly came to life and gradually moved away from the jetty, coming broadside out into the middle of the channel. The ship slowly backed out into a broader channel where she could turn. The Pilot manoeuvred her round with a small touch of his hand. The enclosed TV screens showed the stern sides and bow, and the Pilot glanced at these occasionally as the ship swung round. Soon she was turned and pointing towards the main channel.

The quartermaster took the tiller and Peter took up his position beside the engine controls.

'Keep her amidships and slow ahead please,' ordered the Pilot.

The ship slowly glided towards the main entrance channel.

'Starboard 15.'

The ship immediately responded.

'Ease to 5 midships.'

The ship came into the centre of the entrance channel, heading out to sea.

'Steady at that.'

Cota turned towards Jim, who was positioned behind his chair.

'What do you think of that?'

'Very impressive, Captain. She handles like a toy boat.'

'That's Azipods for you. So simple really. I wonder why we never thought of it before.'

'Possibly because we couldn't,' said Jim. 'We never thought we would see cruise ships like this.'

'Just you wait,' said Cota. 'This is just the start. One day there will be cruise ships with ten, maybe even twenty thousand passengers on them. Imagine, ships where the crew can bring their families with them and live there for several years. Now that would be a cost saving.'

Jim listened. At first he thought that Cota was joking, but it was clear he wasn't.

The ship was a city of light gliding away from one city to form her own at sea. In a way it was arrogance, saying here I am and I'm here to stay. It was like a challenge to the sea: *This is what man can do*. Jim shuddered and felt cold. He began to feel old for the first time, possibly because he realised that, if this was the future, he didn't want any part of it.

As the ship cleared the breakwater, they dropped the Pilot off and increased speed. She began to rise and fall with the slight swell.

'Good,' said Cota. 'First Officer, she's all yours. Secure the anchors, get the stabilisers out and clear the stations.' He looked around the horizon. 'There's not much shipping. Just one coming up from the south, but we will clear her easily. If you want me, I'll be down at dinner. I'll come up later to write the night order book.'

With that he left the bridge.

Jim also left. He took the elevator to the officers' messroom, which was crowded. A number of looks were given in his direction and Jim got the impression that it was unusual for the Staff Captain to come here. He collected a tray and chose a light tuna salad. Seeing both Second Officers sitting together, he decided to join them.

'Excuse me, gentlemen. Do you mind if I sit with you?' They started to get up.

'Sit down,' said Jim. 'Who's who?'

'I am Gaspar Bandissi and this is Mike Prentiss,' Gaspar said.

They looked as if they were both in their twenties.

'Mike, you'll go on watch soon, so I'll be brief. I will be seeing the Senior Cadet in the morning. The proper one, not the oldest. I have stopped their steward service; they're cadets, not officers. I'll be on the bridge in the morning to discuss their training. I want you to bring their record books to the bridge for me to review with you, OK?'

Prentiss looked steadily at Jim. 'If it means we can start getting them into real training, I'm with you, Sir.'

'Good. Now think about what is needed and we'll discuss it in the morning.'

Prentiss looked at his watch, 'Please excuse me, Sir. I have to go on watch.'

Jim waved him away. 'I'm going too. Don't worry, Gaspar. I'll find plenty for you to do as well.'

Jim was making himself a cup of cocoa when the Safety Officer arrived.

'Come in, Jan. Would you like a cocoa?'

'It's a long time since I had that, Sir, but yes please.'

'Sit down.' Jim brought the drinks over. 'Let me give you a view of how I see things. The department seems to function well. Everyone does their job, but it appears as if we go through the motions of what we are supposed to do rather than being committed to doing our jobs. Our first priority is the safety of the ship. Do you agree?'

'Certainly, Sir.'

'Obviously the ship is not in any danger, but we must consider any possible danger and ensure that we can counter that. That is exactly what we do when we are navigating in ice. In a way it is the same on these types of ships, or to be more precise, floating resorts. We are about a hundred seafarers who know what the sea is about, surrounded by approximately four thousand people who don't have a clue. Whether they realise it or not, they are in our care.'

'What you are saying is true, but limits are imposed on us as to what we can do.'

'What are these limits? I'm not doubting you; I just want to clarify that we speak the same language.'

'Well, where do I start?'

'Start with why we didn't have a boat drill before we sailed this evening.'

'We used to before Captain Cota joined, but because the hotel people and the passengers complained to the office, it was stopped.'

'Do you have a written order to that effect or were any written instructions issued by the office?'

'No, Sir. It was all verbal.'

'So, if something happened tonight, as the passengers have not been given any instructions, apart from the chaos, you as the Safety Officer would be hung out to dry.'

'Is this a reprimand, Sir?' asked Jan.

'Not at all; we are two professionals talking. I am trying to establish what is happening here. You're going to help me find any problems and try to improve the safety on board.'

'There's a lot I would like to do.'

'This is the start then. Make a list of where you think improvements could be made. It doesn't matter how impossible they might seem; I'll sort that out. You know the ship and where the problems are. I will also write down where I think the problems might be. As the Safety Officer, you'll have my full support, provided you see me before taking any new steps.'

'You're not wasting any time.'

'Jan, we don't have a lot of time. We only have two cruises before this ship goes north for the Arctic voyages. We will do our wandering up the St Lawrence then head up the Newfoundland coast. We are going to go through the Strait of Belle Isle then steaming full speed 700 miles up to the Davis Strait and then back down the Greenland coast. She will be going fast. Basically we'll be three days in waters where there are limited rescue facilities, hardly any shipping, icebergs and, worst of all, the water just above freezing.'

'With respect, Sir, you are making it sound very difficult. Cruise ships go into ice waters regularly. It's also going to be the summer.'

'They do and regretfully often in ignorance. We're going to make sure that we're prepared. Now, before you go, what's your opinion of the Bosun?'

'He's all right. He'd rather take orders than give them, but he knows his seamanship. I think given the right support he would improve.'

'Maybe he's not being put under pressure.'

'That could be true. The ship has settled into certain routines and us with it.'

'Then tomorrow we start. Bring the Bosun up with you in the morning. One last thing, I have taken the cadets' steward away.'

'About time, Sir. You'll find that we all agree with that. Can I presume they're going to get their hands dirty at last?' Jan enquired.

'You presume right.'

Jan smiled. 'I want to see that. Goodnight, Sir.'

Jim went into his bedroom. There was no noise except for the air conditioning hissing. The ship was as steady as a rock. He sat down on the bed to take off his shoes. As he did, he noticed something glinting in the corner near the bedside table. He bent down and picked it up. It was an earring, an intricate twisted design made in gold with a very large brilliant green emerald. It was obviously from one of Adama's conquests. Jim placed it in his bedside drawer.

Chapter 11

When Rodrigo came into the cabin the following morning, Jim showed him the earring. His eyes lit up.

'Captain Adama was looking for this,' he said. 'So was the lady. She said that I stole it.'

'When was this?' asked Jim.

'Not last cruise but the one before. There was a lot of trouble.' He looked worried.

'It's all right, Rodrigo. You are not in trouble. Who else knows about this? Does the Captain know?'

'Yes, Sir. He also asked me and the First Officer.'

When Rodrigo left, Jim called the bridge. 'When you come down, Peter, could you call in please.'

Jim was sitting at his computer screen when Jan appeared just before eight.

'Good morning, Jan. I've been going through the ship's plans. She's certainly some ship. I didn't realise we had three separate water desalination systems.'

'One is for fresh drinking water, one for washing and the other is for general grey water use, Sir.'

'I've also been going through the stability information. I see we maintain a fairly permanent draught and minimum centre of gravity for the ship, same as on the 'Sea Breeze'.'

'That's right. As weight comes out the bottom, ballast water goes in to maintain it. That centre of gravity is based on a shipload of punters and the swimming pools being full. That means that, as they get off, it gets better. Same with the draught. The maximum is 31ft, but we can get it less if it is needed for getting into a shallow water port.'

'Has she ever needed that?'

'Not to my knowledge. The cruises are planned pretty carefully. All the proposed trips are sent to us for final review before they are advertised.'

'Which decks are aluminium.'

'The top twenty percent, Sir.'

'That's quite a bit. That accounts for her low draught then.'

'I have the Bosun outside, Captain.'

'Good. Bring him in.'

Jan beckoned the Bosun to come in and Jim met him with a smile.

'Bosun, good to meet you. Let's sit down.' He pointed to the corner conference table.

'From the last Staff Captain's report, I see you divide the seafarers into two parts, half to the passenger decks and half to ship maintenance. I see you have two Bosun's mates, so I presume they are in charge of each section. We also have the six quartermasters for bridge duties. Is that enough?' Jim asked.

'Yes, Sir.'

'What about the lifeboats? Do we have a crew dedicated for their maintenance?'

The Bosun looked puzzled and Jim realised he did not understand.

'Do you have special boat men for working in the boats?'

'No, Sir.'

'OK, Bosun. I don't want to keep you. I intend to send boats away in every harbour until I am happy with their handling and the crew's knowledge of the lowering procedures. Is that understood?'

The Bosun nodded. 'Excuse me, Sir, but in port we have to maintain the paintwork on the hull when we are allowed and tend to the gangways. It's also a good time to work on the decks.'

'I understand, Bosun, but the boats must be put first. When I am happy then other work can have priority.'

The Bosun left. 'He's not used to coming up here,' Jan explained.

'How the hell did he get his daily orders then?'

'From your secretary, Celine, usually.'

'From now on, bring him every morning at the same time. I want the crew to know we think he is important. That way he gains status with them and his authority will increase. Now, communications. I want instant access to you and security any time day or night. For that I want us all to carry small walkie-talkies. Do we have any?'

'The deck department have the standard ones, but the security boys have the type you want. They have little earpieces and throat mikes.'

'That's what I want. See if you can get a couple of them for us. Now, do you have anything important for me this morning?' Jim asked.

'Not really. What do you want to do when we have the boat drill?'

'Nothing. I'll walk round and observe how it goes. If it is anything like it was on the *Sea Breeze*, I don't expect anything special. We'll move on to that when we have definite proposals.'

Jan smiled. 'I'd say you have enough already to get started on.'

As Jan left the office, Peter was waiting outside.

'Come in, Peter. I wanted your help on a matter. Please close the door.'

Peter looked puzzled. Jim placed the earring on the conference table.

'Can you tell me anything about this?' asked Jim.

Peter was now looking worried.

'It's all right, Peter. You're not in trouble. I'm interested, that's all.'

Peter shrugged and said, 'It belongs to Adama's woman. She lost it up here.'

'I see. Did she come up here much?'

'She practically lived here,' said Peter. 'She and the other lady.'

'Where do you come into this?' asked Jim. Peter flushed.

'It's all right. You're not in trouble,' Jim repeated.

Peter began to explain. 'Adama used to have parties.' Jim waited. 'They used to get, how can I put this, a little heavy.' Peter was now sweating.

'And you were involved?'

'Only twice. I didn't want to get involved, but they called me in.'

'Who are they?'

'The usual crowd. The general manager, cruise director and his wife, the Purser, the Captain and that dancer he sees.'

'Captain Cota was here?'

'Yes, Sir. He and Captain Adama were good friends.'

'All right, Peter. You've done nothing wrong. This won't be mentioned again.'

'If it helps, Sir, I wasn't happy about it. They insisted I came. That lady friend of Adama wanted me there.'

'That's all right, Peter. I am not interested in the details. Thank you for your honesty. Now forget it. These things happen.'

Jim checked his watch. He still had time before going to the bridge.

Mike Prentiss was waiting for him. He had the cadet training books on the conference table at the back of the bridge.

'I'll take these away to look through,' said Jim. 'Would you say these reflect an accurate assessment of their training?' Jim could see that Prentiss was thinking about what to say.

'They have done the duties that are ticked.'

'I'm sure they have, but if I were to give them a wire to splice or a canvas to sew, could they do it?'

'I'm not sure, Sir.'

'Thank you for your honesty. Have them outside my office by 0930.'

Jim left the bridge and went directly to the Captain's office. The Captain was inside talking to a young woman in a smart white uniform. She had hotel rank markings on her shoulder.

'Good morning, Jim, right on time. Come in and meet Celine. She is our memory bank.' Celine blushed as Jim shook her hand.

'At my age, I'm starting to need one,' Jim said.

'Speak for yourself, Jim. Thank you, Celine. Do you want Celine for anything Jim? I mean legal of course.'

She laughed and blushed again. She brushed past Jim and left the office.

'Come and sit down, Jim,' Cota said indicating the chair in front of his desk. 'Women, they make the world go round, eh?'

'They certainly keep us on our toes, Captain,' replied Jim.

'Keep a few other things tingling as well.' Cota smiled. Jim didn't know how to reply to that.

'You're married I see,' Cota said.

'Yes,' replied Jim. He wondered if he should say 'happily'. Cota sighed. 'Difficult doing this job and being married isn't it? Still, what the heart doesn't see and all that, eh?'

Jim felt uncomfortable.

'Now to work,' said Cota. 'I see you're a cautious man.'

'In what respect, Sir.'

'Navigation. Wait.' He could see Jim about to speak. 'It's not a criticism, Jim, far from it. It is good that you are careful. However, we have made this run many times before and our Cruise Director tells the customers that when they go out of their staterooms onto the balcony they will be able to see palm trees and beaches. You can understand that, when they only see the sea, they wonder what is wrong.'

'I thought that was the idea of coming on a cruise, Sir, to see the sea.'

'Ah, Jim, I wish that were so. All we'd have to do then is sail around in a circle for two weeks then take them back. No, they expect scenery as well, especially if they have been before and are accustomed to it. Jim, we know the area well and have been on the same track many times before.'

'Sir, I was thinking of the possibility of a mechanical failure and was allowing leeway for that.'

'And as I said, I am not criticising you. However, leave the courses as they originally were. We can order the bridge to call one of us if we get a little close to something. How about that?'

And I know who they'll call, thought Jim.

'Sir, can I suggest that we only schedule these close approaches during daylight hours, and during the night we pull back to a safer distance. After all, at night the passengers aren't looking out or, if they are, they want to see the moon, stars and the sea.'

'Very good, Jim. We'll make a romantic of you yet. All right I agree, daytime only. I know you are still settling in, but we have had a complaint about the condition of the upper decks this morning, apparently around the after pool.'

'It would help if they came to me first with the complaint instead of bothering you, but I will look into it, Sir.'

'Good. We must also approve the final routeing for the first Arctic cruise. It's not long now. I'm looking forward to it a lot. Did you know they are all fully booked?'

'I had heard they were doing well,' replied Jim.

'Jim, this means that the Antarctic cruise later in the year is guaranteed to be a sell out. They are planning a Christmas cruise there.'

'That's nice for the penguins,' Jim muttered.

'What?'

'I said that's nice for the passengers, Sir.'

'That's part of the job, Jim, making things nice for them. We must never forget it. Next this morning is the lifeboat drill. Hopefully we can have that over with soon. What are you going to do?'

'I'm going to do a walk around and see how it goes, Sir. Then I'll go and look at this decking problem.'

Jim got up to go. 'By the way, Celine will drop a couple of invitations in your office for this evening. There are a few cocktail parties you should look in at. I've got three already to attend. Oh for the quiet life, eh?'

I bet, thought Jim as he walked back to his office. You love it.

He could see the four cadets waiting outside his cabin as he approached. They were early, but that was a good sign. He walked by them saying come in as he passed.

The invitations were already on his desk and he glanced at them briefly.

'So, names please. And not your first names, thank you.'

The oldest one spoke first.

'Matheson, Sir.'

They were all in uniform, but Matheson looked scruffy. He was tall, with dark hair that was too long and looked as if it hadn't been combed for a week. He looked along the line. 'You,' he said pointing at the female cadet. She was interesting. Certainly Oriental. She had black hair that was pinned up and very delicate features. She was incredibly beautiful.

'My name is Zhou, Sir.'

'From Hong Kong?'

'Singapore, Sir, but I live in England now.'

He looked at the next cadet. 'Kemp, Sir.' He had short blond hair and was a stocky build. Jim thought he was about twenty.

The last cadet was another stocky young man with brown hair and large dark eyes. He wore a turban. He also looked about twenty.

'Bindra, Sir.'

'How do you wear your cap?' Jim asked.

'I put the officers cap badge on the front of my turban,' he replied.

Jim smiled. He was a confident young man.

'Sit down, all of you.'

Jim sat down behind his desk and quickly scanned the first page of each training book, looking briefly at their details.

'You may have noticed that your cabins have not been cleaned this morning. That is because I have withdrawn the steward. He's busy enough without having to look after you, but that is not the main reason. You are being trained and part of that training is to learn how to be an officer. To do that, you must learn how a ship is kept clean. That means keeping your own quarters clean first. Is that understood?' He waited, then Zhou said, 'Yes, Sir.'

'From tomorrow morning, you will be under the Bosun on the lifeboats. There are twenty four boats and each of you will be responsible for six. The Bosun will assign two seamen to each section to assist you. Everything will be checked and cleaned ready for inspection within one week. Next, when we are in Kingston, you will take one of the Fast Rescue Craft and practise picking up a dummy.' Zhou hesitatingly raised her hand.

'Sir, we don't have rescue boat certificates.'

'Pieces of paper won't rescue people. This is how to learn.'

Matheson spoke. 'We are scheduled to go on the tours and report on them, Sir.'

'That's cancelled now. It's just a gimmick so that the ship's staff can go on tours for free anyway. You,' he said, pointing at Matheson, 'will tidy yourself up. Your uniform and shoes are dirty. Also get a haircut.'

'I can't do that. The ship's hair salon is completely booked by the passengers.'

'But the Bosun's salon is not.'

Matheson looked bewildered. 'What's that?' he asked.

'Stand up!' roared Jim. Matheson shot up.

'I think you meant, 'What's that, Sir?', didn't you?' Matheson nodded.

'Who do you think cuts the crew's hair, Raymond and his cronies in the ship's salon? You will report to the Bosun and tell him you have been ordered to have a haircut. Tell him you want it short. When that is done and you have cleaned yourself up, report to the Senior Cadet,' he said indicating to Zhou, 'who will bring you to me. Is that understood?'

'Yes, Sir.'

'Good, now leave. Not you,' he said pointing at Zhou. When the others had gone, Jim relaxed.

'So,' he said. 'Tell me what a young Chinese woman is doing at sea.'

'My father was a Captain,' she said. 'He was a cadet in Blue Funnel. When I was young, I told him I wanted to go to sea. He laughed and told me that Chinese ladies did not go to sea. I wanted to show him we could.'

'I bet he's very proud of you.'

'Thank you, Sir. He's very surprised.'

'Is he still in command?'

She shook her head. 'He's a pilot in Singapore now. He says it is good going home at night.'

'But you said you live in England.'

'I do, Sir. I am living with my aunt until I get my Master's Certificate.'

'You are the Senior Cadet, not that long haired gentleman. I want them sorted out. I don't want to be bothered by cadets so let's make it sooner rather than later. You will report to the Junior Second Officer. Take these training books away with you. Mark in pencil only the subjects you are satisfied you are trained in and then return them to the Second Officer. Anything else, leave clear. At least then we'll know what you need to be trained in. I suspect it will be most of the seamanship subjects. Make sure that the work in the boats is done and not left to the sailors. You will also liaise with the Bosun. He may feel awkward about dealing with you, but you will manage that won't you?'

'Yes, Sir.'

'Good. If you have any problems, you know where my door is.'

Chapter 12

Jim listened to the lead-in broadcasts for the boat drill; they were clear and concise. The passengers were reminded three times to bring their lifejackets and were informed where their stations were. These were based on cabin numbers, with the assembly point being the nearest lounge area.

Before the alarm bells sounded, Jim put on his cap and went down to the assembly area on the main lounge deck. It was the same setup as the *'Sea Breeze'*. The alarms sounded and the lounges started to slowly fill with passengers. They were in no hurry, which was to be expected as it was just a drill. Jim walked outside and could see that a number of passengers were ignoring the drill and amazingly there was also a waiter still serving passengers in a veranda bar. Jim went over to the bar.

'Why isn't this bar closed?'

The waiter looked in surprise at Jim and didn't answer. He looked around for someone to help him. Jim walked away. He was disgusted, not at the waiter, poor sod, but by the passengers who couldn't be bothered to attend and the system that allowed them to get away with it. This was obviously not confined to one ship. Jim was willing to bet it was fleet-wide complacency.

He went back into the foyer, where he saw the Cruise Director, Scott Pierre, talking and laughing with a group of passengers. As Jim approached them, Scott called out, 'Hello Jim!' Then he added with a laugh, 'This is our Staff Captain looking very military in his cap.'

'Could I have a word?' Jim said. 'Please excuse us,' he said to the passengers. He took Pierre's arm and led him to a quiet corner.

'What's with the cap, Jim? We try to discourage wearing those indoors as it takes away from the holiday atmosphere.'

'Scott, you're the Cruise Director not a fashion editor. You know we are trying to get the passengers to take lifeboat drills seriously. What the hell were you doing talking to those passengers when they should have been at boat drill?'

Pierre looked bewildered. 'Jim boy, what's the problem? They're long time cruisers with us and very important people. They've seen it all before. They have suites you know.'

'You idiot!' exploded Jim. 'Do you think I care who they are or how long they've been cruising? It's a boat drill for fuck's sake not some yachties booze up. Now get over there and tell them to go to the drill or I'll go and do it and you won't like my language. Do we understand?'

Pierre nodded.

'Oh and by the way, next time you call me boy, I'll toss you over the side.'

Jim stomped off and then leant against the ship's rail breathing heavily. He could not understand a senior member of the management behaving like this. He stayed there for several minutes, trying to calm down, not noticing the passengers leaving the lounges at the end of the drill.

Jim was roused from his thoughts by a soft voice saying, 'You look a little flustered'. He turned round to see a young woman in a wheelchair. She was lovely, soft brown hair framing a pixie face, but it was her smile that illuminated her face spreading to her twinkling eyes with delicate wrinkles at the edges. Jim guessed she was in her late twenties. She held out her hand.

'I'm Helen Shreiber. You must be the new Staff Captain.'

'Yes. I'm sorry I'm staring. Jim Clariby.'

'I know. I saw your name on the crew list.'

'Crew list? What are you doing with a crew list?' asked Jim.

She laughed. 'You think I am a passenger. I'm the ship's pianist, or at least one of them. I provide light music in the lounges.' She paused. 'Now you're looking at the wheelchair. Really, it doesn't interfere with my piano playing.' She laughed again. 'I can actually walk,' she said pointing to the sticks in a slot on the side of the chair. 'But I get tired very easily so I use this to get around.'

'How long have you been on board?'

'About a month now. I think I got on board as part of their handicapped quota. Three more months to go, then back home.'

'Where's that?'

'New England, Connecticut. I teach piano there at the university but I have a sabbatical to come on the ship. My parents thought it would do me good to get away for a while.'

'Is this new then?' Jim said indicating the chair.

'Oh that. I've been like this since I was a child. No, I was getting stale and needed a break. Too many students playing bad piano.' She laughed again. It was delightful and Jim could feel his mood improving.

'So how do you like our floating palace?' she asked.

'I think your description is very appropriate.'

She looked at her watch. 'I must go and play for the lunchtime drinkers,' she said. 'Perhaps I will see you around town?'

'I certainly hope so,' said Jim.

She gave him a last smile and wheeled herself away back into the lounge.

Jim slowly made his way to the bridge. Peter was going through some papers at one of the work stations.

'How did it go, Sir?' he asked.

'Could have been worse. The same as on *'Sea Breeze'* really. Most of the passengers seemed to turn up though. The announcements were good and distinct, but it's early days.'

'I hope you didn't think that I went to the Captain about the courses.'

'It never occurred to me,' replied Jim.

'When he came up last night to do the night orders, he saw the changes and ordered them back, but this morning he told me to arrange them for daylight only and to call you beforehand if we are doing any really close approaches.'

'Thanks, Peter. That's something anyway.'

'If it's any consolation, I thought about what you said and agree with you.'

'While I'm here, do you know anything about the ballast and flooding control system?'

'Sure, Captain. It's quite simple; the computers do it all for us now.' He led Jim over to an electronic state board on one of the control panels. He switched it on and waited while the display screen started.

'You can see here the state of all the tanks on the ship, including fresh water, ballast and fuel waste. The amount in each tank is entered automatically into the calculations.'

'Manually or electronically?'

'All automatic, Captain, and it's constantly monitored so the information is always completely up to date. The weight of the passengers' baggage and stores is a constant factor, but we can change that manually.'

'What about free surface?'

'Again, when a tank is only partly full, a free surface allowance is automatically made.'

'So how is listing dealt with?' asked Jim.

'The computer is set up to what we require, which is always 0 degrees list. In the ballast cross-over tanks, the computer will automatically move ballast as required to keep the ship in that condition.'

'What about in the event of catastrophic flooding?' asked Jim.

'We can then change to emergency mode. It allows freedom over all the tanks to move what is required to keep the ship upright. We can also override it whenever we wish and operate the tank controls manually.'

'That's quite something,' said Jim. 'I wish I'd had that when I was a cargo officer. One last thing, is the system on the emergency power circuits?'

'All the bridge has secondary back-up power, and as a last resort batteries take over for flood control, communications, lighting, one of the radars and limited manual steering.'

Jim left the bridge and thought about lunch. He didn't want to go down to the restaurant so was intending to head for the officers' mess again, when he saw Zhou and Matheson standing in the alleyway outside his cabin.

'Matheson, I hardly recognised you. I knew there was a cadet under all that hair. Not too difficult was it?'

Matheson smiled. 'Sorry, Sir.'

'Not your fault. They used to train you on cargo ships first. Many companies wouldn't employ you until you had been on other types of ships and had your Master's Certificate. You see, although we are civilians, the Merchant Navy is a disciplined service. We have to be as we are the ones they will look to in times of trouble. That's hard to understand when one minute you're being bollocked for your appearance, then the next you're knocking back cocktails with a bunch of eager young ladies who think you're Hornblower. Learn to separate, got it?'

Matheson smiled broadly and nodded.

'Now go. If it's of any interest, I think you look better. Clean shoes and clean fingernails. That's what they look for.'

'Sorry, Sir?'

'You'll find out. Educate him, Zhou.'

Jim pulled at his bow tie as he walked down the wide corridor of the penthouse deck. Jenny was the only one who could get it perfect. He headed for the open door of the Atlantic Suite, from which the buzz of happy people was emanating.

He didn't bother knocking but walked straight in. Immediately, a waiter offered him champagne. It was a large stateroom, busy with guests, some overspilling through the open glass doors to a balcony beyond.

He was greeted in a haze of names that he could never remember until two women of undetermined age approached him. They were attractive but had been redesigned.

'Hi there, Staffie. I'm Jessie Langton and this is my best friend, Cheryl Huntley. I'm pleased you made our little party. We're on your table. Nothing against you but we thought that Adama was going to be on board. He's quite a man, isn't he Cheryl?'

'You bet your life. He and Augusto gave some great parties.' Jim wasn't paying much attention to the conversation as he was staring at her necklace. It was gold with large green emeralds and was stunning. The gold was twisted in a very delicate pattern that was exactly the same as the emerald earring he had found. This is the mystery woman. No wonder she knew all about Adama.

'Sorry,' he said. 'You were talking about parties?'

'Hell yes. The more the merrier. We've only got two weeks to let our hair down before going home.'

'Sorry, ladies. I'm afraid I've only just joined the ship and I'm still finding my way around. I'm a little too busy for parties at the moment.'

'Don't worry, Jimbo. Cheryl and I will show you how to party.'

The room was becoming increasingly noisy. Smoke from cigarettes and cigars was drifting out the balcony doors. After a few more minutes, Jim made his excuses and went down a couple of decks to the next party. This was no different except that it was a smaller cabin. Again Jim hugged his glass, making it last. After a decent interval, he made his excuses and left.

The restaurant was huge and crowded by the time he arrived. A mass of waiters were hurrying around carrying plates. They wore different coloured jackets signifying their role and, at intervals, the hotel officers, who were now wearing white dinner jackets with gold stripes, were supervising. He had to admire the efficiency of the operation. He asked where his table was and the officer led the way. Jim saw it was full except for his seat, which was flanked by the two plastic ladies. The others at the table were two pleasant couples. Jim settled into the usual small talk, but as the meal progressed it was obvious that the two ladies either side of him were quite drunk.

'So, Jimbo,' said Jessie. 'I suppose you have a trail of broken hearts around the world.'

'Maybe when I was younger, but now, as a married man,' he said pointedly, 'I reserve my affections.'

Cheryl laughed. 'I bet. Christ, we know all about you sailors, don't we Jessie? Adama dropped his trousers to order, didn't he?' The women laughed coarsely and the other two couples looked distinctly uncomfortable.

'So, what have you got planned for Kingston tomorrow?' Jim asked, addressing the table in general, desperate to change the subject.

'The question is, what have we got planned for tonight?' laughed Jessie. Jim felt a hand on his leg.

Christ, at dinner as well. He carefully put his hand under the table and firmly removed the hand. It was Jessie's. He smiled at the others.

'If you can, it's worth getting out of the town and going up the Blue Mountains. The best coffee comes from up there. You can buy it in the shops as well as up the mountains.'

His voice rose as he finished his sentence. Jessie's hand had now moved up to his groin, gripping hard. She looked at him smiling sweetly.

'Are you all right, Captain?'

'I just swallowed something the wrong way, that's all.'

The women grinned at each other. In desperation, Jim knocked his wine glass over. Jessie, pushing back her chair, let go of him. That was all he needed.

He stood up. 'I'm terribly sorry everyone.' He beckoned a waiter. 'Clean this up please.' He looked at his watch.

'Good heavens, is that the time? I am sorry. I promised to relieve one of the officers on the bridge. Please excuse me.'

He hastily left the restaurant and went to the main concourse and found the ship's central office.

'Is the Hotel Manager here?'

'No, Sir. He's having dinner.'

'Then get him to phone me as soon as possible.'

Jim went up to his cabin and sat at his desk. Henry Milau, the Hotel Manager, rang a few minutes later.

'Good evening, Jim. What's the panic?'

'Henry, I am sitting here with my dick in an ice bucket cooling down after being squashed by one of those sea monsters you sat me with at my table. I want them moved tomorrow.'

'Hold on, Jim. It can't be that bad.'

'Not for you maybe, but it wasn't your dick.'

'Are you serious? At the table?'

'At the table. In front of other passengers. Henry, they're both completely pissed. I suggest you keep an eye on them tonight. Either way, I couldn't care less if they fall over the side, but they're off my table or I'm off theirs.'

'Jim, half the ship is pissed. Don't worry. I'll deal with it first thing in the morning. You could of course wear a jock strap,' Henry joked.

'Piss off, Henry.'

Jim watched the latest news and then strolled around the ship. Without a doubt, it was a marvel. The shopping mall was busy. The bars and lounges were all different; they were all busy with music and laughter flowing from them. He arrived at the top deck and walked along to the Starlight Lounge, passing through the casino which was doing a roaring trade. Jim noticed the security officer standing discreetly to one side. The Starlight Lounge was full and one of the bands was playing for a packed dance floor. Jim stood for a moment and then walked back out, looking for a toilet. He saw one off the main alleyway and went in. There, by the washbasins, were two youths snorting coke.

Jim went over and swept the coke off the vanity surface.

'Where the fuck do you think you are? Get out of here! Now!' He wiped the white powder off his hand and followed the youths back into the Starlight Lounge. They went back to join their friends at a table. They were talking and looking over at him. Jim went to the bar and called for the barman.

'That table over there,' he said pointing. 'What is their cabin number?'

All passengers had a ship's credit card with their cabin number on it to use for paying for their drinks. The barman came back.

'There are three card numbers, Sir.'

He wrote them down and handed them over. Jim walked back through to the casino and found the security officer.

'Please call the Senior Security Officer.'

The security officer lifted his arm and spoke into a mike. He listened for a moment.

'He'll be up now.' He looked troubled. 'Is there a problem, Sir?'

'Don't worry. It's nothing concerning the casino.'

The man looked relieved and turned his attention back to the gaming tables.

Bert Fallows arrived and came across to Jim.

'Is there a problem, Captain?' he asked

Jim took him outside. 'I've just come from the toilet over there. When I went in, I found two young men snorting coke. These are their cabin numbers.' He handed Fallows the slip of paper.

Fallows pursed his lips. 'Can we sit down over there for a moment, Sir.'

They found a quiet table in the lounge.

'Sir, every cruise ship has its rackets. The waiters have to pay the suppliers, they then have to pay others for their jobs or promotion. Cabin staff have to pay for sandwiches, wine waiters swap labels and so on it goes. As ships get larger, so do the rackets. Our job is keep it down to a dull roar. This doesn't affect the ship and the punters seem happy enough. We even have had a bunch of hookers working the ship, but as long as it's discreet and they pay their fares, we turn a blind eye. This isn't what we want; it's the company wanting it this way. No fuss, no publicity.'

'I wouldn't say that, Bert. I know the racket situation and when we catch it we usually deal with it. It's been going on ever since ships started carrying passengers.'

'But not to the same extent as today, Captain. In the past, companies have wanted to stop it. Now all they worry about is hushing everything up.'

'Bert, I assure you they don't want drugs on their ships.'

'I'm not saying they do. But we had them on the *'Sea Breeze'*.'

'What? And you knew about it?'

'Yes. I reported it but nothing happened. Admittedly it was only grass, but it was still classed as drugs. But this American fleet is different. Here anything goes. The ship is rotten, Sir. All we are doing is keeping the lid on it.'

'I don't believe you, Bert. You security people see shadows where they don't exist. Of course I know about the bribery and payoffs, but you can't call the whole ship rotten. Have you reported all this? Does the Captain know?'

'Sir, I would like to meet with you once we have docked in Kingston tomorrow morning. I want to bring two of my security men. Can I ask you to say nothing to anyone until we've met?'

'All right, Bert, but this had better be good. You can't make accusations without evidence.'

'Talking of evidence, did you keep the cocaine you saw in the toilets?'

'No. I knocked it onto the floor.'

'So it's only your word about what you saw?' said Bert. Jim nodded.

'The kid will lie his head off.'

'So he gets away with it?'

'Give me the cabin numbers. There are ways. Remember we're in Panama now.'

They got up.

'Come at 1000 in the morning, Bert.'

As Bert walked away, he beckoned to the casino security officer and they left together.

Chapter 13

Jim went up to the bridge for their arrival at Kingston. It was a typical Jamaican morning and the air was warming as the sun rose. Small white clouds were scattered over the top of the Blue Mountains that provided a perfect backdrop to the city. The ship berthed between two other cruise ships. The jetty was already packed with tourist buses, taxis and the usual port debris attracted by a cruise ship's arrival.

As soon as the ship was settled down and the passengers were on their way ashore, they swung the rescue boat out with the cadet crew. At the same time, they lowered one of the lifeboats with a Third Officer at the helm. Once in the water, they circled around. The Bosun dropped a couple of dummies into the water for them to pick up. While the lifeboat returned to the ship, the rescue boat headed off at speed to tour the harbour. Jim watched for a while before returning to his office to continue working.

At 1000 on the dot, Bert arrived accompanied by two security officers.

'I think you'll want to hear what these guys have to say, Sir.'

'First, this is for you.' Bert produced a plastic bag. Inside were some wrappers, a packet of what was obviously grass and some coloured pills. 'We searched those kids' cabins last night and found this lot. It's all logged and witnessed. Can we close the door please.'

'We're being a bit dramatic aren't we?' Jim commented, but still got up and closed the door. They settled in round the conference table.

'A bit of background first, Captain. I arrived on this cruise ship before you joined. I don't know if you heard but on the previous cruise they lost one of the crew over the side.'

Bert looked at Jim as he shook his head, and then continued. 'Well, the crew member was a security officer. He was a steady man, not likely to fall over the side.'

'All kinds of people go over the side, Bert. Just because it was a security officer doesn't necessarily mean anything,' said Jim.

Bert looked at one of the security officers he had brought.

'This is Samuel Gully, Sam for short.'

He was a black man with tight black hair and what looked like a broken nose. He had large hands with scarred knuckles which he rubbed as he spoke.

'Sir, the guy who disappeared was investigating an established drug ring on the ship. At first, we thought that only low-grade crew members were involved. You know, supplying passengers with grass and pills, that kind of stuff.' He shrugged. 'It happens here as well as on the streets of every town and city so it's no big deal, but this was more. He told me about it before he disappeared.'

'Why the hell didn't he go to the Captain or the Staff Captain?'

'There was no proof. He did go to the General Ship Manager thinking there would be cooperation. He was told to wait, get more evidence and then they would go to the Captain together. Shortly after that, he disappeared.'

'That doesn't prove anything,' said Jim.

'There's more,' said Bert. 'Two trips before that, there was a passenger, a woman who was supplying information. One of those involved was screwing her. Anyway, she knew things about the drugs. It was far more than supply. They were smuggling drugs into the States on the ship. She went over the side as well.'

The other security guard spoke.

'I'm Mark Davies, Captain. It's well known to the Florida police that large quantities of drugs are coming in on cruise ships. I was a detective with the Miami police.' Jim looked at him with interest. Mark continued, 'We could draw a chart of the drug increase on the streets of Florida with the increase in cruise ships.'

'Let me get this straight,' said Jim. 'According to you, there have been two murders over the last three cruises, we have a full-scale criminal drug syndicate on board amongst the prostitution and corruption that is going on, and you suspect the General Ship Manager of being involved.'

'Not just him. There must be others as well.'

'Do you realise how ridiculous this sounds? Do you expect me to go to the Captain with this? Just what the hell do you think he'll say? I'll tell you. He'll heave me down the gangway as mentally disturbed, and he'd be right!'

They sat silently until Bert said, 'Excuse me, Sir.' They bent their heads together and whispered amongst themselves. Eventually, they turned back to Jim.

'There is something you should know, Sir. First, please understand you cannot go to the Captain. As I explained, at this stage we don't know how far this goes up the ladder on board. The Captain is very chummy with the hotel side of the ship.'

Jim waited patiently. Sam reached into his pocket and took out a gold badge which he placed on the table. Jim picked it up. It was heavy. At the top, there was an American eagle that surmounted a shield. Around the edge of the shield, it said Drug Enforcement. In the centre were two letters, US, and under them it said Special Agent.

Jim sat stunned. 'This is a cruise ship for fuck's sake,' he muttered.

'It's also a small city with all the problems of one and not under the US jurisdiction,' said Sam. 'It's Panama. That's why the disappearances of the woman and the security guard weren't properly investigated. An empty vodka bottle was conveniently found on the deck where she went over. Only problem was she didn't drink vodka. Her cabin was also clean. Too clean.'

'Are you also police?' Jim asked the other guard.

'No, Captain. Genuine retired ex-detective and now your security guard, but I am, of course, involved.'

Bert brought out a folder which he placed on the table.

'We have identified 18 crew members with criminal records. Here are their details. We aren't saying they are all involved. Not much investigation is done of the lower rated cruise ship crew. That's left to the agencies who employ them so it's natural that may leave some form of record. They've served their time or whatever and are now going straight, but what is interesting is that there is a group who seem to be exclusively recruited in Florida. The same ones go on leave and come back, but there is always a core of them on board. These are the ones we are watching, but it's not them we want. We could pick up about five of the crew who are involved in selling drugs on board, but that's too low down. We want the boys at the top. They have no record.'

'Why are you telling me this if you don't want me to go to the Captain?'

'Because we know you're clean. You have no previous involvement with anyone on board except for Bert here, unlike the last Staff Captain. We need your cooperation.'

'So what happens now?' asked Jim.

'Nothing. You carry on running things as normal. Bert will report to you as required and we'll meet when we have something further to report. If you have anything to tell us, do that through Bert here.'

'You do realise that we still have a ship to run and care for.'

'That's fine, Captain. This will not interfere with that. In fact, we want everyone to act as normally as possible.'

Jim looked at his watch. 'I have to go to the heads of department meeting,' he said. 'And I have to be as normal as possible after what you've just told me - that's going to be interesting. Gentlemen, thank you, I think, for what you've told me. Bert, please report to me each morning at 0900.'

'I'll do that, Sir. It's a lot different to the old passenger ship days, isn't it?'

'You can say that again,' answered Jim.

Jim was late when he arrived at the General Manager's meeting. He apologised and found an empty chair to sit in.

'Got hung up on a security matter,' explained Jim.

The Ship General Manager, William Shelby, sat at one end of the table and the Captain sat at the other. Let's see who speaks first, thought Jim. For some odd reason, he felt truculent. Either these silly buggers knew nothing, which meant they were idiots, or they knew a lot, which meant they were complicit in a cover-up. Time would tell.

'You haven't missed much, Staff Captain,' said Shelby. 'We've just gone through the minutes of the last meeting. Anything serious?'

So that's how the wind blows, Jim thought. OK, let's see.

'Not really. I caught a couple of passengers snorting coke in one of the toilets last night.'

That brought them up with a jolt.

'When was this?' asked Shelby.

'About 2300, outside the Starlight Lounge. Kids. We have their cabin numbers.' He looked at the Captain. 'I was going to tell you this morning, Sir, but, as I say, I got caught up getting the facts before I came to you. Still, we have enough evidence now to throw them off the ship. I don't know if their parents will want to go with them or not.'

'Just a minute,' said Shelby. 'We don't just throw passengers off the ship like that. We must have concrete proof.'

'We have that. A search of their cabins found a nice little drugs haul.'

'You searched their cabins?'

'I didn't. Security did, on my authority.'

'I should have been notified before you did that.'

'Why? Security work for me and I work for the Captain not you.'

'I think the Staff Captain is correct,' said Iain, the Chief Engineer. 'It's time we came down hard on this kind of thing.'

'We haven't had this before,' said Shelby.

'Oh, come on,' said Iain. 'It's been going on under our noses for ages. It's just that you never wanted to see it. Or if you did, you ignored it.'

'That's unfair!' said Scott Pierre, the Cruise Director. Everyone was talking now. Jim looked at the Captain, who was looking distinctly uncomfortable. Come on, he was willing him, take charge. Nothing. The hell with it.

'Just a moment,' Jim said. 'What has happened has happened. We didn't look for it, but we have a duty to deal with it. I don't know what the law in Panama is, but I bet that drug use is a punishable offence. Officially, I suppose we should inform the authorities about this so just heaving them off the ship is the least of their worries. I won't press for involving the authorities if we can agree to that. However,' and here he looked at the Captain, 'I want zero tolerance to drug use on board. I hope that is already accepted by us all. You can bet these kids will have told their friends that they were seen by me. If we don't act, it will send out a bad message.'

Cota cleared his throat. 'It's obvious we can't tolerate drug use on board. However, it is essential we deal with this discreetly so that it does not reflect badly on the reputation of the company.'

Iain the Chief Engineer snorted from the other side of the table. 'I think the reputation of the ship is more important, Captain.'

Cota held his hand up. 'I hear what you're saying, Chief. Now, we have other matters to discuss. I will talk with Mr Shelby and the Staff Captain after this meeting.'

Jim had a list of other things to be dealt with but he felt this wasn't the time to hit them with more problems. Other matters were discussed but nothing of any relevance to Jim and the meeting broke up. As the Chief went out, he stopped to speak to Jim.

'I want to discuss the lifeboat davit maintenance scheduling. Could you come by my cabin once you've finished here?'

Jim nodded in agreement.

The door closed, leaving Jim alone with Shelby and the Captain.

'You've caused quite a stir in just a few days, Captain,' said Shelby.

'It's not of my making, William.'

'I agree, but it would have been helpful if you had waited to discuss this with the Captain and myself privately.'

'I'm sorry. I didn't have the rule book for your meetings. I thought they were to air any problems that have come to our attention. You asked me about it when I came in.' Shelby did not reply.

'What are your thoughts, Captain?' Jim asked Cota.

The normally confident Cota was looking uncomfortable. 'We must obviously do something, but you must understand, Jim, that it would not be in the interests of the company to involve the authorities. If we start throwing passengers off, we must have a valid reason for that. I agree that we have the reason, but if challenged we would have to officially state why.'

'I don't see that,' said Jim. 'They would be happy enough to leave as long as we don't press charges against the kids.'

Cota was silent again.

'Jim,' said Shelby. Not Staff Captain now Jim noted. 'It would be of great assistance if you could be flexible on this.'

Jim pretended to think for a moment.

'I tell you what, William, I'll offer a trade. As you know, I'm not happy with some of the abandon ship aspects. I want the drills to be done before sailing, regardless of what it interferes with. I want to have a meeting with all those involved with the disembarkation procedures, that's all those supervising the passenger movement. I want passenger attendance and the wearing of lifejackets strictly enforced. Zero tolerance. If you agree to that, I'll talk with security and we will move over this incident. Understand the message though. Drugs will not be tolerated, anywhere, at any time.'

Cota looked at Shelby. 'I think we can go along with that, Jim. We were already considering your lifeboat suggestions anyway, weren't we William?'

'Absolutely, Captain. They are good and we support them fully, Jim. You have it. Thank you for your understanding.'

'It shows what can be done when we work together,' said Cota, who was feeling comfortable again and now smiling, although not for long.

'In addition, I want the security team to be allowed to carry out random drug tests on the crew. In the future, I also want to do drug tests on passengers we suspect of taking drugs.'

'What!' Shelby exploded. 'Have you gone completely mad? Cota, tell the man!'

Jim looked at Cota. 'We know there are crew and passengers taking drugs, Captain, all of which is against the law and must surely be against the company's regulations.'

Cota had gone pale. 'Jim, just because you find a few youths with recreational drugs does not mean the ship is drug ridden.'

'I never said that, Sir, but just the knowledge that tests can be done when they have reason should at least make people think. After all, we have random alcohol tests for the deck and engine department, so why not drug tests for the rest of the ship?'

'I knew it!' shouted Shelby. 'You are heading for the hotel departments again!'

'Don't be stupid,' said Jim. 'I'm suggesting this for the good of the ship.'

'How dare you!' cried Shelby. 'I'll remind you that I am the General Manager of the ship.'

'And I'll remind you that the Captain is the Master of the ship and I am under his command, just as you are. I work for him not you!'

'That's enough!' shouted Cota. 'Staff Captain, Mr Shelby is appointed General Manager by the company. As such, I remain in charge of operational matters, but he is in charge of everything on the passenger side, including matters that appertain to them. What do you think would happen if we started giving the passengers drug tests? I'll tell you what. They would be up in arms. Not only that, they would walk off our ships. There are plenty of other companies waiting to pick them up. As for the crew, of course some of them have drugs, just as they do in every single town or village ashore. What do you think it would do to our reputation if we started prosecuting every crew member who possessed marijuana?'

Jim sat silently.

'Now let's calm down. I understand your concerns, Jim, and you have understandably brought them to our attention. We will discuss them with the company ashore. Then, if they wish to take any further action, they will advise us but we do not, and I repeat we do not, take any action that could damage the company without their approval. Is that clear?'

There was silence for a moment. Cota waited.

Jim took a deep breath. 'Perfectly clear, Sir'.

'Good. I am glad that is clarified. Mr Shelby, are you satisfied with that?'

'I suppose so,' he muttered.

'Well, that was an exciting meeting,' Cota said, smiling with relief.

'Thank you, Jim. Are you going down to lunch?'

'After I have seen the Chief, Captain,' replied Jim.

'Watch him; he's dangerous.'

Once Jim had gone, Shelby turned to Cota. 'I don't like him. He's a loose cannon.'

'I understand, William,' said Cota, 'but he's a good officer. He's come up with excellent ideas and we need some of those. Perhaps we are becoming set in our ways.'

'Augusto, an operation like this runs on routine. Just establishing that takes time. We can't change it just because someone arrives who doesn't like it.'

'But what if he's right? Give him a chance. Remember we need him for the northern cruises,' said Cota calmly.

'All right, Augusto, but I'll be watching.'

Jim arrived down on the engineers deck, walked through the crew door and found himself in a pleasant long alleyway of doors. Some were open and others were closed. He passed several offices where officers in white boiler suits were sitting or bending over desks. Soon he came to an open door that led through to the Chief Engineer's spacious office.

'Chief?' he called.

'Come in, Jim!' Iain shouted from his dayroom.

Jim pushed the curtain aside and walked in. Iain was standing with Patrick, the Staff Chief, and another officer with three stripes.

'Jim, this is our electronics wizard, Carlo Secundi, the Chief Electro-Technical Officer, or ETO for short. Without him, everything stops and we go back to something we can understand. I was just telling the lads here about your performance. By God, you put them on edge.'

'That wasn't really my intention.'

'Intention or not, it's time someone brought zero tolerance to the ship. The bloody hotel and shore office people have been running things for long enough. So what's happening? Are we kicking them off?'

Jim smiled.

'Hold on, Iain. I am going to ask for your understanding. I wanted something more important than chucking a few kids off. I did a deal. The kids stay.' He could see Iain's face. 'In return, I get passenger boat drills before the ship sails, not the next day, and zero tolerance for any passengers not turning up or not wearing their lifejackets.'

Iain looked dubious. 'What about the drugs issue?'

'Not forgotten; we just have to wait. We'll act when the time comes.'

'Do you think they will keep to that boat business? You have to watch Shelby. He's a nasty shit,' commented Iain.

'Then we have to be nastier.'

'Are we going to take Jim to the club?' asked Patrick.

'I think we can make him an honorary member,' said Iain. 'Come on, Jim.'

Iain led the way out of the cabin, along the alleyway then down a narrow staircase which led to a door labelled 'Hazardous Space. Strictly No Admittance.'

He opened the door and they entered a crowded room. It was decorated with various items obviously purloined from the passenger area. At one end was a magnificent bar shaped like the side of a ship, complete with a row of bar stools.

'Welcome to the only honest bar on the ship,' said Iain.

'And the cheapest,' added Patrick. 'What's your drink, Jim?'

'A pint please.'

This was placed into his hand and Iain took him away to a corner.

'This is quite something,' said Jim looking around.

'Totally unofficial of course,' said Iain. 'My lads need a place away from the punters to relax. It also keeps them from getting bevvied up in public. They go up there to get women, but they drink mostly down here.'

'Do they bring the women in?'

'Absolutely not. That's what their cabins are for. This is purely for us, and honorary members such as yourself.'

'Any others?'

'Jan, your Safety Officer, and Peter, the First Officer. They're both good lads.'

'I got that impression,' said Jim.

'Jim, watch yourself. This American operation is controlled far more by the shore boys than in the UK and the hotel crowd rule the roost. The Old Man knows which side his bread is buttered. Be careful you don't have the pack after you.'

'Thanks, Iain. I'll remember that.'

'Also, you know where we live. Don't be a stranger.'

Chapter 14

That evening, the ship sailed out of Kingston on the next leg of the cruise. Jim brought Jan up to speed on the events, omitting the drug problem.

'I'm really surprised they've agreed to the boat drills. We've wanted that for some time but never got anywhere. They kept throwing the regulations at us saying within 24 hours of sailing is fine. So, when are you having this meeting with everyone?' asked Jan.

'I want it before the next cruise as it will come into force when we sail from Lauderdale next. Probably in two ports' time. That will be Nassau,' answered Jim.

'We'll have it at 1000 in the morning in one of the crew lounges. Most of the punters will be off. That will give them time to do the lunches without too much disruption. I want you to put some thought into a card that will go into all cabins regarding the attendance at boat drill. Something along the lines that it is a compulsory requirement under the ship's regulations and that it must be strictly adhered to. The one they use at the moment is too soft. How did the boats go?'

'Good. The cadets are getting on with the work. Actually I think they like the change from standing around on the bridge and doing checklists. The officers on the bridge are pissed off mind you, now that they have to write their own log books.'

'Do them good.'

The next morning, Bert Fallows arrived with his daily report.

'As we didn't heave those kids off, I thought we'd have an informal chat with them. I chose the youngest. We told him that the others had named him and that on arrival back in Lauderdale we would be handing him over. It was very easy. He spilled where the drugs came from. It was one of the barmen in the sports bar. He took the order and they were then delivered to the cabin when they were out. The barman was already on our list. Anyway, I thought it would be useful to get it in writing.'

Jim looked at the statement.

'It's all helping to build a picture, Captain.'

Jim spent the next few days on routine matters, inspections, meetings and establishing his stamp on the department. He was on the bridge for the arrivals and departures and saw that Cota handled the ship well. The Captain was always pleasant to him and never mentioned the incident at the heads of department meeting. That suited Jim as he was busy. He continued supervising the passage plans and attending the bridge for the close approaches.

When they arrived at Nassau, Cota surprised Jim by asking him if he would like to make the approach to the Pilot. It was a lovely Caribbean morning. There were lots of small pleasure craft around, but they stayed clear of the channel. Other cruise ships were already berthed and they took their place in the line.

'I see you're having your meeting of the boat embarkation personnel this morning in the main crew lounge. Do you mind if I attend?' asked Cota.

Jim was surprised.

'It would be a pleasure, Captain.'

'Good,' said Cota. 'I'll see you at 1000 then.'

Jim and Jan arrived shortly before 1000 and went to the front of the lounge. It was crowded with all the officers and supervisors who were concerned with the abandon ship drills as well as the security officers standing at the back of the room. The Captain arrived accompanied by Shelby the General Manager, Milau the Hotel Manager and Bella Winchester the Purser.

'We have a full house,' Jim murmured to Jan.

The room was buzzing with noise until Jim stood. He picked up the microphone.

'It's good to see you all here. I know you have other duties to attend to and I will try not to keep you too long. However, I want you to realise that this is a very serious subject and your time here will be well worth it. I have seen the company boat drills being carried out on two ships and one thing is apparent. We are going through the motions rather than being concerned about what is a serious safety issue. It's quite simple. If anything happens to this ship resulting in such catastrophic damage that she begins to sink, our job is to get all the passengers off safely, in the shortest time possible. Images of the Titanic should not be in your minds, but it is essential that we get passengers to their boats efficiently, without delay and above all else without panic. This starts with you. While the seamen get the boats ready, we depend on you to get the passengers ready.

'Preparation starts with the drills. In future there will be no tolerance of passengers either not turning up to their stations or not bringing their lifejackets. You must display confidence and command. There will be no more talking during the broadcast. You will stop it. The bars will be closed. All waiter service will stop for the duration of the exercise. Any passenger trying to make an order will be ignored. Any passenger without a lifejacket will be told to go and get it. The names of those not turning up will be passed to me and the Safety Officer. We will deal with this in future.'

Jim could see that this was causing a disturbance in the front row. The hotel people had their heads together.

'On the next cruise, we will attempt a full demonstration with one boat, using our own crew as passengers. Finally, remember there is no guarantee that an abandon ship will take place in good weather. It could be a gale, dark or cold. You all know the ship is cruising up to the Arctic Circle very soon. Things are very different compared to the Caribbean and we must be ready. The temperature of the water is just above freezing even in summer. You will last about 15 minutes in the water before you die. Even down here you would get hypothermia after an hour.

'Lastly, those of you responsible for getting the passengers into the boats must ensure that the boats are full. Let me tell you why. We do not have enough room for everyone in the boats.'

There was shocked silence around the room.

Someone shouted, 'Why not?'

'Because that's what the regulations allow. Liferafts can be used to replace twenty five percent of the seating capacity. It's not rocket science. Go and count the boats. There are 12 on each side. Multiply 24 by 150 and the answer is 3,600. How many people on the ship? Last time I looked it was 4,200.' Again there was a stunned silence.

'Now my last words to you are this. You are on a ship, not a hotel, regardless of what some would wish. There is a tradition that must be engraved on your hearts. All passengers leave before we do. Don't worry about women and children first, that's not needed as there is enough space for all the passengers, but you stay until they are off the ship. You will get off fast enough, and as the Captain here I must stay until you're off.'

There was a little laughter but it was subdued. Good. He had struck home.

'Any questions?'

Several hands were raised. Jim pointed to one.

'What are we supposed to do if the passenger tells us to fuck off?'

There was faint laughter.

'That's easy. You're hotel staff, so why ask me? It must have happened to you before. I am sure you know how to be firm and courteous while keeping your cool. If you don't then you shouldn't be here. Next.'

It was a young woman. 'Sir, why can't we give them their lifejackets when they get to their stations?'

'Bloody good question. That's what we should do. Just think of midnight, half the passengers up top trying to get down to their cabins for lifejackets and the other half trying to get up to the lounges. How many staircases have we got? Four. Then when everyone gets up to the lounge we have to get them back down to deck three for the boats. But where would we give the lifejackets out? In the lounge? And where would we stow them?'

'By the boats, Sir.'

'Imagine the chaos of passengers putting lifejackets on by the boats. How do we check them? How do the passengers get one if they don't get to a boat or if their boat has gone? I'm not saying you're wrong, but I want you to think of the difficulties of moving so many people off the ship in a short time. I have to tell you, as those in charge of the muster stations will already know, we do have stocks of lifejackets nearby and they will be available to those who don't have them.'

There were several other questions, mostly sensible, and Jim could see that they were thinking, which was the object of this exercise. Jim held his hand up for quiet again.

'We are making up a new pamphlet that will be put into each passenger cabin for the next cruise. This will emphasise the importance of the drill and the fact that they must attend. For this to work, it depends on you. For future drills, I will have deck officers, including myself and the Safety Officer, moving around the boat assembly stations to support you and also to answer any passenger questions. That's it. Thank you for your attention.'

The room slowly emptied.

Jim and Cota walked back together.

'The hotel side don't like this at all, you know. They think you're obsessed with the ship sinking.'

'I'm not obsessed, but the ship's safety is my department's main job. I'm only trying to improve our chances of saving lives if anything does go wrong. You and I know that we haven't got a hope of getting all the people off this ship quickly, even if they don't. The trouble is we are surrounded by all this grandeur and size, and we tend to forget she is a ship with only a few centimetres of steel separating us from the sea.'

'That business about boat availability really hit home. I'm not sure that was wise.'

'Why not, Sir?'

'Because they will talk to the passengers.'

'Would that be so bad? I mean why shouldn't they know? If enough of them complain then maybe we might get enough boats.'

'Look,' said Cota. 'I'm supporting you as far as I can, but cruising is the new world. The companies pour money into the maritime agencies and they have a strong voice. Much more than a few sailors. Be careful.'

Jim was walking along the top deck and as he passed the bar he saw the pianist, Helen. She was sitting in her wheelchair at an outside table with a glass of wine.

'May I join you?' Jim asked.

Helen looked up, shading her eyes. 'How lovely, Captain. Please do.'

'I thought you would be ashore today seeing the sights,' he said.

'I don't want to sound like a wounded bird, but it's a lot of bother going ashore in a wheelchair. Anyway, I'm quite happy here. What about you?'

'I'm not much of a tourist, I'm afraid. I'd rather see things from the sea. Generally it's better than close up. Anyway why go ashore when we have a delightful café by the pool on a nice empty deck and sunshine.'

'I hear you had a busy morning.'

'Word spreads.'

'It should do when it seems there aren't enough lifeboats. You've got people worried.'

'Just a minute. They've been like that for a long time. Anyone can look and count and see it's perfectly obvious. Anyway I wasn't trying to scare them. I wanted them to understand the need of care.'

'You must be careful, Captain. These hotel people don't realise they are on a ship, even if it's like Disneyland. They are actors who suddenly think they are in the magic kingdom, and remember it never rains there.'

'Thanks for that. I'm beginning to feel like the wicked witch.'

She laughed.

'So why haven't you been to hear my piano?'

'Would you believe I haven't had time?'

'Well I'm playing in the after lounge this evening; it's called the Grand Salon.'

'That must be the Versailles end of the kingdom. All right, it's a deal. I'll come along after dinner. But I'm afraid I have to go now as I have to see the fire fighters.'

She waved her finger at Jim. 'You still have to learn. We don't have fire fighters in the magic kingdom. We have fire prevention officers.'

'Thank you, princess. I'll see you in Versailles,' Jim laughed.

Jim met Jan and together they went down to the safety office. The central fire station was next to it and three firemen were inside.

Jan introduced Jim.

'I'm Carlos Benito,' the tallest one said. 'I'm the senior fireman.'

'Where are you from, Carlos?'

'Chicago, Captain. I was in the city fire department.'

It was a productive hour during which they led Jim through all the fire alarm and prevention systems on board. The ship was well covered.

'The state boards here show the detection systems, which are duplicated on the bridge, Sir.'

'What about the fire patrols?' asked Jim.

'We have a watch system, the same as the bridge. Two firemen patrol from 1800 to 0800 and check in with the bridge every hour.'

'In the event of fire, what are your stations?'

'We join in the ship's general emergency muster station, Sir.'

'Which is what?'

'Two firemen to each emergency party.'

Jim turned to Jan. 'Are you happy with that?'

'Not really, but that was what was in place when I joined. I mentioned it to the last Staff Captain, but he said to leave it.'

'What would your people want?' Jim asked.

'Frankly, Sir, if there is a fire, chances are it will be in one place and the main fire party will head there. We'd rather tackle the fire head on with all we've got than spread our people out.'

'Good. We'll change the station bill to reflect that from the start of the next cruise.'

'One last question. How are you going to get all the passengers out of their cabins if the alleyways are full of smoke?'

Carlos looked at Jim calmly. 'The idea is to prevent fire, Captain. That's who we are, fire prevention officers.'

'But you've fought fires as a fireman so I ask you again, how do we get them out?'

Carlos smiled faintly. 'With difficulty, Captain.'

Jim went into the Safety Office with Jan.

'I think we have enough to get on with now. The fire systems are state of the art. Mind you, they have yet to be really put to the test.'

'I agree, Sir. Unfortunately, we can't change the ship overnight.'

'I realise that. Anyway I have to look after the rest of the department. I've looked at the inspection schedule and I'm already behind with that. You carry on with the boat launching routine and let me know when you are having drills and exercises. I see that you've got a full fire and boat drill scheduled for Fort Lauderdale. We'll lower two boats again there and put some of the crew in them to give them a feel for it.'

That evening after sailing, Jim had a rather more enjoyable dinner. He now had three couples on his table. They wanted to talk about the last port and Jim listened with polite interest. It was pleasant to hear their praise of the ship. As he walked along to the after lounge, he agreed the ship was immaculate and a credit to the staff. If only it wasn't floating on the sea.

The lounge was half full. Jim sat at a table overlooking the stern and ordered a coffee. Helen was playing; she was very good. For the first time that day, he relaxed and drank his coffee, letting the music waft over him.

'Hi there!' Jim looked up. It was the Cruise Director Scott and his wife Vivien. 'Mind if we join you?'

Jim didn't have much choice as they settled into their chairs. A waiter immediately appeared.

'What'll you have, Jim?' asked Scott.

'I'm fine, thank you,' said Jim.

'Come on, Jim. Have something.' Jim didn't want to appear churlish.

'I'll have a port if I may, a small one.'

'Heck, Jim, make it a large one. Waiter! Don't forget we have an expense account, Jim. You might as well enjoy it. I'm sorry about the other day. You were right and I want you to know that I'm backing you on tightening up on the drills. I think we needed you to show us that we could do better.'

'That's good. I don't mind a few rocks on the way as long as the message is getting across.'

'I gather you're new to this type of ship, Captain,' said Vivien.

'I suppose you could say that,' replied Jim. 'I have been on many passenger-carrying ships; I was brought up on them to a certain extent, but they were passenger ships that did cruising in the holiday season and then reverted back to being passenger ships for the rest of the year. They were very different. Don't get me wrong. We wanted the passengers to have a good time, but we were always ships first and holiday resorts second.'

The drinks arrived and Jim sipped his cautiously. 'Let me ask you both something. Tomorrow night is the Captain's cocktail party and we have two sets, one for the first sitting and the other for the second sitting. Everyone comes in, shakes the Captain's hand and then sits down. How is that a cocktail party? And we are supposed to mingle, so all the officers should be there to chat to the punters.'

'I'm not sure that's a good idea,' said Scott.

'Why? Because the punters might find out that many can't speak English properly? That's not your problem; it's the company's. Also this line-up business with the spotlights, band playing and nonsense. Do you realise that parading us like some kind of puppet show to a howling mob is deeply embarrassing to most of us?'

'The Captain likes it.'

'With respect, Scott, the Captain is caught up in this cruise ship fantasy that you perpetuate. I'm not criticising it, that's your job, but between you all, you've forgotten we're on a ship. It's my job to remind you of that.'

'On the other hand, Jim, maybe you are wrong. This is the future of passenger ships. Captain Cota has an image of ships becoming larger and larger, almost like floating islands. Just think of the possibilities.'

Jim stood and drained his glass.

'Scott, it's far away from a quiet garden in Somerset where my heart lies. Goodnight to you both.'

Jim walked back through the lounges and bars. It was good to see so many happy people and he wondered whether Scott was possibly right; maybe this was the future. It at least kept them all in a job. He reached the door to the officers' quarters and entered a quieter world. He decided to visit the bridge before turning in and walked to the end of the alleyway. He tapped in the security number and pushed open the door. He was used to a dark bridge, but these days with all the screens and instrument panels that was impossible. Instead there was a constant flickering glow from the different instrument islands, which enhanced the darkness of the view from the bridge windows, not that anyone seemed to be looking out of them. A crowd of passengers were on the bridge, being shown round by the Captain. Extra lighting had been switched on to allow them to move around easily. Jim noticed that some had drinks in their hands.

Captain Cota was showing them one of the radars. He had his arm around a woman in a blue dress. Among the crowd was the General Manager, Shelby, and the Purser. Rather than become involved, Jim quietly pulled the door towards him and retired to his cabin.

As Scott said, maybe this was the future.

Chapter 15

Vacuum Pioneer

Far removed from the world of cruise ships, M.V. 'Vacuum Pioneer' was heading back down the eastern seaboard of the American coast to Galveston. She was empty and the tanks were full of inert gas, making sure that there was no danger of any oil fumes causing an explosion or fire.

Being a Sunday, Karl, the Captain, had completed his inspection of the ship and was sitting in his cabin with the Chief Officer and Chief Engineer having a drink before the Sunday buffet lunch. It was a spacious and modern cabin, with a deep cream carpet and matching cream leather furniture. There were large picture windows looking out over the bow of the ship. They were watching a sports channel on the large flat-screen TV on one of the bulkheads in the cabin. The ship was rolling easily to a beam sea and swell. She was light, having discharged her cargo in the St Lawrence river ports, but had taken ballast in the river before sailing.

The sports channel broke for the commercials and a picture of a glittering cruise ship sailing to some Caribbean port came onto the screen. The image then switched and showed another larger ship advertising a series of cruises called 'Voyage of Exploration to the Arctic Circle'. It was the 'Majestic Sea'. The watching officers all exploded with laughter at the wording.

    'Poor bastards will scream if they even get cold,' said Trond Johnsen, the Chief Engineer.

    'They would sue the company,' responded Eric Aasland, the Chief Officer.

The Captain was more thoughtful. 'It is not good, you know, taking these things up there. They're not ice class and probably don't have ice experienced officers.'

'But it is summer,' said Trond. 'There is no pack ice. Anyway, if the insurers allow it, no one can stop them.'

'The Arctic Council has been protesting about it for a long time,' said Eric.

'Yes,' said the Captain, 'and got nowhere. Don't think I don't agree with them, but these companies are too powerful.'

'There needs to be a big accident,' said Eric. 'That would make them all think.'

'For about two weeks and then back to business. Look what happened when that British ferry turned over. We all said they would do something. Nothing changed except they blamed the Captain as usual. Then that cruise ship sank in the Antarctic. What happened over that?' He looked at them. 'You see, we don't even know, do we?'

The commercials finished and the sport resumed.

Jim was in his office early in the morning sipping his tea, when there was a clack of high heels on the alleyway deck outside. He looked up and caught a glimpse of a blue evening dress hurrying past. It was Cota's lady friend.

He turned his thoughts to his desk, where paper was gathering at an alarming rate. He started to work his way through it until he was interrupted by Jan and the Bosun arriving. The Bosun made his morning report and left. Jan handed Jim a paper. It was the boat drill announcement for the passengers' cabins. Jim read it through.

'That's good. Hard but effective. One thing, you've missed out the bit about warm clothing.'

'Why do we want that, Sir? We're in the Caribbean.'

'It's in the regulations. I didn't write them; the International Maritime Organization did. Anyway, it gets cold at night on the sea, even down here. In the Arctic, it's freezing.'

Jim made the amendment to the announcement sheet.

'Sir, some passengers don't have any warm clothing. Some board with a pair of shorts and a couple of t-shirts.'

'Then this should be sent to them before they join so there are no mistakes. So much junk is put into their cabins for them to read when they join that they tend to ignore most of it.'

'I'll put it in then,' said Jan. 'By the way, it's the cocktail parties tonight.'

Jim scowled. 'Don't remind me. I was enjoying the day until you mentioned that.'

Jan grinned. 'Wait till you see the American audience. They whistle and scream. You're an instant celebrity.'

Jim pointed to the door. 'Go. Get out. Go and chase the cadets or something. One thing you can do, get those small communications devices from Bert.'

'Will do.' Still laughing, Jan left the office.

Jim carried on working until 0900 when he went to the Captain's office. There was no sign of him in the office so he knocked on the dayroom door. Cota called him to come in. Jim found him having breakfast in a blue silk dressing gown.

'Anything important this morning, Jim?'

'No, Sir. We have the pamphlet ready for the passengers' cabins. I've put it on your desk. I also thought we might send this to the company and suggest that they include it in all the passengers' pre-arrival paperwork.'

'I'll take a look at that, Jim. Why don't you relax this morning? You've been hard at it since you joined.'

'Thank you, Sir. I'll consider it.'

'Don't forget the cocktail parties tonight. We have the usual two, one for each sitting.'

'I won't, Sir.'

Jim continued working through the morning until his desk was a neat pile of completed paperwork. He looked at his memo on the computer. There was still so much outstanding, but there was one item that he wanted to get to and that was a visit to the ship's surgery.

He went down through the accommodation until he arrived at an illuminated sign saying 'Surgery and Ship Medical Facility'. On entering, he found a nurse behind a reception desk and two passengers waiting to be seen.

'I'm sorry,' said Jim. 'I didn't phone ahead.' She looked up and saw his rank.

'Sir, is this professional or courtesy?'

'Courtesy I think,' Jim said.

'The senior surgeon is in the surgery at present.'

'I'll come back later then.'

'No, he's alone. Just tidying up. Go on through.' She pointed to a set of double doors. Jim walked through and at the end of a short corridor he passed through another set of double doors. Inside there was a modern operating theatre that would not have disgraced a small hospital. Looking through charts was an officer in a white coat. He was bald, short and wore a thick pair of glasses perched on the end of his nose. Jim put him in his sixties. He looked up as Jim entered.

'Well we are honoured. A visit from the new Staff Captain no less. What do you want? Viagra?'

'No thanks,' replied Jim.

'That's novel. Most of the more senior officers want that. Isn't it strange, women don't want to know about sex for the whole year ashore, then they get on board a ship for a couple of weeks and go berserk. I should do a study for science. The effects of sea and uniforms on the female hormones. So you don't want Viagra. The second most popular request are hangover cures. There's no such thing except don't drink, and you don't look as if you need that anyway.'

He came towards Jim and shook hands.

'I'm Dick Brentwood, Senior Surgeon on this floating embarrassment to the sea. I'm out of retirement and trying to pay a second alimony. What's your excuse for being here?'

'Couldn't find anything else,' Jim said.

'That'll do. I hear you're a member of the Chief's little club. We are a select band.'

'I'm flattered. I thought I would come down and pay you a courtesy call.'

'How kind of you.'

Dick looked at the clock on the bulkhead. 'Sun's over the yardarm. Even if it isn't here, it must be somewhere on the planet.'

He opened a glass cabinet and took out an unmarked bottle. He poured some of the contents into a couple of glasses from under the table, raised his glass and drank. Jim followed.

'That's bloody strong,' Jim said as he spluttered.

'I hope so. Fresh martini, made it this morning.' He appraised Jim. 'I hear good things about you. Well from some anyway; from others you're a pain in the arse.'

'We'll have to see what the jury says then.'

'No need. I know Helen Shreiber. If she likes you, you can't be too bad.'

'Dick, I wonder if you could help me. I know you can't discuss individual cases, but I want to ask you about drug use on board in general.'

'What about it? Does it happen? Hell yes, but you're the first one from the top who wants to know about it. We see some of the results down here.'

'Have you reported it before?'

'Of course I have. Everyone should be well aware of it. I send in my medical reports at the end of each cruise and the statement's in there.'

'Where does this report go?'

'It goes to the Ship General Manager and also the operations department ashore in Fort Lauderdale.'

'What about the Captain?'

'My orders are only to the Ship Manager. I presume he shows the Captain.'

'What do these reports contain?'

'The usual. The number of treatments, what for, any problems. I presume they are thinking of any possible legal consequences.'

'Dick, I want a favour. I would like to see your copies of those reports.'

'No way, my friend. They are confidential.'

He took Jim's glass and refilled it. 'Down the hatch.'

Jim spluttered again.

'Strange, isn't it, how they get stronger the longer you leave it,' said Dick.

'Another scientific study for you to do,' gasped Jim.

'So tell me why you want these reports.'

'We suspect there might be organised drug selling on board.'

'You suspect! You'll have to do better than that. I'll tell you there's selling on board. I've reported it at least twice.'

'Dick, it will be very helpful to our investigations.'

'Who's 'ours'?'

'I'm not in a position to say any more, but as soon as I get clearance I'll bring you in on what is going on.'

'You're not telling me much are you? Come with me.' They left the surgery and went into an office. Dick went over to a filing cabinet, unlocked it and took out a thick file.

'Here you are. One year of reports. I never gave you this. Copy it if you want, but get it back to me as soon as possible in case I'm asked for it.'

'It'll be back as soon as possible, Dick. Thank you for this,' said Jim as he took the file.

'I like a happy customer. Now, one for the road?'

Jim waved him off. 'Dick, another one of those and I'll be in my bunk.'

'And here was I thinking that you sailor boys were drinking men,' Dick teased.

When Jim returned to his office, he rang down to the crew messroom and asked for sandwiches to be sent up. He then spent the afternoon going through the reports. Jim made notes as he went through them and then logged onto his computer. He entered the department general file and found the crew lists. He printed out the crew lists for the last year, and then did the same with the ports of call.

By late afternoon, Jim was ready. He called Bert Fallows.

'Bert, can you come up and bring your two buddies with you please. Also, could you bring your reports of drug cases over the last year?'

When they arrived, Jim had stuck a chart up on the bulkhead in the office. He closed the door. Bert had a large file with him. He also put two small communicators on Jim's desk.

'As requested, Captain, one for you and one for the Safety Officer. We monitor these 24/7.'

'Thanks, Bert. I want the three of you to look at this. This line represents the incidents of drug abuse our surgery dealt with in one year on board the ship. You can see it peaks at various places along the time scale. Now, here is the overlay of the places the ship went over that year. You can see that there is a correlation between two ports, San Juan in Puerto Rico and Orangestad in Aruba.'

'It could be because the passengers bought drugs there.'

'I agree except that the doctor's report states that at least eight of the passengers bought the drugs on the ship.'

'That's still not conclusive,' said Mark Davies.

'No, but there's more. These are the crew lists from the last year. I haven't bothered with all the junior ranks as that would take about a week, but look at the more senior people. Again overlay and look. For those ports and those peaks of drugs, we see the same names.'

Mark now looked with interest.

'We have five names. Captain Cota, General Manager Shelby, Bella Winchester the Purser, a man called Curtis, who I've never met but I believe is the shopping mall manager, and the head hairdresser Shawn Gregory.'

'Keep those crew lists up for a moment, Captain,' said Bert. He drew out a list of crew members. 'These are the names of those lower down the pole we know about. I'll call them out and let's see how it looks.'

As he called the names, Jim marked them on the chart. 'We have four out of five matching again.'

Mark was now standing looking at the chart. 'I think we may have something here. What made you start this?'

'A chance meeting with the ship's surgeon. He mentioned that he was sending in reports about drugs and nothing was happening.'

'Where did the reports go?'

'To Shelby and the operations department in Fort Lauderdale.'

They sat in silence for a minute.

'Now what?' asked Jim.

'We tread very carefully, that's what,' said Mark. 'Even if this is right, we don't have any real proof.'

'But we now know where the drugs will be coming on board and who may be waiting for them.'

'When are we going to these two ports next?'

'Next cruise.'

'The ship hasn't been for two cruises so a large shipment may be due. Can you do one more thing, Captain? Can you get hold of the passenger lists for the last year?'

'I've no idea. What do you want them for?'

'It's just an idea. What if others came on as passengers?'

'Would they keep passenger records on board?'

'They may well be on the computer somewhere. What about the Purser's office?'

'It's possible. I'd have to think of a reason though.'

'The one thing we don't want to do is alert anyone.'

'I realise that. Leave it with me.'

The first cocktail party went exactly as they did on board the *'Sea Breeze'* except the band was larger, the spotlights brighter and the cheering crowd even louder. The Captain made a longer than necessary speech with the usual pleasantries about how they all enjoyed having their 'guests' on board. For Jim and some of the others, the embarrassment was just the same. Jim didn't go to the second party. That was too much to take. Instead he walked down the top deck towards the café by the pool. He ordered a coffee and sat down, turning his chair towards the sea so he could look out into the night.

'I thought I'd find you here.' It was Helen, who had silently wheeled her chair along the deck behind him. She also ordered a coffee.

'I was watching you during the cocktail party. When the Captain called you onto the stage, you looked dreadful. You were scowling at the passengers.'

'No I wasn't. I was scowling at what they were putting me through. Like some performing seal.'

She laughed. 'I should have thrown fish!'

Helen paused for a moment and then said, 'You don't like it here, do you?'

Jim hesitated. 'It's not the ship, it's the attitude. It's as if we have forgotten the sea. Something like this is hardly a ship. It's a hotel, a glittering holiday resort that floats. The more of these, the more we destroy the places we visit. You see it in the ports we go to. It's not just one ship. It's several all crowding in for space. We submerge what were once lovely quiet towns with thousands of punters all scrabbling to get ashore for a few hours to say they've been there. Then they rush back in time to sail for the next poor bloody place. Look at the pollution in the Caribbean from these monsters. It's as if I'm waiting for the sea to rise up in outrage at the sheer audacity in building these things. And now we're about to head to the Arctic Circle, taking the fun palace there. So in answer to your question, no. I'm a seaman. I have no part in this fantasy, but at the moment it pays the mortgage.'

'What about your family? Are they going to join you?'

'They would like to, but I won't let them. If there is a serious accident, we won't get all these people off in time. We all know that, but no one is willing to say it publicly.

I'm not going to put my family into such a position, especially when I'm responsible for getting everyone off. I would worry about them instead of getting on with my job.'

'Jim, you're worrying me.'

'I'm sorry, Helen. Look, the chances of anything happening are very remote.'

'I'm pleased to hear that. I gather you visited Dick the Doc.'

'He makes a mean martini.'

'That he does. The first time I met him I couldn't play the piano all afternoon. I had to say I had a tummy bug and go to bed.'

Jim laughed.

They sat and talked into the night, enjoying each other's company as men and women do who are attracted to each other and continue to revel in that attraction. People came and went, and slowly the café filled up with late night people. Eventually Helen looked at her watch.

'It's been a lovely evening. Thank you for staying with me. I'm sure there are many others who would like your company.'

'Probably, but they can't play piano like you.'

Jim pushed her chair back along the deck to one of the ship's lifts.

'Where do you live?' asked Jim.

'I have a passenger cabin. It's nearer to the boat deck.'

'Then I'll say good night.' He bent down and gave her a peck on her cheek. 'Thanks for listening.'

When Jim got back to his cabin, he picked up the phone and called Jenny. It rang several times before a sleepy voice answered.

'I was missing you,' he said.

'Do you know what time it is here? It's four in the morning.'

'Sorry, it was impulse.'

'What's wrong?'

'Nothing, I just wanted to say hello.'

'Well hello to you, sailor. If it makes you feel better I miss you too, but there's not much we can do about it is there? How's it going?'

'It's all right.'

'That sounds ominous. You're back at sea on a stunning ship, surrounded by gorgeous women hanging on your arm, eating fabulous food and there are dozens of bars. A sailor's heaven. You should be ecstatic.'

Jim sighed. 'It's not all it's cracked up to be.'

She softened. 'Well I could always come out and join you.'

'No, you really wouldn't like it.'

'Try me.'

He laughed. 'Hell no. Why do you think I married you? Just stay there keeping the house, doing the garden and looking after the children. Then I get my money's worth.'

'Be careful. You could come back to find I've sold the lot and run off to Australia with the plumber.'

'You said you didn't fancy him.'

'He's here and you're not.'

He laughed again.

'I love you, Jenny.'

'And I love you. Come home soon, Captain.'

The day before arriving back in Fort Lauderdale, Jim went down to the Bureau. He waited until lunchtime when he thought that Bella Winchester, the Purser, would be away from the office. The counter was busy as usual. He went round the side to the main office door and went in. Two women officers were sitting in front of computers. Jim approached one of them.

She looked up and smiled. 'Can I help you, Sir?'

'I hope so. I am trying to do a study of passengers to see their ages. This is part of the ongoing look at the lifeboat recommendations for the company. Do you have these lists on file?'

'Sure do. I can give you it now.'

'I want information for several voyages, say over the last year.'

'Heck, Captain. That's a lot of cruises.'

'I know, but do you have those on file in the computer?'

'Let's see,' she said. Her fingers rapidly worked over the keys. 'Yes, here we are. You say you want the list for the past year?'

'That's right. Can you download them to my computer?'

'One moment.' She called up another list. 'Here's your name.' She then pressed send. 'It's all yours, Captain. Enough there to keep you busy for some time.'

'You seem pretty good on the computer,' he said.

'I should be. I majored in IT.'

'Can I ask you something? On these files of passengers over the last year, would it be possible to call up repeat passengers?'

'You mean the ones who are travelling with us twice or more?'

'That's right.'

'Why didn't you ask? We have a list of those. They are graded into colours, so we have silver guests, gold guests and platinum guests.'

'Could I have a copy of that list as well please?'

More fingers flew. 'You got it, Captain.'

Jim left the office. That had been easier than he thought.

By mid-afternoon, Jim had a list of names. He used the small communicator to call Bert. It worked instantly.

'I've got something for you, Bert.'

'I'll be up right away, Sir.'

The phone rang. It was Bella Winchester.

'Good afternoon, Jim. I gather you wanted something?'

'Hi, Bella. Yes I did, but one of your staff was most helpful and fixed me up.'

'I wish you had waited for me, Captain. I would have liked to have been there. Can I ask what this is about?'

'It's just to see the type of passengers we are dealing with for the lifeboats, Bella. Nothing important.'

'Then why did you want to know the gradings of the passengers? That's confidential information.'

'Surely not from me? It was just a thought I had. If you remember, the problems we had with passengers not attending the drills concerned those who had been before and thought they knew it all. I wanted to see just what proportion they made of the overall number.'

'Captain, they are not a 'problem' as you call it. I cannot see what purpose that list will serve.' The phone went down. Now why was she so pissed off, Jim wondered.

Bert and Mark arrived and Jim closed the door.

'Look,' he said. 'I have nine names. Six men and three women. Three couples and three single males. They came on all the cruises that went either to one of these ports or to both.'

Mark took the list. 'Does anyone know you have this?'

'Unfortunately, yes. Bella Winchester is very upset that I have it.'

'Shit! Never mind, it can't be helped. Captain, you have been very useful. Now please don't get involved any further. If I want any more help, Bert will keep you advised.'

Chapter 16

Jim stood on the bridge watching the Fort Lauderdale breakwater slide by. It had been an eventful cruise and he was glad it was over. At last he felt he was getting to grips with the department. He had implemented various changes, and overall the improvement could already be seen. The officers and cadets were showing more interest, the security side knew they had support and administration was going well. The boat training was progressing and the two fire control exercises had been satisfactory, especially now the firemen were integrated into the main emergency party. Even his relations with the hotel side were stable. The next cruise was going to be the test of the new passenger drill routines and he expected the usual dissent over that.

As they approached the berth, he could see the swarm of vehicles and people waiting for their arrival. Time was important. They had to disembark more than 3,000 passengers and then after a short pause take on the next group. By 1900 that evening, they would be sailing out again.

Cota was in a good mood. He had the usual group of passenger friends on the bridge watching the show, as he called it, and punters were looking through the bridge window. At least they hadn't brought their drinks with them this time, Jim thought.

The ship glided through the harbour and came gracefully alongside her berth. Jim stayed on the bridge until the gangways were in place and the officials started streaming on board.

Jan was waiting for him in his office. 'I think we are ready for the boat drill, Sir. As you will see from the ship's programme, it is scheduled for 1700.'

'Which allows plenty of time before the departure time of 1900.'

'Are all the passenger cards ready to be distributed to the cabins?'

'Yes, Sir. They will be put there with the other pamphlets. The hotel personnel are briefed, so we will see how it all goes.'

'Good. Thank you. Jan. At least we'll get the drills right at last. I want all the cadets involved. Bring them up here at 1600 for a briefing.'

'During the next trip, we are going to get the boats down. I want to try to put all the boats from one side in the water at once and time how long it takes.'

'That's a major operation, Sir.'

'I know. That's why it's rarely been done. I'm thinking about asking for passenger volunteers.'

'The company would never allow it. Imagine if a passenger gets injured.'

'Then we'll have to make do with crew. I also want to run a major fire exercise. The firemen have a plan ready and it looks good. They want to have it in the galley.'

'Christ, Captain. Be careful. You'll have the hotel people screaming blue murder.'

Jim laughed. 'Just wait till I show you what I am proposing to the company.'

At that moment, there was a tap on the side of the door, which was open. It was Celine, Jim's shared secretary.

'Excuse me, Captain, but Captain Cota would like to see you immediately in his office.'

'Just a moment, Celine. I'll be along shortly.'

'Sir, I think you had better come now.'

She looked very serious, almost frightened.

'Sorry, Jan. I have to go. I'll see you at 1600.'

Jim straightened his uniform and walked down the alleyway to the Captain's office. Captain Cota was standing behind his desk while to the side was Shelby and the Cruise Director, Pierre. Sitting at the conference table was Bob Hinchley, the Senior Vice President, and John Zachary, the Fleet Operations Manager. They were on each side of a man Jim had not seen before. There was an ominous air in the office.

Cota cleared his throat. 'Come in, Captain. We have received a serious complaint.'

'About what?'

'Regarding yourself and your behaviour.'

'Just a moment, Sir. Before we go any further, why are all these people here?'

'This gentleman is Congressman Langton and the others are here at my request,' explained Cota.

'With respect, Captain, this has all the appearances of a tribunal. If that is the case, these people have no right to be here.'

'That's enough bullshit!' It was the congressman from behind Jim. He was now standing and glaring at Jim, his fat face red with anger. 'You felt my wife up and tried to get her into your cabin.'

'I what?' exclaimed Jim.

'You heard me, Captain. I should beat the crap out of you! I want him off this ship now!' said the congressman angrily.

'Just a moment, congressman. We'll deal with this,' said Cota. 'Have you anything to say,' he said turning to Jim.

'I've one hell of a lot to say,' Jim replied, 'but not before this bunch. This is bullshit.'

'We've got witnesses, Clariby. Her friend was there,' Langton shouted. 'Now are you guys going to deal with this or do I take it to the President of the company?'

'One moment, Sir. We will solve this now.' It was Hinchley. 'Captain, your services are no longer required. You will pack your bags and leave as soon as possible.'

'No, I won't. All of you wait here. I have something that may interest you.'

Jim hurried out into his office. He called Bert Fallows on the communicator. 'Bert, has disembarkation started yet?'

'No, Sir.'

'Good, then hold everything. I want you to go to the Atlantic Suite and see if two ladies are there, Mrs Langton and Mrs Huntley. Bring them up to my office immediately. Tell them if they don't come I will tell the congressman everything about the parties.'

Next he called the bridge. 'Peter, do me a favour. Locate my steward and bring him to my office as soon as you can.'

He willed himself to calm down. His hands were shaking. His anger was threatening to overwhelm him and, if it did, he would explode with rage. Next he called Jan.

'Jan, come up to the office immediately.' He needed a witness.

Peter and Jan arrived first. 'I've sent for Rodrigo,' said Peter. 'Can you tell me what this is about, Sir?'

'I haven't time to go into it. You'll have to wait I'm afraid. Sit down at the table both of you. Now don't say anything until you're asked.'

They waited patiently.

They heard Bert coming along the alleyway, or more truthfully they heard the women coming. Mrs Langton was complaining loudly. Bert ushered the women in and closed the door.

'Good morning, ladies. I'm sorry to drag you in here like this. Mrs Langton, your husband is in the Captain's office. You know what this is about, don't you?'

She looked determined. 'If it is about your assault on me, then yes I do know. What are you doing dragging me in here?'

'I'm trying to save your embarrassment, Mrs Langton, and probably your husband's career.'

There was a tap on the door. Bert opened it and Rodrigo entered. As soon as he saw the gathering, he tried to back out.

'It's all right, Rodrigo. This is not about you. Come in and stand over there.' He indicated the corner of the office.

'I will be quick, Mrs Langton. 'He took out the earring.' Is this yours?'

She hesitated.

'I'll answer for you. It is yours and it matches your necklace. Do you know where I found this? In Adama's bedroom.'

'I went in there to use the bathroom.'

'Funny that it was under the bed then. And it wasn't the first time you'd been into the bedroom was it? Rodrigo here can witness that you were a regular bed mate.'

'That's a lie!'

'The First Officer was also dragged into these rather strange parties of yours in Adama's cabin. I haven't asked what kind of parties they were, but I can guess. Now, you have two minutes to decide on the truth or we can all go to the Captain's office where the whole sordid mess will come out. That involves you as well, Mrs Huntley. I shouldn't think your husband will be very pleased either, especially if it gets to the press.'

'Hey, don't involve me. I have nothing to do with this.'

'But you are a witness.'

'No, I'm not. I saw nothing.'

'Cheryl!' Mrs Langton cried out in dismay.

'Hell, Jessie. I told you not to get involved in this. Captain, I have nothing to do with this stupid business.'

Mrs Langton was looking miserable.

'One more question, Mrs Langton, before we face the music. Whose idea was this?'

She was silent. Jim opened the door. 'Right, let's go and see your husband then.'

'It was Shelby and that woman Purser,' she said hurriedly.

'You and your chum here are going to go to the Captain's office and are going to tell everyone that this was a dreadful mistake. I don't care how you do it, but you will exonerate me completely. Are we clear?'

'Yes,' she said hurriedly.

'You're a sad woman. You tried to destroy my career with no thought whatsoever. We don't matter do we?'

She was beginning to cry. 'I'm sorry.'

'Stop the waterworks. It's a bit late to be sorry. Now, get your arse in gear you two. Come on. The rest of you stay here in case you're needed.'

He hurried the women out the door towards the Captain's office. They could hear heated voices coming from inside. Jim didn't bother to knock. He opened the door and ushered the women inside. Langton sprang up and grabbed his wife. 'What the fuck is going on?' he shouted.

'Shut up!' said Jim pointing at him. 'Mrs Langton wants to tell everyone something.' Jim saw Shelby looking agitated.

'I'm very sorry for causing any problem, but there has been a dreadful mistake.'

She started to sob again. 'I didn't mean any harm.'

Cota took her arm. 'Please carry on, Jessie.'

'Captain Clariby didn't do anything. I wanted to get back at him for moving us from his table.'

'Why the hell did you do that?' shouted Langton.

'Shut up, Gus!' called Mrs Huntley. 'It wasn't the Captain's fault. He was right. We had a few too many drinks and upset the other passengers at the table. That's why he asked for us to be moved. We agreed to it.'

Clever, thought Jim.

Langton calmed down. 'So the message I got last night was wrong then?'

'I'm sorry, Gus. You know me. I sometimes go overboard.'

'You damn well did this time. Look at the fuss you've caused. I had to break off a meeting to get down here.'

'Never mind trying to ruin my career,' said Jim.

'That too, of course,' muttered Langton.

'Well I'm glad that is cleared up,' said Cota. 'No harm done, eh?'

Jessie turned to Jim.

'I'm so sorry, Captain. I have been very stupid.'

'You have, Mrs Langton, along with a few others.' He put his hand in his pocket. 'I believe this is yours. It was found by one of my staff.'

He passed the earring to her.

'Thank you, Captain,' she said. 'You've been very gracious.'

Jim turned to Hinchley.

'I presume I can unpack now?'

'What? Oh, of course, Captain. You do understand I had to take the action that I did.'

'Actually no I don't. But that's your problem not mine.'

Jim left the office and returned to his. The others were all standing waiting.

Jim turned to Rodrigo. 'Thank you, Rodrigo. You can go now.'

'There is no trouble, Captain?'

'No, no trouble, at least not for you.'

When he had gone, Jan turned to Jim. 'What the hell is going on, Sir.'

'It's a bit complicated,' said Jim. 'You'll have to bear with me for a while. I'll tell you the whole story when I can.'

'If it's sorted, Captain, then I'm glad,' said Jan, 'but we'd like to know more one day.'

'Soon,' promised Jim.

When they had gone, Bert looked at Jim.

'Well, they've shown their hand. Do they know that she spilt the beans?'

'I don't think so. I didn't say anything in the Captain's office.'

'Is he part of all this?'

'I don't know. Bert, let the disembarkation carry on now.'

When Bert left, Jim sat down at his desk. What a fucking morning.

Chapter 17

At 1600, Jan arrived with the cadets in tow.

'Come in and sit down,' he ordered. 'As you know, we are having the boat drill at 1700 today and this one is going to be by the book. I want you to spread yourselves around the lounges where the passengers are being assembled and see to it that all the passengers have their lifejackets. Those that don't have them are to be politely told to go and get them and that you will wait till they return before allowing the checks to continue. I want the names of all passengers who fail to turn up. We can't delay the proceedings indefinitely waiting for them, but we can ensure they are dealt with later. Once the passengers are wearing their lifejackets, you can check that they are being worn correctly. Anyone not wearing appropriate warm clothing is to be told that it is essential this is done. Again, we can't hold the ship while they get dressed.

'Next, all bar and waiter service is to stop during the drill. You must all wear your caps. The idea is to get the passengers realising that you are not hotel staff but from the deck department. In others words, this is a seaman, listen to him,' continued Jim.

'Take your walkie-talkies and keep in touch with me if there are any problems. Any passenger who gives you lip, don't try to deal with it, call me. You mustn't give lip back; I can and will. Bert and his boys will also be on call if required. I want to show everyone, both passengers and hotel people, that we mean business and that nobody is going to fuck us around. Now, boat number 8. Whoever is dealing with that boat, I have a little surprise for you.

Inform me once the check is completed and I will tell you to order the embarkation manager for that boat to take the passengers to the boat. I have arranged with the Bosun for that boat to be lowered ready for embarkation. They won't embark, but I want you to keep timings for how long it takes to get them all down there, ready to get on board. Don't forget that, when you get them to the boat, you must check the names again. That will ensure that none have strayed on the way. So far so good. Any questions?' asked Jim.

'What about the talking, Sir?' It was Matheson. 'I mean the passengers not listening to the announcements.'

'Good point. Call me if there is a problem and I will make a further broadcast.'

Zhou raised her hand. 'What if we see the hotel people not doing their job, Sir? It has happened in the past and we have said nothing.'

'Take their names.' The cadets looked at each other and smiled.

'This is not a 'get your own back' or intended to deliberately find fault. It's about the passengers being given the best briefing we can give them. Where corrections are needed, we will make them. Is that clear?'

They all nodded.

'Good. Then out you go and let's make sure this is better than before.'

The preliminary announcements started at 1630. Just before 1700, Jim went down to the muster lounge areas. As usual, the vast majority of the passengers were sitting with their lifejackets waiting for instructions. The warm clothing was a different matter. It was difficult for them to understand that this was required for the Caribbean. Jim knew that it would be essential for the next two cruises. The alarm signals sounded and more passengers arrived. It was flowing well. He noticed that all service had stopped and that the bar personnel were no longer in attendance. The embarkation managers for each boat had their signs clearly marked and their checkers were doing their best to list their boat passengers. Jim wrote 'Bar coding' in his notebook.

All seemed to be going well, but then Jim had a call from Zhou. 'We have a problem, Sir.'

Jim arrived to find her standing beside three passengers who had no lifejackets.

'Can I help?' he said. The passengers had obviously been drinking. They were middle aged. Two were men and there was a rather large woman in a bright florid dress.

One of the men said, 'This girl here wants us to go down and get these stupid life vests or whatever they are. We've told her we've been on lots of cruises and they've never bothered us before.'

'This 'girl' is the Senior Cadet Officer of the ship and speaks with my authority. The ship is under new regulations, Sir. I must ask you all to go and get your lifejackets now please, as we will have to hold up everyone until the regulations are complied with.'

'Come on, George,' the woman said. 'Let's do what the man says.'

'No. I'm here. What more do they want? Look, Captain or whatever you are, just go away and do your sailor thing and leave us alone.' He turned away from Jim.

Jim called into the walkie-talkie. 'Mr Fallows?' Bert acknowledged. 'Will you bring your security team to the forward lounge at the double.'

Jim saw the Hotel Manager, Henry Milau, hurrying towards them.

'Is there any problem, Jim?' he asked.

'Not for me. For them, unless they get their lifejackets pronto. Don't worry, Security will be here soon.'

Henry looked desperate. 'Excuse me,' he said to the passengers. 'I'm the Hotel Manager. Perhaps we can sort this out.'

'Just get this man to go away,' said the belligerent passenger, 'and then it will be sorted. We have attended and that's enough.'

Henry grabbed Jim's arm. 'What are you going to do?' he whispered.

'I'm going to throw them off the ship, Henry, that's what I am going to do.'

'You can't do that,' Henry squawked in horror.

'Just watch me,' said Jim. Bert arrived with all of the security team. Jim turned to the passengers; the woman now was pale.

'This is your last chance. You either get your lifejackets now or I will have to ask you to remove yourselves from the ship.'

Around them, other passengers were now watching the scene. Someone called out, 'You tell 'em, Captain!'

The passengers made no move.

'I must now ask you all to leave the ship,' said Jim.

'Wait!' said the woman. 'I'll go and get my lifejacket. Come on, George.'

She and one of the men stood up and scurried away. They were now left with the remaining man.

'I'm not going anywhere,' he said.

'Mr Fallows, assist this gentleman off the ship.'

As the security team moved in, the passenger stood and took a swing at Bert who ducked and then grabbed him around the waist. Two others moved in and wrestled him to the ground, where they took hold of his hands and feet and then between them picked him up and carried him out of the lounge.

Henry looked at Jim in horror. 'You're mad!' he said. 'You can't do this!'

Some passengers stood open mouthed and others started cheering.

Jim ignored Henry and followed the group out of the lounge. When they reached the foyer area where it was quiet, Jim ordered Bert to put him down.

'Now, I will give you one last chance,' he said. 'Are you going to get your lifejacket or do you want to go down the gangway like this?'

The man was red in the face and panting from his struggles.

'You bastard!' he shouted.

'Never mind what I am. Which is it to be - lifejacket or gangway?' There was no reply.

'Off the ship,' said Jim. As the security men moved in again, the man held his hands up.

'OK! OK! I'll get the fucking thing. You haven't heard the last of this I promise you!'

'Bert, please escort the gentleman down to his cabin and then, once he has his lifejacket, back up to the lounge.' He looked at the man. 'Have a nice day, Sir.'

Jim went back up to the mustering area and saw that the checking had nearly been completed. He went through until he arrived at the assembly point for boat number 8. The embarkation manager was waiting for him.

'We're ready to start the evacuation procedure, Sir.'

'OK. How are you going to address them?' The manager looked puzzled. 'I'll have to shout.'

'All right. Get on with it.'

The manager cupped his hands and shouted for the passengers for boat number 8 to follow him. Those closest stood up, but most just sat. The manager looked haplessly at Jim.

'It's all right, not your fault. Tell your checkers and any other staff to go round telling them to follow you.

You go and stand over by the door you're going to lead them through.'

He called up Zhou and Jan.

'Zhou, I want you to go with the passengers to number 8 boat. Don't say anything, just observe. Jan, go and wait down by the boat.'

Gradually, the passengers stood up and moved towards the door where the sign indicated the boat number. Jim saw the sign bob up and down and then disappear through the doorway followed by a crocodile of passengers except for two passengers in wheelchairs and one with crutches. He walked over to where one of them was sitting. The passenger smiled.

'I suppose I'm to join the Captain and go down with the ship.'

'No, Sir, you're not. This is our balls up. You should have crew helpers assigned to you. Please don't worry about this. I'll get it organised so that if anything does happen you will be looked after.' He went over to the other two passengers and repeated the same message.

An announcement came over the ship's broadcast system telling all the passengers that the drill was over and thanking them for their attendance.

Jim went down to deck 3 where he could see along the alleyway to the crowd at boat number 8. When he arrived, he managed to ease his way through and found Jan at the boat.

'There's not enough room to get them all out onto the embarkation area by the boat,' he said. 'We have to leave some of them inside.'

'Which on a dark night with the ship sinking would certainly have them worried.'

'I bloody well would be,' said Jan.

'Right, have they all been checked off?'

'They are doing it now the best they can. Apparently, while there is a procedure for checking them off at the muster point, there is not one for checking them off at this end.'

'Which means that anyone who strays away from the party would not be noticed or reported.'

'Exactly, Sir.'

'The whole thing shows that the drill should include all the passengers coming from the muster point down to the embarkation area.'

'Or change the muster point to here.'

'There's not enough space for that, Jan. There would be chaos.'

'Then they should have made the muster area down here much bigger.'

'Of course, but then they would lose cabin space and that eats into profits.'

The embarkation manager pushed his way in through the crowd. 'We are several passengers missing, Sir, but it's hard to tell. There's no room to do this properly.'

'Don't worry. We've seen all we need. Thank all the passengers and tell them the drill is over.' Jim and Jan went round helping and gradually the passengers dispersed.

'Imagine doing that on a dark night with the ship sinking,' Jim said to the embarkation manager.

'Sir, I really don't want to think about it. I just want to make sure I'm not here if it ever happens.'

'Gather all the times together and we'll have a look at them,' Jim said to Jan as they walked back along the alleyway. 'Once we've had a review of them, I'll ask the Captain to meet with us and we can discuss them with him. Talking of which, I see a storm coming my way.'

Up ahead, Cota and Shelby were walking briskly towards them.

'Jan, get going. I have a feeling this is not going to be pleasant.'

'I'll stay, Captain.'

'No you won't! Go!'

Jan hurried away in the opposite direction.

'Captain Clariby, what the hell do you think you are doing?' hissed Cota. 'Mr Shelby has told me you tried to throw a passenger off the ship. Is this true?'

'Not tried, Sir, threatened. Until the passenger saw sense, that is.'

'How dare you! I'm the Captain of this ship not you. You have no authority to do that.'

'Sir, it was a case of dealing with a situation when a passenger directly confronted the good order and discipline of the ship. We had no other choice.'

'You see, Augustus,' Shelby snorted. 'I told you. He thinks he's on a battleship. Discipline and good order of the ship! Have you ever heard such nonsense? You belong in a bygone age, Clariby.'

'I belong in an age of seamanship, Shelby, and that is desperately needed on this ship!'

'That's enough, Clariby! Mr Shelby is the General Manager of this ship and you will treat him with respect. You have also had passengers running around with their lifejackets on.'

'That was part of the drill, Captain.'

'No it wasn't,' said Shelby. 'The drill doesn't include trying to put them into the boats.'

'They didn't go into the boats. Just a minute, who the hell am I talking to? You or the Captain?'

'Captain Clariby, come with me. Now!' said Cota.

Cota led the way up through the ship to his cabin without speaking.

Jim was seething but tried to get his temper under control. This was turning into one hell of a day.

Cota walked into his office and Jim followed him in.

'Close the door,' snapped Cota.

As Jim turned back, Cota had moved to stand behind his desk.

'Captain, since your arrival on board I have had nothing but problems. Nothing seems to be to your satisfaction. While Captain Ricci was here, everything ran smoothly. Worst of all is your relationship with the hotel side of the ship. I have a litany of complaints from them regarding you and your staff, who you are apparently encouraging to copy you.'

Jim drew a deep breath.

'Captain, it is not my intention to quarrel with you and I am very sorry that we find ourselves in this position. But we, as the seamen of the ship, have one job above all else and that is the safety of those on board. If this upsets the hotel side, I suggest that is their problem,' Jim said.

'There you see, it's your attitude that is at the root of all this. First this safety business, I agree that is very important but, Captain, look around you. This is not like one of the little ships from your last company. This is one of the largest cruise ships in the world. We have every conceivable device on board to ensure safety. Everything is duplicated, even the generators that allow us to keep our power.

In the unlikely event that anything should happen, although I agree we must be prepared, then it is highly unlikely that we would need to abandon ship. Even if we did, we have large specially designed lifeboats to cope with that. Do you really think there is so much wrong with what the company has laid down for boat drills and the design? It is a very successful company. The classification society has approved the safety plans and the design. The International Maritime Organization has approved the boats and all the safety equipment. The flag state has also approved it all. In other words, everyone concerned in the safety of this ship has unanimously given their approval. Except you. What makes you such an expert?'

'Are these the same organisations that approved the lifeboat hooks that are breaking and killing hundreds of seamen?' Jim asked. 'The same ones that are letting hundreds of seamen die in enclosed spaces without adequate equipment? The same ones who have approved manning which causes such fatigue that we are wrecking ships because tired officers fall asleep? Are they?' demanded Jim.

They both paused like two tired fighters.

Cota leant forward on his desk. 'Here it is, Captain. No more changes to the drills or exercises. They go back to how they were. Next, I want the cadets back on the bridge. The officers are complaining that they have to spend more time on paperwork than they used to do. Anyway, learning to grease wires is hardly preparing them for life as a cruise ship officer. Finally, you will improve the relationship between the deck department and the hotel department. If you still feel strongly about the safety situation on board, you may prepare a report that can be forwarded to the head office in Southampton. In the meantime, Captain, we have a ship to run, and run smoothly. If that cannot be done, I will request your removal from the ship. I don't want to do that. You have expertise in ice that we need.

'Think man! You have only this cruise and two more after that, and then you go on leave. You came here with an excellent report. You could still have a good career here. It's up to you. Now, we also have a ship to sail. I'll see you on the bridge.'

Vacuum Pioneer

Captain Karl Johnsen was a happy man. The 'Vacuum Pioneer' had arrived in Galveston the day before and was now loading a mix of oil products for a return voyage to Canada. The new Third Officer, Ivo Milanovic, had arrived on board and was taking over from Ramon, who was heading off that evening back to the Philippines for his wedding. The ship had given him a farewell party the night before and had collected a wedding present adding up to a month's wages.

The Captain was pleased with the new Third Officer. He had been in ice as a cadet and therefore already had experience. Karl was now waiting at the airport for the arrival of his wife, Gerdy, and daughter, Briget, who were joining him for the summer. Briget had just qualified as a doctor and was taking time for a well-deserved holiday before starting work at their local hospital. Now that the children were educated, he and Gerdy could look forward to having time to themselves, making up for all the years apart.

After two more days in Galveston, the ship would head back up to Halifax, then up the St Lawrence to Quebec and Trois Riviere. What happened after that was up to the charterers, but now that the ice was melting, he expected orders to take her further north.

Gerdy and Briget came through the doors into the arrivals lounge pushing their trolleys. As usual, they had packed for a desert island. They look so alike he thought. Both had blonde hair and blue eyes. Gerdy had a large smile on her face. He swept them both into his arms. It was good to be together again.

Chapter 18

Jim stood on the bridge and watched the ship perform her departure dance again and head down the channel out to sea. The intensity of the flashing red and green lights of the channel buoys diminished as the brightness from the ship's thousands of lights passed by. The open decks were packed with excited passengers while those who had been many times before were already in the bars planning their evening.

It had been a bloody day. All his gains in the lifeboat management improvements were gone and the ship was back to square one. Worse, he and the Captain were now at odds with each other and that bastard Shelby and his cronies would make the most of that. On the bridge, the Third Officer came over and advised Jim that the Safety Officer was on the phone.

'Captain, I've got the senior cadet with me and I have the drill times for you.'

'Bring them up to my office. The cadet as well.'

Jim went over to where Cota and the Pilot were standing.

'I'm just going down to a meeting, Sir, unless you want me for anything.'

'Very good, Captain. I'll see you in the morning.'

Jan and Zhou were waiting for him in his office. Jan looked at him and raised his eyebrow.

'Don't ask,' said Jim. 'I'll tell you later. Right, let's have a look at the times.'

Jim looked down the list.

'It's very uneven. Some boats completed in 30 minutes and others took over 40. What about the timings on boat number 8?'

'It took 20 minutes to get them down to the boat and assembled there. The second check was attempted but wasn't completed as it was impossible in the space.'

'Zhou, what about the transit from the lounge to the boat?' asked Jim.

'The front section followed well, but towards the end we had many stragglers. Three passengers stopped on the way to sit down. They were elderly and two had sticks. They couldn't keep up on the stairs. I had to direct them after they had rested.'

'So, if we said it would take an average of one hour from the alarms sounding to when we get them ready for embarkation, we would be pretty accurate.'

Jan and Zhou agreed.

Jim looked at the times for a minute.

'That's unacceptable. The ship could easily sink while they are still heading down the stairs.'

'If we added a mass of people trying to get up the stairs at the same time,' said Jan, 'it would be even longer. Also people would get mixed up.'

'Sir,' said Zhou, 'I don't think people would stay with their boat managers in that situation. I think that once they were mixed up they would head for the nearest boat.'

'Especially if it was dark and the ship was listing,' added Jan.

'Really the whole of deck 3 should be just for embarkation,' said Zhou.

Jim laughed. 'Zhou, you have a lot to learn about ship owners. Think of the money they would lose.'

'Then they should put their prices up.'

'If any country was brave enough to require that, every cruise ship that was registered there would change flags the same day.'

'Why can't we have the boats back where they used to be then? Up on the top decks near the assembly areas.'

'Because the regulations now stipulate that they should be lower down so there is less swinging when they are lowered. Thank you, Zhou, for your help and your comments. Are you back on watches now?'

'No, Sir. The others are.'

'Then tomorrow I want you to get me a list of all the passengers who are over 65 and also a list of all those who are infirm in any way, wheelchairs, sticks, whatever. That should easily be available as the Captain is supposed to have that before sailing.'

When Zhou left, Jim beckoned Jan into the dayroom. He went over to the cabinet.

'What would you like?'

'Beer, please.'

Jim poured a beer for Jan and a large scotch for himself.

'Regrettably, the decision has been made to stop all further changes to the embarkation system. As of now, we revert back to how it was before I joined. The cadets are also back onto the bridge. However, we will carry on with the boat lowering and exercises in port. Cheers.'

'Where has this come from?'

Jim shrugged. 'The office? The Captain? Who knows. But there will be no change and I have to keep my head down.'

'I'm sorry, Sir. I thought we were beginning to make headway.'

'So did I. Anyway, carry on as normal. Obviously the fire exercise in the galley is cancelled. They can also revert to their standard training and smaller exercises.'

'What are you going to do now?'

'You know, I think I shall enjoy the cruise like everyone else.'

The next morning at the heads of department meeting, Jim handed out the boat timings report to everyone.

'I thought you should all see this, just in case you are ever asked about it.'

'Why should we be?' asked Shelby.

'Well, if anything ever did happen, it's the kind of thing that courts of inquiry tend to ask about.'

Cota looked at Jim carefully, but said nothing.

'What do you expect me to do with this then?' Shelby said.

'I couldn't care less. What you should do about it is think very carefully and send it to the company. What I expect you to do with it is bugger all.'

'That's enough, Captain,' Cota warned.

Jim shrugged.

Shelby carried on looking at the report. 'It is based on speculation not substance. The conditions it was done in are all artificial. Obviously in a real emergency everyone would move a lot faster.'

'If you say so.'

'I do say so. Captain, what do you think?'

Cota was careful. 'I think it is worth considering. However, I see that the report states that the passengers were ready to embark within one hour and I consider that acceptable. Even if we ever were to sink, it would take far longer than that.'

'There we are,' said Shelby.

'I think that Staffie is right.' It was Iain, the Chief Engineer. 'Although for the life of me I don't see what we can do about it.'

'Jim,' Cota said, 'may I suggest that you include this in your general recommendations to the company?'

Jim nodded and then added, 'Can I ask that you all note the problem of the disabled passengers and also the elderly?'

'We have a full list of those who stated they have a disability on their ticket application forms, Captain,' stated Bella Winchester.

'We might have that list, but we're not doing much about it. Do we have crew assigned to each of them?'

'We have provision for that.'

'Jim,' Cota said, 'we have discussed this enough and there are other matters we must move on to.'

When the meeting was over, Cota came over to Jim. 'I presume you are going to write up a safety report.'

'Yes, Sir. That's my intention.'

'Good. I look forward to reading it.'

That evening, Jim listened to Helen playing the piano. During the interval, she came over to where Jim was sitting. She smiled at him and placed her hand on his. 'I hear you had a strange day in Fort Lauderdale.'

'You could say that, although I had a coarser description of it. Listen, I didn't come here to talk about that. Tomorrow we're in Kingston again. Have you ever been to the Blue Mountains?' She shook her head. 'I've heard of them but never been there.'

'Good. I've hired a car for tomorrow. We're going there for the day.'

'Are you sure?'

'Why not? I need to get off the ship and it's far from the crowds.'

'I would love to come,' she said.

'Bert Fallows, the Security Officer, will have a collapsible chair ready for you in the morning. It will be waiting at the gangway for you.' He got up. 'I'll see you on the forward gangway at 0900.'

He bent down and gave her a kiss on her cheek.

'See you in the morning. Don't forget to bring a jacket and insect spray,' he added.

Jim arrived down by the gangway to find Bert already waiting with Helen in her chair wearing a lovely dress and a large white sunhat.

'It seems far too hot to wear this,' she said indicating the blazer on her lap.

'Just wait till you get up the mountain.'

They found the vehicle at the end of the jetty and, once the driver had given Jim the keys, they set off through Kingston. Initially, it was very busy and the traffic was dense. As they reached the northern outskirts, they passed the university and then the road started to rise out of the city.

'How far can we go up?' Helen asked.

'The mountains are 7,000 feet high, but the road goes up to 5,000 feet.'

'That's high enough.'

They passed through a few small settlements and arrived at Irish Town.

'Do you know the way?'

'Just about, there's only one road. We're going to do a tour. Do you know anything about Bob Marley?'

'Of course, I'm a fan.'

'Good. Chris Blackwell, who produced Bob Marley's records, bought an estate called Strawberry Hill, 3,000 feet up in the mountains. The house was destroyed in a hurricane in the 80s but they've built a cottage there. The bar has a whole collection of music memorabilia. We're going to Strawberry Hill for an early bite and then I thought on to John Crow Peak and Sir John's Peak, a tour of a coffee plantation at Mavis Bank, and finally down to Bull Bay and back to the ship, hopefully in time to sail.'

'Jim that sounds wonderful.'

'Sit back and enjoy.'

She did. She was enchanted with Strawberry Hill. They sipped Planter's Punch in the bar while hearing about the history and seeing the musical mementos. They then sat by the pool and looked out over the views of the island. They toured the coffee plantation and of course bought some Blue Mountain coffee. Before returning to the ship, they sat by the sea at Bull Bay. They admired the beautiful view, conversation flowing easily. It was the perfect end to a special day.

'Jim, thank you so very much. It has been wonderful,' said Helen

'No, thank you. It has done me a lot of good getting off the ship. Given me time to think.'

'What have you thought or shouldn't I ask?'

'No, I don't mind. Mainly, I'm not cut out for these hotel ships. I think you have to know only this kind of life, then perhaps you can go along with it. Don't get me wrong. There are many who love it and I understand that, but it isn't for me. I see it as a money hungry machine. There are so many people that it feels like an impersonal conveyor belt spewing out the same product at the end of each cruise. Worse is that those who run them have forgotten they are ships just like anything else out there. Size is of no concern to the sea.'

'So what are you going to do?'

'I'm going to resign and make a lot of people happy, including myself.'

'What about a job?'

'Something will turn up. It always does.' He smiled. 'Do you know, I already feel happier now that I've made my mind up.'

They drove back to the ship, arriving on the jetty late in the afternoon. Jim arranged for the car to be returned and then assisted Helen to board the ship.

'Are you all right Jim?' she asked.

'Never better.'

He took the lift up to the bridge deck and entered his cabin, showered and changed. He looked at the clock on the bulkhead. The ship would be sailing in two hours. Plenty of time. First he would phone Jenny.

He heard the phone ringing at the other end and then she picked it up.

'Hello, sailor,' she said. 'Guess what? You didn't wake me up.' It was so good to hear her voice and her cheerfulness.

He told her so. 'I have to be cheerful,' she said. 'It goes with the territory of being married to a sailor.'

'I've had a few problems,' he said. He then related the events of the last few days.

'Come home, Jim.'

'I was thinking of resigning.'

'Don't think, just do it. We don't need the money that badly. Leave them to it.'

'Are you sure, Jenny?'

'Of course I'm sure. I sensed there was something wrong. Don't worry. We'll get through this.'

He finished the call feeling as if a weight had been taken off his shoulders. He sat down at the computer and wrote his short resignation. There was no need to explain why. He printed the letter out and read it briefly before signing it and placing it in an envelope.

It was time to go to the bridge for sailing so he took the letter with him and as he passed the Captain's empty office he placed it carefully on the centre of his desk.

Chapter 19

They were in another port by 0700 in the morning. Jim was just about to go down to breakfast when his phone rang. It was Cota.

'Please come to my office.'

Jim arrived and found Cota standing there with Jim's letter in his hand.

'Come in and sit down, Jim.'

He put the letter down on the desk between them.

'This is really not necessary.'

'I'm sorry, Captain, but I discussed the situation with my wife last night and my decision is that the circumstances now require this.'

'Not by me, Jim. I want you to take this back.'

'Sir, thank you, but it really is for the best.'

'And you won't change your mind?'

'No, Sir. I would like to be relieved as soon as possible.'

Cota sighed. 'In that case, I will advise Southampton this morning.'

'Thank you, Sir.'

'I want you to know that I do appreciate what you tried to do. It wasn't always like this you know. I've been in this company for years. When we were independent and had smaller ships, it was much easier. We could run the ships as we wanted, but then we became bigger, became a group, expanded into larger and larger ships. You know what I think? This is the future. We are going to see larger and larger ships and one day they will call the hotel or ship manager, Captain.'

'I don't want to be here to see that, Sir.'

'It is a matter of compromise, Jim. The whole sea is changing.'

'Then I'll leave it to you, Sir.'

'All right, Jim, it's your decision. I won't say one word of this to anyone else and I ask that you keep all this to yourself until Southampton have made their arrangements.'

They sailed in the late afternoon and Jim went down to dinner in a happy mood. The passengers on his tables at both sittings this trip were very pleasant. On this sitting, he had two school teachers who had a delightful repertoire of funny school stories, a couple who had just retired after years building up a business and a young couple on their honeymoon. Nice normal people as he had requested. They went up to one of the lounges for coffee before they went to the ship's theatre to see the show. They were thrilled with the ship. As he listened to them, Jim found himself actually questioning himself about the ship. Maybe they really were big enough to survive any disaster. He walked through the bars, which were full of happy people, and then past the dance floors, again with the sound of laughter. It was good to see people happy. He didn't notice Samuel Gully walking towards him until Sam spoke.

'You're deep in thought, Captain.'

Jim started. 'Sorry, Sam, you're right. I was just thinking about how much people were enjoying themselves.'

'So they should be. That's what it's all about. Captain, we've been investigating the list of passengers you gave us. It was very interesting. We have eliminated everybody except for two males and both have criminal records, both from Miami.'

They sat down at a nearby table.

'So, what now?'

'Things are moving up a notch. We have two other passengers on board, both from the DEA. We don't want to involve you any further, just keep you advised. We are going to keep an eye on these passengers as we see them as key to the whole operation. If we can determine that drugs come on board and where they are, we then intend to follow them to their source. That will lead us to those running the show.'

'You seem very cool about this, Sam,' Jim observed.

'Heck, Captain, there are so many drugs flying around. As soon as this is over, there will be another case and then another. It never stops. Even if, or should I say when, we arrest those responsible, others will take their place. There's so much money involved. Just think, what do you guys get? I mean as a salary? If I suggested not more than 100 grand would I be right?'

'Certainly neither the Captain nor I get that. I don't know about the hotel side. They probably get more.'

'Well, if you were involved in the smuggling, you could get at least 250 grand from one trip. How about that? If you do this just four times in a year, that's a million in your pocket and no taxes, and in the drugs business that's small change. This is not the only cruise ship doing this by the way. We are watching others.'

'Can I ask how you are going to find out where the drugs are hidden?'

'These people aren't stupid, but then neither are we and they tend to forget that. We have people on the ground in Aruba and San Juan watching. They know the drug barons there. We have a very good chance of wrapping this up. Now, Captain, please understand, I've told you more than I should but that is because of your help. You have been invaluable. From now on, leave it to us. I've enough on my plate with Bert wanting to be the Lone Ranger without the Sheriff riding into town.'

Jim laughed.

'Believe me, Sam, I really want nothing to do with this. I look forward to hearing of your success.'

That evening was again cocktail party time and Jim managed to get through it, hiding his feelings. After dinner, he accepted the Chief's invite to visit the club. It was crowded with a noisy darts match going on. He and Iain found a corner of the bar to wedge themselves in.

'Where's Patrick tonight?'

'Ah,' said Iain, 'he's entertaining. A private party.' He tapped his nose with his finger. 'I think he's showing off the golden rivet.'

They laughed. 'Thanks for the information about the ice precautions, Jim,' said Iain. 'We've gone through most of it already, but it doesn't do any harm to repeat it. We won't be going into any hard stuff, will we?'

'Better not,' said Jim. 'it would cut her open like a knife through butter. No, we'll probably see icebergs going up the Strait of Belle Isle on the way out of St Lawrence and a few drifting around in the Davis Strait, but that's all. The ice reporting service is excellent at keeping tabs on them. It won't even be too cold, although the water will be just above freezing. That doesn't change much.'

'So you don't expect freezing on deck?'

'No. If the sun is shining and you're sheltered from the wind, you can even sunbathe.'

'I'm looking forward to it,' said Iain. 'I've been at sea all these years and I've never seen an iceberg.'

'Most sailors are the same. It depends on which company you grew up in. They are starting to learn now though. The Arctic is going to open up and, once it does, there will be another gold rush. There are more ships going up there than ever before.'

'What about cruise ships?'

'There will be more of them, which is worrying because not many of them are ice class. Worse, like this ship, they don't have double hulls. Still, at this time of year, there's no real problem provided they stay in open waters.'

Jim finished his pint.

'A final thought though, according to regulations, we are supposed to do ice damage control exercises,' said Jim.

'What the hell are those?'

'On a ship like this, God knows. I can't see us rushing around with wooden spars or wedges can you? Don't worry. I don't think any of the other large cruise ships do them either. On the ice ships though, they are done regularly. But then a lot of things were done there that we don't do here. C'est la vie.'

Just before going to bed, Jim was sitting at his desk adding items to his report when he glanced up and saw a flash of a red-headed woman in a white dress followed by Cota. As only Jim's desk light was on, Cota did not notice him.

The next morning, Jim was with the Safety Officer at one of the boats. They had assembled all the deck department, together with a group of waiters lent by the restaurant manager.

'Don't worry,' Jim said to those assembled. 'We're not lowering the boat to the water. We just want you to go inside, sit down and strap yourselves in.'

One of the cadets was in the boat to direct the seating. The sailors started to file in. It was apparent that the large lifejackets were causing a problem as they squeezed into their seats. 'Keep going,' shouted Jim. 'We can't have any stops.'

Twenty minutes passed before the last seaman was packed into the boat, which was now jammed full.

'Thank you all,' said Jim. 'Get them out and hoist the boat.'

Jan was looking at his checklist. 'That took 20 minutes with a trained crew in calm conditions.'

'So, from the emergency signal to getting people sitting in the boat, we can say it'll take one hour twenty minutes then.'

'That would be the best time, Sir. But the environment wouldn't be so calm.'

Jim nodded. 'But that's speculation. One hour twenty minutes we can prove.'

'Are you going to tell the Captain?'

'No. I think he already knows but doesn't want to face it. I'll put it in the report.'

Jim's pager went off. 'Talk of the devil. He wants to see me. Thank you, Jan. You can get on with your boat exercise now.'

Cota was waiting for him when he arrived.

'Sit down, Jim. Southampton wants to speak to us both. I'll put it on speaker phone.'

It was West. 'Good morning, Captain Clariby. I am sure you know what this is about. I have spoken to Captain Cota who assures me that your leaving is not his wish. I understand there have been a few difficulties while you adjust to the company ways and such a large ship, but Captain Cota is satisfied with your professionalism.'

'That's very good of him to say so,' said Jim.

'In that case, Captain, can you explain why this sudden resignation?'

'It is all explained in a report that I am sending to you,' answered Jim.

'What's it about?'

'It is an overall review of the safety situation on board the ship.'

'What specifically? The navigation, engines, the crew?'

'Basically, Mr West, I am concerned about the inability to evacuate the ship in sufficient time if required.'

There was a momentary silence.

'I think you had better send me this report as soon as possible.'

Jim looked at Cota. 'Provided the Captain does not mind, I can email it to you this evening.'

Cota nodded.

'In the meantime, Captain, if you remember, we recruited you mainly because of your command experience in ice waters. Now, if your decision to resign is final, I would request that you give us appropriate notice and remain for the first cruise north. At least those on board will then have some experience of the conditions before you leave. Could you do that for us?'

That was fair thought Jim. 'Very well, Mr West.'

'Thank you. Are you happy with that, Captain Cota?'

'Yes, Mr West.'

'Good. Then I look forward to receiving your report.'

Jim spent the rest of the day on the report. When it was finished, he invited Jan to come to the office and read it through. Jan sat quietly while he turned the pages. When he finished, he put it back on Jim's desk.

'Well?' Jim asked.

'I'm just trying to think if there is anything you haven't covered. You've mentioned the lifejackets, muster points, lack of trained crew, boat capacity, smoke escape hoods, warm clothing, harder passenger drills, recognisable uniforms for the deck department and taking away all the gold braid from the hotel people. They'll hate that; they love their braid. Overall, I think this gives them enough to get on with. Of course, Sir, you do recognise that they know all this. I mean we all do. Ever since I joined this outfit and I came on these beasts, I realised that we had an impossible job. No one wants either of us around to remind them of the problems. We're a bit like sick men wandering around reminding them of their own mortality.'

'Well, at least I have tried.'

'You're the first Staff Captain I've seen take it this seriously and go to such lengths. I hate to say this, Sir, but you do know that you won't succeed. In fact, if you send this in, it could be the end of your career here.'

'I know that, Jan. This report will most probably be filed away with all the other bits of unpleasant news. With regard to my career, I will be leaving at the end of the next cruise.'

Jan was shocked. 'Have the bastards fired you?'

'No, not at all,' Jim said. 'In fact, they asked me to stay. This is my decision.' He could see that Jan wanted a further explanation.

'I realise I don't have the right attitude for these ships. Maybe I should say 'frame of mind' for want of a better expression. Don't get me wrong. I have no problem with passenger ships. I've been on enough of them and was very happy commanding them, but they were ships, Jan. Ships where safety and order came before anything else and were given priority. That doesn't happen here. This is not a criticism of anyone on board nor am I saying that they don't care about these things. Huge floating palaces like this have reached a critical point. They are too big for us to cope with if anything does happen. Maybe this size is possible, but we have to think about double hulls, where we send them, how we are going to cope with the elderly and infirm. There needs to be a complete rethink of how we get the punters off and forget this idea that everyone can stay until they're rescued. Maybe detachable modules like small ships that can separate from the mother could be used. Unfortunately, it needs another Titanic for anything to be done, and even then I'm not sure that would be enough. Maybe the odd pleasure palace sinking is acceptable. The insurance companies certainly have accepted that.'

'I don't think I will be around long enough to see that,' commented Jan.

'Just make sure you're not around on one that sinks. Now to more cheerful matters. I'm having my tables up for drinks tonight after we sail. I'd like you to join us.'

'Thank you, Sir. With pleasure.'

'One last thing. No mention of me leaving. There are those who would like to start celebrating and I don't want the party to start too early!'

The evening went well. Jim had dropped off a copy of his report with the Captain and then sent it by email to West in Southampton. Cota had called in for a drink before carrying on to his other engagements. By the time the second sitting passengers were being entertained, Helen had managed to get her wheelchair in the dayroom and was talking to one of the Second Officers and Zhou. She had a large glass of wine in her hand that had already been replenished once. She was obviously not playing piano tonight.

Eventually, the guests and officers filtered away one by one until only Jim and Helen were left.

'I suppose I had better get you down for dinner,' Jim said.

'I'm not going in the restaurant tonight, Jim,' she said. 'Could I have another drink please?'

'Of course you can. I'm not bothering either.'

Helen was looking at a picture of Jenny that Jim had on the bureau.

'She's a very lovely woman.'

'I know,' said Jim. 'I'm a lucky man.'

'I think she's a lucky woman.' Jim let the remark pass.

Helen was silent for a moment and then suddenly asked, 'Would you like to kiss me?' She looked away from him in embarrassment. 'If you don't then it doesn't matter.'

Jim knelt down by her chair and took her hand.

'Helen, I would very much like to kiss you, but I'm not going to because I know what would happen. Once I start, I wouldn't want to stop. Then what do I say to a certain lady who is waiting for me?'

'Is it the leg or the wheelchair? I am fully capable.' Jim put a finger on her lips. 'You credit me with too much gallantry. I assure you that if there wasn't a certain lady over there watching us ...' He paused. 'You are a very beautiful and desirable young woman. I am very flattered. Now, while I still can, I'm going to take you home.' He lifted the drink from her fingers and wheeled her chair out of the cabin.

At her cabin door, Helen put her hand on Jim's arm. 'Are we still friends?'

He bent down and, lifting her chin, kissed her softly on her lips.

'I cannot think of anyone else on board who I would rather have as my friend. I'll see you tomorrow at the piano. Now I'm going away to have a cold shower and kick myself.'

She laughed. 'Well, if you get too frustrated, you know where I live.'

'That's another problem I have to cope with,' he called as he walked away.

'Jenny, if only you knew what I do for you,' he muttered.

Chapter 20

The ship arrived on schedule in San Juan in Puerto Rico. It was an overcast day and the clouds were sullen with rain, but it didn't stop the passengers evacuating the ship for the various tours or to just amble round the port.

Cota had also gone ashore with one of his lady friends and the ship was quiet. Jan had reported that, by the time the ship returned to Fort Lauderdale, all the lifeboats would have been lowered and sent away and that all the equipment was in good order.

Jim made good use of the quiet to get on with the inevitable paperwork. The pile of various training books reduced as he scanned through them as well as the confidential reports for the crew changing at the next call in Fort Lauderdale. The deck department store requisitions were on the computer for him to scan through. Even though the deck department was reduced from the years when Jim first came to sea, it was still large enough to generate a mass of paperwork and computer-generated forms to be sent to the office ashore.

After a brief lunch in the officers' mess, Jim went to the bridge for a passage planning meeting with Peter and the deck officers. They were scheduled to sail from Fort Lauderdale for New York, then into the St Lawrence River to Quebec, down the Saguenay Fjord to La Baie, then through the Strait of Belle Isle and the dash to the Davis Strait for the Arctic Circle pass, then back to Halifax, Philadelphia and Fort Lauderdale. The officers were looking forward to the cruise as it would be their first time heading north into the Arctic Circle and, even though it was summer, they were pleased to be going somewhere new instead of the usual tour round the Caribbean. The ice navigation manuals he had requested had arrived and these were now around the bridge. The various cold weather precautions were also ready, although most would not be required in July. Still, it did no harm to be ready.

Later in the afternoon, the passenger tour buses returned and once again the ship stirred into life. She sailed in the late evening and headed for her home port. After dinner, Jim went to the piano lounge and listened to Helen. When she finished, they went along to the café by the pool and ordered coffees.

'I had too much to drink last night. I'm so sorry,' she said.

'If you did, I never noticed. I remember a very lovely young woman flattering me and making me feel young again.'

'Thank you, Jim. You were very understanding.'

'So were you.'

'I'm leaving after the next cruise,' she said. 'I was thinking of going before that but I want to say I've been to the Arctic.'

'A lot of other people want to say that apparently. We have a full ship. I'm also leaving at the end of it, by the way.'

'Then it's a good time for me to leave. I don't know if I will be able to settle down as a teacher back in Connecticut again after this.'

'You will. Think of this as an extended holiday. Not real, but a nice interlude in your life.'

'But this is your life.'

'That's right. The interlude for me is when I'm on leave.'

'You can't stay at sea forever. What happens then?' asked Helen.

'I haven't really thought about that. Perhaps if the life out here carries on changing like this, I'll be happy to leave. A bit like the comedian whose jokes aren't funny. He has to know when to leave the stage. Very few seamen stay on all their working lives, you know.'

'Why is that?'

'Lots of reasons. Married life is the biggest one. Then lots realise the opportunities they are missing ashore. There are more career opportunities there and the salaries and rewards are better. Life at sea is changing. A lot of my friends don't like that. The shipping companies are also changing. We now mostly work for faceless people, in a company we hardly know. There is no pride now in the flag we sail under. The ship is part of a country we know nothing about. Don't get me going! Come on, I'll take you home.'

'Yet you're still here.'

'Clinging on by my fingernails.'

The ship arrived off Fort Lauderdale early in the morning. When Jim appeared on the bridge, Cota asked, 'Do you want to take her in, Jim?'

Jim sat down in the command chair and, after the handover, took control. A ship is a ship and most generally behave in the same way, but this ship was particularly easy because of the various propulsion systems. He went to the wing of the enclosed bridge to watch the Pilot approach, then headed the ship for the channel. By the time the Pilot arrived, the ship was already setting course for the breakwater entrance. As always, the ship went through the berthing procedure with ease and soon the ship was being secured alongside.

Jim went down to his office and found Bert Fallows and Sam Gully waiting for him.

'Sam wanted to come up to say cheerio,' said Bert.

'All good things come to an end,' Sam said with a smile. 'It's been a pleasure knowing you, Captain.'

'And you, Sam. Can I presume if you are leaving that the investigation is completed?'

'At this end yes, Captain.'

'Am I allowed to know anything else?'

'Officially no, but as you were instrumental in solving the puzzle, drugs have come on board, a large quantity by the way, we know where they are and who is involved, but we need a few last pieces before we can proceed. All we need are the kingpins ashore and then the case is wrapped up.'

'What about those on board?' asked Jim.

'I'm sorry, Captain. I can't discuss that. All I can say is 'watch this space'. There are about ten DEA agents on the berth watching so we are treating it seriously but no moves will be made yet.'

Sam stood up. 'Once again, Captain, your help is appreciated. It's been a pleasure to meet you.'

Bert left with Sam, and Jim returned to his desk just as his phone rang. It was West in Southampton.

'We have your safety report here, Captain, and I must say we are very disturbed by what you say.'

'Perhaps you can tell me what disturbs you.'

'It's the overall tone, Captain. You seem to think our whole attitude is at fault.'

'No, Mr West, not at all.'

'But you criticise the design. You say there aren't enough staircases.'

'True. Not if four thousand people are trying to use them, half going up and half going down all to get off in thirty minutes. It can't be done.'

'How do you know?'

'Sheer common sense. Anyway, you have our timings.'

'They are all artificial.'

'True. They were done in calm circumstances,' explained Jim.

'What about the lifejackets? We have been using that type for years.'

'There is no grab strap at the top. How the hell are you meant to lift someone into a boat or a liferaft if you can't pull them up?'

'They are approved by the coastguard.'

'Who have never tested them. They have just rubber stamped someone else's approval.'

'You say the lifeboats are too big.'

'They are. You can load a boat with 50 people faster than you can one with 150. How long are you going to hold a large boat waiting for the last passengers to arrive? The faster you load them, the faster you get them off the ship.'

'You want a limit on the number of older and infirm passengers.'

'I do. How are they going to go up and down stairs without help if the ship is listing? How are you going to push a wheelchair? If they are in the water, they can't get into the liferafts. It's impossible. Christ, it's bad enough for a young fit person getting into them. We all know that but rarely talk about it, do we?'

'There's no point going on, Captain. You are asking the impossible.'

'No, Mr West. Nothing is impossible. These things should have been thought of before these huge floating resorts were built. I notice you didn't mention warm clothing. From the records, you have never told passengers to wear warm clothing for the muster drills. Do you know it is a regulation?' There was silence.

'I hope that you have told the passengers coming on the next cruise about that. We are going into icy waters.'

'I have already discussed this report with Captain Cota. He agrees that many of your conclusions are wrong.'

'I expected that.'

'I can see, Captain, that we are not going to agree. Perhaps you are right to give your resignation.'

'I never doubted it, Mr West.'

'On that basis, we'll arrange your relief after this cruise.'

The line clicked off.

Sod you, thought Jim.

He got up and went to Cota's office. He was talking with Bella Winchester.

'I'll be with you in a minute, Jim,' he said. He signed the papers that Bella had taken to him, and then she left. 'Just getting the last of the port papers signed. So, what can I do for you?'

'I just wondered why you disagreed with my report to Southampton, for my own interest.'

'Jim,' Cota said, 'I didn't disagree with what you wrote.'

'Strange, that's what West said.'

'Look,' said Cota, 'it was the way it was said. You have to be diplomatic with these people.'

'You mean I should have said 'probably the stairs might not be able to accommodate all the people at once' or 'maybe the boats are a little bit too big?' Come off it. I told it like it is. I'm a seaman, not a politician. So are you, or at least you used to be.'

'Don't be insolent, Captain!'

'Well then, Sir, what was wrong?'

Cota slumped. He looked tired. 'Captain, I have worked hard to get where I am. When I first started, it was far easier. You did your job on the ship and went home. Even when I got command, it was easier. I then joined this company and have grown with them. They weren't always like this. But they grew and were taken over, and slowly it all changed. You're leaving. I'm here to stay. I have to get on with them. I do that by smiling when they want me to and by saying what they expect me to say. I keep my job.'

Jim said nothing. As he turned to leave, Cota said, 'Bend with the wind, Captain. It's a cold world out there.'

Jim didn't reply.

Throughout the afternoon, passengers poured on board while on the jetty the loaders dragged masses of stores into the ship for the prolonged cruise. Crew were also changing. The crew who were joining arrived just after the ship had berthed. After handover, the leaving crew were heading for the waiting buses to go to the airport. One of the Purser's staff was down by the buses checking off the departing crew. In the vicinity, another two cruise ships were going through the same routines.

Vacuum Pioneer

The 'Vacuum Pioneer' was heading back up the east coast of America. They had rounded the Florida keys and were now heading up the Florida Straits assisted by the strong Gulf Stream current that drove up the Straits from the south. Gerdy and Briget were sunbathing on the bridge deck while watching the coastline pass by.

The new Third Officer was on watch and the Captain was keeping an eye on him, but he was showing that he was both competent and confident in his position as Officer of the Watch. The ship had a full load of different oil products ranging from aviation fuel to heating oil. The crew were painting the bridge front in gleaming white and some were working on stages rigged along the front while others tended the lines.

The Bosun had made sure the ladies weren't disturbed by the work. The Captain's steward had also brought them ice cream and fresh orange juice. Curled up in the shade nearby was the ship's cat, Biscuit, which officially didn't exist but was now a seasoned seacat after being on board for over five years. In fact, he had been on the ship longer than anyone else.

The Chief Officer was also standing nearby watching the crew on the stages. He was in his white uniform and relaxing after the delicate art of loading the hazardous cargo. Briget was lazily watching him through one open eye. He was certainly a good-looking man she thought, especially in his uniform, and he was unmarried. This voyage could prove more interesting that she had anticipated. Her attention had not escaped her mother either, who smiled discreetly.

Part Three

The Arctic

So all were lost, which in the ship were found,
They in the sea being burnt, they in the burnt ship drown'd.

John Donne

Chapter 21

The ship sailed from Fort Lauderdale in the evening. Under new orders, the ship's boat drill had reverted to the previous routine, meaning it was scheduled for the next morning. The hotel staff were busy settling the passengers in, although the bars were doing a roaring trade and the casino was packed full. The ship had a very faint vibration, only noticeable to those who were not new to the ship. It was caused by the ship's speed being increased.

There was a different air about the ship, probably due to the fact that, for most, the ship was going to places they had never been before. It was also going to be a longer cruise with more time between ports. The ship would take two and a half days to get to New York. The cruise would really start with the visit to Canadian waters.

Jim met the deck officers on the bridge next morning before the boat drills.

'Be as courteous as you can, but emphasise that they must be wearing warm clothing. They will probably tell you that they weren't told about that and they will be right. Just get across that if there is an emergency then they must get it if they can. It's a conundrum. We want those in their cabins to bring their lifejackets, but we don't want those on the entertainment decks trying to go and get them. It would cause a complete blockage on the stairways. Frankly it's a mess. They should have been told all this before they joined, but the company won't hear of it. Never mind, we just have to do what we can. You should all wear your caps and walk around. Make sure the hotel people are doing their job and answer any questions when asked,' explained Jim.

'Should we be completely truthful?' asked Zhou. Jan glanced at Jim and raised his eyebrow.

'As much as you can be, but nothing to cause panic or get them disturbed. Do that and the proverbial hits the fan. We've got one of the top suits from the Lauderdale office on board and he's a shit. Look, they're here for the holiday of their lives. Let's make sure they enjoy the cruise, OK?'

The drill went as Jim thought. Without pressure, the hotel staff were noticeably more relaxed. Still, a few more weeks and it wouldn't be his concern. Reports came in from the others about passengers without suitable clothing or lifejackets and failure to pay attention, but he let it go. The last thing he wanted was conflict at this stage.

Bert Fallows was waiting for him when he got back to his cabin.

'I've had a very interesting conversation with the Ship General Manager, Sir.'

'Sit down and go on,' said Jim.

'He wanted to talk to me about the security log books, you know the ones I bring you every day.'

Jim nodded. These logs were similar to the bridge log books. They listed all the events of the previous 24 hours, except in the security books they recorded any incidents involving the passengers or crew and how they were dealt with. Mostly these were petty incidents, such as drunkenness, but there was the occasional more serious incident involving a passenger or crew member being detained, which was usually the last resort. Also common were off-duty crew in the passenger quarters, or passengers in crew quarters. The latter usually involved women and often those old enough to know better.

'He called me in and I thought it was about the shoplifting we had last trip.'

'That was sorted wasn't it? The passenger handed back the goods and he's now been banned from cruising with us again.'

'Yes, that's right, but it wasn't about that. It was about changes to the log book system. We now have to keep two log books. One is for ship operational matters, which as far as I can understand is anything involving safety or ship's crew, and the other is for all events involving passengers or hotel staff.'

'That seems a bit silly,' said Jim. 'Just more paperwork.'

'There's more,' said Bert. 'That last log book is for him and not you. You get the one about the ship's crew.'

Bert saw Jim's face. 'I had a feeling you didn't know about this, Sir.'

'No, Bert, I didn't.'

'I did tell him that I was responsible to you as head of the department, but he told me that this had the Captain's approval.'

Bert waited. 'What do you want me to do, Sir? I'll do whatever you say, sod them.'

Jim thought for a moment.

'You'll have to do what they want,' he said. 'At least for the time being.'

'I'm sorry, Captain, there's one more thing. You know we carry certain, shall we say, pacifiers on board, pepper spray, handcuffs etc?'

Jim nodded.

'Well, we've been told to hand them in to his office. I told him again that I would have to consult you, and again he told me this had been cleared by the Captain.'

Jim drew a deep breath, trying to stay calm.

'Bert, I don't know what is going on, but for the time being just do what he says. I'll try and sort this out.'

As Bert was about to go, Jim stopped him.

'Bert, I'm going to ask you a question. Do you or any of your team have any firearms? I'm not interested in their legality or the company rules. It's a question for my own knowledge that's all.'

'This is just between us then, Captain. Is that right?'

'Completely, Bert.'

'They were here before I arrived, Sir. I'm not trying to get out of anything. If they hadn't been, I would have got them myself. You know that, back in the good old days of proper liners, we used to carry them. We didn't have security officers then; we had quartermasters. The weapons were kept locked up by the bridge, but they were always there just in case, not that I ever saw them being used. Today, it's a different game. Just as discipline is breaking down ashore, so it is here. There are 4,000 people out there and just ten security people. The deck department is no longer allowed weapons so what are we supposed to do if some passenger, or worse a bunch of them, or crew go berserk? Wave pepper spray at them?' exclaimed Bert.

Jim waited.

'So we have to do what we have to do. Other cruise ships are the same. A lot of Captains and even suits ashore know about it, but it's a case of no one really wants to know, if you get my meaning. If there is any problem, we can always chuck them over the side.'

'You still haven't told me what you've got.'

'Each of us has a small automatic, except our friend from the Miami police. He's got a bloody great magnum like Dirty Harry.'

'What about the new man who joined to take Sam's place?'

'One for him as well. He's ex-army, good man.'

Bert stood there looking at Jim.

'So what now?' Bert asked.

'What about?'

'The guns.'

'What guns?'

Bert grinned. 'I'll carry on, Sir, if I may.'

'I trust the items we have been talking about are well hidden.'

'That's guaranteed, Sir. If the security team don't know where to hide things on this beast, then no one else bloody well does.'

Jim thought for a moment and then walked along to the Captain's office. Cota was sitting at his desk when Jim walked in. Only then did he see Hinchley behind the door on a couch.

'I'm sorry, Sir. I didn't see you had company. I'll come back later.'

'It's all right, Jim. Mr Hinchley here's one of us.'

Jim was uncomfortable.

'It's about the new security arrangements, Sir.'

'What's the problem, Captain?' said Hinchley from behind him.

Jim deliberately ignored him.

'I don't mind the two security log books, Sir,' he said to Cota, 'but apparently my security chief has been told that I'm not to have the one relating to the hotel staff and passengers.'

Cota was about to reply when Hinchley spoke.

'That's correct, Captain. We had a meeting about this and decided that this was the way to go. That way, we avoid any unpleasant problems between the ship and the hotel side.'

Jim turned.

'I was unaware that you were commanding the ship, Mr Hinchley.'

'This wasn't the Captain's decision. It was a company one. We will be bringing it in on all the ships. Well, the ones operating out of Lauderdale anyway.'

Jim looked at Cota. 'How do you feel about this? You know what it does. It takes any control of the passengers or the hotel staff away from us.'

Cota looked resigned. 'It's out of my hands, Captain.'

'Did you know about removing the pacifying equipment from security?'

'Again it was a company decision,' said Hinchley. 'We can't have a bunch of untrained people wandering around the ship with this kind of thing, Captain. Hell, if they used them, we could get sued for millions. Anyway, it's illegal.'

Jim turned back to Hinchley. He was getting angry.

'If you want them trained better, then train them, but that costs money doesn't it? Another thing, what they have isn't illegal. This is Panama don't forget, at least that's what the ensign and registration written on the stern showed the last time I looked. Next, you're interfering directly with the Captain's authority on the ship. And mine. How dare you order the equipment to be handed in to Shelby without discussing it with me first!'

'I'll remind you that I am the company's senior representative on board!'

'And I'll remind you that you have absolutely no authority on this ship or over me while the Captain is in command and if he isn't, then I am!'

'Not for long!'

'Please, gentlemen, stop this!' Cota was now standing behind his desk.

'Captain,' he said to Jim. 'I agreed to these changes. I am sorry. Yes we should have discussed them with you.'

Jim looked at him with disgust. 'No wonder we Captains are losing our authority to these bastards ashore. I know this didn't come from you. It came from him behind me.'

'Either way, Captain,' said Hinchley, 'it's the way things are and if you want to keep working at sea, you'd better get used to it.'

Jim walked out. It was pointless saying any more. If he stayed he would really lose it and that wouldn't do him any good.

On the second night at sea, Jim attended the Captain's cocktail party charade and then went down to dinner for the second sitting table. As he passed the Captain's table, he noticed that Hinchley from the Lauderdale office and his family were sitting on the table.

For a change, Jim had a young family on his table, Harvey Inch and his wife Shirley, together with their two teenage children, Andrew and Nicola. They were joined by a retired doctor and his wife, David and Isobel Chancery. Both were in their eighties but still fit. Once they found out that Jim had worked in the Arctic and Antarctic, their questions grew, especially from the children. He managed to convince them that where they were going they would not see sheet ice nor would the ship be breaking through any ice, much to the children's disappointment.

'I've been to most places,' said David, 'but always wanted to say I've been to the Arctic. It seemed so strange that we have been all over Asia yet, just a few miles to the North, there was this ocean we've never been near. Same with Canada; we've been to the cities but never up the St Lawrence.'

Jim smiled. 'You won't be disappointed. The St Lawrence is quite a place. The Saguenay is breathtaking and Quebec is one of my favourite cities, a breath of Europe in the heart of Northern America.'

'Do you know New York, Captain?' asked Shirley.

'I've been there a few times, but not really. I'm not a big city lover. Most sailors tend to only know the areas around where the ship is berthed. In the good old days, they were very lively areas and sailors didn't have to stray any further to find what they wanted. Generally that wasn't a museum or an art gallery. Now ports have become more industrialised, so many just stay on their ships, even if they're allowed ashore.'

'Can the Captain stop them?' asked Andrew.

'It's not the Captain, it's the ports that stop them.'

'But can they do that?' asked their father.

'It's a good question. Not really, but they use security as the reason and you know how serious that is especially in the States. To most ports, it's a good excuse to rid themselves of the problem of sailors wandering through the port area.'

'If I couldn't get off the ship, I wouldn't go on the ship in the first place,' said Nicola.

'Regrettably that's what a lot of sailors decide, especially if they can get better jobs ashore. Then they can earn enough money to come on a cruise ship and pay other sailors like me to take them around the ports instead.'

Jim said it with humour and they all laughed.

'Are you going ashore tomorrow, Captain?'

'Unfortunately no,' said Jim. 'We have a few safety drills to go through and as usual paperwork to catch up on, but I'm sure you are all going.' They all nodded.

'Isobel's brother lives there,' said David. 'They're meeting us when we arrive in the morning.'

Chapter 22

The ship sailed into New York early in the morning, but the decks were already packed with passengers watching the Statue of Liberty on the port side. Shortly afterwards, they berthed at the Manhattan terminal on 12th Avenue.

As the ship was between United States ports, there were not too many formalities. Jim was therefore surprised to see officials in the alleyway when he came off the bridge. Some were in civilian clothes, but others were in uniform. As Jim neared, he could see they were New York City Police. Two of them stopped him.

'Who are you?'

'I'm the Staff Captain of the ship. Just who are you?'

One of the officials spoke into a microphone in his sleeve.

He turned to Jim. 'Would you please go into the Captain's cabin, Sir?'

When he entered, the office was full of people, including Shelby and Winchester. She was crying. An official told Jim to continue on into the cabin. The cabin held several people, but was far less crowded. Cota, looking pale, was sitting on the edge of one of the chairs and around him there were other officials. One of them was Samuel Gully.

He looked up as Jim entered and smiled. 'Hi, Captain,' he said getting up. He came across and shook Jim's hand. The other officials were also getting up.

'Captain, I would like you to meet my boss, Senior Agent Brian Wheeler. Mr Wheeler, this is Captain Clariby.'

Wheeler extended his hand. 'A real pleasure, Captain. Sam here has told me what you did and we owe you our gratitude.'

'Can I ask what is going on, Sam?'

'Sure, we're arresting crew members who have been identified as being part of the drug racket. You will have seen Shelby and Winchester outside. They're both under arrest, but I don't think that will be a surprise to you. We've also got several others including the shop manager, hairdresser and head barman. Once they start talking, I have a feeling we'll have more, but they will be lower down the chain. We have the main culprits.' He smiled. 'Your Captain's in shock,' he said indicating to where Cota was sitting.

'What about him?' asked Jim.

'Clean so far.'

'I'm pleased.'

'It doesn't explain how this could have gone on under his nose for so long though,' said Wheeler.

'You have to know him to be able to answer that,' said Jim. 'He only sees what he wants to see. It's a company-wide problem.'

Jim went over to Cota, who looked up as he approached.

'I gather you knew about all this.'

'Yes, Sir,' replied Jim.

'Why didn't you tell me?'

'Because you might have been involved. You were thick with Shelby and Winchester.'

'They were my friends.'

'No they weren't, Captain. They were using you.'

'I've got some more bad news for you, Captain,' said Sam walking over. 'We're putting an extradition warrant out for Captain Adama Ricci.'

Cota said nothing.

Hinchley arrived. 'What's going on, Captain? The ship's rife with rumours about some officers being arrested.'

'I'll answer that, Hinchley,' said Jim. 'Your General Manager and Purser are under arrest for drug smuggling.'

'And others,' said Sam. 'There could also be more serious charges. Two people disappeared on the ship. We suspect they were murdered.'

Hinchley sat down. 'Jesus, what's the company going to say?'

'Probably going to deny that the ship belongs to them,' said Jim.

Hinchley looked at him. 'That's not funny,' he snarled. He turned to Wheeler. 'Is this going to interfere with the ship sailing this evening?'

'Not if we can get this cleared up quickly,' said Wheeler. 'We may have more questions when she returns though.'

'What still needs to be done?'

'Well, we have forensic teams in the rooms where the drugs were stored. They are taking fingerprints and samples of residues to establish that the drugs were carried there. We will want statements from a number of crew, including the Staff Captain, the surgeon and a few others.'

'We will give you all the cooperation possible,' said Hinchley. 'Clariby, everyone is busy here. I would like to use your office to talk to Lauderdale and Southampton.'

'Be my guest.'

Hinchley left the cabin.

'What are you going to do with those people out there?' asked Cota.

'We'll get them off the ship now, Captain,' answered Wheeler. 'We won't cuff them until we get them off. We don't want to cause any fuss. Hopefully, our teams will be finished by early afternoon, and then we will give you permission to sail.'

'I'll just go out and say goodbye to them,' said Cota.

When he was gone, Jim shrugged. 'They have been friends for a long time,' he commented.

'That's what we find puzzling. As yet there is no link, but I reckon that woman will sing like a bird. We'll get all the story.'

'Either way, this is going to hit the papers,' said Jim. 'His career is finished regardless.'

'That's not my concern, Captain. I just put the bad guys away. By the way, did you know that the DEA has a reward policy? From what I see, you are going to get a substantial award.'

'I never thought of that.'

'Well, if you have a mortgage, it will certainly take care of that.'

'Really? Well, I'm not going to be noble and say I don't want it. When I leave here, it will come in very useful.'

'Good. I'm pleased.' Wheeler looked at his watch. 'Time to be on our way. We've given them long enough to say their goodbyes next door. Sam will keep in touch with you, Captain. I gather you're leaving after this cruise.'

'That's right.'

'Then be careful. This isn't the only cruise ship where we are arresting people. The FBI also hopes to set up an investigation into all the disappearances of people on these ships. There are just too many for them all to be accidents.'

'Don't worry. I'm heading for a proper ship.'

'Best of luck, Captain.'

They left the cabin and, after collecting their prisoners, they headed off ashore. There was silence again.

Cota appeared and sat down.

Jim went to go, but Cota waved to him. 'Stay please, Jim. Sit down.'

He looked at Jim. 'I really never knew. You have to believe that,' pleaded Cota.

'Strangely, I do, Captain.'

'I'm finished now, you know. They will blame me.'

Jim knew he was right but said nothing.

'All these years for nothing.'

'There are other ships, Captain. Other companies.'

'Who the hell will want me? All I know is cruise ships. And it appears I don't know much about them either.'

Hinchley came back into the cabin.

'The company is naturally very upset. They are getting their damage control people onto this now and their lawyers. As long as there are no more delays, it looks like we will sail on time tonight. The Deputy Purser has been promoted temporarily to Purser. That's no problem and there is no problem in the assistants of those lower down who have been arrested going up one grade. Southampton has decided that, as I am here, I will take over as General Ship Manager for the remainder of the cruise. It will give me good experience and I'm looking forward to it. We will make no official statement on board. The vast majority won't give a toss and in two days they will have forgotten all about it.'

'The crew will talk,' said Jim.

'Let them. They're always talking. No one listens.'

He pointed at Jim. 'You knew about this.'

'Obviously.'

'Then why the fuck didn't you tell me?'

'Because you might have been involved.'

'Me?'

'Why not. Think of all the cover-ups that have taken place over incidents on board. How were we to know you weren't covering this up?'

'The company won't forget this. They'll tell other companies. You won't find it easy to get a job as Captain after this.'

Jim got up and bent over Hinchley.

'Don't threaten me,' he said softly. 'I'm not the Captain. If I were you, I would worry more about your own career than mine. Just a thought for you to take to bed tonight.'

Vacuum Pioneer

*The 'Vacuum Pioneer' had arrived in Halifax in the early
morning, and Briget and Gerdy immediately headed down
the gangway for the downtown shops. They returned in
the early afternoon and, as there was no cargo work that
night, were now with the Captain, Chief Engineer and
Chief Officer in a club on the waterfront, after a superb
seafood dinner.*

*Gerdy and the Captain were watching Briget and the
Chief Officer dancing. The Chief Engineer was chatting
to a blonde at the bar.*

'There's no future in it,' Karl said to Gerdy. 'He's
determined to stay at sea.'

'He's a nice young man though, and it didn't stop us
did it?' said Gerdy.

'It works sometimes.'

'Still, let her have her holiday romance.'

'As long as she doesn't tire him out. He has to do a
watch.'

'I seem to remember you had no trouble.'

'What do you mean had? Come on.' He took her hand
and they joined Briget on the dance floor.

*The Chief, Trond, was making good headway with the
blonde lady, who turned out to be a dentist at the city
hospital. They were of a similar age and she liked his
easy going approach and his blue eyes. They went onto
the dance floor and then joined Karl and his family at
their table.*

'Susan here tells me that there is a late night jazz club
not too far away,' said Trond. 'We're going on there.
Would you like to join us?'

'Not me,' said Karl. 'We're heading back to the ship,
but maybe Briget and Eric would like to.'

'Yes please,' replied Briget. They said their goodbyes and headed off, leaving Karl and Gerdy.

After another dance, they left and went outside into the street. Despite it being summer, there was a chill in the air. Gerdy huddled close to Karl. 'Let's walk for a while,' she said. 'Briget's growing up. She'll be on her way soon.'

'You'll be able to join me more often then,' said Karl.

She said nothing for a moment.

'You know they're looking for Pilots in Bergen,' she said. 'My cousin Lars loves piloting there and he says they would employ you if you applied.'

'You've been talking to him about it then?' Karl asked.

'It came up in conversation. It would be nice to have you home after all these years. I've never asked you to leave the sea before, have I?'

'No, you haven't.'

'And I won't this time, but it's just that it would be so good to be together as a family for a while before she goes and then when she's gone we would be together.'

'Let me think about it.'

'You will?'

'If it's what you want.'

She stopped him. 'No, Karl, that wouldn't work. It has to be what you want as well.'

They stood on the pavement and he put his arms around her. 'Strangely, these last few years, the sea has begun to lose its appeal. It's all changing out there. Tell you what, when you go back, tell Lars that I am interested and we'll fix an interview for my next leave.'

Her eyes sparked.

'Karl, that will be wonderful!' She hugged him closer.

Karl flagged down an approaching taxi. 'I only said an interview, mind.'

'That's enough,' said Gerdy.

Chapter 23

Eventually the various agency officials left the ship. The returning passengers were curious about the events that had taken place, but nobody seemed unduly perturbed. The ship sailed on time out of New York harbour at sunset and onto a calm sea. Captain Cota had been on the bridge throughout the transit, but as soon as the Pilot departed, he left the bridge without a word. Jim remained on the bridge until the ship had cleared the heavy traffic in the approaches and then ordered the courses and speeds required. Peter, the navigator, had the watch.

'The Captain seems a bit upset,' he remarked.

'He's had a trying day. Give him a little time.'

'Is it all sorted now?' asked Peter.

'I certainly hope so. Now, let's concentrate on the ship rather than the Captain's health.' Jim looked at one of the radar screens. 'Looks like we're clear of the main traffic, just the usual coastal stuff, north and south bound. Keep an eye out for fishing boats. I'm going down now; she's all yours.'

Jim went down to his cabin and changed for dinner. At his table, the passengers talked animatedly about their day in New York.

'So, you didn't make it ashore, Captain?' said David Chancery.

'Regretfully no. We were a little busy.'

'So we heard. You lost a few people, I gather.'

'Not for too long. They'll be returning for the next cruise.'

'Let's hope so.' David wasn't stupid. He didn't pursue it and the conversation reverted back to New York.

Jim made his excuses as soon as he could. As he passed Jan's table, he indicated with his head for Jan to follow him.

Jim waited outside the restaurant for Jan who quickly joined him.

'I presume you know what has been going on?'

'Can hardly avoid it. The galley radio is buzzing.'

'Well, I intend to give a briefing to all the department officers on the bridge tomorrow morning, so you can come along to that. Hopefully the affair is over now.'

'At least we got rid of Shelby and the Purser.'

'Unfortunately, only to be replaced by a bigger bastard. I don't know how Winchester got involved though.'

'That's easy, Captain. Shelby was screwing her.'

'Stupid man. Standard rule: screw passengers, don't use the "ship's bicycles".'

'Sorry, Captain?'

'It's a very crude expression from long ago on passenger ships. The female staff who played around were referred to as "ship's bicycles".

Jan laughed. 'Not to their faces obviously!'

'Bloody right. These days you would probably get hauled in front of some tribunal. I'm going to hang around the cabin this evening. The Captain is still a bit disturbed by the events. I'll see you with the other officers at 0900 tomorrow. Tell the Chief Security Officer to attend.'

Jim spent the evening working in his office, catching up on emails, reports and various bits of paper that seemed to grow on his desk overnight like mushrooms. Before going to bed, he visited the bridge. It was a calm night and the sky was clear with the moon and stars only dimly showing because of the bewildering array of lights from the ship that illuminated the sea around them as she followed her course. The ship moved easily to a very light swell on the starboard bow. All the traffic from the

New York area had disappeared and the ship was alone except for a distant light on the horizon.

The Junior Second Officer had the watch along with one of the Third Officers and a cadet. They were anxious for news about the events of the day.

'I'm having a meeting on the bridge in the morning,' Jim said, 'so there is no point in repeating myself. I'll see you then.'

He went down to his cabin and turned in.

The phone went. Jim woke instantly thanks to long years of training. He pressed the speaker button. It was the Senior Second Officer on the bridge. 'Nothing serious, Sir, but it's 0200. The Captain hasn't been up to sign the night orders.'

'Thank you, Second Mate. Leave it with me.'

Jim put on the light and swung out of bed. He grabbed his bathrobe and headed out of the door for the Captain's cabin. The office was in darkness, but light was coming from under the door of the dayroom. Jim knocked. There was no reply so he knocked again. Nothing, but there was the faint sound of music playing. He opened the door cautiously and looked inside. The dayroom appeared empty, but then Jim noticed one of the easy chairs drawn near the forward looking window. Cota was slumped in it.

'Captain?' Jim queried.

Cota didn't answer. Jim approached slowly and called again.

Cota opened his eyes.

'Staff Captain.' It was a statement rather than a question.

'Yes, Sir.'

Jim could smell the alcohol as he got closer. He could also see there was an almost empty bottle of whisky on the table by the chair and that Cota had a glass in his hand.

'I'm sorry to disturb you, Sir, but the bridge was concerned that you had not written the night orders. I'll go up and write them on your behalf.'

'Get yourself a drink,' ordered Cota.

'Sir, it's better that I …'

'I said get yourself a drink and sit down!' Cota was slurring his words.

Jim took a glass from the sideboard, sat down by Cota and poured himself a small whisky.

'So you won.' Cota raised his glass, his arm swaying and spilling some of his drink. 'Here's to you.'

'Sir, no one has won. This wasn't a competition.'

Cota looked blearily at Jim.

'They used me. I thought they were my friends.'

Jim said nothing. Let Cota talk, he thought.

Cota sighed heavily. 'Even Adama.'

There was silence again.

'So stupid. How could I have been so stupid?' He looked at Jim. 'You must understand. I knew nothing about the drugs. Yes, I knew they were on board, but they're on all these ships. They convinced me that we should accept that. Part of the life you see? Party time. Always party time.'

'Sir, there's no need …'

'Shut up!' exploded Cota.

There was silence for a while and then Cota continued.

'She'll talk you know, that bitch. She got me involved. She gave me money. She said it was my share of the usual business. You know, the scams. You were Captain of a cruise ship; you must have taken money as well.'

'I knew about the scams and stopped what I could, but I never took any money.'

Cota leered at Jim. 'Of course, Saint Jim.'

'Captain, it's late. Why not go to bed now?'

'I'm finished, you know.'

'Captain, listen to me. No one knows what will happen, but until then, whatever is decided, we have a ship to run. You have a ship to command. You can either sit here for the voyage feeling sorry for yourself or you can take command again. We can't change what's happened, but we can run a proper ship.'

Cota was watching Jim, not speaking.

'Sir, regardless of what's happened, I'm your Staff Captain.'

'It's too late.'

'Bullshit! It's never too late! Think what you used to be like when you first got your command, before you got involved with all this shit. When you were a proper seaman, not some toy sailor. You can do it again.'

For a moment, Cota said nothing. He just carried on looking at Jim.

'One last try. Who knows? Maybe we could. I don't know. I'm tired,' slurred Cota.

The glass dropped from his hand.

Jim got up. 'Come on, Sir. Time for bed.' He bent over Cota and helped him to his feet. He eased him to the bedroom, where Cota fell onto the bed. Jim removed Cota's shoes and undid his bow tie and shirt.

You poor bastard, he thought. He put the lights out and quietly shut the door, leaving the cabin.

Jim went up onto the bridge.

'The Captain has asked me to write the orders up tonight.'

He checked the visibility and traffic, and then scribbled the standard phrases.

'You'll note that I have said to call me if there are any problems,' he said to the Second Officer.

'Yes, Sir.'

Jim had one last look around before leaving the bridge. It was still a calm night, at least outside the ship if not inside, thought Jim.

Chapter 24

The deck officers, cadets and Bert Fallows were assembled on the bridge in the morning when Jim arrived. He ran through the basics of what had happened in New York.

'What is the Captain going to do?' asked Peter.

'I'm not aware he should do anything,' said Jim, 'unless you would like to make a few suggestions?'

No one offered any.

'Let's get one thing straight. The Captain was as much in the dark as all of you were about what was going on. Obviously, as they were senior officers, he was involved with them, but that's as far as it went. I don't want any speculation on things that don't exist. These things happen at sea, although hopefully not too often. Best of all, it's over now and we can settle back into normal ship routine. What I don't want is you speculating with the punters. It's none of their business, so let's keep it that way.'

At 0930, Jim presented himself at the Captain's office. Cota was working at his desk and beckoned Jim to sit down.

He looked a little embarrassed. 'Jim, I want to apologise for last night.'

'Sir, there is nothing to apologise for.'

'Yes there is. I was drunk.'

'What Captain hasn't been? You're not going to repeat it and you had plenty of reason to, shall we say, indulge.'

Cota smiled faintly. 'Thank you for putting it so nicely. If it helps, I don't feel very well this morning.'

'It's forgotten, Sir.'

'As you said last night, we have a ship to run. So, what now?' asked Cota.

'It's in your hands, Sir. We have a heads of department meeting at 1100 with our new Ship Manager.'

'You know, I've never liked the idea of Ship Managers, or Hinchley for that matter.'

'There are a few things that I want to raise with you before we go down.'

'Go on,' said Cota.

'As you know, I objected to the interference with the security personnel, particularly the log books and removal of equipment.'

'And I didn't support you, did I?'

'No, Sir,' Jim answered.

'Anything else?'

'Drugs, Sir.' Jim waited. Cota said nothing. 'I fully believe we have stopped the main problem on board, but we should remain vigilant. We need a zero tolerance regime regardless of the company image. We must be allowed at least random checks of the crew, and the ability to remove any passengers suspected of drug abuse, regardless of who they are. That way we keep the gains we have made.'

Cota nodded. 'I have a feeling that Hinchley and the hotel crowd won't be very happy about that. Right, Jim, as always with you, it should prove an interesting meeting. I'll see you down there. Tell them to start without me.'

Jim arrived to find Iain and Patrick already sitting there. Iain winked at Jim as he sat down. Hinchley ignored his arrival and continued to shuffle his papers. Jean Sinter, a smart black woman newly promoted to Purser, sat by his side. Around the table were the Cruise Director and his wife, Scott and Vivien Pierre, and Henry Milau, the Hotel Manager.

Eventually Hinchley looked up. 'Where's Cota?'

'You mean where's *Captain* Cota,' said Jim. 'He's on his way. He said to start without him.'

Hinchley looked disconcerted. 'We'll wait for him,' he said. They sat in silence for a few minutes.

'How are you, Jim?' asked Iain.

'Fine, Iain,' said Jim. 'How are you, Iain?'

'Fine, Jim,' said Iain.

'How are you, Patrick?' asked Jim.

'Fine thank you, Captain. How are you?'

'I'm fine, Patrick. How are you, Vivien?'

'Stop it!' shouted Hinchley before she could reply. 'You're behaving like children!'

Iain had a broad grin on his face. Jim yawned and then stretched. Patrick looked at his watch.

The door opened and Cota walked in.

'Hope I'm not interrupting anything?' he said.

'We were waiting for you, Captain,' replied Hinchley.

'Didn't Jim tell you to carry on without me?' asked Cota.

'He did,' said Iain, 'but Mr Hinchley decided to wait.'

'Please sit down, Captain. We have a busy schedule. Now, I want to discuss the bridge broadcasts for going up the St Lawrence.'

'Drugs,' said Cota.

'I beg your pardon?' said Hinchley.

'Drugs. We will discuss drugs first.'

'The issue has been dealt with.'

'Not by me it hasn't. Now it will be.'

'Captain ...'

'Mr Hinchley, I'm speaking.'

Hinchley's mouth opened, but no sound came out.

'Thank you. Now, as I was saying, drugs. We know what has been going on in the ship. I'm not talking about the smuggling, but about the sale of drugs to the passengers by crew. From now on, our policy is zero tolerance both for crew and passengers. The Staff Captain will give orders to the security staff this morning to that effect. I also expect all ship's officers to watch out for this and to take action when required. Anyone found in possession will be treated exactly as if they were ashore and will be handed over to the authorities.' Jim had been holding his breath and slowly let it out.

'You can't do this, Captain,' said Hinchley. 'You know the company policy on involving the shore authorities. It must be approved by the office ashore.'

'Not any more, Mr Hinchley. I've had enough of this interference in operating the ship. The ship will now be operated according to marine law and the laws of Panama. Also, if you try to stop this by calling the office, I will have no hesitation in giving a press conference in Quebec on some very interesting private orders I have had in the past. I keep a record of these, Mr Hinchley.'

'That's blackmail!'

'Probably. But just think how bad it is that I have to do that in order to get control of the ship back from you people.' He stood up and looked at them all.

'You know, I actually thought you were right. This was the way to the future. I let myself be taken in by all the glitter. I stood by and watched you all covering yourselves with gold braid and said nothing. I saw sensible seamanship standards changed to suit the hotel instead of the passengers' safety and I did nothing. We worry more about whether the surf machine works or the palm trees look real than whether we can cope with emergencies. I'm not blaming you. You're ignorant of the sea, but I'm not. I'm supposed to be a seaman and I should have protested. Well, now I am.'

Pierre, the Cruise Director, interrupted. 'It's a bit late in the day, Captain, to suddenly get on your high horse. You forget that we know things about you.'

'Of course you do. We're all linked, aren't we? But, I tell you, the lunatics are no longer in charge of the asylum. All I ever really wanted was to come to sea and become a Captain. I'm not a celebrity; I'm just a seaman. Now, I've talked enough. Mr Hinchley, while we have this General Manager business, then by all means carry on, but you do not interfere in any safety aspect of the ship. The Staff Captain is my deputy and whatever he wants for safety you will comply with, as will everyone else on board. Now, if you will excuse me, I'll leave you to your meeting.'

They sat in stunned silence when the door closed. Even Jim hadn't expected that.

'He's finished,' said Hinchley.

'He's having a breakdown,' said Scott, his wife nodding in agreement.

'I'll tell you what he's doing,' said Jim. 'He's taking the ship back, and even if it's for this one cruise, I am under his command and support him.'

'Well said,' said Iain.

'Another thing. No one will speak in any derogatory way again about the Captain in my presence. Do you all understand that?' He looked round the room at each officer.

'You have to admit he went a bit far, Jim,' said Scott.

'Mr Pierre, I admit nothing. You forget he's the Captain. You are a comedian in a uniform. He has the responsibility for all on board. You hang around the bars waiting for passengers to buy you drinks. There is a hell of a difference.' He saw Scott about to speak.

'Don't! Don't say a word. Now, let's all calm down and get on with the meeting. One more thing, Mr Hinchley. Certain equipment belonging to the security staff was taken by the previous General Manager. That will be returned immediately after this meeting. The Senior Security Officer will collect it.'

He looked at Hinchley, waiting. Hinchley looked back and realised this was not the time to argue. Instead, he looked down at the agenda.

'Gentlemen, we will return to the meeting.'

The meeting ended forty minutes later. Outside, Iain grabbed Jim by the arm and, together with Patrick, led him to a quiet place.

'Christ, Jim. That was something. Does he mean it?'

'I hope so, yes.'

'About time. Mind you, I wouldn't like to be in his shoes when the ship gets back to Fort Lauderdale. Hinchley will have his scalp.'

'Iain, the Old Man knows that he's through, certainly on this ship and maybe in the fleet. He's trying to set things straight before he goes.'

'If only he'd started this way when he came here.'

'He probably thinks the same, but if he had been intending on doing that, do you think he would ever have been appointed? They want politically acceptable Captains on these ships, not seamen, although from my short experience, they need bloody street fighters as well.'

'Well, Jim, good luck to him and to you. For what it's worth, you have the backing of my department.'

Vacuum Pioneer

Far from the social world of cruise ships was the technical world of the 'Vacuum Pioneer'. The complexity of her various cargo tanks was monitored from the cargo control room. The state board ran down one side of the room, the coloured lights and dials showing the state of the tanks and the filling rates.

Because of the dangerous nature of the cargoes and the gases they generated, the strictest safety precautions were maintained throughout the ship, especially during cargo operations, which were regarded as the most dangerous time. Cargo operations on all ships are the domain of the Chief Officer or Mate. On the 'Vacuum Pioneer', Eric had watched over the Second and Third Officers during their watches from the control chair and occasionally went on deck. The work, while hazardous, was routine for the ship. Eric was especially pleased with how Ivo had handled his cargo watch.

The cargo discharge was completed in the early afternoon, just as the Captain and his family returned to the ship. Once the departure formalities were completed, the Pilot boarded and the ship eased out of her berth, turned and sailed through Halifax harbour. Once the Pilot had been dropped off, they headed out of the outward separation channel to the sea. Once clear, they turned towards the north east, heading for Cape Race on the Newfoundland coast before turning northwards for Nuuk in Greenland.

Briget joined Eric on the bridge in the late afternoon. When she arrived, she made coffee for them both and they sat in the command chairs looking out over the sea. Biscuit, the cat, was sitting contentedly on top of the flag locker, having just finished a plate of fish courtesy of the

Cook. It was a fresh day with the wind picking up from ahead. A swell was coming in from the east causing the ship to roll easily. There was a chill in the air, the heat dying from the sun as evening approached.

'Whenever we head this way, I always feel like we are leaving civilisation behind,' Eric said. 'When we cruise the coast in other parts of the world, you always see lights from the towns and houses scattered along the coast. Here, once we get up to Cape Race, there is nothing except for St John's.'

'How far is it?' asked Briget.

'About 450 miles to Cape Race and then just over a thousand miles to Nuuk. I like the trip. Let me qualify that; I like it in summer, like now. The weather is usually pleasant, although it can still blow up. In winter, it can be bad, especially with the ice.'

'What about Nuuk?'

'Same, up and down. I've been there in summer when it's been 23 degrees. Then again, it can be 9 degrees.'

'Is it a big place?'

'Not really. It's more like a town than a regular capital, very pleasant though. Nice people, some great bars and restaurants. You'll like it there. Anyway, being Norwegian, we're meant to be used to the cold.'

'Doesn't mean we have to like it. What's the local food like?'

'I suggest you give the whale blubber and seabirds a miss, but the cod is the best you've ever tasted.'

He got up from the command chair and looked at the radar. Then he picked up his binoculars and looked astern.

'We've got one of those huge hotel ships coming up on us,' he said, passing the binoculars to Briget. She took them and looked astern.

'It seems to be crossing over our stern.'

'She's heading for the St Lawrence. Next port Quebec.' Eric was standing over the automatic identification system display.

'She's the 'Majestic Sea'.'

They watched as the ship gradually overhauled them and crossed their stern to appear abeam on their portside.

'Why are her boats so low down to the sea?' Briget asked.

'I really don't know,' Eric replied. 'I've enough to do knowing all the tanker regulations without worrying about theirs.'

'Won't they get damaged or washed away in bad weather?'

'They're not built for bad weather.'

Briget put the binoculars down. 'It looks so ugly.' She came to him and put her arms around him, giving him a kiss. 'I'll see you tonight.'

Eric glanced quickly towards the bridge door.

'Every time you do that, I think your father is going to come through that door.'

'Don't worry about him. He's lovely.'

'To you, yes, not to a Mate who's sleeping with his daughter.'

Briget laughed. 'My Mother knows.'

'Your Mother's not the Captain. Now go. I have work to do. See you tonight.'

Chapter 25

That evening after dinner, Jim was sitting in the piano lounge with Jan, Iain, Patrick and the ship's Surgeon, Dick Brentwood. The waiter arrived with their drinks. Dick spluttered as he tasted his.

'Give this back to the barman and tell him it's for the ship's Surgeon not a punter.'

The waiter disappeared. 'Some of the barmen have changed,' Dick said. 'Not that I'm complaining, it's just that I had finally taught them how to make a good martini. Now I'll have to start again.'

Many of the passengers were sitting or standing at the glass windows on the port side of the lounge. The lights on the shore were visible and ships frequently passed by.

'We are just passing the northern coast of New Brunswick on the approaches to the St Lawrence,' Jim explained. 'About 50 miles to go to the river.'

'When do we pick the Pilot up?' asked Patrick.

'In the morning at Escoumins. A couple of Pilots board there, and then we head up to Quebec, getting there by early afternoon.'

Dick's martini arrived. He tasted it and smiled.

'Thank the barman please. Tell him he gets a free consultation on penis enlargement.'

He looked at them all.

'Seriously, the lads are heavily into it. I once had a sailor who hung heavy nuts and bolts from the engine room on his. Trouble was he went to his bunk which was one of the upper berth ones and jumped out next morning leaving the weight in the bunk. Very messy,' Dick said grimacing.

'We're going ashore tomorrow night, Jim. Coming with us?' asked Iain.

'I'd like to, but it all depends on how things go.'

'As the ship's in until the next evening, we can relax a little.'

'I'll certainly try to make it.'

'Good. We'll hold you to that.'

'What's the Saguenay like?' asked Jan.

'Stunning, like all of Quebec. It's unique because it's the only fjord in Northern America. They've recently built a passenger terminal there so we can go alongside at La Baie, not that there's much there, but you can go up to Chicoutimi or Lac Saint-Jean. Really the visit is for the scenery.'

Helen finished playing the piano and wheeled her chair over to join them.

A waiter followed bringing her drink with her. She raised it.

'Can I say congratulations?'

'As long as you don't say it too loud,' said Jim smiling. They all raised their glasses.

In the morning, the ship closed in to the shore at Escoumins and briefly slowed to allow the two Pilots to join before picking up speed again for the busy river transit to Quebec.

Jim met with Jan in his office to plan the fire exercise for the next morning when most of the passengers would be ashore. They scanned through the drill lists that had been undertaken over the past month.

'We seem to have exercised just about all the crew at various times so we are up to date,' said Jim.

'We haven't ever run a major one in the passenger accommodation.'

'Which deck do you want to use?' asked Jim.

'I thought deck 4 on the starboard side. It should be quieter with the ship alongside on the port side,' explained Jan. 'That's where we will start from, but I expect you will spread the fire.'

'Make sure all the fire teams have shoe covers on. The last thing we want is the hotel people screaming about their bloody carpets.'

'I thought you could decide on the fire and limits and give the situation to me in the emergency control room. From there, I will direct the four teams.'

'That makes sense. I'll base myself on the bridge so we can also monitor the communication between yourself and the bridge. You'll need observers with each team and a senior officer in the emergency room vetting you and your staff there.'

'All organised. The Staff Chief Engineer will be watching over me and I have arranged other non-involved officers for the teams. Surprisingly, the new Purser will be one of them. She's all for it.'

'So, we're going to call the entire engine department and deck department to full emergency stations and a part of the hotel side for those involved in the fire parties.'

'That's right.'

'What about involving the shore brigades?'

'No, Sir. I want this to be a ship at sea scenario.'

'The medics?'

'All arranged. They will be stood too, as well as the first aid parties.'

'You seem to have it all covered. I look forward to this.'

Shortly after Jan left, Bert appeared.

'Got all your equipment back then?'

'Yes, Sir, without a murmur. I have brought the log books for the last few days with me.'

'Sit down, Bert.'

Jim scanned through the logs, which contained the usual minor theft and drunkenness reports but nothing untoward. 'I'm sure that most of these small thefts are people simply leaving things lying around. They don't look deliberate to me, just opportunistic.'

'That's right, Sir. The report by one of the shops last voyage was simply a mistake in stock-taking.' Bert shrugged. 'It happens.'

'I see we have the usual female underwear missing. That's been going on ever since I set foot on passenger ships.'

'They can't remember whose cabin they left them in.'

Jim laughed.

'Just one drug report then.'

'Yes, Sir. I understand the zero tolerance policy, but I used my discretion over that. It was a fourteen year old girl with a small joint. I think she had been given it. I took her to her parents and they gave her hell. I thought that was enough.'

'Good. That's exactly how it should have been handled.' Jim gave the log books back to Bert.

'So far it looks like a quiet trip. Let's hope it stays that way. Now, I want to talk to you about something. When I joined the 'Sea Breeze', I had the idea to form a small squad which, for want of a better term, I called the panic squad. The idea was that, in the event of an emergency and if things started to get out of control, they would act as a control group to deal with any problems, like a rush to get on the boats or something similar.'

Bert nodded. 'Some of my mates in different cruise ship companies told me they had a similar thing, unofficial of course. Not when the ships were run with well-trained crews, but later when they became a cruise company and lots of half-trained crews started coming on board. We've often talked amongst ourselves about what would happen here.'

'What were your conclusions?'

'Bloody chaos, Sir.'

'Hell, Bert. That doesn't give me much confidence.'

'You asked, Sir. I mean what do we expect? We don't have enough boats, except for those silly liferafts and we have a thousand odd crew from twenty different nationalities, many of whom don't understand English. They've had a few days training and most have certificates that aren't worth the paper they're printed on. Mix them together with three thousand punters, most of whom are pensioners, and if anything serious happens, it's a recipe for disaster.'

Jim was tapping his desk with his pen. Slowly, he said, 'Suppose I told you very quietly and discreetly to form a group. Let's call it an emergency control group. This would be formed around your security team. Add in the fire control people and the cadets. That should give you a good team.'

'Not enough,' said Bert. 'We need more than that. What about some of the sailors?'

'No. They are all needed for the boats. You're going to have to draw them from the hotel side. What about the fitness centre? There are a few there. Some of them must have been in the forces.'

Bert thought. 'Leave it with me. I will have a look around and see who I can use. You know that this will get out as soon as we start approaching them.'

'Make it casual, as if it's your idea. Don't mention me. When you've got a list then I'll meet them.'

'What about weapons?'

'Are you suggesting that we arm them? That's impossible.'

'Captain, you're going to have to face this. They won't be able to do much with their bare hands if things get rough.'

'No, Bert. I accept that you have your weapons, but I cannot arm the others.'

'I'm not talking about guns, Sir, but they should at least have truncheons. Do you remember, they used to be normal in the old days? I remember when we were quartermasters doing the rounds on the passenger ships, we always carried them. They also used to give the deck officers making the rounds at night thick rubber torches. They weren't just for lighting the way.'

'These are different times, Bert.'

'And now the problem is far worse!'

'How would we get them?'

'If you give me permission, I'll see if I can make contact with the police suppliers in Quebec. Police will be on the berth and we always liaise with them at all the ports. It's not as if we are asking for anything illegal. You'll have to pay for them of course.'

'That's not a problem. We can lose it in the department budget. Bert, if you can, get them, but don't issue them. Just have them ready. Is that understood?'

'Completely, Sir. This is between you and me. Are you going to tell the Captain?'

'No. He has enough on his plate without this, especially as there is only a remote chance they will ever be required.'

'There's just one more thing, Sir. This is awkward, but just in case anything should ever happen and we have to use this team, there will be questions afterwards. You know, there always are. Punters will complain, lawyers, whatever. Could I have some kind of authority from you for this? I swear it won't ever leave my possession, but it will at least give me some kind of protection if things go pear-shaped.'

'One moment.' Jim reached for a sheet of paper and wrote several lines on it. He then signed the paper and handed it to Bert.

'This states that you will be forming an embarkation control group and that I have authorised it to be equipped with pacifying equipment. Is that sufficient?'

'That's all I want, Sir. I'll keep you advised as to how this goes.'

In the afternoon, the green roof tops of Quebec came into view and shortly after the ship was berthed at the passenger terminal. For the American passengers who had never been to Europe, this first view was fascinating, as Quebec has a lovely aged look that does not exist in the United States. Before long, most of the passengers had left and the ship became quiet again for a while.

That evening, Jim went ashore with Iain, Helen and the others. They went into the old town to a French restaurant that Iain had pre-booked. It was packed, with just their table available. The waiter came over to them. 'I will speak in French or English, whichever you prefer.'

'I think you had better make that English,' said Iain. 'My French is rusty.'

'You are Mr Macgregor?'

'That's me.'

'The piano is over there,' the waiter said pointing towards the wall.

'I didn't know that you played piano, Iain,' said Helen.

'I don't.'

'Then who's it for?'

'It was meant to be a surprise,' muttered Iain.

'Like you were going to look around and say, Oh look there's a piano! Why don't you give us a tune?'

'Something like that.'

'Give him a break, Helen,' said Jim laughing.

The evening was a great success. Helen did play the piano; she had a surprising repertoire of French songs. The whole restaurant joined in the more popular ones. Bottles of wine appeared on their table from various grateful customers.

'I think I'll marry the girl and stay here,' said Iain. 'Send her out to work and live on the proceeds.'

They had intended to go on elsewhere from the restaurant, but when another customer appeared with an accordion, they decided to stay. Shortly after midnight, they climbed into taxis and returned to the ship. Jim went to sleep as soon as his head hit the pillow.

The next morning the security officers sealed off the exercise area. The few remaining passengers had been asked to vacate their cabins for an hour or remain inside.

The broadcasts had warned those remaining on board and they were all set. Jim was on the bridge with one of the Third Officers and a cadet. The ship's deck plan was laid out and set up on the computer screen.

They watched the bridge clock approaching 1000 hours and then Jim gave the signal and the cadet sounded the fire alarms.

Within minutes, the reports of the stations manning came in.

'Tell them we have a fire report on deck 4, port side, cabins 56 to 58.'

They waited a moment and then Jim spread the fire. 'More sensors indicating fire 56 to 68.'

'Safety Officer reports moving fire parties from aft and forward in towards the fire. He's also joining the two central parties into one.'

'Tell him we have phone calls from passengers trapped in cabins 60 and 68. Numbers 2 pax in one and two in the other. Also fire sensors show smoke on deck 5 above 56.'

'Safety Officer requesting permission to open fire doors on deck 4 to get the hose parties in.'

'Permission granted.'

'Safety Officer reports after fire party designated boundary cooling and sent to deck 5, cabin 56. All electrical circuits isolated deck 3, 4 and 5 port side. Cabins 40 to 70.'

Jim smiled. 'Let's turn the heat up. Who's leading the after fire party?'

'Junior Second Officer, Sir,' replied the cadet.

'Tell him he's injured and out of play. Tell the Safety Officer there is heavy smoke on deck 5 area. Cabin 56, six passengers trapped. Also reports that the deck is hot in area cabin 56, deck 4.'

'Safety Officer reports the forward fire party moving down to deck 3 for investigation under cabin 56. Cadet Zhou is now in charge of aft fire party.'

'Fire party 4 reporting four breathing apparatus manned and searching for pax. Deck 5.'

'From Safety Officer, fire is now contained on deck 4.'

'Tell him he has four casualties, two burns and two pax smoke inhalation. Tell after fire party they have four pax casualties. Tell the forward fire party the fire is endangering the lifeboats. Lower lifeboats 3, 5 and 7 down clear of the embarkation area deck 3. That'll give them something to think about.'

The exercise continued for several more minutes and then Jim called a halt.

'Tell them all to stand down. The exercise is completed. I want the Safety Officer, all the auditing officers and leaders of the fire parties to report to my cabin at 1200 together with the ship's Surgeon. The security officers can take the barriers down and let the passengers move again. Please thank the passengers on the Captain's behalf for their cooperation.'

At 1200, Jim's cabin was ready and soon it was full. He had arranged waiters to be present and a buffet table was laid in the office. The chatter was incessant as each team leader and the auditors discussed and argued together. Captain Cota was also there.

'It's certainly got them going,' he said to Jim.

'That's what I was hoping for. We have everyone mixed in together, even some from the hotel side. And they are all talking about fire and how they did. Look at the Purser.'

The Purser was in animated discussion with the Safety Officer, Zhou and the Chief Engineer.

'Of course we have to wait for the collation of the reports, but I am certain that this was invaluable. Have you heard anything from Hinchley, Sir?'

'Not a word. He's probably laying low, waiting for an opportunity.'

'Anyway, Sir, thank you for this.'

'No, Jim, we should have done it a long time ago. Let's just hope the ship never has to use it.'

Later that evening, the ship sailed from Quebec. Some passengers had gone on tour and would join the ship in Saguenay the next day. The passage was at slow speed and was timed for the passengers to see the scenery of the fjord at breakfast time.

At dinner that night, the Inches and the Chancerys were regaling Jim with their trips ashore in Quebec.

'I'm so pleased you enjoyed it. It's one of my favourite cities,' said Jim.

'It's so different to America,' said Andrew Inch.

'One day, you'll go to Europe and see many cities and towns like that,' said Jim.

'Is it like that in the Saguenay?' asked David Chancery.

'No, not really. It's more like the standard Northern American town places. You will find that not too many people speak English though.'

'Why is that?' asked Nicola Inch.

'Because Quebec was once a French province and many of the people are of French descent, so they speak French. It's a lovely language.'

'I can speak a bit of French,' she said.

'Then it's a good time to practise,' said her father.

'What's the route after Saguenay, Captain?' asked David.

'We'll drop the Pilots at Escoumins, where we picked them up coming in, and then we head for the Strait of Belle Isle. That's the passage out of the St Lawrence to the north rather than the southern route we took coming in. It's the strait between Newfoundland and the Canadian mainland and is so called after the island we'll pass as we come out of the Strait.'

'How wide is it?' asked David.

'It's about eight miles at the narrowest part.'

'Will there be any ice?' asked Isobel Chancery.

'Not covering the sea, but you may well see icebergs, especially at the top end. They drift down there from the current at sea and then ground in the shallows of the strait.'

'Is it dangerous?' asked Isobel.

Jim laughed. 'No, it's not dangerous. If it was, we wouldn't be going through there. Anyway, we will have a special Ice Pilot with us who knows these waters very well to advise us.'

'Are there any towns in the Straits?'

'None. Just fishing villages. There's a ferry station that goes across and that's about it. If you go to the observation lounge above the bridge, you can see the whole passage laid out for you and watch the ship's track in real time.'

'We're going to the theatre tonight. Are you going Captain?' Isobel asked once dinner was finished.

'Not tonight,' said Jim. 'I have to be up early for the Saguenay transit and the berthing at La Baie. I hope you all have a good night.'

The ship arrived at the approaches to the Saguenay just after dawn. The decks were already crowded with passengers. It was the start of a beautiful day, and the last red streaks from the rising sun were disappearing into the deepening blue sky. The deep cliffs of the land rose above the ship as it entered the passage. The green forests covering the mountains darkened the still waters close to the sides. Dolphins cavorted in the water, delighting the tourists as they swept into the passage.

On the approach to La Baie, the ship emerged from the fjord and ahead lay the town and waiting tugs.

'Hard to imagine this place ice bound,' said Captain Cota.

'In winter, Captain,' said one of the Pilots, 'we have to use ice breakers to get ice class ships in. Even then, it can take several hours to get them alongside.'

'Rather them than me. I don't like the cold. Give me the warm Italian sun anytime.'

Vacuum Pioneer

In Nuuk, it wasn't too cold in the daytime, but in the evening it was below freezing. The ship was alongside trying to discharge her cargo of aviation fuel, but problems ashore with the receiving tanks had caused a halt. It was simply that there wasn't sufficient room for the cargo.

That afternoon, Karl and Eric had a meeting on board with the agents and the receivers' representatives. The situation didn't look good, with a possible holdup of several days. This would be very costly to all concerned, and the charterers had been contacted for instructions.

While frustrating to those ashore waiting for the cargo, most ships welcomed any stoppage that gave the crew the opportunity of shore leave, especially in a ship-friendly port like Nuuk. That evening, most were ashore. For a small town, there was a surprising number of bars and restaurants, and two of the bars had live music. Karl and his family, along with Eric and Trond, the Chief Engineer, were also ashore well wrapped up in their parkas. The women were in the supermarket with Eric, while Karl and Trond were sitting in the bar of the restaurant drinking beer in front of a roaring fire.

'What do you think they'll decide, Karl?' asked Trond.
'They're not going to let us sit around here for a week drinking beer, that's for sure. It'll come down to costs. The receivers are stuck with the bill if we stay and the charterers have other contracts to fill. They've got most of their cargo so I reckon they'll sail us tomorrow or the next day at the latest.'
'Where to?'

'Who knows? They are probably looking around right now to see if they can discharge the cargo anywhere else. These oil companies have arrangements between themselves so it wouldn't surprise me if we don't get orders by tomorrow.'

'How much cargo is left?'

'Not a lot. About 5,000 tonnes in No 3 starboard tank.'

At that moment, the women returned, with Eric following as bagman.

They settled down and ordered drinks.

'I swear that if you were in the middle of the polar ice cap, you'd find a shop,' commented Karl.

'Are we going dancing later?' asked Briget. 'They told us in the supermarket there's a lovely bar close by where they have dancing every night.'

'I suppose we could,' said Karl.

'Where do you think we'll sail next?' asked Gerdy.

'I really don't know. The cargo is jet fuel JP4, so whoever wants it, that's where we'll be heading.'

'What's JP4?'

'Highly flammable jet fuel,' said Eric.

'Could it catch fire?' asked Briget

'Not while it's inerted,' replied Karl.

'Which means what?'

'We pump in an inerting gas which takes out the oxygen. Without oxygen, you can't have a fire. It's the vapour from the fuel that catches fire not the liquid.'

'What about an explosion?'

'Only if the burning vapour is restricted, such as in a box. Now, let's look at the menu and talk of nicer things.'

Chapter 26

Shortly after the ship arrived at La Baie, Graham Chesney, the Ice Pilot, boarded. Once he had settled into the pilot cabin next to the bridge, Peter, the First Officer, brought him round to Jim's office. After introductions, they went to the bridge. They showed Graham around and then brought up the passage plan in the electronic chart system.

'What's the situation with icebergs in the Strait of Belle Isle?' asked Jim.

'Not bad at all,' Graham replied. 'Nothing big and mostly grounded in the shallows. We'll still find enough of them for the passengers to photograph.'

'The idea is to set the speed so we can get to the end of the straits in daylight to give them a chance to see any before we hit the high seas.'

'That's no problem. From the ice reports, we have a clear run up to the Davis Strait. There are some iceberg reports, but at this time of year everything is well reported. For the moment anyway, the weather report looks good, but of course up there it can change very quickly.'

'We'll keep hoping for it to stay good. I've ordered rock salt for the decks in case we get frost at night, but provided we don't get a blow from the north, it may even be sunbathing weather.'

'If I may, Captain, I'll correlate the ice reports and plot any berg reports on the chart, with the navigator's assistance. Then I'll keep a watching brief on the bridge throughout the passage there and back. It'll be nice seeing Halifax again. I look forward to an evening there before flying home.'

'I'll leave you two together then,' said Jim. 'Anything I can do to make your stay more comfortable, just give me a call.'

Just before lunch, Jan phoned Jim. 'I've got the results of the observers' reports from the exercise, Sir. Can I bring them up?'

'Good idea. Tell you what, call the officers' messroom, order them to send up a plate of sandwiches for us both and we'll have a working lunch.'

Jan and the sandwiches arrived together. Jim got two beers from the refrigerator and they sat down at the conference table in the office.

Jan sat quietly as Jim looked through the various reports.

'In general, it's good for communication, command and control, but we fall down on teamwork.'

'That's not surprising considering we don't often do such a large exercise. We're more used to doing standard drills, Sir.'

'Well, that shows which way we have to go, doesn't it? Lack of adequate equipment is highlighted. I quote: "Impossible to rescue all the passengers when ordered to get them out of their cabins, owing to a lack of BA sets for rescuers and rescued." The problem is, of course, that the passengers have no knowledge of BA sets anyway. Don't our existing ones have a buddy system, you know a way of allowing someone being rescued to share the air?'

'No, Sir. It's not a required bit of kit.'

'Well, it bloody well should be. I mean just how are we supposed to get a whole bunch of passengers out of their cabins?'

Jan didn't answer. There was no point.

'I see that, when I ordered the boats to be cleared from the fire, it was too much for the after party. They didn't have enough people to cope with everything. That's my fault. I should have realised and sent other crew for that.'

'Who would you have sent? All the sailors are in the fire teams.'

'Good point. So we have the usual problem; we can't cope with two different emergencies at the same time. You know, that's not right. We have a thousand crew on board. We should be able to give them sufficient training for them to deal with most of the fire fighting, leaving the sailors to deal with the boats.'

'Then we would need a specialised course in fire fighting in confined spaces, again not a requirement. Anyway, another comment you'll note is that, when fire parties 1 and 2 combined to fight the main fire, there were too many people for the narrow alleyways. On that deck, the alleyways are narrower. Higher up, they are wider.'

'Why is that do you think?'

'Cheaper cabins.'

'Can you see that in the adverts, that deluxe cabins have a better chance of survival?' Jim grumbled. 'Never mind, we do what we can. I won't be here, but what you need to do next trip is start using the fire teams to get a small group trained up. If they can do that and repeat it over time, we should have a hotel team capable of acting as fire fighters.'

'You're not going to get that, Sir. It'll require too much time from their duties.'

'Then that's the ship's problem not mine. I'll be well gone.'

'Any idea where you may be going?'

'Not a clue. From experience, there's not too much around for older Captains.'

'For what it's worth, Sir, everyone taking part thought it was an excellent exercise. The fire prevention team agreed.'

'Good. Thank you, Jan. I'll précis these reports and then give a copy to the Captain for sending on to Southampton, who will no doubt file it away with all the other reports requiring equipment and training.'

The ship sailed in the afternoon and again the deck was packed with passengers for the Saguenay transit. Jim brought Helen up to the bridge and installed her in one of the command chairs.

'Just don't touch anything.'

Cota arrived on the bridge.

'Hello, Helen. Can you run things for a moment while I borrow Jim?'

They walked over to the back of the bridge where Cota handed Jim a message. It was brief and to the point, ordering that no further fire exercises were to take part in passenger accommodation while passengers were embarked.

Jim looked at Cota. 'Hinchley?'

'Has to be. No one else.'

'It certainly wasn't the passengers. We checked with them before we had the exercise and the few that were remaining had no problem with what we were doing.'

'I know, but you can bet that's not what Hinchley has told the office. Have you got the report of the exercise?'

'It'll be on your desk this evening, Sir.'

'It can wait till morning if you like. As soon as I get it, I'll send it on to the office. That might just keep them quiet for a while. How did it go anyway?'

'Very well, Sir. The teams did better than I expected, but of course the problem of dealing with such an incident in such a confined space is difficult to imagine.'

'Fire prevention, Jim. That's what we concentrate on. We have the latest detectors and mist sprays. At the first sign of a fire, they will come on.'

The ship was coming to the end of the Saguenay passage and ahead was a gathering of small boats.

'What are they doing there?' asked Helen.

'They are tourist boats looking at the whales and dolphins.'

'I never realised just how beautiful Canada is,' said Helen. 'Where do we go next?'

'From here, we head to Escoumins and drop the River Pilots. Then we head for the Strait of Belle Isle. That's about 500 miles from Escoumins. We pass in between the mainland and Anticosti Island. The Strait is about 70 miles long to Belle Island. Then it's north to the Arctic Circle. Turn around and head back to Halifax.'

One of the River Pilots overheard the conversation. 'Anticosti Island is called the graveyard of the St Lawrence. Over 400 ships have been wrecked there over the years.'

'Does anyone live there?' Helen asked.

'There's a small fishing village on the western tip. A few hundred people live there. In the summer that doubles.'

Helen and Jim stayed on the bridge for the approach to Escoumins, and then they went down.

'Are you coming to the piano lounge tonight?' Helen asked.

'I would like to, but I'll hang around up here while we're in these waters,' Jim replied. 'Once we get out to sea, I'll see you there.'

The phone woke Jim. He instantly picked it up, thinking it was the bridge. It wasn't. It was Bert.

'Sir, we have a problem. Serious. Can you come down. Cabin 106, deck 5.'

Jim looked at his watch, 0245. He instantly threw on his clothes and then put his pullover with epaulets on, grabbed his cap and headed for the cabin. When he arrived, there was a security officer outside the door, which was open and light was coming out into the alleyway. He went inside. Sitting on one of the twin beds were two sobbing girls. Bert was standing with a notebook in his hand. The girls were wearing party dresses. Jim could see they looked dishevelled and one girl's dress was torn down at one corner revealing her bra. She also had a red swelling to the left side of her face. The other girl had scratch marks on her bare shoulder. Both girls had mussed up hair and their lipstick was smeared on what appeared to be swollen lips. Bert came over to Jim and spoke in a low voice.

'Sexual assault, Captain. I just got here.'

'Have you called the medics?'

'Not yet, Sir. I wanted you here first.'

'Call them now. I want the Senior Surgeon here as well.'

'I have their names, Sir. They are Joyce Larman and Holly Backerman. Both are students and they are sharing this cabin. The cruise is a birthday present from one of the girls' parents. The security guard outside found them running from the crew quarters.'

'Shit, crew involved?'

'That's not unusual, Sir.'

'It is to me. Quickly, what happened?'

'Apparently, one of the barmen invited them down to his place with another barman when the bar closed. They were told they were going to a party. When they got there, they were given drinks and then the party started, but it wasn't what they wanted. I haven't gone into the details of what happened, but as far as I can tell it wasn't rape. They managed to get away and that's when they were found.'

'All right. Thanks.'

Jim knelt down by the girls.

'Hi, I'm Jim, the Staff Captain. Now, I know that you're very upset, but can you tell me what happened?'

The girls repeated what Bert had said. 'I want to know what they did to you,' Jim said gently. They looked embarrassed. Just then, Dick, the Surgeon, appeared with two nurses.

'Good morning, Jim. We'll handle this now. The nurses will take them down to the surgery and we'll examine them there. We'll find out what happened and then I'll be up to see you.'

They hustled the girls away.

'What have you done with the two barmen?' Jim asked Bert.

'I have two security officers with them now in their cabin.'

'Put them in the brig. I want them locked up tonight. Whether they did anything or not, they contravened regulations by having passengers in their quarters.'

Like most cruise ships, there was a special imprisonment area that was not talked about. It was officially called the 'confinement area', but to the ship's seamen it was known by the traditional name of the 'brig'.

'Also, give them an alcohol test and check them for drugs. I want their cabin searched. Strip them of their clothing and bag it.'

'I've got Mark, my ex-detective, onto it, Sir. He's already started doing that.'

'I can't do much down here. When you're finished, come up to my office with the detective chap and bring the Hotel Manager with you.'

Jim went back through the ship, attracting curious glances from a few late night passengers going home.

An hour later, Bert arrived with his assistant and Henry Milau, the Hotel Manager. Also with them was Dick, the Surgeon. They all sat round the conference table. Jim waited until they were settled.

'Dick, what can you tell us?' asked Jim.

'The girls have bruising to their faces and on their breasts. One of them also has bruising on her inner thighs. The bruising is in line with what they told us happened. They haven't claimed they were raped. My report is here. I have no doubt they were attacked. Both girls had drunk alcohol and would be unfit to drive if that is any criterion, but in my opinion, they had not drunk an excessive amount.'

'Where are the girls now?'

'We're keeping them in the hospital overnight, officially for observation, unofficially to let them calm down and sober up,' Dick replied.

'Bert, what did you get?'

'They were invited down to the barmen's quarters and went voluntarily. They were told it was for a birthday party. They were given drinks and that is when the attack happened. They were grabbed by their private parts and the crew tried to force them into sexual acts. The girls asked for more drinks, and while the crew were getting these they ran from the cabin. They were pursued, but a security officer appeared and the crew went back to their cabin.'

Jim nodded towards Mark Davies, the security assistant.

'I called two other security officers and we questioned the men. They claimed the girls went with them fully knowing what to expect. They were demanding more drink and making noise. The men tried to quieten them to avoid waking other crew members. That's when the girls started to fight them and how the bruising occurred. They are now in custody. Both tested positive for alcohol.'

Jim turned to Henry.

'Have you got anything, Henry?'

'I also spoke to the men in the brig. They are saying they are innocent and that they were mistreated by the security staff. They are bruised about the face.'

'They resisted arrest and had been drinking,' said Mark. He appeared unconcerned.

'I will protest this to the Ship General Manager in the morning,' said Henry.

'That doesn't excuse them bringing passengers down to crew quarters,' said Jim.

'It's not exactly a serious offence, Jim,' said Henry. 'It goes on all the time.'

'Well, it shouldn't. If it wasn't so 'acceptable' to you, this wouldn't have happened. So, what now?' Jim asked.

'It's the girls' word against the barmen's,' said Henry.

'Yet the evidence is overwhelming. We're not in a court of law; we're under Panamanian maritime law. Anyway, it's for the courts ashore to decide, not us.'

'If it gets that far,' said Henry. 'If that's all, I'll see you in the morning.' He left the office.

'What do you think?' Jim asked Dick.

'The bastards tried to screw the girls. It's bloody obvious. They thought it would be easy after getting them drunk, but the girls resisted. If they hadn't got away, they would have been fucked left, right and centre and then tossed out. But I've seen this before. I have no say about what happens next. I patch people up and send them on their way. It happens on all these ships. The younger they are, the less likely they are to complain. The crew know that. They are too ashamed or embarrassed, or the crew get their mates to give statements saying they were begging for it. As soon as they go down into the crew quarters, they're fair game. It's strange how we then tend to almost blame them for it as if they should have known better.'

Jim looked at his watch. 'It's not up to me. I'll see the Captain in a few hours and he can decide. Bert, please prepare a report for the morning meeting and stand by to be called. Dick, I should be grateful if you would attend the heads of department meeting. With that, I suggest we all get a few hours' shuteye.'

Jim was ready to go to the Captain's office when Jan appeared with the Bosun.

'Sorry, Jan. I have no time this morning. I have to get to the Old Man's office. Is everything all right?'

'Yes, Sir. I just wondered about any orders for salting down the outside decks.'

'Keep the salt handy. If we get any frost, we'll put it down as required. If we do get any, it will be at night and the sun will quickly melt it in the morning. It's only for the next few days.'

Chapter 27

Cota was not in his office so Jim tapped on the door frame to the dayroom. The door was open, but the curtain was drawn. Cota called for Jim to come in. He was sitting with a coffee reading the ship's morning newspaper. He looked up.

'I can guess what this is about. I've already had Hinchley on the phone. Sit down, Jim. Coffee?'

'Please, Sir. I would be interested in what he had to say.'

'Well, first he was pretty upset that he wasn't called last night.'

'There was no need. We dealt with it and called those who were needed. There was nothing he could have done at that time.'

'Next, he has lodged a complaint about the mistreatment of these barmen by the security people.'

'How about the assault of the girls by those barmen?'

Cota shrugged. 'The barmen are sticking to their story, of course. Jim, you must understand this is not unusual. Occasionally, you'll read about this sort of incident in the press, but most don't get that far. All cruise companies have a policy of trying to deal with this kind of thing in house. You can imagine the publicity if it became general knowledge that this is a regular occurrence. You must have had the same kind of policy in your last company.'

'If we did, I didn't know about it. I suppose it was because we had smaller ships. I can only remember one such case and the crew involved were handed over to the police in Cape Town for trial. They are doing time in Pollsmoor prison now.'

'Well, it's different here. If there had been a rape, we would of course have to treat this very seriously, but I'll tell you confidentially that they don't always get to court either. We work to one rule here. Avoid adverse publicity at all costs. We are not the law and anyway, as you often say, we are in Panama. I can't see them sending the police out to investigate this. In fact, I can't see them sending police to investigate anything here bar a mass murder.'

'So, what is going to happen?'

'Look, Jim, we'll leave it till the meeting. See what Hinchley wants and take it from there. Is that fair enough?'

'Agreed. I've requested the surgeon to attend the meeting.'

'That should be interesting. As you may have heard, Dick tends to say what he thinks.'

Jim and the Captain went down together. Hinchley was already there with the others and Dick arrived soon after.

'The first item on the agenda is the incident in the early hours of this morning. I regret that I was not called, but it was dealt with by the Staff Captain. Briefly, two young girls alleged that two of the barmen assaulted them in the crew quarters at around 0230 this morning.'

'There is no doubt that they were sexually assaulted,' said Dick. 'The bruising, and where the bruising was, confirms that. They certainly didn't do it to themselves.'

'Well, whatever. It doesn't matter now as the girls have dropped the charges.'

'What!' exclaimed Jim. 'When was this?'

'About an hour ago. If you had called me last night, this would have been dealt with then. Anyway, they realised they had been where they shouldn't have and that they were inebriated. They went to a party and, shall we say, play got a little out of hand. So it's over. Now we deal with the security officers' assault on the barmen.'

'Just a minute,' said Jim. 'It's not bloody well over. What do you mean the play 'got a little out of hand'.

Those bastards tried to rape those girls and you say it's over? What happens next month when they try the same thing? How do you know they haven't done this before?'

Hinchley's lips tightened. 'You obviously aren't listening, Clariby. I said the girls had dropped the charges. It's over. There is no case, no complaint. For God's sake, get real. This kind of thing happens. Girls get drunk, want to fool around and then cry stop when the men are all worked up. What do you expect? What did they think was going to happen, a little kiss? Anyway, no damage was done. They just got felt up a little. I bet they weren't virgins anyway.'

There was a bang. Jean Sinter, the acting Purser, stood up and threw back her chair. She glared at Hinchley, but said nothing as she stalked out of the meeting.

'Well done, Mr Hinchley. You should join the women's lib movement,' remarked Iain. Hinchley ignored the remark.

'I see you have your Senior Security Officer here, Clariby. Bring him in please. I want to find out why these men were assaulted.'

'I'll get him,' Patrick said.

Bert came in and Jim gestured to an empty chair. 'Sit down, Bert. Mr Hinchley wants to know about those two creeps you apprehended last night.'

'No, I don't want to know about them, Clariby. I want to know why they were beaten up.'

'They weren't beaten,' said Bert. 'They resisted being taken to the brig.'

'On whose authority?'

'Mine.' It was Cota. 'I told you, the Staff Captain is acting on my authority and this is an operational matter, not hotel.'

'It is when two of our staff are beaten for no reason,' spat Henry.

'For fuck's sake, Henry! What do you mean no reason? The little bastards tried to rape two passengers!' protested Jim.

'No, they didn't! There are no charges against them and that makes them innocent.'

'And I suppose they will be back working in the bar again tonight?'

'Of course.'

Jim looked at Cota. 'Captain?'

'There's nothing we can do. The charges have been dropped so there is no offence. Sorry, Jim, but that's that.'

'Mr Fallows,' said Hinchley. 'You're lucky these men don't want to press charges against you and your men. This must not happen again. Do you understand?'

'Bert, you can go now,' said Jim. 'Please thank the men for their assistance last night. You all did well regardless of what has been said here.'

As Bert left, Dick snorted. 'So, how did you get the little girls to drop it Hinchley?'

'That's none of your business, Doctor.'

'Oh, but it is. You see I have my medical log which shows their injuries.'

'That log belongs to the company, Doctor, as you well know. As such, it comes to me in the office.'

'How much?'

'How much what?'

'How much did you give them? Two students like that, probably frightened their parents would find out they'd been drunk in crew quarters. I should imagine you only had to give them a few thousand dollars. Am I right?' Dick turned to Jim. 'That's the company's standard amount for an assault. Well, it's good to see justice prevailing again over avarice. I'm off to the Chief's club before I really say what I think. See you there, Iain.'

'I want those two men off the ship at the end of this trip,' said Jim. 'They had passengers in their quarters and were drunk. That's against the regulations, so get them off.'

'That's not a problem,' said Henry. 'That was my intention.'

'And out of the company.'

Henry looked at Hinchley. Hinchley nodded. 'Agreed, out of the company.'

The meeting broke up shortly afterwards. 'Provided Dick has left us anything to drink, are you joining us in the club?' asked Iain.

'I would like to,' said Jim. 'The way I'm feeling now, I would probably stay there all afternoon, but we're still in the river and I want to be around for the bridge. Thanks though.'

During the night, the ship slid between Anticosti Island and the mainland. Morning found the *'Majestic Sea'* in the long approach to the Strait of Belle Isle. Again, the decks thronged with passengers, although many had elected to stay inside and watch through the windows. Those with balconies were standing or sitting out on them.

Graham Chesney, the Ice Pilot, and Jim were on the bridge swapping battle stories.

'What are you going to do next then, when you leave this ship?' asked Graham. 'I presume from what you've said you don't want to come back to these ships.'

'I really don't know. There's not a lot left out there for European Captains. The owners all want the cheapest.'

'Have you ever thought about coming out here, Jim?' asked Graham.

'I'd love to,' Jim replied, 'but unfortunately my wife is wedded to England.'

'That wouldn't matter. You wouldn't have to live out here if you became an Ice Pilot.'

'An Ice Pilot? I'd never thought about that.'

'Well, you should. You've got all the necessary ice experience. There's a shortage you know, especially with the ice melting and more ships going into the Arctic. They'll continue to increase at a time when there's less and less command experienced people around.'

'Is that what you did?'

'Damn right. I was like you, running around trying to keep my job on the ships when no one really wants us anymore because we're not willing to work for rice, so I thought to hell with it. I looked around and found this. I was living in Liverpool, but after doing this for about two years my wife came out and loved it, especially when she saw the standard of living here. So we moved out and here we are four years later. Now if I want to panic her, I talk about going back to the land of lager and social security.'

'How would I go about it?'

'No problem, I'll put the word in for you if you like. You will have to go through the usual interviews and probationary period, of course, but then you're in. It's a bit like being at sea. You do four or five months over here during the season and then go back for your leave. Better pay and leave as well. You should think about it.'

Jim went down to his cabin in a thoughtful mood. His phone rang; it was Iain the Chief.

'Good morning, Jim. I've just got your orders regarding the watertight doors. That's a pain in the arse. Is it really necessary?'

'Sorry, Iain, but yes. All watertight doors must be closed each night we are up in these waters.'

'I thought we weren't going near any ice.'

'That's my intention, but up here you never know so, just in case, we adopt the standard precautions.'

Iain sighed. 'OK, Jim, if that's what you want, but will you let me know as soon as we can open them again?'

'I will, Iain. I've trimmed it to the hours of darkness, 2000 to 0600, so it won't bother the day workers too much.'

'Have you heard from Hinchley and his crowd yet?'

'Not yet. Why?'

'You will,' Iain chortled. 'Have a nice day.'

Jim considered what Iain had said. Obviously, he knew something. Still, there was work to do. He carried on checking through the computer messages and sent out the replies that were required. There was a pile of discharge books on his desk for the deck crew who were leaving at the end of this cruise. Celine, the secretary, had already stamped them. All they required was Jim's signature and she would put the dates in when they left the ship.

He was working his way through these when the phone rang again.

It was Hinchley.

'What's this nonsense about closing watertight doors?'

'It's a standard precaution for ships going into ice waters,' replied Jim.

'I've asked around and everyone says that they have never seen this before.'

'They probably haven't,' said Jim, 'but then they probably haven't ever been in ice before.'

'Do you realise the problems this is going to cause?'

Jim was trying to stay calm.

'Mr Hinchley, I am not closing these doors to cause problems. They are part of the safety requirements for this ship and in the interests of all on board. I will rescind this order as soon as we are clear of the ice waters. I anticipate it will be in force only for two days hopefully.'

'That's not good enough. I have both the Hotel Manager and the Purser here complaining about this. You do realise that you are closing these doors during the second sitting.'

Jim lost his patience. 'Hinchley, I couldn't bloody well care if it was the second coming. They are closing and that's that.' He banged the phone down and then picked it up again. He called the Captain's office. When Cota answered, Jim relayed the conversation. 'I expect you'll be hearing from Hinchley shortly, Sir.'

'I have that strange feeling as well, Jim. Still, you are quite right. No argument from me. However, I noticed that you want to lower the lifeboats to the embarkation decks. You really can't do that.'

'That's another standard precaution, and only each night, Sir.'

'Jim, think what it would do to the passengers if they see boats being prepared for what they think is a little jaunt up north. It will send some of them into a screaming fit. No, Jim. Not the boats.'

Jim knew when he was beaten.

'I understand, Sir. No boats.'

'Good. Come for a drink in my cabin this evening, 2000.'

When Jim arrived that evening, the cabin was pleasantly occupied with a mix of passengers and officers. Dick, the Surgeon, was holding forth on how to mix the ultimate martini, while Peter, the First Officer, and Jan were talking to two attractive women. Cota was with Hinchley and his family. Seeing Jim, he beckoned him over. Reluctantly, Jim joined the group. 'Jim, I don't think you've met Mr Hinchley's family. This is Barbara Hinchley, David and Janet.' Barbara was an attractive woman in her early fifties, slim and with a sparkle in her eyes. The two children were in their teens and had that teenager 'I don't belong here' look.

'So, at last I meet the man who has been giving my husband a hard time,' said Barbara. 'Good. He needs it. Most people always agree with him, except me and apparently you.' She was looking at Jim with interest, as were the children.

'He really doesn't like you,' said Janet.

'Janet,' said Hinchley in a warning voice.

'That's all right. I don't like him,' said Jim. 'Imagine how boring life would be if we all went around liking each other.'

'I hear you're leaving, Captain,' said Barbara. 'What are you going to do next?'

'I really don't know. I might come out to Canada. Who knows?'

'You don't have to leave,' said Hinchley. 'It's your choice.'

'I think after my last conversation with West in Southampton there is not much choice.'

'He's a little prick.'

'At last we agree on something,' smiled Jim.

Jim made acquaintance again with his table, arriving slightly late and apologising.

'Did you see the icebergs?' he asked the children.

'Lots. We took photographs,' announced Nicola, 'but we didn't see any whales.'

'You will tomorrow,' said Jim. 'The bridge will announce whenever whales are near the ship.'

'Will we go close to them?' asked Harvey.

'We will go as close as we can, but we have to be careful. Sometimes they are asleep on the surface and we don't want to hit them. If we go too close and they are awake, they will go down. It's called 'sounding'. They don't like over a hundred thousand tonnes of ship getting too close. I don't blame them. I wouldn't like it either!'

'When do we get to the Arctic Circle?' asked Shirley.

'It'll be around one thirty in the morning.'

'And then what?'

'We turn round and head back down to Halifax.'

'It seems a little strange, coming all this way to see nothing.'

'Yet we have a full ship of people that wanted to come to see nothing. Anyway, you'll see the coast of Greenland.'

'I think the draw of being able to say they have been in the Arctic was the reason,' said Harvey. 'And we have the Arctic party tomorrow night to look forward to.'

'What party?' asked Andrew.

'Not for you,' said his father. 'It's for grown ups. You're going to the children's party in the theatre.'

Andrew wrinkled his nose. 'I don't want to go there.'

'It's Captain's orders,' said Jim. 'All children must attend or walk the plank.'

'What plank?' asked Nicola.

'It's a plank that we keep for punishing bad crew and passengers. In the olden days when I first came to sea, there was no video or TV so to keep us amused we used to make people walk off the plank into the sea. This was after the Sunday floggings.'

The children were looking suspiciously at Jim.

'Don't believe a word he says, children,' said Shirley. 'He's never done any of that.'

'No,' said Jim. 'But at times it's a nice thought.'

Chapter 28

Vacuum Pioneer

Karl walked into the officers' mess for breakfast and sat down with Eric. The steward came over and poured fresh coffee. The smell of freshly baked bread came from the galley. Along the side of the mess, the breakfast buffet bar was laid out and officers were helping themselves.

'The ladies are having breakfast later in their cabins,' said Karl. He held a piece of paper in his hand. 'It looks like the charterers have finally lost their patience. They have given the receivers until midday to take the cargo otherwise we sail for Seven Islands in the St Lawrence.'

'That's good,' said Eric. 'This place is too expensive. Good fun, but it's time we left. Do you think they can take the remaining cargo, Sir?'

'No, not a hope. I have just come off the phone to the terminal manager. It seems the problem is that the airport has been hit severely by snow and ice this winter and they have a surplus of fuel.'

'I'll set up the sailing then. What time do you want the engines and bridge equipment tested?'

'Better make it 1100, and then we can sail as we want after that. I've already told the Pilots provisionally 1200.'

Eric finished his coffee.

'I'll stop shore leave now, although I don't think anyone wants to go ashore anyway - they've got no money left. I'll also let the engine room know.'

Jim met with the cadets in his cabin in the morning. They were sitting around the conference table, their work books scattered in front of them.

'I think you all realise the subjects you are deficient in. Your watchkeeping, navigation and bridge work are all up to date, but your seamanship side is sadly neglected. At least we have you back on the deck again, but there's not much time left. Two of you are due to go back to college in two months and that's the last of your deck time before you qualify as officers. Seriously, do you think you're ready?'

There was silence.

'Look. It's not your fault. You're on the wrong ships. You should be on ships where you can hone your skills in seamanship as well as the bridge. There's no doubt you can give orders to a waiter and amuse passengers, but how about dealing with a sullen mixed race crew who haven't been allowed shore leave for months and now you have to drive them out on deck to secure containers in bad weather?'

Again silence.

'Am I talking to the bulkhead?'

'Sir, it's not our fault. We have to go where we can get berths. The cruise companies have them and there are not many other companies who will agree to carry cadets. That's why we end up here.'

'You're right,' said Jim. 'I suppose I want you to realise that, while you have your sea time in, and with that you will become officers, you have a lot to learn about the sea.'

'We do understand, Captain.' It was Cadet Bindra. 'I am already applying to other companies.'

'Good. Remember, you can always come back to these ships once you have your Master's qualification. I seriously recommend you go onto the oil field support ships. If you can, try and get onto the anchor handlers or standby vessels. That's where real seamanship is practised. Now, to other things. I presume you have had a meeting with Mr Fallows, the Chief Security Officer.'

'We've had two meetings, Sir,' said Zhou, 'but we are still unclear about our position in an emergency. Presently, I am with the main fire party, Bindra is on the bridge, and Kemp and Matheson are with the forward and after fire parties. Then if we go to boat stations, we are designated to each take command of a boat.'

'Officially that stays, but if the ship goes to boat stations, instead you will join Mr Fallows' team. As such, you will be under his orders. The boats can be run by the seamen designated to each boat. They can get by without you.'

'It's just that we have no experience of controlling passengers, Sir,' said Matheson.

'No one on board has. That's why it's hard to tell you what to expect. It's not really the passengers that bother me. They will generally do what they are told to do, provided they have confidence in those giving the orders. It's the crew I'm concerned about. If they get out of hand and the passengers see this, it will spread like wildfire. Your job is to present a calm, authoritative presence.'

'Mr Fallows seems to think it may be more than that. More like riot police,' said Kemp.

'He has to look at the worst possible scenario,' explained Jim.

'Can I ask, Sir,' said Zhou, 'why there is no training as regards breakdown of discipline?'

'That's simple Zhou, because if there was, we would be admitting to it being a possibility. If that were the case, do you think the punters would continue to pack the ships? Anyway, that would require a complete rethink of so many things on board. That is now beyond the ability of many companies and would mean a drastic increase in the cost of running these huge ships. Most companies would go out of business.'

'So, what is the answer, Sir?'

'I hate to say it, but a bloody great accident. Even then it's not guaranteed that anything will change. Zhou will understand when I say, too many rice bowls to break.'

Zhou smiled.

'Anyway, this is only a project to see if we could have a different way of doing things, that's all. We won't have to get worked up about it. The good thing is that hopefully it has made you think. Never stop questioning what exists on your ships. There is always room for improvement and always remember that the safety of those on board is your first priority.'

An announcement came through the loudspeaker system. It was the bridge telling the passengers that whales had been sighted on the starboard bow. Jim could see the cadets looking interested.

'Lecture over. Off you go.'

They left his cabin quickly and he could hear them hurrying along the alleyway to the bridge.

That afternoon, Jim walked along the upper deck. It was a clear day and there was a hot sun beaming down. The upper deck was well sheltered from the wind and many passengers were lying out on deckchairs. Even the swimming pools were in action and the surf pool was full of teenagers. He stopped at the after pool bar and sat down at an outside table, where he ordered a beer. It was good seeing so many people enjoying the ship and being on the sea, except the only way to see it was to go to the side and make the effort to look.

He finished his drink and strolled back down the deck into the accommodation. He made his way down to the next deck, where the main public rooms were located. Crew were scattered around putting up various decorations for the Arctic Night party. The main colours were silver and white, icicles were predominant. In the theatre on the next deck down, the dancers were going through their rehearsals for that evening's show. Again, ice was the theme. Further down, he went into the ship's main 'town square'.

Jim still marvelled at the way it had been constructed inside the ship. High up at the top was a huge dome letting in light. Suspended above was the glittering chandelier that was more for decoration than light. The deck was made from real cobbled stones from France complete with street lamps. The whole square was surrounded by shops, even a mini supermarket, just in case anyone wanted to buy food. Incredibly, this shop was busy. Most of the shops though were high class boutiques with many famous brand names on display. One shop hired out costume wear and was busy with people getting ready for the party. As Jim passed by, he saw Helen inside the shop. He noticed that she was on crutches rather than in her chair.

'I see you've decided to get some exercise,' he remarked, startling her.

'What are you doing in here?' she asked. 'Surely not getting fancy dress?'

Jim laughed. 'If the gold braid and cap badge size continue to increase, we will already have one. No, I'm just strolling around like any other tourist. What's with the crutches?'

'The clever people who built the town here didn't consider wheelchairs on cobbles. Our wonderful Cruise Director has decided that I have to wear a costume to get into the swing of things tonight, so I'm trying to find something that I can play a piano in, but most of the appropriate costumes have gone.

'Why not just wear a plain white evening dress. With your figure, that would look stunning.'

'Good lord, Captain, you noticed!' she said. 'I would if I had one.'

'Come on,' Jim ordered.

'Where to?'

'The dress shop.'

'Jim, no way. Those dresses cost thousands. I can't afford them and there is no way I would allow you to buy one.'

'Don't worry. I can't afford them either. We're not going to buy one, we're going to borrow one.'

They went across the square to a large dress shop. The manageress was by the counter and smiled as they entered.

'Well, I am honoured, the Staff Captain and the ship's pianist. To what do I owe this visit to?'

'A small problem, Madame,' said Jim. 'The young lady here has been told to wear something appropriate for this evening's party and there is nothing in the fancy dress shop. You on the other hand have some very beautiful dresses.'

'So, where is the problem?'

'We can't afford to buy one.'

'That certainly is a problem.'

'On the other hand, the young lady would provide a most charming model for one of your dresses, just for this evening.'

'So, you are suggesting I lend her a dress?'

'That's certainly one way of putting it.'

The manageress thought for a moment. 'Well, she certainly can't go anywhere with it can she.' She walked around Helen. 'Can you show your legs or do you want to keep them hidden?'

'I can show them; it's the muscles that are the problem.'

'OK. I have a couple of dresses in mind. Come with me.'

Jim waited. From experience, he knew he should have brought a newspaper.

Eventually, they emerged from the changing room. Helen wore a stunning slim white dress. It was low cut showing her cleavage and a slit on the side revealed a very shapely leg.

Helen waited. 'So, what do you think?'

'You're very beautiful.'

'She is, isn't she?' said the manageress. 'Just a moment.' She picked up the phone and spoke for a moment then turned back to them. 'We wait,' she said.

After a few minutes, a young man in a grey suit appeared bearing a velvet box.

'Hi, Martha. Is this the young lady?'

The manageress nodded. 'Please sign here.' He presented a receipt pad and a pen. Helen, looking a little bewildered, signed her name.

'Thank you. Now, like Cinderella, this only lasts a certain time. Please return these to our shop first thing tomorrow.' He turned to go and then looked back and smiled. 'You look stunning by the way.'

After he had gone, Martha opened the box to reveal a diamond necklace and matching earrings.

'We had to finish the ensemble off,' she said. 'After all, if you're going to be my fashion model, we have to have you looking your best.'

Helen was stunned. She looked at the box. 'Oh my God, it's Bulgari. I'm terrified to wear it. I'm terrified to wear any of it. Even the dress is Chanel.'

'Nonsense,' said Martha. 'Enjoy it while you can.' Helen went to change back while Martha put the dress in a box. 'She's a very nice girl, Captain.'

'I know she is Martha, and no there's nothing between us except friendship.'

'She doesn't think so.'

'That's her problem. I have a lovely wife waiting for me at home and, in about a week's time, I will be there.'

'That's good, Captain, and, if I may say so, for you officers that's unusual.'

When Helen emerged, Martha presented the box.

'The jewellery is inside. Now both of you go before you take anything else.'

Jim carried the box as Helen hobbled along on the cobbles.

'I left my chair over by the after square entrance,' she said. They walked over and Helen settled into her chair.

'Thank you, Jim. I really don't know what to say to you. There's so much I want to say, but I can't.'

'Helen, in any other circumstances, I would carry you away. Your face will be with me for a long time after I have left the ship. I will wonder how you are, what you are doing and who you are with.'

'I'll write,' she said.

'No,' said Jim. 'That would be worse. We both have our lives to live and that life is with other people.' He bent down and kissed her gently. 'I will see you in the piano lounge after dinner.'

Vacuum Pioneer

The 'Vacuum Pioneer' sailed shortly after 1200. Karl, Gerdy, Arturo Emita (the Second Officer) and the Pilot were on the bridge. The Quartermaster was on the wheel. Shortly outside the breakwater, the Pilot departed and Arturo set the course for the Strait of Belle Isle.

Some ice was floating around, mostly bergy bits and a few growlers, with the sea occasionally washing over them, their green grey colour matching the ocean waves. The ship eased through them as it went down the sound towards the open sea.

There was a northerly wind blowing and they all had their parkas on. Even though the bridge was warm, outside on the bridge wings, the wind was blowing and it was very cold. Once the ship cleared the ice, Karl ordered the ship to full speed and shortly rang full away. Eric, up forward in the bow, secured the anchors and quickly piped down his mooring party. Shortly afterwards, he arrived on the bridge and went immediately to the coffee pot, rubbing his hands.

'The anchors are secured, Captain,' he said. 'The Bosun and crew are checking around the valves and tank covers. I don't think we'll get any frost tonight, but I've left the hydraulic heaters on just in case.'

'I've set speed for 16 knots,' said Karl. 'That should get us to Seven Islands in time.'

'Have we heard where we go after that?'

'No, but I guess we'll head back to the Gulf.'

'At least it's warmer there,' said Eric. 'That was one of the reasons I used to like going out east, especially to the Philippines.'

'The girls are nice there,' said Karl.

'*Never you mind about the girls,*' interrupted Gerdy. She turned to Eric. '*When we were courting, he used to try to make me jealous by telling me about the girls there.*'

'*They are beautiful,*' said Karl.

'*I quickly realised that every girl is beautiful to sailors after six months on a large tanker,*' said Gerdy.

'*Come on,*' said Karl. '*Let's leave the Second Officer to get on with his work.*'

Chapter 29

That evening, Jim had two cocktail parties to attend before dinner, one in a penthouse suite and the other in one of the balcony suites. He made his usual polite small talk in the penthouse before excusing himself and continuing to the next engagement. This was more enjoyable as it was the Inches' suite. The Chancerys were also there, together with a small group of other passengers. The men had all put on their white tuxedos in recognition of the white theme for the evening and the ladies were all in some form of costume that glittered.

The waiters offered drinks with frosted rims. Jim took one and sipped it cautiously. Vodka, he might have guessed.

'Where are the children?' he asked Shirley.

'They've gone to an early dinner with their friends, and then they're going to the children's show in the theatre. They pretended they weren't interested, but they left us fast enough.'

'We were just talking about what we are going to do tonight,' said David. 'The problem is that there are so many things going on. There's a show in the theatre and there are three different dances. There's another show in the night club and then there is the casino.'

'Which he is staying away from,' interrupted his wife Isobel. 'If he wants to throw money away, he can throw it at me.'

'Do you gamble, Captain?'

'I once went into a casino in Adelaide in Australia. I had an hour to waste so went in and put a dollar on black; it came up red. So I doubled and again it came up red. All I wanted was my money back. In five minutes, I lost 500 dollars. The chap running the wheel said that he had never seen a run of reds like that, but he probably told everyone that. Anyway, I realised I wasn't a gambler, walked out and have never gambled again.'

Harvey Inch tapped his glass. 'Sorry to be a party pooper folks, but it's gone eight so I think we should head down for dinner.'

Gradually the cabin emptied and they made their way down to the restaurant. The staff had done an amazing job with the décor and the huge room now looked like the inside of an ice palace. The dinner was suitably splendid to match. David insisted on champagne and two bottles were placed on the table.

The room was noisy with the passengers in a festive mood. Jim could see that it was going to be an enjoyable evening. It was certainly one way to visit the Arctic.

Jim kept himself to just one glass of champagne. He had left his drink in the penthouse suite untouched and only finished half his cocktail with the Inches. It was a nuisance keeping a count, but essential in an atmosphere like this. Each time he left a ship, he always enjoyed an evening in the local pub where he could relax. It wasn't that he couldn't handle the drink, but the fact that all the happy passengers who would thrust drinks on him would be the first to point a finger if something went wrong. Iain, the Chief, had it right by providing his unofficial club for his officers. At least the drinking was out of sight.

The dinner came to an end and the restaurant started to empty as the passengers left to get their tables at the various entertainments for the evening.

'Are you joining us, Captain?' asked Isobel. 'We're heading for the main ballroom.'

'Sorry, but I'm going for coffee in the piano lounge.'

'Where the lovely pianist plays,' said Harvey.

Jim found himself blushing. 'Not at all. She is a very good pianist.'

'Leave the man alone,' said Shirley. 'You have a good evening, Captain.'

Jim walked away quickly. Harvey's remark bothered him and he wondered whether others were thinking that way. The trouble was, he was attracted to her, and she knew it. It was just that he didn't like to think it was obvious to others. He wished he was one of those who could leap in and out of bed with such ease on these ships and then go home to their family and do the garden without a second thought. As one captain explained to him, it was like going to the toilet. Relieving yourself, as he crudely put it.

Jim entered the piano lounge and walked towards the table where Dick, the Surgeon, was already sitting. For the first time, he was aware of people watching him, or at least he thought they were. Did they think that he was sleeping with her, he wondered.

Helen's beauty took Jim's breath away. She looked stunning. The dress shimmered and the necklace sparkled in the light from the lamp on the piano. She glanced up as he passed the piano and her smile sank into his heart.

'Come and sit down, Jim,' called Dick. 'Stop interfering with the piano player.'

Jim sat down and a waiter brought him a coffee. Shortly after, Iain and Patrick arrived.

'Bloody hell,' muttered Iain. 'Helen looks gorgeous tonight.'

'Doesn't she?' said Dick. 'A fact that has not escaped our Captain here. He can't take his eyes off her.'

Jim started; he hadn't realised he was staring. 'I'm sorry, gentlemen. Yes I was looking and she is lovely.' He paused and then added, 'So is my wife.'

Dick and Iain looked at each other and said nothing.

The noise was growing in the room as more passengers arrived in a party mood.

Dick finished his drink. 'I'm heading off to the nightclub. Anyone coming?'

'We're with you,' said Iain. 'How about you, Jim?'

'No thanks. I'll have another coffee and then I'm off to bed.'

Iain clapped his hand on Jim's back as he went by. 'The question is, who with?'

They laughed as they left the table.

Vacuum Pioneer

It was approaching 2000 and Eric and Briget were sharing the bridge sitting in the side-by-side command chairs. Briget had Biscuit the cat sitting on her lap. The duty sailor was watching out through the bridge windows on the starboard side.

'Tell me about home, Eric.'

'Not much to tell. My father was at sea and he was very happy when I enrolled at the marine college and went to sea like him. He died a few years ago when his ship sank in a hurricane off Japan. I have a younger brother, who wants to become a doctor, and two sisters, one married and the other engaged. My mother and sisters live in Trondheim.'

'Are you going to stay at sea?'

Eric shrugged. 'Who knows? I want to be a Captain. I haven't come this far to leave without getting command. It's a good life, you know, for a man anyway. I think then I may be like your father. Once you get command, you don't want to let it go. There is still so much of the world to see and there's no better way of doing it than being at sea.'

'My father has invited you to stay when you go on leave.'

'I know, but I have to get home first. I keep a watchful eye over my mother and sister. I would like to come, though. I have seen pictures of your home by the fjord. It looks very beautiful. Maybe I can come before I join my next ship.'

'I would like that,' she said.

Eric looked at the clock. 'It's almost 2000 and I have to write the log book before the end of the watch.'

Briget got up and gave him a quick kiss. 'I'll be waiting in the cabin.'

Helen had finished playing and was sitting with Jim. 'It's too cold to go to our café tonight,' he said. 'Do you want to go anywhere else? The party is going on all over the ship and it's not late.'

'No,' she said. 'I'm just happy being with you.'

He was feeling very warm. It was a pleasurable warmth, but also a guilty one.

'We only have a few days left, Jim, until we go back to reality again, you to your Somerset countryside and me to my small apartment in Connecticut. It will be as if this never happened. That's what these ships provide, a brief illusion.'

'We all need illusions sometimes, as long as we know that's what they are.'

'Then let me have my illusion, Jim. Take me down to my cabin.'

It was as if all movement had stopped. He could see people talking and laughing, but no sound came. He found he was trembling. He looked at her and she smiled and again that smile drove down into his heart and warmed him.

He stood up and without a word took the handles of her wheelchair and pushed her out of the lounge.

Chapter 30

On the bridge, it was a pleasant enough evening. A northerly wind was blowing causing a slight head sea and swell into which the ship's bow dipped gently. It also added a wind chill factor to the cold air outside the warm bridge. It was a cloudy night, with the sky mostly overcast, shadowing the full moon that lurked behind. There was a very slight tremble on the bridge caused by the engines running at a high revolution to keep the schedule of a quick run to the Arctic Circle and back to Halifax.

By tradition, the 8 to 12 watch is the junior watch of the ship and the Junior Second Officer, Mike Prentiss, had the watch with a Third Officer and Cadet Matheson. A Quartermaster stood by as a lookout, ready to take the wheel as required.

The '*Majestic Sea*', with her radar scanners higher than those on the '*Vacuum Pioneer*', saw the other ship first, the echo on the screen showing up faintly at just over 21 miles at approximately one point on the starboard bow. The radar plot showed that the ships were almost on a collision course with a time to intercept of 30 minutes. The ships were still a long way away, certainly out of visual range and the '*Majestic Sea*' continued her course.

Vacuum Pioneer

When the 'Vacuum Pioneer' picked up the first echo of the 'Majestic Sea' at 17 miles, it gave similar intercept information. On the bridge of the 'Vacuum Pioneer' were the Third Officer, Ivo Milanovic, and the Quartermaster, Corazon Montejo.

As the ship approached, the computerised radars continued to silently update the information. The ships' names, their course, speed and destination were also displayed on the Automated Identification System.

The '*Majestic Sea*' was the give-way vessel and, at 2223, Mike Prentiss ordered the Quartermaster to the wheel and gave a course alteration to starboard. The Quartermaster did this; it was with only 5 degrees as large cruise ships tend to list heavily if too much wheel is used.

Mike had ordered a course that would take the ships past each other at a distance of two miles. As the '*Vacuum Pioneer*' did not have to alter course, Ivo did not change from autopilot.

The officers on both ships were relaxed. With the alteration of course by the '*Majestic Sea*', the ships were on a parallel course and would pass two miles away from each other, a perfectly adequate distance.

Vacuum Pioneer

Ivo and Corazon were both looking at the 'Majestic Sea' through their binoculars.

'How would you like to be on board that?' Ivo asked Corazon.

'The money's not good, Sir. Much better here.'

'I wouldn't mind trying it,' said Ivo. 'Just think of the girls there.'

'You would have to take them ashore and buy them drinks,' said Corazon. 'Very expensive.'

Ivo laughed. 'Let's have a coffee. I bet they get theirs served by waiters.'

On the bridge of the *'Majestic Sea'*, they were also watching the approach of the tanker. The officers on the *'Vacuum Pioneer'* were experienced in ice, but those on the *'Majestic Sea'* were not. They had a talk from the Staff Captain and read the books, but none of them had been in ice waters. They did know, however, what ice could do to a ship, especially one such as theirs which had no ice strengthening and only a single hull. They also knew that, if the ship went into any ice, this could be catastrophic for the ship, but they had been told that the only ice expected would be isolated icebergs and that they should call the Ice Pilot, who was in his cabin next to the bridge, if required.

At that moment, a rift appeared in the cloud cover allowing moonlight to shaft down to the sea immediately ahead of the *'Majestic Sea'*, illuminating an extensive sheet of ice on the water.

The Third Officer shouted 'Ice!' and pointed ahead of the ship. Mike Prentiss looked in horror as he saw an ice field stretching across the bow from the port side and going into the distance on the starboard side. His brain functioned with experience. He knew the ship could not stop in time, nor could he go to starboard as the ice stretched further that way. Therefore, his only option was to bring the ship to port. Luckily, the ship was in hand steering and he immediately ordered hard to port. The ship began to swing to port, slowly at first, and then picking up momentum. At the same time, she began to heel over to starboard, increasing with the speed of the turn. Papers, books and instruments began to fall off the tables and shelves on the bridge, and the officers had to hold on tightly to the rail that ran along the bridge front. Mike waited for the crunch of ice against the ship's bow, but none came. Instead, he watched as the sea rippled ahead, revealing the optical illusion of the moonlight, and highlighting the inexperience of the crew. Mike was about to order the ship back to starboard when he slipped and fell, his body sliding rapidly across the bridge and slamming painfully against the starboard side.

The ship continued to turn across the path of the oncoming tanker.

Vacuum Pioneer

On the 'Vacuum Pioneer', they were waiting for their coffee to cool when, to their amazement, they saw the 'Majestic Sea', which was on a perfectly safe course three miles away, suddenly turn towards them and heel to starboard.

'What the fuck are they doing?' Ivo screamed. 'Get on the wheel!'

Corazon ran to the wheel and put the ship into hand steering. Ivo watched for a few seconds longer, but the 'Majestic Sea' continued to turn across their course, now only two miles away.

Ivo was a good officer, but still lacking in experience. A more experienced officer would have been able to assess the situation and realise that if they turned the ship away from the 'Majestic Sea', even with her cutting across their course, they would be able to avoid a collision and turn the ship round in circle. This would have avoided heading towards the 'Majestic Sea' and reduced the speed of advance. Instead, Ivo acted from instinct. He saw the 'Majestic Sea' was now heading across his course from his port to starboard, so he ordered the ship hard to port. This would take the ship around the stern of the 'Majestic Sea'.

The Third Officer slid down beside Mike Prentiss to help him up. Mike was pretty dazed, but realised that the ship had to alter back to starboard to clear the tanker. 'Hard to starboard!' he shouted. The Quartermaster immediately put the wheel over to starboard. The ship did not respond immediately as the momentum was still taking her to port, but this gradually slowed and then stopped. After a slight hesitation, the ship began to come back to starboard and her original course. Mike picked himself up and, looking out of the bridge windows, he stared in disbelief as he saw, just a mile away, the 'Vacuum Pioneer' crossing his bow from port to starboard.

The two ships, with a collective weight of 200,000 tonnes, were now heading for each other at a combined speed of 40 miles an hour.

Vacuum Pioneer

Ivo saw that the 'Majestic Sea' had now reversed her course and was heading back to her starboard. The navigation lights, which were meant to show this aspect, were diminished by the thousands of bright lights from the passenger accommodation. All Ivo could discern was that the 'Majestic Sea' was now heading back the other way and had altered her course to starboard again. In a last desperate act, Ivo order the wheel back to his starboard.

At the same time, on the 'Majestic Sea', Mike ordered his wheel back to port. It was the last act of a tragic dance. Mike's last order altered the head-to-head final approach to opening the bow of the 'Majestic Sea' to the oncoming tanker, which now approached slightly on the starboard side.

Jim and Helen had reached Helen's deck and could hear the noise from the cobbled town square, which was on the same level. Opening from the foyer, they could see into the square where a large crowd was watching a jazz band playing in the centre. At that moment, Martha from the dress shop saw them and beckoned them over. Helen looked up at Jim.

'Just for a moment, can we? I want to say thank you again.' Jim smiled and pushed her into the square, carefully avoiding the cobbles.

Martha came over and noticed Helen's right hand covering Jim's as he held the chair.

'Helen you look beautiful. You both look so happy. Isn't it a lovely evening?' She swept her arms out to encapsulate the moment of gaiety from the band and the crowd. Suddenly she staggered. There was a moment of puzzlement and then the band stopped playing and the ship heeled over to starboard. People started screaming and some stumbled and fell, dragging their companions down with them. Jim fought to hold on to the wheelchair. The ship carried on heeling and more people fell over. Now they were all starting to slide to the starboard side except for a large pile around the fountain in the middle. Band instruments were flying now. Jim, in desperation, grabbed Helen from out of the chair and threw her onto the deck with him holding her. Martha was swept away by a collision of bodies that passed like a wave. Then the heeling stopped.

'Jim, what is going on?' screamed Helen in fright.

'I don't know,' he shouted. He gritted his teeth in pain as he desperately tried to counter the slide. 'It could be the stabilisers.'

Slowly the ship began to come back upright and the pressure on Jim's arms eased. He held Helen tightly. She was shaking. 'It's all right,' Jim gasped. 'We're back up again.'

In the ballroom, chaos reigned. Hundreds of passengers had been swept off their feet into a jumbled heap along the starboard side. Worse, all the tables and chairs had toppled down on top of them. Among the screams were groans and cries of help from the injured. The band had toppled off their podium and the piano had slid over and crashed on top of one of the players, killing him instantly.

The scene was repeated throughout the ship. In the bars, casino, nightclub and other lounges, passengers and crew were thrown in disarray against the starboard side, causing massive damage and multiple casualties.

In the engine room, one of the engine crew had been thrown off the second level platform to land on the bottom engine gratings, where he lay semi-conscious with a broken back. As yet, he had not been noticed in the urgent scramble to check the various engine systems and deal with the alarms that were sounding in the control room.

In the ship's hospital, the phones were ringing incessantly for the duty nurse, who was still picking herself up from the deck as the ship came back to her upright position.

In the nightclub, the cadets, who had been given special dispensation to attend the party night, were all sitting at a table when the ship heeled. Their drinks slid off the table, drenching Zhou in beer and causing her to shout in dismay. The next moment, all the cadets found themselves on the floor, sliding uncontrollably amidst the tangled furniture and the struggling mob of passengers.

Captain Cota was talking with Iain and Patrick when the heel occurred. The air conditioning was having difficulty coping in the main ballroom and they were standing outside in the main staircase area, away from the noise, to discuss the problem. The heel caused them to pause and then as it increased they staggered and groped for the rails at the sides of the foyer. Iain and Patrick found the rail in time, but Cota missed and was thrown partly down the stairway, ending up stunned and bleeding against the side of the stairs. As the vessel straightened, Iain and Patrick helped him up.

'Fucking hell! What's going on?' shouted Patrick.

'I must get to the bridge,' mumbled Cota still dazed.

Iain noticed Cota's leg bent outwards at an angle from his body.

'Fuck, his leg is broken. Patrick help him!' shouted Iain. He looked around in desperation and saw two waiters getting to their feet further down the stairs.

'You two come here, now! Help the Captain to the bridge!' he turned to Patrick. 'I'm going to the engine room. See you there when you make it.' He dashed away as Patrick and the two waiters helped Cota to his feet and started to help him to the bridge.

Vacuum Pioneer

The heel on the 'Vacuum Pioneer' was nothing like as pronounced as on the 'Majestic Sea'. The 'Vacuum Pioneer' was what is called a 'light' ship with only 5,000 tonnes of cargo remaining. She was fully ballasted which meant she was stiffer in the water and, therefore, although her heel was quick, it was short. Even so, it was very noticeable, especially to those who were familiar with the sea. The Captain woke instantly beside Gerdy and grabbed the phone. After a few rings went unanswered, he leapt from the bed and quickly dressed.

'What's the matter, Karl?' asked Gerdy.

'I don't know, nothing probably. Go back to sleep.' He was just about to leave the bedroom when the collision occurred.

On the bridge, they had made their final fatal move and all they could do in the few seconds remaining was to watch the two ships hurtle together. The 'Majestic Sea' loomed over the 'Vacuum Pioneer', and then came the screaming and screeching of metal smashing together. The impact knocked the bridge crew off their feet, even though they were holding on. In the seamen's mess, where they were holding a video evening, the unsuspecting crew were picked up like rag dolls and thrown against the bulkhead, where they slid down to the deck, leaving streaks of blood on the white formica. One of them never moved again. Another two lay there groaning from broken bones.

In the engine room, the duty engineer who was doing the rounds was thrown from the platform on which he was standing onto the top of the port generator some twenty feet below. He landed on his skull, which cracked open like an egg. He never knew what happened.

Karl was thrown backwards back into the bedroom and landed on top of Gerdy. This softened his impact and together they were then thrown against the wardrobe. Luckily, this was only a short distance, leaving them bruised and gasping for air but alive. It was a similar story for the rest of the crew who were in their bunks. Briget and Eric were curled up together and were protected by the duvet they were snuggled in.

Chapter 31

On the *'Majestic Sea'*, the Ice Pilot picked himself up from the deck where he had landed after rolling out of his bunk. He grabbed his jacket and staggered to the door and, managing to wrench it open, fought the short distance to the bridge door. Flinging it open, he pulled himself onto the bridge as the ship came upright. In the darkness, all he could see was the enormous dark shape of the approaching tanker. Her navigation light huge and glowing was only seconds away. Then came the impact. Once again, he was hurled onto the deck, this time banging his head against one of the instrument islands.

The ice-strengthened bow of the *'Vacuum Pioneer'* struck first at a slight angle directly under the *'Majestic Sea's'* bridge. The impact was shattering. Both ships reeled and a scream of tortured metal drowned out all other sounds.

The *'Vacuum Pioneer'* tore into the side of the *'Majestic Sea'* like a tin opener. Even though she was high, having discharged most of her cargo, she still had a substantial draught and deep down her ice-strengthened bulbous bow gouged into the *'Majestic Sea'* below the waterline. Higher up, the bow scythed along the starboard accommodation level with number three deck. It ripped apart the cabins and destroyed the row of lifeboats neatly parked in their davits. The screeching of the metal tearing and breaking overcame the screams of those hapless passengers who spilled from the shattered cabins out into the night. Many fell onto the deck of the tanker, where their bodies lay shattered. Some were left crawling in agony on the steel decks amid the pipes. Others fell in between the two ships to be ground into a red pulp. It was endless as the two ships ground together.

The savage impact of the collision threw everyone off their feet. Fixings broke loose and the windows cracked and smashed. The public rooms were a total disaster of wrecked furniture and bodies. The screaming of the frightened and wounded could be heard throughout the ship. The cabins weren't spared. People were thrown from their bunks and then further injured by furniture breaking loose and toppling onto them. Those who were able staggered out of their cabins in search of loved ones, desperately trying to find out what had happened. Others simply sat around on the decks in stunned shock.

In the cobbled square, Jim was thrown down and spun around. He lost his grip of Helen. Looking up, he saw the huge glass dome shatter and the glass start to fall down as if in slow motion. The chandelier started to swing heavily and then broke loose. Jim screamed, 'Helen! Look out!'

Jim covered his head as the glass shards began to hit the cobbles all around him. Suddenly there was a massive crash as the chandelier hit the ground, narrowly missing him. Jim scrambled to his feet and, turning round, he saw that the square was covered in broken glass and bodies, some moving, others trying to stand, but some lying still. In the centre was the wreckage of the huge chandelier. Martha was lying underneath, her body covered but her face staring at him with sightless eyes. To his horror, he saw Helen lying beside Martha, her white dress covered with blood, her eyes closed.

Patrick and the waiters carrying Cota fell awkwardly as the ship shuddered from the collision. Cota cried out in agony as his broken leg was flung heavily against the side of the alleyway. He grabbed hold of Patrick by his collar.

'Get me to the bridge! Whatever happens, get me there!' They picked him up again and carried on up the stairs.

Vacuum Pioneer

The 'Vacuum Pioneer' continued to scrape down the starboard side of the 'Majestic Sea', sparks flying into the air as it tore its way through the thin metal hull. The ice-strengthened hull of the tanker gave protection only so far along the hull. With the hulls tight together, the frames on the side of the 'Vacuum Pioneer' started to buckle under the tremendous force being exerted on them. With a noise like thunder, the steel plates bent and ripped apart, exposing the side tanks. Even the double hull failed to stop the tearing as the rupture continued into the inner hull, exposing the cargo tanks. One by one, they smashed open.

The cargo tanks were all empty except for No 3 tank where 5,000 tonnes of highly inflammable aviation fuel was sloshing around. In seconds, the tank ripped open and air rushed in. Immediately, the fuel poured out and streaked down the hulls of both ships.

Sparks showered down on the fuel and the open cargo tanks. There was a flash of bright white light and then an explosion of sound. The decks of the tanker heaved upwards and a ball of flame hurled skywards, expanding outwards. On the port side, it expanded into the air and sea. On the starboard side, it blew into the side of the 'Majestic Sea'. A ball of flame and hot fuel blew into the gashes in the hull. It blew upwards searing the upperworks of the 'Majestic Sea', blackening and blistering the immaculate white paintwork. It burnt to a crisp the bodies of the dead, dying and injured passengers on the deck of the tanker as it passed over them. Its hot flame seared those in the cabins in its path. It was mercifully quick. Hundreds died in the blink of an eye. Its hot breath then licked at the front of the accommodation *of the tanker and swirled around the bridge. Ivo and the Quartermaster were enveloped in flame as they and the bridge around them were engulfed in a ball of fire.*

The explosion at last subsided with a shaking of both ships for a third and final time.

Chaos reigned on the bridge of the '*Majestic Sea*'. Lights were flashing on many of the panels with the corresponding alarms howling. Mike Prentiss was in total shock, holding onto the forward rails staring out, not even hearing the pleading of the Third Officer. Peter, the First Officer, hurled himself through the bridge door and took in the scene with horror and bewilderment. Graham, the Ice Pilot, was staggering to his feet, holding his head which was bleeding copiously on the left side where he had hit it on the side of the navigation console. Peter was about to speak when he saw the main mast of the tanker about to come abreast of the bridge just a few feet apart. He opened his mouth. At that moment, the bridge turned white and all sound stopped. The air was sucked from the bridge and in an instant the bridge turned glowing red as, with a roar, a blast of hot air hit the back of the bridge shattering all the windows. Fortunately, the bridge staff were not standing on the starboard side as the hot blast swirled through the bridge and shattered the armoured front glass of the bridge wing.

Jim cradled Helen in his arms as the ship shook and the sound of the explosion coursed through the accommodation. Her eyes were closed, her body crushed and blood was trickling from the corner of her mouth. Jim was oblivious to the destruction around him. His world for a moment was just the two of them, a cocoon of denial surrounding them. Helen murmured, 'Jim.'

'It's all right,' he said. 'You've been hurt, but don't worry, I'm here.'

Her eyes fluttered open and she smiled weakly. 'I knew.'

'Don't talk. I'll get help.'

'Oh Jim, I knew. I had you for a moment.' He squeezed her hand.

'You'll always be with me.'

'I can't feel anything, Jim. I'm frightened.' He held her close and kissed her lips.

There was a faint smile on her face. She whispered, 'Jim,' then closed her eyes. She died without any further sound.

Jim gently laid Helen down. Gradually the sound around him returned and he began to comprehend the devastation. There was a haze in the air and then he smelt smoke. The ship was also listing slightly. He ran over to one of the shops and found the telephone. He dialled the bridge.

Peter rapidly came to his senses and instinctively staggered to the engine controls and put the throttles to stop. On the after fire panel, rows of red lights were flashing. Warning lights were also showing on the ballast control panel indicating the automatic ballasting functions in action. Phones were ringing on several panels. Other islands of instruments were silent, their functions destroyed by the collision and shock.

He answered the phone on the main control panel. It was Jim. 'Thank Christ you're there!' shouted Peter.

'Calm down!' said Jim. 'Just tell me what has happened.'

'We've been in a collision with a tanker. She has scraped down the starboard side, then exploded. Several fires are burning on the starboard side. We haven't seen the Captain, and the Safety Officer isn't answering from the emergency control room.'

'Who is on the bridge?'

'Me, the Ice Pilot, but he's injured, one of the Third Officers, Cadet Bindra and Mike, the Junior Second Officer who's in shock.'

'Right, now listen to me. Call everyone to their evacuation stations. Tell them not to return to their cabins. Lifejackets will be issued to them at their stations. Send out an all ships distress call and give our position. We want immediate assistance. Tell them the ship is sinking. Tell them we have 4,000 persons on board, many injured. Have you got that?'

'Yes, Sir. Are we already sinking?'

'I don't know. Now just listen. Call the crew to emergency stations. I'm going to the emergency control room and I will call you again from there. Have you heard from the engine room yet?'

'No, Sir.'

'Call them. Advise them of the situation and tell them that we have severe damage on the starboard side and we need all the pumps on. Right, get on with all that. I'll call again shortly.'

In the engine room, water was surging in through a gaping hole in the side of the ship. Engineers were swarming around equipment and various panels, trying to cope with the different alarms and getting what pumps they could on line. Iain and the First Engineer were desperately standing in the control room watching the huge control panel readouts.

'She's listing,' said the First Engineer.

'I know. I can feel it. Never mind the main engines, we have one job now, to keep the generators on line as long as possible. Have we heard anything from the bridge?'

'Nothing yet. Poor bastards have got their hands full. I have a team standing by in the emergency generator room just in case.' Iain was watching the water level in the engine room. 'I have a feeling that we'll need them soon.'

The direct bridge phone went. Iain grabbed it immediately. Peter hurriedly explained the situation.

'Who is in command?'

'Presently the Staff Captain, but he's heading for the emergency control room. We can't contact the Safety Officer.'

'The Captain?'

'We don't know.'

'Right, tell the Staff Captain I have all the pumps running, but that the engine room is flooding. I will concentrate on keeping the generators on line and maintaining the fire main pressure. Keep me informed.' Iain slammed the phone down.

Cota and Patrick reached the bridge with the two waiters. 'Good luck, Sir,' Patrick said, before disappearing and racing down to the engine room.

Peter grabbed Cota and assisted him to the command chair where he sat down heavily, sticking his leg out to the side.

'Go to your stations,' Peter said to the waiters, who also disappeared.

'What has happened?' Cota demanded. Peter briefly recounted the collision.

'On the Staff Captain's orders, the ship is at emergency stations and we have ordered all passengers to their embarkation stations. We have started lowering the boats to the embarkation deck on the port side. We have sent out an all ships distress call and have two ships responding, but the nearest is ten hours away. We are in touch with the Canadian Air Force at Gander and have asked them for liferaft drops and any other assistance they can give. The Canadian Coastguard will sail as soon as possible and we have boats coming out of Greenland. As I have said, the nearest is ten hours away.'

'Next, what's the situation on board?' asked Cota.

'Confused, Sir. We know we have several fires on the starboard side, and all the lifeboats on that side are gone or wrecked. The ship has a list to starboard, indicating we have damage to the hull. The list at the moment is increasing at around three degrees every five minutes. We have not established communications with the emergency control room. The Staff Captain rang in just before you arrived and said that he is going to the emergency control room and will call from there.'

'What about the engine room?'

'The Chief says that the engine room is flooding and that he is concentrating on the pumps, the fire mains and keeping the generators on line as long as possible.

'The First Electro-Technical Officer is now on the bridge. He came a few minutes ago and is taking over the outside communications. The Third Mate and Cadet are dealing with internal communications.'

'How long ago did the collision happen?'

Peter looked at the clock. '15 minutes ago.'

'What about the other ship?'

'She's astern of us, on fire but still afloat.'

Cota rubbed his eyes. 'Dear God.'

Vacuum Pioneer

Karl had been saved from incineration by five seconds. He was at the bottom of the stairs to the bridge when the explosion sent the fireball through the bridge deck. He was also saved by the fact that the bridge door was a fire door. He was thrown back and hit the bulkhead. He lay there dazed for a moment. Thank God for thick Norwegian skulls, he thought. He crawled up the stairs and, feeling the heat through the door, had the sense not to go through. Instead he staggered back down and went to the port side door. Opening it, he went out onto the deck. The smoke was swirling around and the heat was intense. He went round the back of the accommodation and stared in disbelief at the burning side of the 'Majestic Sea' just astern of them. It seemed as if most of the starboard side of the ship, for about a hundred metres of the length, was ablaze. The sky was red, with black smoke billowing across before disappearing into the darkness of the night. Even the sea around was in flames from the spilt fuel. The stench of acrid smoke and petroleum filled the air. Karl felt a hand on his shoulder. It was Eric.

'Thank God you're all right, Sir. We've collided with that cruise ship and the starboard tank has blown. We have a hole in the main deck big enough to drive a bus through.'

'What about the side?'

'I don't know yet, but we have a list of about 5 degrees. I can't get to the bridge so I phoned the engine room and asked them to put the pumps on all the starboard side tanks. They reported that at the moment the engine room is dry.'

'She's down by the head as well,' said Karl and he pointed ahead where the bow was down in the water.

'I've got the fire party ready on the port side of the accommodation and I'm ready to try to get out onto the main deck to see what's happening.'

He gave Karl a walkie-talkie. 'I don't think this will be much good at the moment. That cruise ship is on every channel. They are in real trouble from the sound of it.'

'More than we are?'

'We haven't got thousands of passengers.'

'What about the boat party?'

'The Second Mate is standing by with two sailors on the embarkation deck. I've told him to get the port boat lowered ready for embarkation.'

'I want both boats down!'

'The starboard boat is bust up, Sir. We only have the port.'

'That will have to do, and we've got the liferafts. I'll organise the boats. How's Briget?'

'She's fine, Sir. She's with your wife. We've got some injured crew. Briget is down in the messroom treating them and your wife is assisting.'

Karl nodded relieved. 'On your way then. Be careful, I don't want any heroics. Your lives are more important than the ship.'

Karl went back into the accommodation. There was no one there. He picked up the phone to the engine room. Trond answered. Karl briefed him quickly about the situation. As ever, Trond was calm.

'All the engine systems are fine, Captain, apart from some minor damage from the shaking. I regret I have one man dead.'

'I'm sorry, Trond. There are a lot of people dying tonight.'

'The fire pumps are on. All the pumps are on the starboard side tanks. I feel it is pointless though as the *sea is coming in faster than we can pump it out. Looking at our control board, we have three cargo tanks breached on the starboard side. I have counterflooded on the port side which is why we don't have much of a list. We also have flooding in the bulbous bow area forward and I have pumps on that.'*

'Well done, Trond. I'll leave that in your hands then. I've ordered the lifeboat to be lowered ready to use if we have to. Eric has the emergency party out on deck and is trying to see what is going on and getting an idea of the damage. I've told him no heroics. The weather's not bad and if I can't get anything definite soon we'll abandon her. No sense in any more casualties.'

He put the phone down and went out onto the short embarkation deck. The enclosed port boat was already down and the hatches were open. Arturo was standing by with two sailors. They were all in their orange survival suits. Black smoke was building around the deck.

Arturo was coughing 'The boat is ready, Sir.'

Karl nodded and held his hand up. The Mate was talking on the walkie-talkie. 'We're on the main deck, Sir, and I have two hoses rigged. All I can do is boundary cooling down the accommodation front at the moment. There's a huge hole in the deck over No 3 tank, but I can't see any damage over the side on the starboard side yet. The port side looks all right. I've sent the Bosun and a sailor up onto the bridge deck. There's smoke coming from there so it seems likely there is a fire up there as well.'

'At least the smoke is blowing forward.'

Karl turned to Arturo. 'Take your men up to the bridge deck and take charge of the fire fighting there. Do what you can.'

He spoke again to Eric. 'I've just sent the boat party up to the bridge as well.'

'Sir, I think you should know, there are a lot of burnt bodies on the main deck'.

'What!'

'Bodies, Sir. So far, we have seen about twenty. They are very badly burnt and there are a couple of children among them.'

'My God, they must have fallen from the ship. Look, do what you can forward. If most of the fuel has spilt out, there won't be much left to fuel the fire. Just keep it from the accommodation. I think the fire will go out on its own. I'll go up and take charge of the bridge fire team. One thing, I haven't managed to send out a distress signal as I can't get to the bridge, but I'm certain the other ship will have. Keep in touch.'

Gerdy and Briget were with the Cook in the crew messroom dealing with the wounded. Two crew had broken bones and were lying on the mess tables. There was a body in the corner, covered with a blanket. Other crew had called by to have various cuts patched up and then disappeared again. Briget's hands kept shaking.

'I'm sorry, Mother,' she said.

'It's all right, Briget. I'm frightened as well.'

'Do we know what is happening?'

'No, but don't worry. They'll look after us. We must get on here.'

At that moment, the messroom phone rang. The Cook went over and answered it. He listened for a moment and then called Gerdy.

'It's the Captain.' She rushed over and grabbed the phone.

'Karl, are you all right?'

'Of course I am. What about you?'

'We're fine. Briget is here with me looking after the injured.'

'How many are there?'

'Two. One broken leg and another with a broken arm, but he's also hit his head hard and I think he is concussed. I don't know, I'm not a doctor. Briget is dealing him. There's also one dead, the steward.'

'That makes two. We have one dead in the engine room as well.'

'Is help coming?'

'I don't know, Gerdy. If there is, it'll be a long time. At the moment, we're on our own, but don't worry. We still have the engines and power. The ship is listing, but it looks like we have stabilised that. The Mate is dealing with the fire on deck and I'm going to the fire on the bridge.'

'What about those on the bridge?'

'I don't know, but I fear the worst. Now, can you move the casualties up to the boat deck if we have to?'

'Not without help.'

'OK. Stay where you are. If we need to get them up, I'll send help. It's better to keep them in the warmth as long as possible. I'm going now. I love you.'

'I love you too,' Gerdy replied.

Chapter 32

The starboard side of the ship from decks 2 to 5 was well alight. The hull, blackened with blistered paint, was also on fire.

Jim arrived at the emergency control room when he saw Cadet Matheson running towards him.

'Hold it!' Jim shouted. 'Where are you going?'

'To the emergency control room, Sir. I'm to stand by there.'

'Where is the Safety Officer?'

'He's with the fire party.'

'Damn it. He's supposed to be here.'

'He was here, Sir. Then he went to assess the situation.'

'So, what's happening?'

'We're missing a lot of people from the fire parties so the Safety Officer has made two parties. One is on deck 3 and the other is on deck 4. Sir, there are a lot of passengers trapped in the cabins and we can't get to them. There are bodies lying around everywhere!'

'Come inside and calm down. Now, sit down and breathe deeply.'

Jim picked up the phone and called the bridge. He was passed to Cota.

'Good to hear you, Sir. I've found the Safety Officer. He's directing the fire parties at the scene of the fire. Apparently, passengers are trapped and we can't get them out. I want to go and see the fire situation, and then I want to get up to the assembly areas.'

'What about boarding the boats, Jim?' asked Cota.

'We don't have enough boats for everyone. I want to get the security people organised to deal with that situation. I'll get them ready now. I think we know that she's going down. Even if she doesn't, we have to be ready.'

'Mr Fallows has already called the bridge. He is in the assembly lounges with his team. He says that there are hundreds of injured passengers. At the moment, most of the passengers are in shock and things are quiet. I've called the medical staff and they have moved their team up to the embarkation areas and set up a hospital in the forward lounge. That's the best place at the moment as the ship's head is still coming up to wind and they are away from the smoke. We've got help coming, but it's several hours away. Jim, the water is rising in the engine room and they don't know how long they can hold on there. We may well lose the main generators before long.'

'Do we know the extent of the damage to the hull?'

'As far as we can tell, there is a tear along the side of the ship, probably caused by the tanker's bulbous bow. In some areas, it's bad, in others not so. The worst seems to be alongside the engine room and then down aft. Our flooding indicators up here show serious flooding along the starboard side in three areas covering five sections of the ship. We know that most of deck 1 is now flooded on the starboard side. The ballasting computer is still compensating, but the list is increasing.'

Jim looked at the heel indicator on the bulkhead. It was reading 6 degrees to starboard.

'Sir, with this level of damage, she is going to go down. I suggest that we get the boats down as soon as we can and start getting the passengers off. Even if we're wrong, they can always come back, but looking at that heel, I don't think we have much time. Can you send someone down with one of the bridge loud hailers to meet Mr Fallows and tell him I will join them shortly?' Jim asked.

'On the fire indication board, the whole of the starboard side of the ship from amidships aft from decks 3 to 5 is showing fire.'

'Sir, if that is the case, all we can do is to try and hold the fire off the port side boat embarkation area. What worries me is that she will heel over too much before we can get the boats away.'

'If you think she is going down, then we can override the computer and use manual control to flood as much to the port side as possible. One problem is that most of the large tanks are down aft. It will put her further down in the water aft, but it may slow the list.'

'I think list is our biggest problem, Sir.'

'Then we will do that.'

'Do we have any estimate of how long we have?'

'Based on the present rate of heel, it could be as little as one hour, two at the most.'

'We have no time to waste, Sir. As we don't have enough boats, we must only take the injured, then the women and children.'

'I agree. I'll make the announcement now.'

'Do you want me on the bridge?'

'No, Jim. You carry on below. Keep me informed about the situation. Where are you going now?'

'I was going to see the fire situation, but as we will be starting embarkation, I'll get the boat launching organised and see what the situation is in the embarkation lounges.'

Cota turned to the officers on the bridge.

'You all heard that. The Staff Captain is getting the boats ready for evacuation. Peter, override the ballasting and get what you can into the port side. Cadet, bring me the microphone.'

Jim spotted a row of walkie-talkies in their charging stations. 'Grab some of those,' he said to Matheson as he helped himself to three. 'Take them down to the fire parties. There's no point staying here. Just keep me briefed about the situation there. I'm heading for the lounges.'

On the way to the lounge, Jim called Jan. It took several attempts before he reached him.

'Give me a report, Jan.'

'We have all the fire equipment now distributed between decks 3 and 4. The problem is not manpower, but that we can't get enough men in the narrow alleyways. We are losing deck 3 but at the moment we are holding deck 4. Unfortunately, fires are being reported from other areas further away. The latest is smoke on deck 5.'

'Who have you got with you?'

'Gaspar, the Senior Second Officer, two Third Officers, two Cadets, an Electrical Officer, two Engineer Officers, the Bosun, about 30 seamen and assorted hotel staff.'

'I want one Third Officer, one of the Cadets, the Bosun and half the seamen to go immediately to their boat stations and start lowering the port boats to the embarkation deck.'

'I won't be able to carry on with boundary cooling if you take them away.'

'Don't worry about that, Jan. Have you seen the list? We don't have much time. Just hold the fire back on deck 3 from the port side while we get the boats away. If necessary, take your crews away from deck 4. Deck 3 has the priority.'

'What about the passengers trapped on deck 4? We're trying to get to them now.'

'Jan, I've told you. Do what you can, but keeping the fire away from the port boats is imperative. You have a few passengers trapped. We have thousands to get off. Now, send those seamen immediately. Tell the Third

Officer and the Bosun to start lowering the boats as soon as they get there.'

'Aye aye, Sir.'

'What about the passengers on deck 3?'

'I don't think there is much left of them, Sir. If you could see it down here, you would understand.'

A temporary hospital area had been set up in the forward lounge, and Dick and his staff were trying to cope with the avalanche of casualties that had descended on them. One of the nurses was directing several hotel staff who were ferrying supplies, while the remaining three and the junior Doctor were attending to the most seriously injured. The entertainers and dancers had been recruited to assist. The floor of the room was covered with sheets and mattresses that had been dragged in, and lying on these were hundreds of passengers and crew mixed together. Many relatives of the injured were sitting with them. Fresh casualties were being brought in continuously.

Hinchley appeared beside Dick. 'Don't stop, Doctor. Just wanted to update you. Cota has advised me that help is coming, but it is several hours away. He says that will be too late. We are going to have to abandon the ship soon.'

Dick looked up. 'Just how the hell are we going to abandon ship with these people? Half of them can't walk!'

'What do you need?'

'About three hundred stretchers. We're running out of bandages and have hardly any morphine left. We've run out of Entonox, so I can't relieve pain. All we can do is give aspirin and put patches on. We need medical supplies. We need a miracle. Can I smell smoke?'

'Yes, you can. The starboard side of the ship is on fire and we are losing the battle'. He keyed in his walkie-talkie to the bridge. 'Captain, I'm with the Surgeon in the forward lounge. It's bad here. There are hundreds of casualties and there are no stretchers to move them. We need medical supplies urgently.'

'We'll relay that to the Air Force. They are preparing their planes to fly out. We have asked for liferafts to be dropped. We'll see if they can parachute medical supplies as well.'

In the embarkation areas in the other lounges, some passengers were standing in groups and others were sitting on the floor. Many were weeping in distress and fear. More passengers were arriving, many without their lifejackets. Some were in their night clothing or still in evening or party dress. Bert Fallows and his men were walking among them reassuring them and trying to keep the panic down. Henry Milau, the Hotel Manager was also directing the hotel staff to assist the elderly and infirm. Several of them were going around distributing lifejackets from the stores on the upper deck.

There was a large group of crew doing nothing. They were sitting around with their lifejackets. Hinchley went over to Henry.

'I want a sweep of the accommodation. There must still be many down below needing help. Get the crew to search through the decks, starting from the lowest ones.'

'I've tried, but they won't go back down below.'

Hinchley went to them and shouted for them to get up and join the others who were helping. Most would not look at him and turned away.

The loudspeakers made an announcement. 'Your attention please. I repeat, your attention please. The Captain will speak to you.' There was a noticeable hush in the lounges. Cota spoke; he sounded tired.

'This is the Captain. As you know, we have had a serious collision with another vessel. The result of that collision is that we have a fire on the starboard side of the ship and a hole in the side. That is why the ship is listing to starboard. Help is on its way from several ships and planes but, as a precaution, I have decided to disembark the passengers only. I repeat, passengers only. All crew except for the boat crews will remain with the ship at this time. If the situation improves, we will re-embark the passengers. We will only use the port side boats. Therefore, do not pay attention to your previous boat numbers.

'Many people are injured and it is my intention to disembark them first. When we are ready, we will need volunteers to assist with carrying casualties down to deck 3. Once there, you will hand the casualties over to the boat crew and leave the area. You will not get into the boats. Once the casualties are embarked, women, children and the infirm will be embarked.' Immediately, the noise grew in the lounges with people crying out and shouting. 'I repeat, women, children and the infirm. There is to be no argument about this. It will be done in an orderly manner. I promise you the world is watching us. Let the world be able to look with pride on us at this time. Shortly, I will advise you about the boat embarkation. Anyone needing help to the boats, please indicate to the ship's staff. Thank you.'

Hinchley looked at Dick. 'That was a good speech. Do you think it will be enough?'

'It will hold them for a while, but sooner or later they will realise that those remaining are walking dead and then we will see. I think we will have trouble with the crew.'

'I'm just going to say goodbye to my wife and kids,' said Hinchley, 'and then I'll come back to help organise the casualties.'

Jim walked into the main lounge and was instantly mobbed by passengers. He tried to reassure them as he passed through, but their questions became more and more strident. He then saw Zhou with the loud hailer, standing beside Bert Fallows. Bert was like a rock in the stormy sea. The passengers ebbed and flowed around him and he stood unperturbed. This imparted a calmness that radiated in his immediate vicinity. He was pleased to see Jim though.

'Good to see you, Sir. Bit of a mess on our hands tonight though.'

'That's one way of putting it, Bert. How are things here?'

'At the moment, calm but edgy. I think a lot of them don't realise what is happening. The Captain's broadcast helped somewhat. We are going to have to carry wheelchair users down to the boats as we can't push them with the list. We are going to need time, Captain.'

'The seamen are lowering the boats right now, Bert, and when the first few are down, we'll start. We need to start moving the injured now. I want you and your men down by the boats. Do you have any 'equipment' with you?'

'Yes, Sir, but well concealed.'

'Only in extreme circumstances, Bert.'

'I understand, Sir.'

Hinchley appeared. 'You can see what's going on here?' he said.

'All we can do is the best we can.'

'It's going to be chaos.'

'Only if we allow it. It's our job to hold everything together for as long as possible and care for those who need it.'

'What happens at the end then? When all the boats are gone and they realise they are going to die?'

'Hinchley, let's deal with saving who we can first. Once that's done, then we will see what happens. But we will never give up. There must always be hope and that is what we can give them.'

'Even when there's none?'

Jim didn't answer. He called the boat party.

'We've got three boats down ready to go, Sir,' said the Third Officer.

'Right, we'll start with the casualties. Spread them out between the three boats. If anyone is wearing a lifejacket, take it off them as they get in.'

'Take off their lifejackets, Sir?'

'Son, we only have boats for less than half of those on board. We need the space if we are going to cram as many as we can into the boats. Understand?'

Next Jim called Cota on the bridge. 'We're ready to start the embarkation, Sir. Can you call for the casualties and infirm first.'

The loudspeakers made the announcement and gradually a stream of casualties helped by volunteers began to come out of the forward lounge.

'The list is getting worse,' said Hinchley.

'I know, but I'm trying not to think about it. Just keep the passengers moving.' Around them, families were holding on to each other, sobbing at the thought of separation.

On the bridge, two Electro-Technical Officers were now handling the communications. Messages were pouring in. Cota had spoken briefly to Fort Lauderdale and Southampton, but was now ignoring them owing to their incessant questions. There were now seven ships heading towards them and he had been informed of the first plane leaving Gander Air Base in Newfoundland. They would be overhead in 30 minutes. Mike Prentiss was sitting in the corner. He was still in shock and not speaking, just staring out to sea. In normal times, they would have arranged immediate medical attention, but these were not normal times and he was left alone. Graham, the Ice Pilot, was assisting on the internal phones that were calling from different parts of the ship. Then he was plotting the fire situation on the ship's plans laid out on the chart table.

Jan and his fire teams were already exhausted. Water was flooding along the alleyways and the sprinklers were still operating, soaking everyone. Empty air bottles were rolling against the port sides, and exhausted men in fire suits sat against the bulkheads taking short breaks before taking their place on the hoses. The fire party from deck 4 came on the walkie-talkie. 'Sir, we have a problem here. Passengers are interfering with the fire party!'

'Shit,' Jan exclaimed aloud. He quickly left his position at a temporary command desk he had established and hurried to the stairs. The injured passengers were already coming down the stairs being assisted by a mix of passengers and crew. The smoke was causing some of them to cough as they passed.

'Keep to the port side,' Jan shouted.

The stairs were leaning over at an angle as Jan clambered up to deck 4 and then on to where he could see the fire party. Smoke was swirling around on this deck and it stung his eyes. He could see two passengers being held back by Matheson and the Third Officer, Alan Drury. As soon as they saw him coming, they ran to him.

'You must help! Our children are in their cabin along the alleyway here.' It was the Inches. Shirley was screaming.

'Please understand, we can't get into the cabins along there. They are completely blocked off by smoke, and the fire is also blazing in many of the cabins.'

'But you're not trying! Look! Your men are taking the equipment away. Why aren't you trying?' Shirley was distraught and howling her pain. Her husband was trying to comfort her.

Jan was just as upset. 'I'm sorry. I need these men. We have the rest of the passengers to save. There cannot be anyone alive down there and I cannot risk any of my men to search. You must go back immediately to the embarkation lounges. The boats will be leaving soon.'

He turned away, with the parents shouting abuse after him. Shirley collapsed on the deck in hysterics with her husband bent over her.

'Get these men and equipment down to deck 3 as soon as you can,' Jan said to Alan. 'I'm so sorry. I really am.'

He hurried back to the stairs.

Matheson looked at Alan. He grabbed a fire suit and started pulling it on.

'We've been told to withdraw,' Alan said.

Matheson said nothing and carried on putting the suit on.

Alan looked at the parents huddled on the deck. 'Fuck it,' he said and took hold of another fire suit. He turned to his fire team.

'I want you to keep the hoses on us as we go in and keep them on for when we come out,' he ordered the hose party. 'If we do,' he muttered under his breath. They picked up new sets of breathing apparatus and checked the air pressures. 'How do we get them out if we find them?' asked Matheson.

'Get some fire blankets and we'll wrap them up best we can,' Alan replied. Matheson now with his face mask on nodded.

Alan bent down and shook Harvey Inch. 'Which cabin are they in?' Harvey looked up. 'Cabin 68. Their names are Andrew and Nicola.' Shirley sprang to her feet 'Oh God! Thank you, thank you.'

'Don't get your hopes up. All we can do is try.'

Alan turned to the two hose teams. 'Just keep the spray on us. As we go in, try to advance as far as you can. Give me one of the hoses. Keep paying out the slack.' He clipped the guide line on. 'Come on,' he said to Matheson. 'Follow me and hold on to the guide line.' They put their helmets on and, picking up their crow bars, set off down the alleyway towards the red glow ahead in the smoke.

Vacuum Pioneer

Eric had managed to get the fire out on the bridge. The fire party were still spraying water on the steaming metal and smouldering woodwork, but it was out. Carefully, Karl entered the bridge. It was a blackened mess. Everything had been burnt, and even the ship's wheel was now just a set of metal spokes standing out from the steering column. His foot sank down and something crunched. He looked down and saw he was standing on a blackened body. He jumped aside. It was impossible to see who it was. Then he noticed two further bodies, one beside what remained of the steering wheel. He guessed that was the Quartermaster. There was nothing to be done here so he left the bridge and went back down to his cabin. The whole ship reeked of smoke and everything was covered with a greasy black film.

He called the engine room.
   'How is it going down there?' he asked Trond.
   'We are still dry down here and the bulkheads seem to be holding. We are getting nothing out of the other cargo tanks that are not flooded. So far, it looks as if we are stable, but I don't know how long the bulkheads will hold. God knows what strain has been put on the girders.'
   'So, at this moment, we are not sinking?'
   'No, but who knows what will happen. How's the weather?'
   'Still holding.'
   'That's good. We might just get away with it. Have we been able to contact anyone yet?'
   'No, the whole bridge has gone. I found the bodies of the Third Mate and the Quartermaster.'
   'That makes four dead then.'
   'Yes and two injured. Gerdy and Briget are looking after them.'

'How's the Mate doing on deck?'

'He's keeping the accommodation front cool, and it looks like the fire might be dying down. I'll keep you informed.'

Karl went out onto the deck and saw that Eric was still directing the hoses on the front of the accommodation, but he had also advanced further up the deck and had hoses spraying the twisted metal surrounding the hole on the deck. As Karl approached, Eric took his helmet off and rubbed his eyes.

'Fuck knows how she's holding together,' he said, 'but she is. We're still afloat. If we hadn't been ice class, we'd be on the bottom by now.'

Karl nodded.

'What are we going to do then?' Eric asked.

'At the moment, we stay here until help comes. We have nothing left on the bridge. Even the magnetic compass has been destroyed. The engine works and we can steer her from the emergency steering position in the steering flat. But we have to know where to go.' He looked up. 'The clouds are covering the sky so we can't even see the stars. Anyway, I don't know what damage there is to the hull. Any forward movement might damage her even further.'

'I agree,' said Eric. 'That ship must have sent out distress calls, so help will be coming.'

They both looked over at the 'Majestic Sea', which was now listing over at about 10 degrees, still burning fiercely with thick smoke billowing from the starboard side.

'I have a feeling that we're better off over here,' murmured Karl.

Chapter 33

Alan and Matheson could feel the heat through their suits. The smoke was thick and they had to feel their way along the bulkhead. The first cabins they came to had their doors open and had already been searched. They moved further along, with Alan holding the hose tightly as it bucked with the pressure of the water. The heat was increasing all the time, radiating from the deck below. Even the bulkheads were hot. They were sweating inside their masks. They came to a closed door. Alan played water onto it. They stood to one side as Matheson tried the door. It swung open, but no flame came out. They looked inside through the smoke, but it was empty.

The next cabins were the same on both sides of the alleyway. In one of the following cabins, they found the bodies of two elderly passengers. Alan bent down and turned them over, but found no sign of life. Two more cabins along, they found more dead passengers. All of them had been asphyxiated by the smoke. Matheson tapped Alan on the shoulder and indicated his pressure gauge. Alan also looked at his and found it was low. He realised he was panting; this was using up the air faster than normal. They had just cleared cabin 66. There was no time to waste. Alan turned and gave the hose to Matheson. He unclipped his guide line, put it on Matheson and took the fire blankets. He pointed at himself and then ahead. Matheson nodded. Alan felt the water on his back and saw it hit the smoke ahead of him as he felt his way along.

The fire was now a stronger red glow through the smoke, and Alan knew it was getting close from the intense heat.

He reached cabin 68. The door was shut. He managed to open it slightly, but it was jammed. He took the crowbar and edged it in and then put his weight behind it. Gradually the door eased open. No flames came out. He pressed down on the crowbar again and the door opened enough for him to get through. The cabin was blackened by smoke and he could see that someone had propped a mattress behind the door to try to stop the smoke coming through.

There was no one in the room. So who had put the mattress there? He was about to leave when he noticed that the glass door to the balcony was closed. Just in case, he went over and looked through. There in the flickering red firelight he could see two huddled bodies.

His heart sank. He pushed open the balcony door and stepped out. The balcony was partly wrecked and on one side the rail was torn away. Poor kids. The boy was on top of the girl, obviously trying to protect her. He bent down and tried to turn him over. Suddenly the boy moved.

Alan found himself staring at a blackened, frightened and tearful face, the eyes wide with terror. Then the girl moved as well. He took his face mask off. Immediately the smoke stung his eyes.

'It's all right. Your parents sent me. I've come to get you out, understand?' The children nodded and the girl began to sob.

He looked at his pressure gauge. He reckoned he had about five minutes at the most and presumably Matheson had the same. He gave the children the fire blankets.

'Wrap yourselves in these, now.' He roughly shook the girl. 'Do you want to live?' She nodded again, still crying. 'Then save this till later. Get these around you now. Wait here!'

He took a deep breath and ran back into the cabin and into the bathroom. He turned the tap. Water was still running. He grabbed two towels and held them under the tap. He then put his mask on and took a deep gulp before taking it off again. The towels were soaked and he ran back to the balcony. The two children were standing with the blankets wrapped round them.

He looked at the boy. 'Can you stand and walk with that wrapped around you?'

'I think so,' Andrew replied.

'Good. Now listen, both of you. There's no fire outside, but it's very hot and smoky. I want you to put these towels around your heads and keep your hands inside the blanket but hold it tight to you and don't open it. Andrew isn't it?' The boy nodded.

'OK. Andrew, you will hold on to my belt at the back here and just walk. Don't open your eyes and keep the towel on your head.' Then he turned to Nicola. 'I will carry you. We have one chance at this, but we can do it if you do exactly as I say. Now are you ready?' They nodded again.

'Right. When I hit you, I want you to take a deep breath and hold it.'

He looked at the boy and smiled, and then put his face mask on. He picked the girl up and turned her over so her face was pressed into his shoulder. Then he hit them both on their backs and felt Andrew's hand on his belt. He walked quickly to the door and turned into the alleyway. It was thick with smoke and the red from the fire was perilously close. He walked as fast as he could, holding the girl and feeling his way along the bulkhead on the side. There was no spray of water coming, but there was water running on the deck. As he walked, the water became strong and then looking down he came across the body of Matheson sprawled on the deck. He stepped over him and then heard a coughing behind him. The boy let go. He turned around and with one hand ripped off his face mask and the towel from the boy's face and pressed the mask on.

'Breathe!' he screamed. The boy grabbed the mask and took several breaths. Alan seized the mask away from him and, putting it back on, he grabbed the boy with his free hand and began to run down the alleyway dragging him behind. The girl was struggling and coughing as well. The heat from the fire behind him was more intense and he was slowing down. There was no more air in his mask. His vision was becoming blurred and the children were sagging in his arms. Then he felt the spray of water on his front. A few steps more and he could see the dim shadows of the hose party. He fell into them and they dragged him and the children out into the foyer where their parents were waiting. They laid the children down on the deck and the parents clutched hold of them, crying. Alan collapsed onto his knees.

'Let them breathe, for fuck's sake!' he shouted. 'Get me another breathing set! You put one on as well and follow me!' he said pointing at a sailor. 'Get the resuscitator ready!' He staggered up and took the new set that was passed to him and got it on. He took a few deep breaths and, without waiting for the sailor, plunged into the smoke in the alleyway. The smoke was even thicker now and the heat intense. The fire was spreading. He was so tired, but staggered on, passing the guide line through his hands. Eventually he came to Matheson's body. He bent down and, holding him under his arms, began to drag him along the deck back the way he came. It seemed to take a lifetime. Every step was agony. Then out of the smoke came the sailor. Between them, they dragged Matheson clear into the foyer. Here the parents were still around their children, who were now both crying and clinging on to them.

'Get the resuscitator on him!' Alan shouted to the fire team. They laid Matheson out and put the face piece on him. The machine started. Alan helped by a timer pressed down on Matheson's chest. Minutes passed; there was no reaction. The cadet's eyes were open and unseeing. Alan sat back exhausted against the bulkhead and wept.

One of the sailors came up and shook him gently. He looked up.

'Sir, what do you want to do now?'

Alan pulled himself together.

'Go down to deck 3, all of you. Report to the Safety Officer. Take all the equipment. We're finished here.' He closed his eyes for a moment and then felt a hand on his shoulder. Harvey Inch had seen the dead cadet.

'I'm so very sorry. He died saving our children.'

'That's our job,' Alan replied. 'Go to the boats otherwise they will leave you behind and he will have died for nothing.' Harvey hesitated. 'Go now!' Alan shouted.

In the engine room, Iain and Patrick had done all they could, but now they realised the end had come. The water had risen steadily and they had slowly shut down the main engine and the various auxiliaries as the water had closed on them. 'We'll shut down the generators now, and then go up to the emergency generator room and keep those on line as long as we can,' said Iain. 'We should have brought a bottle of the hard stuff if we'd known we would be down here for so long,' said Patrick. Iain smiled and slapped him on the back. 'When this is all over, I'll buy you every drink in the bar.'

Iain rang the bridge. Cota answered.

'Sorry, Captain, but we have to abandon the engine room now. The Staff Chief and I are going up to the emergency generator room. We'll keep the generators on line as long as possible.'

'Thank you, Iain. I couldn't have asked for more. I'll make a broadcast to warn everyone that some of the lighting will be going off, just so they don't panic.'

'How's it going up there?'

'We've already got some of the boats away. It's been slow as they have been getting the casualties off first, but now it's women and children. I gather from Jim that it's pretty horrific.'

'I can imagine. How much longer have we got?'

'Well, we are over 16 degrees now. We have done all we can to keep her level, but we can't do any more with the tanks so she will now continue to go over. I reckon 40 more minutes, maybe an hour at the most.'

'She's lasting longer than I thought she would,' said Iain. 'I'll be in the emergency generator room.'

'Iain, can you send your officers to the Staff Captain at the port side embarkation deck,' said Cota. 'He needs help there.'

'Will do,' said Iain. 'Patrick and I can run what's left.'

The boat embarkation deck was in chaos. They had managed to get the casualties off, but it had taken valuable time and boat space. Jim had now got the women and children boarding the boats from both ends of the embarkation deck to speed things up. The list was now causing serious problems with movement, especially among the elderly. There were still people on board in wheelchairs who had missed the casualty boats, and waiters were being ordered to carry them to the embarkation deck. Casualties were also still being found and directed to them. A number of crew who brought people down were trying to board the boats and had to be dragged off to make room for the passengers. Another problem was men being parted from their women and children. They were coming down to the embarkation area and the place was clogged with people clinging to each other not wanting to let go.

At least they were getting the boats away now. Jim was seeing boat 6 away. It was packed with 250 passengers, 100 more than the boat was designed for. Piles of lifejackets were scattered all over the deck area, but at least it meant they could get more people in. Jim had half of the security team down with him and they were going round forcing people apart and assisting the women into the boats. Luckily there weren't many children, but the elderly were causing a problem. Hinchley was proving a tower of strength in the lounges and he was keeping the flow going from there.

Jim turned to Zhou. 'I want you to take four seamen and start getting the liferafts inflated and swung out. We'll start boarding them as well. We don't have too much time. The list is increasing. We have to get everything away before it gets to 30 degrees.'

'Aye aye, Sir.' Jim was startled. He had never heard her using the traditional response before. He looked at her. 'I thought it was a good time to say it, Sir.' She smiled brightly and disappeared into the crowd. Jim shook his head. The engineer officers were now arriving and Jim spread them out along the embarkation deck. He also had the assistance of some of the hotel officers, but most were with Hinchley in the lounges. Another boat was lowered and the various officers were moving the single men away back to the lounges. Many were weeping.

Jim's walkie-talkie crackled. It was Bert. 'Captain, can you send up my security people. I need help. There are a few hundred crew and some passengers in the after bar. They have broken in and are loading up on drink. The fat Cruise Director and his wife are with them. It's starting to get ugly. The Cruise Director is telling them they are going to die if they stay. I think they are getting ready to rush the boats. If they do, it could start a panic.'

'Where are you now?'

'I'm standing outside on deck near the bar on the port side.'

'I'll be there shortly. I'll get your men on their way. He called across one of the security men. 'Get your people to Bert. He's outside on deck by the after bar. There's trouble.' The officer saluted and hurried away, calling to the other security officers.

Jim called Jan.

'Jan, I need someone here to take charge. Can you send the Second Officer up?'

'I might as well, Sir. We're pretty well at the end of our resources down here. Everyone is shattered and we seem to be beaten whatever we do.'

'Not so, Jan. You've held the fire back and you're helping us get the boats away.'

'Are they all gone?'

'No, but they will be before long.'

'We'll keep going as long as we can, Sir, but we've run out of air. There's no time to recharge the bottles. Passengers are still trapped in cabins and we can't get to them. The fire is still spreading through the ship. It's now on decks 3, 4 and 5 and smoke has been reported on 6.'

'Jan, just keep at it until we get all the boats and liferafts away.'

'Sir, I've got two of our firemen here. They say we have to close down the forward staircase. The fire and smoke is too dangerous.'

'Hell no, Jan, not yet. We need that staircase!'

'I'm sorry, Sir, but it's bad. I've already sent men to the stairs to stop any more coming down.'

Jim thought desperately. He called Hinchley. 'No more passengers down the forward staircase. It's blocked by fire.'

'Then where the fuck do we send them?'

'Use the two after ones. Send the fit ones outside on deck aft. They can go down the outside ladders there to deck 3 and along to the boats.'

'That's going to take too long.'

'It's all we've got left. You must do this otherwise we're not going to even get all the women off.'

'I'll get crew to show them the way then.'

Jim walked down to where the next boat was filling. The usual scenes of tragedy were taking place and the ship's staff were forcing people apart and pushing the women into the boats. The screaming and shouting was terrible to hear. Jim helped to push the male passengers away from the boat hatch as it was closed on the packed people inside. Immediately the boat started to lower down. The next boat along was already filling. Zhou came on the radio.

'The first of the rafts is ready on the davits, Sir.'

'Get them away as soon as they are full, Zhou. No delay now.'

Jim turned to the Second Engineer, who was directing the passengers. 'Move them forward to the liferafts. We're going to use them as well.'

The Senior Second Officer appeared. He was streaked in sweat and black smoke, his white boiler suit just as filthy as his face.

'Take over Gaspar. Cadet Zhou is lowering the liferafts and we are streaming passengers there as well as to the boats. We've got over half the boats away. Pack them in tight. It doesn't matter how full the boats are. I'm going aft for a few minutes to deal with the problem in the after bar.'

As Jim hurried aft, he called Hinchley. 'How many women and children left?' 'About five or six hundred, and we have about three hundred female crew.'

'The passengers take priority.'

'I agree,' said Hinchley. 'There are also a number of women up here who will not leave their husbands. Mostly elderly.'

'That's to be expected.'

'How many do you think we'll get off?'

'If we can get all the women and kids off, then we'll be lucky.'

'Christ, Captain. That will leave over two thousand on board.'

'You're forgetting the dead. I reckon it'll be more like twelve hundred. All we can do is get as many off as we can. I'm heading aft. I'll have a look at the new passenger route to the boats.'

Jim was called again. It was Zhou. 'Sir, many of the passengers don't have much to wear. They are still in their party clothes and some of the women are already freezing.'

'What the hell do you want me to do about it, Zhou?'

'The liferafts will also be freezing, Sir. They will get hypothermia.'

'Just get them in, Zhou. Never mind the cold. If you pack them tight enough, they will keep each other warm. How many rafts have you got away?'

'Three, Sir.'

'That's bloody good. Just keep going. One thing, Zhou, I want you to coordinate the rafts when they are in the water. You will go on the last one.'

There was no reply.

'Zhou, that's an order. Is that clear?'

'Yes, Sir.'

Jim approached the stern and saw the first of the passengers coming down the outside ladders from the open decks. They were being led by the Purser.

'Keep going,' Jim said. 'Don't stop. When you get to the boat deck, send some further forward to the liferafts. The more elderly can get in the boats.'

'I can't separate them. It's bad enough just getting them down here.'

'Just do your best. There are officers down there to help.'

Jim had to push his way past the passengers up the ladder to the upper decks. The heel of the ship was making it difficult for the passengers to hold on. He got to the upper deck and went inside the accommodation to the after bar. Bert was standing there with his men. They had closed the bar doors and barricaded them.

'I've locked them in, Sir. I thought that was the best way of containing the problem.'

'Leave one of your men here. As soon as all the boats are gone, they are to be let out. We can't leave them there when the ship sinks. I want you to take your men to the lounge and put yourself under Hinchley's command. Help him all you can. We have a problem getting the passengers to the boats. It's taking a long time to get them from the lounges to the embarkation deck and now we've lost the forward staircase because of the fire. Do what you can to hurry them along.'

'Anything else?'

'There are apparently a lot of women passengers who won't leave their husbands. We are going to have to get them out onto the upper deck soon. I want you to tell Hinchley to get the hotel crew organised to go round the upper deck cabins and strip them of their bedding and curtains, anything to give to these passengers to wrap themselves up. It will be cold when they go outside.'

'Is there any point in going out, Sir? I mean, if they are going to drown, why not let them drown in the lounges?'

'Bert, if we admit to that, we stop trying. Our job is to keep them alive as long as we can.'

'I'm on my way, Sir. I presume you'll give Hinchley or me a shout when you want the remaining people moved.'

'I will. Just get going. I don't think it will be long.'

Jim came outside onto the deck and grabbed hold of the ship's rail. He looked astern at the tanker, which was stopped about a mile away. Her lights were burning brightly. They seemed to have put the fire out and, although she was listing, that seemed to have stopped as well. Jim turned away and then stopped.

'My God!' he shouted, and raced up the outer ladder to the upper deck and then along that. He ran as fast as he could with the list on the ship. It was a long way to the bridge. He was gasping as he entered the accommodation and climbed up the last stairs to his deck and then along to the bridge. The door was fastened open and he ran through. The bridge was brightly lit and several officers were talking into phones or crowded round the instruments. Cota was sitting in one of the command chairs, with Peter, the First Officer, by his side.

'Staff Captain, Sir,' said Peter when he saw Jim. Cota turned and he grabbed Jim's hand.

'Jim, are we going to get them off?' It was more a plea than a question.

'Sir, the stairs are holding us up. We have too many decks to go down and we have now lost the forward staircases. I must act quickly. Do we have contact with the tanker?'

'No,' said Peter. 'We've tried, but they're either not listening or their radios are out.'

'What about Morse? Have we tried using the signalling lamp?' No one spoke. 'Give me the signalling lamp!' Cadet Bindra quickly opened a bridge locker and pulled out the lamp and plugged it into the battery.

'Let's hope it's charged,' said Jim. 'Put the bridge lights off!' he shouted. The bridge was plunged into darkness. Jim lifted the lamp, pointed it at the tanker and started flashing the call-up signal.

Vacuum Pioneer

Karl and Eric stood together on the main deck looking at the smouldering hole in the deck. The steel was still too hot to touch around the edges, but the fire was out. The crew were still spraying water on the deck and smoke continued to come out, but there were no flames.

'As long as the weather stays like this, we will be all right,' said Karl. 'The good thing is that we still have power and machinery. That means we can take a tow and get her into port.'

The Cook appeared in the starboard alleyway. 'I've got tea and sandwiches for the crew. Can we bring them out, Captain?' Eric looked at Karl.

'It's safe enough now.'

'All right, Cook, get them out here.'

Immediately behind the Cook, Briget and Gerdy appeared with trays. They brought them to where Karl was standing and the crew crowded round.

'I think we're all right,' Karl said to Gerdy. She squeezed his arm.

'Sir,' said one of the crew, 'the cruise ship is signalling us.'

Karl looked across. 'It's the general call sign. Shit, we can't answer. We've no light.'

'I've got a halogen light in my cabin,' said Eric.

He dashed off and returned a minute later. He gave the light to Karl who instantly replied to the cruise ship. There was a pause and then Karl, reading the returning signal light, said slowly, 'VHF channel 16.'

He picked up the walkie-talkie. 'I listened on this before, but all there was was internal chatter. This is 'Vacuum Pioneer', Captain.'

'Captain, 'Majestic Sea'.'

'I am listening, Captain.'

'We have assistance coming, but not for several hours. How are you?'

'We have several dead and have lost the bridge. The fire is out, the ship is stable and we can wait for the rescue ships.'

'Captain, our situation is critical. We have lost half our boats and are sinking. We have over one thousand persons without boats to get them off.'

Eric whistled. 'Did he say one thousand? Fucking hell!'

'Vacuum Pioneer, can you help us?'

'What the hell does he think we can do?' said Eric.

'I think I know,' said Karl. 'What do you want us to do?'

'Can you come alongside?'

'He's mad!' said Eric.

'No, he's not mad, he's desperate.'

Eric looked at Karl. 'You knew he was going to suggest that didn't you?'

Karl nodded. 'It's what I would have asked.'

'So, what are you going to do?' Eric asked. 'We have our own safety to consider. There's Gerdy and Briget as well. We're safe now. Any force against the ship or even movement could cause the bulkheads to go and then we go down like a stone.'

'You decide.'

'Me? I'm not the Captain, you are!'

'What do you think we should do?'

Eric looked over at the cruise ship. 'I bloody well know what we should do if we had any sense, but I know what we are going to do.'

'And you agree then?'

'We're seamen. We have to go.'

'Good man. Now, how is the bow on the starboard side?'

'Completely smashed up. Almost the whole of the forecastle deck is gone.'

'What about the starboard side on the main deck?'

'Apart from a bloody big hole, not too bad. The main deck rails have all gone.'

'Could they get down onto it?'

'Yes.'

'Then I'll use the starboard side against their port quarter. That saves trying to turn around and then manoeuvre the port side alongside with that fire raging. It would be too close to the accommodation.'

"Majestic Sea', this is 'Vacuum Pioneer'. We're on our way. I will come alongside your port side after quarter with my bow.'

'God bless you, Sir.'

"Majestic Sea', can you keep this channel open and clear now?'

'I will be here all the time.'

'The handling may be a little rough. We are on emergency steering and all controls are with the engine room.'

'Just as long as you get alongside.'

'How long have we got?'

'As soon as you can, Captain.'

'Eric, send Arturo down to the steering flat. I want the Chief on the walkie-talkie in the control room, you forward. Tell everyone what is happening. As soon as we get alongside, Arturo can come up on deck. I'm going up to the bridge.'

Karl headed up to the bridge and stopped at his cabin to ring Trond.

'Trond, we're going alongside the cruise ship. I've no time to explain, but we're still pointing in the right direction. Arturo is coming down to the steering flat.

I'll give him the course to steer from the bridge. He's bringing a walkie-talkie for you. I want slow ahead on the engines now.'

Chapter 34

Passengers were still dying. On the port side, some passengers were still trapped in their cabins by the smoke. The thick fumes stopped any movement in the alleyways, which were the only way to escape. In cabin 106 on deck 5, David and Isobel Chancery had desperately stuffed towels and bedding around the bottom of the door to try to stop the smoke from entering, but now the smoke and heat from the fire had forced them out onto their balcony. David had tried to see if he could reach the balcony above, but it was too far away. Also, with the heel of the ship, he couldn't balance. He had wrapped his wife up in the duvet from the bed. He could see other passengers on their balconies as well. Isobel was praying quietly.

He looked down. The fires had gone out on the water, but the sea was black and he knew it was icy cold. He felt so helpless.

'I'm so sorry, Isobel darling. I brought you into this.' He held her tightly. 'Quiet,' she said. 'This isn't your fault. Just hold me. I love you so much. All the years we've had. We've been so lucky.' They talked of their children, of their memories together of their past, but most of all they talked of their love for each other.

There was a sudden roaring and the lights of a very low plane flashed overhead with white boxes tumbling from it. An airforce plane had arrived and was dropping liferafts into the water. They inflated as soon as they landed and their yellow domes with flashing lights were now scattered on the sea around the ship.

David could see that passengers were jumping into the sea from their balconies. He went back into the cabin and found their lifejackets.

'Here, put this on,' he said to Isobel. 'We're going to swim to one of the liferafts.'

'I'm scared,' said Isobel.

'We have no choice, my love. If we stay here, we will burn.'

David put the lifejacket over her head and tightened up the straps before putting his on.

They looked down at the water.

'It looks so cold,' she whispered. The nearest liferaft looked about 50 metres away. They could see and hear some of the passengers in the water.

'It won't be long,' David reassured her. 'Just hold on to me and hold your breath.'

'Kiss me,' she said. He took her face in his hands and kissed her as he did when he first met her.

'I love you so very much,' he said through his tears.

Isobel was crying as well. David tenderly brushed her tears away.

'Are you ready?' David asked. Isobel nodded. They climbed up the rail and sat at the top. He held her hand tightly.

'Go!' shouted David. They fell from the rail and hit the sea untidily in a splash. The water was ice cold. David came to the surface first and then Isobel bobbed up beside him. Her eyes were closed. David grabbed her and pulled her towards the liferaft. It seemed so far away. What David didn't realise was that the liferaft was drifting away from him as the wind blew across the water. He didn't give up, but put every effort into his legs.

'We're getting closer,' he shouted to Isobel.

Slowly, so slowly, the raft came closer. David was exhausted but didn't stop. At last he bumped against the yellow rubber and held onto the hand line on the side.

He was so tired, but he couldn't feel the cold now. All he wanted to do was rest. Forcing himself on, he worked his way round the raft and then saw the opening in the canopy and ropes hanging down. He reached for these and tried to pull himself up, but he was overcome with exhaustion. He held Isobel close.

'Just a moment, darling. I'll get my breath back and then we'll get in.'

Isobel didn't reply. She never would. When she hit the water, the hard foam flotation block in the front of the lifejacket had jerked up and hit her chin, snapping her neck like a matchstick. David didn't know, nor would he. He made two more attempts to board the liferaft, each time getting weaker and weaker. His body was numb from the cold and hypothermia was setting in. He still held on to the raft, but he was no longer there. He was with Isobel on a beach. They were young again and running with their dog. The sky was blue and they had the whole world ahead of them. He went to sleep still holding on to the raft. He died happy with Isobel.

Other passengers who jumped that night tried to get into the rafts. Some succeeded and were able to help out others to safety. Many cried out that night. They cried to their various gods, they cried to parents long dead or still living, they cried in pain, despair and loneliness. The sea has no ears. It has no knowledge of gods. The pleas for mercy fell wasted onto the surface of the black sea.

Jan was in trouble. The fire team had done everything they could, but the fire was too much and was advancing through the ship's heart from the starboard side towards the port side. The problem was that his team were now cut off from the rest of the ship and all he could do was retreat towards the bow. He had 16 men and they were exhausted. He called Jim on the walkie-talkie but got no reply, so he called the bridge. Peter answered.

'Is Staffie there?'

'Yes, but he's busy.'

'Who isn't? Can you tell him that we're finished down at the fire. There is a party aft of the fire but I'm cut off from them, so I am moving my people forward towards the bow.'

'Can't you get through?'

'If I could, I would. But no, the fire's spreading across the ship. You'd better get those liferafts away as fast as you can.'

'I'll tell them, Jan. Good luck.'

'Same to you. We'll need it.'

Zhou was loading the last liferaft. She was waiting for more passengers to arrive, but at the moment there were none. She looked down the long boat deck and could see all the people clustered around the remaining boats. She had a few more places left. The bridge called.

'Zhou, get your liferafts away as fast as you can and get out of there. The fire is out of control and spreading across to where you are.'

She turned to the three sailors who were standing by.

'Get in the raft.' They hesitated. 'Get in. Now! I'll lower you.' They piled in through the canopy opening and Zhou instantly released the brake.

With the list on the ship, the raft rubbed and banged against the side of the ship as it went down, but it hit the water with a splash and then released. It was just in time. Zhou could see flames now coming through the open doors to the deck and ran aft towards the remaining boats.

Jim put down the signalling lamp and called Hinchley.

'How is it there?'

'We have a major problem. The stairways are still clogged with passengers trying to get down to the remaining boats and now the crew are joining them and trying to push their way through. Fallows and his men are there, but it's hard to separate the crew and passengers. Jim, it's starting to descend into chaos. The crew are pretty good, but I want a search of the passenger accommodation and they are reluctant to go. I can't blame them. They're all pretty scared.'

'So is everyone. Does that mean there hasn't been an organised search of the accommodation?' asked Jim.

'Partly, but I can't rely on it having all been done. They're not trained seamen, Jim. They're just hotel people. We mustn't expect too much. I just don't know how long it will be before panic starts.'

'Hold on. We've got the tanker coming alongside on the port side down aft. I'll make an announcement in a minute. When the tanker gets alongside, we'll try to get the passengers off first, but I have a feeling that by then it will be every man for himself.'

'Are there many women and children left?'

'No children up here, but I don't know about the stairways. There are several women still here and most of the female crew also.'

'As soon as I make the announcement, start moving them out of the lounge down aft. I reckon if you get them down to deck 4 and out onto the deck spaces that should be about right. The gymnasium is down on that deck. Take fire axes and smash through the windows there on the port side as well. That will give you more space.'

'How are we going to get them onto the tanker?'

'We're going to have to do whatever we can. Get a bar top or something to make slides. I don't know. I wish I had an answer, but I don't. The main thing is keep everyone clear while she's coming alongside and have men standing by to make her lines fast.'

Jim picked up the microphone. He glanced briefly at Cota, who gestured Jim to continue. 'This is the Captain speaking. We have a rescue ship coming alongside shortly on the port side aft. That's on the left-hand side at the back of the ship. All passengers and crew should start to make their way down there. Crew will direct you. I remind all of you, crew and passengers, that your conduct so far has been superb. Keep this up and we will get everyone off. We are relying on you. Passengers must follow orders from the crew without question. Crew you will help those passengers who need help. Now, please start going to the back of the ship immediately.'

Graham, the Ice Pilot, was standing in the corner together with the ETO. He was the best dressed of everyone, having his yellow survival suit on and an inflatable lifejacket.

'We've just about been in touch with every station that is within reach,' said the ETO. 'We have help coming from all over, ships, planes, even fishing boats out of Greenland, but they're all going to arrive hours late. Graham has been helping keeping them informed.'

'I don't think there is much more we can do, Captain,' said Graham.

Jim looked around the bridge. 'Where's Prentiss?'

There was a moment of silence. 'He went over the side, Captain,' said Graham.

'I'm sorry. I should have realised. I saw him slumped in the corner not saying much. The Captain questioned him and we got some of the story, but he was in a real state. We should have taken care of him, but there wasn't time with everything going on. The Quartermaster saw him at the back of the bridge, but it was too late to stop him. He had climbed up over the rail and just jumped.'

'Poor bastard,' said Jim. 'Now they will be able to tear him apart without any worries.'

He went to Cota.

'Sir, we don't need the bridge party here anymore. Can I send them to help with the evacuation down aft?'

'Let them go, Jim.' He waved his hand weakly.

Jim called the '*Vacuum Pioneer*'. 'Captain, I think that, once we get people across to you, we are going to need urgent medical attention for many of them. If I ask for personnel and equipment to be parachuted down, can you pick them up with your boat?'

'If they can do that then yes, we can. We have a doctor on board.'

'Our own medical staff will also be on board shortly and they can assist.'

'We are under way now and will be alongside shortly.'

Jim turned to the ETO. 'One last broadcast. Tell all ships and stations we are now abandoning ship and that many people will be on the tanker. We need urgent medical attention. Ask Gander if they can parachute medics and equipment in and the tanker lifeboat will pick them up.'

While the ETO was busy sending out the last messages, Jim turned to the others on the bridge.

'Gentlemen, you've done a great job. There's nothing else left to do here. I want you all to go down aft and assist with the evacuation when the tanker gets alongside. As you go aft, I want you to go through the passenger decks that you can reach and make sure they are clear. Peter, hold on. We'll carry the Captain down.'

Jim rang the generator flat. Iain answered.

'We thought we had been forgotten. What's up?'

'We're abandoning her, Iain.'

'I thought that would be soon. She's really heeled over now.'

'The tanker we collided with is coming alongside aft on the port side. Make your way there and do what you can to help control the crowds.'

'Are there many?'

'Over a thousand I'd say.'

'Bloody hell. Right, we're on our way. We'll leave the gennies running; hopefully they will keep going a bit longer. Even if they don't, the batteries will click in. See you there.'

Iain turned to Patrick. 'It's time to go. The tanker's coming down aft to take us home. Jim reckons there are over a thousand still on board.'

'As usual, the engineers are at the end of the queue,' said Patrick.

'He wants us to help control the mob.'

Patrick picked up a large spanner. 'I reckon this may come in handy then. I hope there's a bar on the tanker.'

'If there is, the first thing we're doing is getting pissed. Come on.'

Jim called Jan next. 'What's your situation?'

'We're moving forward, Sir. All my people are exhausted.'

'How many are there?'

'14 of us, but we've found a bunch of passengers.'

'How many?'

'Haven't counted, but about 10 or so.'

'The tanker's coming alongside down aft.'

'That's great, Sir, but sorry we won't be there. I'm taking everyone down to the forward mooring deck to use the liferafts there.'

'Call me when you get there. I'm on the bridge now with the Captain. I've sent everyone down aft.'

'How's it going?'

Jim looked at the inclinometer. 25 degrees. The clock showed that it had been one hour and ten minutes since the collision.

'Touch and go. She's over 25 degrees now so it won't be long. Hinchley's got problems with crew in the lounges. It was to be expected. They've been bloody good up to now, better than I thought.'

'For the record, Sir, my teams have been superb. I'm so proud of them. Even the Bosun here has stood with me throughout. I just want that known.'

'It will be, Jan, you can tell it.'

Jan turned to the Bosun. 'We're getting off the ship now.'

He looked at the passengers. Four women were among them, being held by their partners. 'Come on, everyone. We're getting off the ship. There is a liferaft on the mooring deck and we're going to use that. Follow me.' It was becoming difficult to walk now, but they staggered along behind Jan.

Gaspar Bandissi, the Second Officer, called from the boat deck.

'Sir, I'm filling the last boat now. It's hard against the side, but I think with the weight it will go down on the skates. I have even managed to get twelve into the fast rescue craft. One of the Bosun's Mates has taken it away.'

'Well done, Gaspar. Did you hear the broadcast about the tanker?'

'Yes, Sir. I still have a whole bunch of passengers down here and there's no more room in the boat for them. They are reluctant to go aft.'

'Once the boat is down, Gaspar, they'll go believe me. There's nothing else they can do. You lead the way and they'll follow.'

'There are some elderly people here, Captain, and they are finding it very difficult to walk with the ship heeled over like this.'

'Get people to help them. Christ, Gaspar, there's nothing else we can do! If they can't or won't go, they'll die. It's as simple as that. Tell them that. Inform me when the last boat is launched and, once that's done, get aft and get that tanker secured.'

Jim leant against the bulkhead and rubbed his forehead. He was exhausted. He noticed his hand was trembling. He grabbed it with his other hand and held it tightly. Smoke was now swirling around the bridge. That would soon be out, he thought. He sensed someone behind him and turning saw Cadet Zhou.

'What the hell are you doing here? I told you to go!'

'I let my sailors go, Sir. They had done so well and there was no one else to go in the liferaft so I gave them the places. I had to lower them down.' She gave that bright smile again.

My God, thought Jim. If she can hold it together so can I.

'Go down to the after boat station and find the Second Officer. He needs help getting the remaining passengers aft.'

She smiled again and left the bridge.

Jim looked out of the bridge window astern. The tanker was approaching. Its accommodation was lit up and there was lighting on the forecastle and foredeck. He went to Cota.

'Sir, it's time to go.'

Cota was silent for a moment.

'I'm not going anywhere, Jim.'

'Sir, this is nothing to do with you. This is not your fault. There's no need to go down with her. She's just a great heap of garish metal and plastic. The seas are better off without her. Come with me now.'

Cota smiled weakly. 'Jim, it's nothing to do with heroics. I'm dying. Look.' He took his hand away from the middle of his body and Jim could see a dark patch against the white uniform. 'It's blood, Jim. When I was thrown down the stairs, something went into me as well as breaking my leg.'

Jim was angry. 'Why the hell didn't you get this seen to?'

'Who by? The doctors were busy with the passengers.'

'Sir, I can still get you down aft and we can get you attended to on the tanker.'

'Jim, to move me you'll need a stretcher, but there's no point. Look at me. I wouldn't last a minute if you try to move me.'

Jim was in despair. 'There must be something I can do.'

'There is. Get the people off. That's your concern, not me. When it's all over, tell everyone about these ships. Just maybe someone will listen. Now, send the First Officer down.'

Jim paused. He knew Cota was right.

He turned to Peter. 'You heard the Captain, Peter. I want you to take charge of securing the tanker. Use our ropes or theirs, it doesn't matter, just as long as we can hold her in tightly to avoid any gap between her and us. She'll only be putting her forward part into us so I reckon there will be about 50 metres of us together, but that's enough. Once secure, I think that no matter what we have said, it will be a free for all. I want you to get Bert and his men to assist the elderly or anyone who is reluctant, you understand.'

'Yes, Sir.'

'I mean it. Throw them over if you have to, but get them off. Last thing, get lighting rigged if you can. Good luck.'

Peter went to the Captain. 'I'm sorry, Sir.' Cota took his hand. 'Thank you, Peter. You did well. God be with you.' Peter stood back and saluted, then turned and quickly left the bridge.

Gaspar called Jim. 'That's the last boat gone, Sir. It was touch and go, but we got her down. I'm heading aft now with the passengers. I've got Cadet Zhou with me and some of the engineer officers. We're managing to keep them going.'

'Jim, you must go as well. There's nothing to do up here now,' said Cota. 'They need you on deck. Just hold them together a little bit longer. You have been a fine Staff Captain. I'm proud to have met you. A lot of people owe their lives to you tonight. I also owe you for reminding me that I was a seaman.'

Cota held his hand out. Jim took it and gripped it tightly. Cota pulled him down. 'Remember me. Tell my family my last thoughts were of them,' he whispered. 'Tell them what we did together. Take command now, Jim. She's all yours.'

Jim stood back and saluted. Cota weakly raised his hand and returned the salute. Jim hurried off the bridge without looking back. He staggered down the deck towards the stern. He slipped a number of times. In the end, he worked his way along the side rails. He could see the tanker now, close to the stern.

Chapter 35

Vacuum Pioneer

Eric was organising the crew to be ready for the survivors on the foredeck. They had roped off the hole in the deck, and had the two gangway safety nets ready to be hoisted on board the 'Majestic Sea'. They had decided to use the gangways to form makeshift bridges between the two vessels. Cutting through the wires was the quickest way to free the gangways and the Bosun was desperately trying to unbolt the first one from the top platform. Other members of the crew stood by ready to lift it and drag it forward.

Finally, the lines were ready to secure the bow. The crew had dragged their mattresses onto the deck and formed them into a small square to break the fall if any passengers jumped. Eric knew there was only limited space along the length of the deck alongside the cruise ship, but it was the safest option.

He was standing on the forecastle now with three of the crew, who had heaving lines ready in their hands. Other crew members also had heaving lines that were attached to the gangway nets. The crane on the deck had been destroyed in the explosion so everything would have to be lifted by hand.

He could now see many hundreds of people crowded on the stern of the 'Majestic Sea'. Bloody hell, he thought. We can't get them all on board.

He called Karl. 'Have you seen the people, Captain? There are hundreds of them.'

'All we can do is let them get on board,' said Karl. 'We'll worry about them once they're here. How are you getting on?'

'We have the safety nets ready. If they hoist them on board and make them fast, they can scramble down them. We've got all the mattresses out on deck for people to jump onto. God knows if that will work, but it's all we can do.'

'It's all right, Eric. You've done the best you can. I'm most concerned about the elderly; they don't bounce so easily'.

'That's why I've got the gangways coming. If they can haul them up then they can put the older people down those.'

'I'm going to suggest that they send the fittest men first. They can then help you get the others on board. Once the main bulk of the survivors are coming, get them to move aft as soon as possible. We'll fill the accommodation up with the women and elderly first. Men can go down to the engine room. Once that's filled up, we will have to settle the remainder down on the deck. I'll hold her alongside as long as I can. Don't worry about the lines. When the time comes, I'll give her full stern and break away. Just keep clear.'

Karl couldn't raise the engine room with the walkie-talkie due to all the steel between him and the control room, so he moved down to his cabin and used his telephone to give the steering and engine orders. He was watching the stern of the 'Majestic Sea' getting closer.

He called the ship. Jim answered.

'Captain, we're as ready as we can be. We have nets and a gangway for you to hoist up. My men will throw you heaving lines. I will also send you heaving lines for two bow ropes and two spring lines from further down the deck. That should hold her alongside. We've also got *a square of mattresses on the deck in case people want to jump. There's not much more we can do.'*

'Captain, just coming is good enough,' Jim said. 'I'll get the people on board.'

'I suggest that you get a bunch of fit men on board first as they can then help the others. You can use the gangways for the elderly,' said Karl.

'I'll organise some of the crew to jump on board when you arrive alongside,' Jim responded.

'Finally, if your ship starts to go or we take damage that might endanger us, I will break away. Is that understood?'

'Completely,' said Jim.

'Right, Captain. Here I come.'

Karl put the walkie-talkie down and ordered starboard 10 degrees dead slow ahead. The next few minutes were going to be the most momentous of his career. He was risking his ship and the lives of his crew. It was against everything in the book.

Jan and his party arrived forward on the mooring deck. The liferafts were gone. Jan stared at the empty cradles. At that moment, he was joined by Alan, the Third Officer.

'It must have been crew. No one else knew they were here.'

'Fuck them!' said Jan. 'Check the lifejacket locker.'

Alan did so and shook his head. 'Empty.'

Only the passengers had lifejackets on. The fire teams could not wear theirs to fight the fire and had left them at their emergency stations.

'I'll take one of the firemen and get some lifejackets,' said Alan. 'There are plenty lying around.'

'Don't be long, Alan. Time's running out.'

He looked around at the passengers. They and the rest of his party were sitting on the deck, some with their heads slumped down in their arms. One woman was crying loudly, with her husband trying to comfort her.

He called the Bosun. 'Go down to the store and get anything that will float. Paint stages, oil drums, whatever, understand?'

The Bosun called some of the seamen and the group went off to the deck below.

Alan and the fireman hurried back through the accommodation. The smoke was dense in parts. They could hear the fire roaring and crackling as it spread through the ship. They searched around, but found nothing.

'Let's try the next deck down,' said Alan.

They found the staircase and went down. In the foyer area, there was a pile of lifejackets.

'Grab what you can,' Alan said as he started picking up the jackets.

'Stop! Listen!'

They could hear a cry.

'Where's that coming from?'

'It's down the forward alleyway.'

This was untouched by the fire. They worked their way down the alleyway and found it was coming from a cabin. The door was open and inside sitting on the floor beside an overturned wheelchair was an elderly woman. Sprawled beside the woman was an equally elderly man.

'I thought we had been abandoned,' the man said.

'These cabins were supposed to have been checked by the hotel staff,' said Alan.

'They're probably the ones who took the liferafts,' replied the fireman.

'I can't get him off the floor,' the lady cried.

Alan and the fireman started to right the chair, but then Alan said, 'This is no good. There's no way we can push the chair with the ship at this angle. We'll have to carry him.'

He turned to the woman and said, 'We're going to carry him. You follow us.'

'What?' she said.

Alan spoke louder. 'I said follow us.'

'It's no good,' the man said. 'She's deaf.'

Alan beckoned her to follow them.

'The alleyway is not wide enough for a fireman's lift,' said the fireman. 'We'll support him on each side.' Turning to the man, he asked, 'Are your arms strong?'

'That's one part of me that does work,' he replied.

'OK, put your arms around our shoulders.'

They lifted him up and carried him out of the cabin and staggered down the alleyway with the woman following. They reached the foyer and collapsed.

'Go and get help,' Alan said. 'I'll stay here with them.'

The fireman hurried off.

'I'm deaf,' said the lady.

'I know,' said Alan and nodded at the same time.

'It's a lovely boat,' she said.

Alan looked at her in amazement.

'She's also a bit daft at times as well,' said the man.

'Can I ask you why you came here? Didn't you think that you were coming on a ship and there might be problems?'

'Son, we come from the Midwest. We've never even seen the sea before except on television. We saw the adverts, but they didn't advertise this. Our doctor thought it would be good for us.'

Alan listened in amazement and then inanely started to laugh. After a moment, the man joined in and the woman seeing them laugh did so as well. That was how Jan and the seamen found them.

'I'm bloody glad you can all laugh,' Jan said. 'Come on, let's get going.'

'One's deaf and the other's crippled,' said Alan. 'But they're both funny.'

'As if we need any more problems.'

They picked the man up. Alan led the woman by the hand and they returned to the mooring deck.

Jan distributed the lifejackets. On the deck around them lay a pile of junk from the store. There was a paint stage, some old netting, oil drums and several heaving lines and lengths of rope.

'Are we building an ark?' asked Alan.

'This is all we could find. It's nothing, but it's something. Look Alan, we have to do something. There has to be hope, understand? We may know what's going to happen, but there's no need for them to know.'

'I'm with you, Sir. I just wish I didn't know.'

Jim arrived down aft. It was a seething mass of people. Most of the crew were at the back, but many were mixed in with the passengers. To one side, Dick and his staff were tending to people on stretchers and a few others who were sitting on the deck. Jim pushed his way through the crowds until he could see Peter together with Hinchley. Peter had various sailors and officers along with Bert's men facing the crowd trying to keep a distance between the after rails and the crowds. The problem was that those at the back were constantly pushing those at the front.

Peter had the loud hailer and told the crowds to stop pushing, but it didn't seem to do much good. Peter saw Jim and called to his men to get him through.

'Give me the loud hailer!' Jim shouted.

Peter handed it to him. Jim climbed up onto the after rail and held tightly onto the flagstaff with one hand.

'Listen to me everyone! This is the Captain! I repeat listen!'

The noise gradually dulled.

'First, everyone stop pushing. Right now. All of you, stop pushing. We have to get the ship secured and then get the gangways hoisted. Once they are up and ready, you will start to board the tanker. Now I promise you, you will all get off, but only with order and discipline. The first to leave will be the passengers. I want all the ship's crew to move to the back. Once we get them off, we'll be able to leave. There is plenty of time so everyone will get off the ship, but the rule is injured first, then passengers, then the crew, then the officers. Last of all is me so I'll make sure you all get off.'

Jim saw Iain and Patrick approaching.

'Let them through please. They are needed on the rails.' Iain and Patrick managed to get through and joined the crowd of officers and crew around Jim.

'Next, I want you all to look around you. If you are near a woman or an elderly or infirm person, I want you to look after them. Now, anyone who is injured or handicapped, please put your hands up.' A number of people did.

'Right, you've all seen them. Those next to them, they are your responsibility.

'You will all wait until I give the order for you to embark. There will be no pushing and no arguments. The first off will be the injured and the medical staff. There are gangways for the elderly and the injured. There is a jumping zone marked on the deck with mattresses. Be careful those who want to try this. Once you get on board, please move to the back of the ship as we must keep the landing area clear. Follow the instructions of the tanker crew.

'Finally, you will obey the orders my officers give you without question. You will keep calm. Any troublemakers will be dealt with. My officers are armed and, if required, I will give the order for them to use their weapons.

Enough people have died tonight. Don't make it any more.'

The crowd seemed quieter and the pushing had stopped for the moment. Jim climbed down.

'Well said, Jim,' said Hinchley. 'Although I don't know how long they will remember it.'

Hinchley was standing with his son.

'I thought you got your family off.'

'We got the women off, but we men stayed, didn't we?' he said, turning to his son.

'We did, Dad.'

'We Hinchleys might be bastards, but we're not cowards, Jim.'

Jim smiled. 'I can see that.'

He turned to Bert, who was standing beside him.

'Bert, what about the drunks?'

'Still there, Captain.'

'Let's start getting them out.'

'Do you want them up here now?'

'No, but we have no choice. Some might be incapable of standing and will have to be carried. Take four of your men, Bert, and be ready with your pepper sprays. I want you to keep them separate from everyone else.'

'We'll try, Captain. No guarantees.'

Jim turned back to the rails. The tanker was very close now. He could see the burnt-out bridge and the blackened front of the accommodation and wondered how the hell the Captain was steering her.

Vacuum Pioneer

Karl was watching the final approach very carefully. The scene was like an artist's impression of Hell. The sky was red, with flames soaring into the air from where the fire had broken through onto the upper deck of the 'Majestic Sea'. Black smoke and thousands of sparks billowed into the sky from the amidships part of the ship, which seemed to be completely on fire. Flames gushed out of broken port holes and windows on the side. He could see the crowd of people very clearly now. On the foredeck, his men were standing by with the heaving lines in their hands. The Bosun and his men had made a super-human effort and had managed to drag one of the aluminium gangways up the deck. It was now propped against the rails. They even had the remaining pilot ladder ready to be hoisted.

He stopped the engines. The ship was parallel to the 'Majestic Sea', only feet apart. The 'Vacuum Pioneer' glided by the stern and the sailors threw up their heaving lines to those waiting on the deck. The ship continued forward another 50 feet before Karl came astern on the engine. More heaving lines were thrown up by the sailors further down the deck holding the spring lines. The ships ground together and the 'Vacuum Pioneer' stopped. The lines were hove tight.

The tanker crunched alongside. As the heaving lines landed, the crew immediately pulled them on board bringing the mooring lines. They made them fast to anywhere they would hold. Once fast, Jim crossed his hands above his head and the tanker heaved them tight. Suddenly, there was a surge of people towards the rails.

'Hold them back,' shouted Jim. The thin line of crew pushed the people back.

Further lines were thrown by the *'Vacuum Pioneer'*. Again the crew grabbed them and hoisted the safety nets and ladders up. Jim looked down. There was approximately a three metre drop onto the tanker's deck. It was enough to break bones but not kill. Some were already jumping onto the mattress area, but others were landing on the steel deck. Some were obviously injured as they crawled away or stayed motionless.

The tanker crews were still busy. A gangway was now being hoisted up. As soon as it reached the *'Majestic Sea's'* rails, it was lashed into position and people started to pour down. Next, the safety nets were made fast and these were also swarming with people. People were helping each other though. Jim could see that the injured and older people were being assisted. Some of the younger women were going down the nets or even jumping.

Cadet Zhou was struggling to reach Jim.

'It's the Safety Officer, Sir. He's trying to call you.'

Jim hadn't heard him over the noise of the embarkation.

He pushed his way out of the crowd and pressed the walkie-talkie to his ear.

'There are no liferafts, Captain. We think some of the crew have taken them. Anyway, they're gone.'

'Is there anything else up there?'

'We've looked. We've found some old oil drums and a few bits and pieces, but nothing that's going to help.'

Jim knew the answer but had to ask. 'Is there any chance you can get aft?'

'It's impossible, Sir. The whole amidships section of the ship is ablaze.'

'How many people have you got there?'

'Fourteen in the fire party and twelve passengers including two infirm.'

'Just a moment.' Jim called up the *Vacuum Pioneer*.

'Captain, we have a problem forward. We have the fire party and a few passengers trapped up in the bow. When you break free, can you do a pass of the bow and take them off. I'm sorry to ask, but there's nothing else we can do.'

'Captain, have you seen the list on your ship? I reckon she's ready to go over.'

'But she's not gone yet,' replied Jim.

'First, let's see if we can get all these people off. If you're still afloat then we'll give it a try. There is a problem though. Your bow is high up.'

'They're on the mooring deck, which is underneath the top deck of the bow.'

Karl sighed. 'All right, Captain, but it will be just a pass. I won't secure the ship.'

'That's good enough.'

'Jan, the tanker's coming along to you after we've got the people off down aft here.'

'I thought we were finished.'

'You thought wrong. Now, you will have to judge the height of their deck from your position and somehow get to the right level or have lines ready to lower people down. The tanker will not be securing alongside, so you're going to have to be quick.'

'Like greased lightning, Sir. Just watch us.'

At that moment, there was a commotion behind the crowd of people. It was the hundred or so crew and passengers who had been locked in the bar. Jim pushed his way through to the back of the crowd. He could see immediately that many of them were very drunk. Some of the women were only partly clothed and one was naked. It was the Cruise Director's wife.

The rest of the crew were getting restless as well, and a number of them were surging forward starting to shout.

Bert was walking backwards with his men, keeping the drunks apart from the passengers who were still boarding. They had their pepper sprays in their hands ready for use and were shouting at the drunks to keep back.

Jim called to Peter, 'Send some men!'

As the drunken crowd and crew advanced, Iain and Patrick broke through the back of the passengers, accompanied by their engineer officers and a number of crew. Some of them had spanners or other tools in their hands and they looked ready for business.

Iain came alongside Jim. 'Every time you deck lads have a problem, you always call for us engineers to sort things out.'

Some of the drunks were throwing bottles they had brought up from the bar.

'There are more, Sir,' said Bert. 'Some are unconscious in the bar. We tried to wake them, but they're completely out of it.'

'How many?'

'About five or six.'

Jim saw Gaspar, Zhou and Peter helping passengers over the rails. The two other cadets, Bindra and Kemp, were also there. He also saw the Purser assisting. He called to them. 'Gaspar, take Zhou and some of the sailors down to the after bar and start bringing out the drunks. See if the doctor has any spare stretchers. I doubt it, but try anyway. Otherwise just drag them out.'

'Should bloody well leave them where they are,' said Patrick, threatening a drunk who got too close. 'They wouldn't know if they drowned.'

The Cruise Director staggered up to Jim.

'Jimbo, you know me. What's the problem? Let us get off.'

'When the others have boarded, Scott. That's the rules.'

'You fucking deck officers. Always bloody rules. Look what you've done tonight with your bloody rules. You've fucking well sunk the ship, that's what you've done, hasn't he boys?' He turned to the others, who cheered. 'Now, let us through.'

'Where's your wife, Scott. You should be looking after her.'

'Fuck her!' shouted Scott. Then he paused. 'Everyone else has tonight!' Then he roared with laughter as if he had said something funny.

'You're going to wait your turn, Scott.'

'Fuck you, sonny,' Scott said and charged at Jim. Patrick caught him neatly with a swing of the spanner across his head and Scott went down like a log.

'Nicely done,' said Iain

'It's all the golf,' explained Patrick.

The thin line of officers and security staff was being pushed back now by the pressure of the crowd. The peppers sprays were being used, and occasionally a crew member fell holding his eyes. Bert and his men had drawn their rubber truncheons and were using them to drive back the crowd.

The sailors were coming up from the bar, dragging the remaining drunks behind them. Jim looked behind him. Gradually the deck was clearing. The passengers were still streaming over the rails, being assisted by other officers and crew.

Bert called to Jim. 'We can't hold much longer, Captain. Can we use our firearms?'

Jim thought desperately. 'No, Bert. We're not going to shoot our own crew. Just hold a little longer.'

The line continued to resist until at last there were gaps at the rails. The last of the passengers were now going over the side.

'OK. Let them through!' shouted Jim.

The mass of crew now rushed the rail. Jim called Karl.

'That's all the passengers on board now. The crew are now following. I'm sorry to say that some of them are very drunk.'

'You seem to want to give me problems tonight, Captain.'

'I would leave them behind if I could, but when they are sober most of them are probably all right.'

'Let's hope they sober up quickly then.'

Chapter 36

Vacuum Pioneer

The foredeck was a sea of humanity as the survivors poured on board. Down ladders, nets, gangways or jumping they continued to come. The crew were assisting them off the embarkation area and moving them down aft. Briget and Gerdy were also there doing what they could to assist. Briget was looking for the more seriously wounded to get them to the crew messroom while Gerdy was guarding the main door to the accommodation for the elderly and wounded. Inside the ship, the accommodation was filling fast. The messrooms were all full, as were most of their cabins. Now they were squatting in the alleyways, anywhere to get warmth.

Suddenly, there was a muffled thud from deep in the heart of the 'Majestic Sea' and the ship gave a sharp lurch further to starboard.

Karl held his breath. For a moment, he thought the ship was going over, but she seemed to stabilise. He called Jim.

'Captain, I suggest you get out of there as soon as possible. I think she will go at any time.'

'I know, Captain. We're doing all we can. The crew are boarding now. There are a lot of them, but they are moving fast.'

Karl called Eric.

'Eric, we can't just head away as I wanted. You will have to let the lines go. We're going to move further up the ship to the bow. There are some people trapped there.'

'Right, Captain. I'll stand by to let go. Watch that fire as you go past. It's pretty fierce.'

'I see that, Eric. Once you've let the lines go, make sure everyone is on the port side as we go along the hull.'

Many of the passengers could not find room in the accommodation and were huddled together in groups on the deck. The Cook and other crew were going amongst them distributing the remaining bedding. The deck was covered with white sheets and duvets, mixed with curtains from the cabins and even canvas and plastic from the stores.

Dick and the 'Majestic Sea' medical staff had joined Briget and were set up in the crew messroom where they were already dealing with the injured. The medical supplies of the 'Vacuum Pioneer' were quickly being used up.

Portable lights had been rigged around the deck, providing pools of light for people to work by. They also provided some heat for those close by. There was a crash of sound from another plane going overhead dropping more liferafts into the water. The seas around them were full of bobbing yellow liferafts and twinkling lights. This ship's liferafts were huddled together around the lifeboats in a mass of orange and yellow about a hundred metres from them.

There were many other lights as well. They were dimmer, and Karl didn't want to think about them. They were the lights on the lifejackets of those in the water. There were many of them and Karl knew they were all dead, probably due to the intense cold of the water. Those without lifejackets had a quicker and more merciful death. Karl shivered.

Peter came to Jim.

'They are boarding fast now.'

The crew were surging past. As the officers stood clear, they hurled themselves at the rails. Some scrambled down the nets. Other used the ladder and gangway, but most jumped over the rail.

Coming up the ladders from the deck below, Gaspar and the sailors were helping to carry up the last of the drunks.

'Throw them over,' said Jim. 'There's no time. Is that all of them?'

'Yes,' said Gaspar.

'OK. Let your men go.'

Jim turned to the officers. 'That's it everyone,' he shouted. 'Abandon ship!'

The remaining crew and officers scrambled over the rails and dropped or jumped down onto the tanker deck. Jim and Bert waited to board.

'Where's Zhou?' Jim asked.

'She must be on the tanker,' said Bert.

The 'Vacuum Pioneer' called.

'Captain, we have to break away. The ship is going over further. Is everyone on board?'

'The last are coming now, Captain,' Jim replied. 'Bert, you go. I'm going to find Zhou.'

'Captain, no! It's too late!' Bert shouted.

Jim scrambled away and called to the tanker.

'Break away, Captain!' He reached the ladder going down, swung down the rails and then crawled toward the bar doors.

'Zhou!' he shouted. 'Zhou!'

He went into the gloom. The lights were still on in the wrecked room.

'Zhou!'

'Help!' Her voice was desperate and came from the corner by the bar. Jim went over to the bar and there in the corner was Zhou, pinned to the deck by two drunks.

'Are you crazy!' Jim shouted. 'The ship is about to go over! Get out!'

They looked up. 'You bastard,' one of them shouted. 'It's the fucking Staff Captain.' They lurched up forgetting Zhou and stumbled towards him. Jim saw they had wicked-looking knives in their hands.

'Zhou, run for it!' he shouted. She struggled to pick herself up. Jim recognised the two barmen. All he had was a walkie-talkie.

'This is madness! For God's sake, get off the ship! We're sinking!' he shouted. It was no good. They came for him. What a stupid way to die, Jim thought, murdered on a sinking ship. The first one reached him and raised his knife. From just behind Jim came an earshattering explosion and the first assailant fell backwards, his head exploding in a red foam. Another explosion rang out and the second assailant went over backwards with his chest a spurting mass of blood.

'Come on, Captain. Let's get the fuck out of here.' It was Bert. He had a huge silver automatic in his hand.

'A present from Sam,' he said.

They grabbed Zhou and stumbled to the door and then to the ladder.

Vacuum Pioneer

Karl saw the last of the survivors jump onto the deck of the ship and shouted, 'Let go!' Immediately, the crew let the lines go, leaving them trailing from the 'Majestic Sea'. Karl put the engines ahead. With the ropes let go, the ship began to make its way down the side of the cruise ship. He ordered the rudder to port to take the ship off the side to avoid the heat and flames from the still burning fire, although the starboard side was now a blackened ruin of twisted metal. The 'Majestic Sea' was now over at an angle of approximately 40 degrees. She could not last much longer. The enclosed starboard wing of the cruise ship's bridge was now level with Karl's cabin, although he could not see inside. He could not see any sign of life remaining on the ship. It was an incredible sight looking at the leaning top deck of the ship. The ship's lights were still on and the hundreds of coloured lights around the swimming pools still flashed. The deck was covered with various areas of amusement. Some of the trees on the main street were still standing, although most had tumbled to the side.

Another plane roared overhead, scattering more liferafts on the water like confetti at a wedding, rather than wreaths at a wake. They were wasted; no one was alive in the water now. The 'Vacuum Pioneer' continued slowly along the length of the hull, the ship pushing through the flotsam from the wreck.

The phone went beside Karl. It was Eric.

'Captain, I have a man down here demanding to speak to you. He says he is the Ship General Manager, whatever that is.'

'Make it quick. I need the phone.'

'Captain, my name is Hinchley.'

'What is it, Mr Hinchley?'

'Sir, we have left the Captain behind on the stern. He was searching for a missing officer when you left.'

'He told me to go, Mr Hinchley.'

'Sir, he is the one who saved most of us tonight. We must save him.'

'I can't go back, Mr Hinchley. I will try to take off those on the bow and then get away. She will be lost any minute now.'

Eric came back on the phone. 'Sir, let me take the port lifeboat. I'll take a couple of our crew and ask for volunteers from the survivors. I'll see if I can get them.'

'It's very risky, Eric. If the ship goes while you're there, you could go with it or get smashed by the wreckage.'

'I'll take that chance.'

'Only volunteers, understand?'

'Understood, Captain.'

Eric ran onto the main deck, where he called to the Bosun.

'Two sailors, Bosun, immediately up to the port boat.' He then ran up the ladder followed by Hinchley.

'I'm volunteering. So is my son here.'

Eric stopped them. 'Where are you going?'

'Taking the lifeboat to get the Captain! Want to come?'

The boat was down ready for launch. Eric jumped in and started the engine.

'Get in!' he shouted to the others. 'There are lifejackets inside.'

The Bosun lifted the brake and the boat instantly ran down the side of the ship and hit the water with a splash. Eric then released the hooks and put the engines full ahead.

Karl was concentrating on the approach to the bow. He picked up his walkie-talkie. 'Captain?'

There was no reply.

From the bow, Jan could see the tanker moving slowly down the side of the ship towards them. He had put all the mooring ropes out over the side and had found safety harnesses in the store, which he distributed to the women and elderly passengers. They had even found plenty of hard hats.

'You and I will stay till last,' Jan said to Alan, 'and then I'll lower you down.'

'Who'll lower you?'

'I'll jump.'

'If there's not much time, we'll both have to jump, Sir.'

'I thought of that as well.'

There was a rumbling from inside the ship and she lurched another few degrees.

'Fuck, this is getting serious,' said Jan. 'Line up everyone.'

He lined up those with the lines on first and had three men for each line.

'As soon as I say go, climb up onto the rail and sit on the top. Don't worry about overbalancing. If you do, we will hold you.'

He went down to where the disabled man was sitting with his wife.

'Sir, we will hoist you up and then push you over. Your wife will be alongside you. That's the best we can do.'

'Son, have you ever done this before?'

'No, Sir.'

'Has it ever been done before?'

'I doubt it.'

'At least it doesn't matter if I break my legs. Can't feel the damn things anyway.'

'I don't intend breaking them.'

'Just get me and my daft lady off this boat, son. All I want to do is see the rolling hills again and I swear I'll never set foot on a ship or even see the sea ever again.'

'At the moment, I feel the same way.'

Vacuum Pioneer

Karl could see the people on the bow now. They were leaning out of the ship through the mooring ports in the side of the bow. Even though the ship was heeled over, they would still have a drop. The bow was heeled over so far that it formed a ledge over the sea below. He wondered. There was no time for a considered decision. He ordered the ship hard to port and the bow started to lift off the side of the 'Majestic Sea'. The distance increased between the ships' bows. Then, keeping the engine ahead, Karl ordered hard to starboard. The turn to port stopped and gradually the ship came back to starboard. Instead of stopping the ship, Karl kept the speed on. Then when the bow was starting to head in towards 'Majestic Sea', he came amidships with the rudder. Then he increased speed.

Jan saw the manoeuvre and immediately realised what the tanker was about to do.

'Everyone down off the rail!' he shouted. 'She's going to ram!'

He was right. Karl had decided to ram the bow of the '*Vacuum Pioneer*' into the bow of the cruise ship and provide a platform for those on board to get onto the tanker.

'Get down on the deck and hold on,' Jan shouted. He grabbed the disabled man and held him. He peered over the coaming of the bulwark and saw the tanker surging towards them. Then there was a crunching and rendering of metal. The deck shuddered under them as the tanker ground into the hull. The ship pushed on into the cruise ship until it finally stopped. The mooring deck now overhung the tanker.

'Quickly!' shouted Jan. They grabbed the passengers on the lines and put them over the side. Now, there was only a short distance to lower them down and there were many people waiting to grab them. Once the passengers were off, the sailors followed until only Alan and Jan remained.

'Right lad, let's go,' said Jan.

They looked down and then at each other and jumped, landing amongst the grasping hands of those below. They fell down in a jumble of bodies, but safe at last.

Chapter 37

Jim and Bert helped Zhou up from the lower deck onto the stern. They slid down against the rail, which was now only a short distance from the sea. The lights had finally gone out, but the batteries had clicked in for the emergency lights, giving a ghostly light over the scene.

'I'm so sorry, Captain,' Zhou said.

'You've nothing to be sorry for,' said Jim. 'It wasn't your fault. I'm just pleased we reached you in time.' He looked at her. 'It was in time, wasn't it?'

She smiled. 'Yes, it was.'

'It was Bert here who saved us,' Jim said.

'Thank you, Bert,' said Zhou.

'But we don't know how, do we?'

'What?' she said in a puzzled tone. Then she realised. 'Of course not.'

'Think of me like a lavatory cleaner,' said Bert. 'I just did the world a favour. So, now that I've saved you, what next, Captain?'

It was very cold now. Jim leant against the rail, with Zhou huddled against him. 'Bert, I really don't know.'

He looked out along the steeply sloping deck. It was chaos and here they were, a small huddle of humanity in this enormous mass of steel, waiting to die.

'We can stay here or we can jump into the sea,' he said.

'I can't swim,' said Zhou.

'What!' said Bert.

'That settles it though,' said Jim.

Even now, Jim smiled. 'I don't think that matters. What's your first name?'

'Mei,' she said. 'It means beautiful.'

'That you are, Mei.'

'I thought you didn't call cadets by their first name.'

'With you, I make an exception.'

'Will it be quick?' Zhou asked, indicating the water.

Jim didn't know how to answer that. This was wrong. He turned to Bert. 'How far do you reckon the nearest liferafts are?'

Bert stood up holding on to the rail and looked out at the nearest flashing lights.

'Difficult to say, Captain. Deceptive at night. I reckon about half a mile.'

'We can make it. It's better than staying here.'

'I agree, let's give it a go. Zhou, we're going to give you a swimming lesson.' Bert scrambled around picking up lifejackets. They put them on and Jim gave Zhou an extra one.

'Hold this in front of you as well. It will give you extra support.'

Then they heard an engine and out of the dark came a beam of light on the stern.

'It's a lifeboat!'

They started shouting, but of course no one could hear.

Frantically, they tried to attract the attention of the boat. Even as it got closer, it was still playing the light around looking for them.

'Block your ears,' said Bert. He had drawn his automatic. He pointed it out to sea and fired. The noise was deafening, but more important was the flash from the barrel. He fired again, and again. The light from the boat pointed directly at them, momentarily blinding them. The boat came in under the rails where the pilot ladder, nets and ropes from the *'Vacuum Pioneer'* were still hanging.

'Quickly!' Jim said to Zhou. 'You first! Can you hold on?'

'Yes, Captain.'

Zhou climbed over the rail and started down the pilot ladder, which swayed and twisted as she went. The boat had the light on her and moved in. There were figures standing out on the small walkway on the deck of the boat, holding the ladder and reaching out for her. They grabbed Zhou and thrust her into the side hatch. Bert was already on his way down. He was faster. Jim waited until he was almost at the bottom before climbing over the rail.

His hands were icy cold. He held the ropes of the ladder in his arms as he went down, swinging and twisting in the air. He felt hands grabbing his feet and then he was pulled into the safe warmth of the boat.

'I'm the last,' he gasped. Jan immediately turned towards the helm position. The noise from the engine made speech impossible so Jan crossed his hands above his head. Eric immediately rammed the throttle ahead and steered directly away from the ship. Hinchley closed the hatch and the warmth from the engine seeped into them as they sat shivering on the bench seating. Jan came up. In the dim light, Jim could see he was grinning. Jan grabbed his hand. Jim looked around and saw that they were all grinning at each other. He felt so tired and his head slumped down. He slept.

Vacuum Pioneer

As soon as the last person had landed on his decks from the bow, Karl put his engines full astern. The ship shook, but the stricken cruise ship still held on to her as if she didn't want to die alone. Karl ordered the rudder hard to starboard and then hard to port. He repeated this several times, until gradually the cruise ship let go with a mournful rendering of steel. With the rudder amidships, the tanker came astern, picking up speed until Karl stopped the engines and let the ship drift to a stop. He could see his lifeboat returning and the crew were standing by ready to hoist it back.

The 'Majestic Sea' was still burning fiercely and listed over at an impossible angle. She was now sinking rapidly by the stern. The after mooring deck was under water and, as Karl watched, more of the stern disappeared under the water. As the stern sank, the bow began to rise. The clouds had cleared and in the moonlight, out of the flames and wreckage, the bow was rising towards the sky like an accusing finger at the heavens. The tanker rails were lined with people watching the end. They were very quiet. Some wept as they remembered loved ones lost and left on board, others fearful not knowing where theirs were. The bow had now risen almost straight up and the sea appeared to boil with the air escaping from her innards.

On the bridge, Captain Cota sat alone. Driven by batteries, the radios still chattered. Occasionally, more alarms sounded and lights flashed, but he ignored them. He wondered whether Jim had managed to get the passengers off. He heard the aircraft overhead and then gradually drifted into unconsciousness.

The final lurch of the ship caused Cota to fall from the command chair and slide to the back of the bridge. He felt no pain. Disorientated, he had no idea where he was on the vast bridge. The bow continued to reach further into the sky.

Cota opened his eyes and realised he was looking out through the bridge windows at the stars. They gleamed in the black sky. In his youth, the stars had guided him. So many ships, so many oceans, but always the same stars. The same stars were shining down on his home and family. It gave him warmth and sadness. It was all over, the ambition, the gold braid, the glitter, all an illusion. So much of it seemed pointless.

He now realised so much, so late. He was going home to the sea. The icy water came quickly. The stars disappeared and the black sea pervaded his thoughts, which faded into oblivion as he died and his body and his ship sank to the seabed.

He was not the last to die. There were others still trapped in the ship, many lying injured, alone in the dark, waiting to endure the terrifying end as the sea burst into their cabins. Their screams went unheard. Even their prayers were unanswered. They were now part of the ship's final agony and their remains were also part of the ship's remains, to lie on the seabed for eternity in the black cold of a dispassionate sea.

Vacuum Pioneer

Karl had moved up to the bridge to watch the ship dying. He heard footsteps behind him and turning he saw a haggard looking man in a torn white mess jacket, open shirt and torn black trousers. One shoulder epaulet was missing but the other shoulder showed four gold stripes. The figure advanced with a hand held out. He took it firmly.

'Are you the Captain?' Karl asked

'Staff Captain. The Captain is dying at this moment. He is still on the bridge.'

Karl nodded. 'It's a strange tradition, isn't it?'

'He had no choice. He was badly injured and could not be moved, but I think this is what he would have wished anyway.'

'It will be quick,' said Karl.

They spoke no more. The bow had risen straight up in the sky and then, with just a faint hesitation, it slid smoothly down into a foaming sea. Then it was gone. The sea boiled up over the ship, spewing up the last wreckage, and then gradually returned to a calmness that was disturbed by an occasional burst of air reaching for the sky.

The sea had once again claimed not just a ship but the arrogance of those who thought that size could conquer an element so insidious in its beauty and fascination. The dangers it constantly presented were masked by a belief that it could be restrained.

From those watching, there was no cry, but a soft sigh as she went down.

Then silence again.

Karl spoke. 'It's not good watching ships sink.'

'This one had to sink,' said Jim. 'She had lost her way.'

Karl was puzzled, but Jim did not elaborate.

'Captain,' Jim said, 'I have to thank you on behalf of all those on board for your actions tonight.'

'You would have done the same.'

'Yes, I think I would, but that does not diminish your seamanship and compassion. You, your officers and crew saved us all.'

'Thank you, Captain. Just thank the Gods that our ship stayed afloat. If it hadn't, you would all be dead. You look very tired. I would offer you my cabin, but it is full of passengers, as is every part of the ship except this burnt-out bridge.'

'Did you lose anyone?' asked Jim.

'Four men, two up here on the bridge.'

Karl left the bridge for a moment and returned with a thick parka.

'Put this on and stay here to rest. Don't worry any more. It's my problem now. We'll do what we can for everyone. I'm keeping the ship here and waiting for the rescue ships. The wind would be too much for those on deck if we try to move. Besides, I can't leave the boats. Hopefully, it won't be much longer.'

Jim was left alone looking out at all the boats and liferafts. The lifeboats were drawing in to the tanker, seeing it as a place of refuge. Some of the lifeboats were towing liferafts. The tanker had launched its boat again. It was going round the liferafts, checking for survivors and bringing them into the fold. It also collected the medical supplies that had landed in the sea nearby.

The sea was covered with wreckage and bodies. Most of the bodies had lifejackets on, but some did not. Some were burnt, others were unmarked. The Chancerys were united in death. David was still clinging to the liferaft with his wife in his arms. Others had also failed to board and were floating peacefully nearby.

The conditions in the lifeboats were appalling. The overloaded boats were packed with survivors, but there were no lavatories or sick bags. Many had fainted or were debilitated from retching due to the stench of vomit and excrement. Others had died from their injuries or burns. Tirelessly, the boat went round transferring the worst and bringing them to the tanker. In other cases, lifeboats came to the remaining gangway and more were taken on board.

But many had been saved. Somehow, against all the odds, the majority of the passengers and crew were alive. Jim knew they had been lucky. If there had been a storm or a gale, most of them would be dead.

On the main deck below, those who had not been accommodated inside the ship were huddled together, fighting the freezing cold. The tanker crew and other volunteers were going round distributing anything that might give them some protection from the cold. Inside the ship, every bit of space was occupied. People were in the alleyways, bathrooms, cabins and even in the engine room spaces. No one complained. They lay or sat numb and silent. Some were traumatised, others were still shaking, not with cold but with the shock of what had happened.

It was quiet on the bridge. The ship was still as it waited for the rescue ships to arrive. Jim stayed there, ignoring the acrid smell of the fire. He sat on the blackened deck and looked at his watch. It was less than three hours since the collision, three hours that, regardless of whatever happened in his life now, he would never forget. He felt a movement beside him. Looking down, he saw that a cat was watching him. It was shivering. Jim unzipped the parka and, after a moment of hesitation, the cat crept onto his lap. Jim closed the parka around them and they gave warmth and comfort to each other.

Jim was woken from a deep sleep by Jan and Hinchley. It was dawn. There was a noise of engines bursting through the broken bridge windows.

'It's the helicopters,' Jan shouted. Jim got up and looked out. Around them was a sea of ships and boats. There were naval vessels, coastguard, merchant ships and fishing boats.

It was a beautiful morning with a bright blue sky that reflected its colour onto the sea.

Stretchers were lined up on deck waiting to be transported by the helicopters. Rescue personnel in bright orange suits were walking among the passengers. There were far too many bodies covered with blankets. It was so tragic to have survived the disaster and then to have died before rescue. On the sea, the liferafts and lifeboats were clustered around the various ships and their occupants were going up the gangways. Fishing boats were pulling bodies out of the water and laying them on their decks. They will have a good harvest today, Jim thought.

Jim turned to Jan and Hinchley.

'You did well, both of you.'

'A lot of people did well, Jim,' replied Hinchley.

'Others didn't,' said Jan.

'That doesn't matter now,' said Jim. 'Enough people did well. Whenever there is a disaster, there are usually enough people who come forward and are counted. They can often surprise you,' he said looking at Hinchley.

Hinchley smiled. 'It's Bob, Jim.'

'How is your family, Bob?'

'They're all well, thank God.'

'You should be proud of your son. He's a fine young man.'

'I am, but thanks for saying it. I have to go now. The 'suits', as you guys say, are calling for me ashore. They wanted you as well, but I told them you are too busy. I've also made sure that your family have been informed that you are safe and well. Your wife, Jenny, passed on her love.'

'Thank you for that, Bob. I want to stay and see all the passengers and crew off and then I'll be free to go. Jenny will understand.'

'I wanted to come and say goodbye and also to thank you on behalf of us all,' said Bob.

'I just did what I was supposed to do, Bob.'

'You held us all together.' He put his hand out and Jim took it. 'You were right, Jim. You were right about a lot of things. Even Cota realised that. I won't forget. Goodbye, gentlemen. I have a feeling we'll all be meeting again soon in far more formal circumstances.'

He left the bridge.

'I suppose he's referring to the inquiry,' said Jan.

'You guessed right. That's going to be a bugger. Every armchair sailor will be howling for blood. Everything we did wrong will be gone over with a fine toothcomb.'

'But we did a lot of things right.'

'Never mind that. It's what we did wrong that will count. They will want blood and ours is the easiest. Have they got an idea of numbers yet?' asked Jim.

'Very rough. It looks like around seven hundred dead. A hell of a lot more injured.'

'God almighty,' Jim whispered.

'A lot of them went in the collision, Sir.'

'They're still dead.'

Zhou came onto the bridge. 'I was looking for you, Sir,' she said.

'I'm glad you found me.' He turned to Jan. 'Her first name is Mei. It means beautiful and she is, even looking like this.' She was dirty and bruised and her hair was matted. 'Your father is going to be very proud of you, as we all are. In fact, all of our officers did well. Regardless of what any inquiry says, we'll make sure everyone knows that.'

'What about the Captain?' asked Jan.

Jim looked at him. 'Jan, he was wounded but still carried on. He went down with his ship, still in command. No man could have done more. That's all there is to it. Now, I suggest we walk around our crew and tell them how well they have done. No one else will. Will you join us Mei?'

'With pleasure, Captain.'

The sun was shining now and warming the air. It was good to be alive.

Chapter 38

Southampton

It had been a day to remember in head office as well. They had been called in the early hours with the news about the collision. Since then, the telephone calls, meetings, briefings, enquiries and demands from the media had been overwhelming. Television, radio and press turned over every stone in their efforts to find new facts or, in too many cases, new fiction to feed the public appetite.

Every facet of the incident had been turned over and speculated on. West had been involved in preparing the press conference details of the safety aspects, and answering the barrage of questions from inside and outside the company. It had been a day of incessant and unending defence of the company and the '*Majestic Sea*'.

It was now early evening. The senior office staff were licking their wounds and preparing for another onslaught the next day. A solitary light shone on the desk of West. As the Fleet Safety Manager, no one was exposed more than him. He knew his career rested on how this was handled. In an organisation like this, anyone could be thrown to the wolves if it served the company's purpose. He had seen it happen several times in the past, and he was determined that he was not going to be the next victim.

On the desk in front of him was a slim file. Inside were several sheets of paper making up a report. It was from Captain Clariby, sent from the '*Majestic Sea*'. Each time he read it, he became more aware of the contents. Words jumped out at him that carried implications far beyond today. The report was an alarm bell that had been ignored and the more he considered it, the colder he became. He shivered.

Purposefully, West rose from his desk and gathered up the papers and the file. He walked over to the corner of his office and stood over a machine which hummed faintly.

Very slowly, he put the file into the top of the machine. The hum changed to a subdued mechanical chatter as out of the bottom thin slivers of paper dropped from the shredder into the basket.

DEVIL'S CAULDRON

by Michael Lloyd

Published by
Monument Series

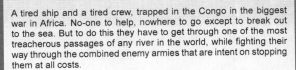

A tired ship and a tired crew, trapped in the Congo in the biggest war in Africa. No-one to help, nowhere to go except to break out to the sea. But to do this they have to get through one of the most treacherous passages of any river in the world, while fighting their way through the combined enemy armies that are intent on stopping them at all costs.

With the British Merchant Navy in a state of collapse, the few remaining British crews are sinking into despair as their Red Ensigns are hauled down and replaced with ensigns of a bewildering array of nations. For many, this signals redundancy and the end of a life at sea.

This is the story of one such ship and one such crew. They are a long way from home, overdue their leave, battling breakdowns, and trapped in the Congo River during the largest war in Africa. The rebel armies are closing in on the port and the ship and, to make things worse, refugees look to the ship as their only hope. They must risk everything to escape to safety, breaking through the rebel army and then through the Devil's Cauldron, a dangerous maelstrom of currents and rocks, and then on to the sea.

It is a story of ordinary seafarers caught up in events beyond their control and who discover the resolve and strength to continue their increasingly desperate attempts to get their ship through against the odds.

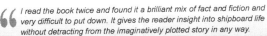

Available to buy
from Witherbyseamanship.com or Amazon

> *I read the book twice and found it a brilliant mix of fact and fiction and very difficult to put down. It gives the reader insight into shipboard life without detracting from the imaginatively plotted story in any way.*
> **(Amazon Review Aug 2012)**

> *I couldn't put this book down. It is a real page turner - I even found myself reading it whilst walking to the bus stop! Great story - I was totally drawn in.*
> **(Amazon Review Sep 2012)**